dArRkK mOoNdDaAyYsS

Other books by Kage Baker include:

In The Garden of Iden
Sky Coyote
Mendoza In Hollywood
The Graveyard Game
The Company Dossiers: Black Projects, White Knights
Mother Aegypt and Other Stories
The Life of the World to Come
The Children of the Company
The Machine's Child (forthcoming)

dark mondays

STORIES BY **KAGE**
BAKER

Night Shade Books
San Francisco & Portland

To Tom Barclay, fellow seeker after truth and the original melody to Dead Man's Chest. Here's to ourselves, shipmate!

CONTENTS:

THE TWO OLD WOMEN

The gulls rose from the evening water, glided out serene and pointed, each little pilot craning its neck to judge its way on sharp-curved wings. So high the sea the bright foam was driven on the wind, and cloudy air rolled in low above the little town. Backlit by the low sun, the long combers threw back manes of white salt mist, thundering up the sand. Boats rocked at anchor, battened down against autumn gales, and she could hear their blocks and tackle clinking even up where she sat.

The old woman gazed down at the harbor.

She wore black, being a widow, a little stumpy lady like a wooden post. When she had been a young wife, sitting in this same place, watching this same harbor, there had still been ships moored in the green water, and the horizon was all masts and spars. Gradually the masts had given way to steam, or diesel. Now only the sailboats bore canvas. Bright summer days they skimmed out there beyond the island, or tacked to and fro in the harbor. Not tonight.

Nobody ventured out tonight, except grandmothers in black. They went to St. Anthony's for evening mass, praying for their dead on All Soul's Night. The old woman, though, remained in her chair. She was not a grandmother.

She sat there still as the sun sank, as the pink twilight fell. When the change in the wind came she felt it first, because her house sat high on the last street. She turned, peering. It was a hot wind, coming over the fields, and it smelled of mown hay and creek water. It flowed over her. It rolled down on the harbor. The mist fled before it, retreated out to sea, and the sea grew glassy and calm.

Her breath quickened, though her expression of stolid patience did not change. She rose, creaking, and went slowly into her house.

1

Inside, her house was spartan and shabby, but scrupulously clean. One bare table with two chairs; one rug with a half-century's path worn across it, sun-faded. Only in one corner was there color, all around the tall shelf where the candles burned in their ruby glass cups before the image of the Blessed Mother. Here the old woman had set a vase of flowers, dark red roses from the schoolground fence, yellow chrysanthemums from her garden.

And here she had hung the pictures: the tinted photographs of a distant wedding day, a smiling bride and groom, a formal portrait of a handsome young man in his best suit.

She took off her shawl, tied on an apron. For the next four hours she worked very hard, pounding spices in a mortar, chopping greens, simmering broth. She roasted a formidable loin of pork with garlic, baked linguica with peppers, and crumbled crisp bacon into the *Caldo Verde*; but she prepared nothing with seafood of any kind. And in no dish did she use salt.

When things could be left over low heat, she went into the front room and laid the cloth carefully, set out the candlesticks. One place set, one bottle of black-red wine from a cupboard, a single fine glass. Half an hour before midnight, she set out the tureen, the platters of meat, the pan of cornbread. She poured a single glass of wine. She lit the tapers. She took another candle, a blue one, and set it in the window, carefully tying the curtains back.

Then she took off her apron, drew her shawl around her shoulders, and walked down to the harbor.

The wind had not changed. The air was clear, the darkness full of little flickering lights. It took her longer than it had used to, to get down to the mole, but she arrived before midnight. She waited, staring out into the night ocean.

At midnight she saw the white sail gliding in, as she had known it would. The black water was smooth as glass, the little fishing boat moved over it without a sound. She could see it clearly now. The timbers were rotted and festooned with rank weed, the paint bubbled and chipped away, and all the ironwork risen like biscuit with rust. But the sail was white and whole, belled out with phantom wind, bright with phantom sunlight. His face was bright, too, where he sat at the tiller.

He was still young.

He brought his craft up to the mole easily, tossed a loop of seaweed around a bollard and moored; stepped lightly out, with his duffel over his shoulder. He leaned down to kiss her. His lips moved as though he were speaking to her, gleeful and excited, but he wasn't making a sound.

He chattered away in perfect silence, all the way back through the town. He outpaced her easily, on his young, long legs, and more than once had to stop and wait for her at a turn in the street. He looked a little puzzled at her slowness.

But they got to the top of the hill at last. He bounded up the steps of their house, opened the door for her, slung down his duffel and stood rubbing his hands together, eyeing the food greedily. As she closed the door, he was already pulling off his jacket and knitted cap. Where he dropped them they became a soaked mass of rotten wool, and the duffel was black and sodden too.

He hitched his suspenders, sat down at the table, rolled up his long sleeves. Grinning, he helped himself to the food. Knife in one fist, fork in the other, he ate heartily, steadily, and set the fork down only to gulp the red wine. She sat across from him and watched. He smeared melting butter on the corn bread. He savored the pork crackling. Once or twice he looked around on the table, hunting for the salt; but as it wasn't there, he shrugged and went on eating.

When he had done, when the white candles had burned down a quarter of their length, he pushed his empty plate back and said something to her. He winked broadly. She rose and went into the bedroom, and he followed her.

There her young heart went out of her body, and the old woman sat weeping in a chair watching the young woman undress, and slip into bed. He shucked off his boots, his clothes—they fell to pieces on the floor, and water spread there in a dark stain on the rag rug. He climbed into bed with the phantom girl, and she lay in his arms.

Far into the night, as the young husband and wife slept, the old woman rose from her chair. She was moving more stiffly now, and her eyes were swollen from so much weeping, so she felt her way as though she were blind. She gathered up the ruined garments in her apron, carried them out to the garden, and lay them at the base of a tree. She collected the food from the table and carried it out there too. She got a shovel. Gasping, her old heart laboring, she dug a hole under the tree and buried the rags, the remains of the feast.

Then she went back into the house. She took a box from a cupboard and carried it outside again. Walking the perimeter of the garden fence, she laid down a line of white powder, very carefully. When she had drawn an unbroken circle around her home, she went back indoors. The sky was just getting light in the east.

She blew out the candles. The smoke rose, coiled.

• • •

The other old woman, in her house down the hill, woke a little while later. She dressed herself and, kneeling at her corner shrine, said a rosary. Sometimes her gaze was on the Blessed Mother's kind, inscrutable face; sometimes on the framed photograph of the old man, sitting in after-dinner ease with a grandchild on either knee, and the ash falling from his cigar caught by the camera in midair forever.

But as she told her beads, the other old woman became aware of a sound. It could be heard above the diesel motors rumbling to life in the harbor, the raucous screaming of gulls following the trawlers out. After a moment she identified it as someone hammering, irregularly.

It continued as she rose and went to the kitchen. It counterpointed the rocking of the wooden bowl as she kneaded dough. It was still going, three taps and a pause, three taps and a pause, as she sliced potatoes and set them to fry in bacon grease.

At last she turned from the stove and went to the window above the sink. Parting the checked curtain, she squinted in the direction of the sunrise. There was her sister's house, on its high ridge. She peered, rubbed her eyes, retrieved a pair of spectacles from her apron pocket and slipped them on. She saw a man on a ladder, putting new shingles on her sister's roof. The sun, just now reaching him, lit him up in gold.

The other old woman nodded in approval, and went back to the stove.

After a moment, though, she frowned. She looked out the window again, wiping her hands on her apron. At last she turned down the heat and left the kitchen, walking through the house.

Marco's bed was empty, neatly made, because he was away at boot camp. Danny was still asleep on his side of the room, snoring. The other old woman shook her head at the sport jacket lying where it had been thrown, the cigarette butts on the floor, the guitar. She picked up his discarded socks and went on.

Margaret Mary was in her room, sound asleep under the sultry gaze of Elvis on her tacked-up posters, and the other old woman spared her no more than a glance in before moving on. She looked in on the twins by habit, and caught them awake and clandestinely eating Halloween candy. One basilisk stare was all it took and they scrambled back into bed, huddling there as she retrieved tiny underwear and socks from their hamper.

Celia woke when she opened the door, though John slept through it. The other old woman left without a word, and had the first laundry load going when Celia shuffled into the kitchen in her bathrobe.

The hammering was still going on. Tap tap tap, pause.

"The wind's changed. It's coming from inshore, can you feel it? Going to be hot today," said Celia.

"Mm," said her mother.

"Mama," said Celia, clearing her throat, "you don't have to fry up so much linguica in the morning. The kids want Corn Pops."

"Danny likes it," said her mother. "Did you tell Rosalie to get Jerry to fix Tia Adela's roof?"

"No, Mama." Celia yawned, and got a can of coffee down from the cupboard. "I told you, Danny's going to do it. He promised me."

"Well, somebody's up there now," said her mother, parting the curtain once again. Celia blinked, came and stared.

"Who's *that*?"

"Not Danny," said her mother.

"Huh," said Celia, troubled. But she went to the breadbox, methodically laid out sandwiches for the school lunches: Peanut butter for the twins, tuna salad for Margaret Mary. Three brown paper bags, three oranges, three dimes for milk. Rituals for the living.

Not another word was said on the subject of Tia Adela's roof, as the household was fed, as the children were sent to school, as John went to work at the boatyard, as Danny was coaxed out of bed, bullied into eating linguica and onions despite his hangover and sent on his way to the new job at the fish market, as the clean, wet clothes went out on the line to dry.

But when the house was quiet and well-ordered again, the other old woman looked meaningfully at her daughter and pulled on her shawl. Celia followed her out the door, fanning herself with a piece of newspaper.

"Mama, it's hot," she complained. "You don't have to wear that thing." But her mother ignored her, and they were silent the rest of the way up the hill to Tia Adela's house.

The hammering was still going on. They could see the edge of the ladder poking up over the roofline, but they could not see the workman until they walked out to the edge of the street and turned.

The other old woman said nothing, but she made the sign of the cross involuntarily. Celia shaded her eyes against the sun with her newspaper. "I'm sweating to death, Mama," she muttered, studying the workman. Nobody she knew, though he was certainly good-looking: long lean back bronzed by the sun, a mermaid tattooed on his right arm. His hair was a little long; his wool trousers were a little tight.

"Hello?" she called. "Mister?"

He did not reply. He did not even turn his head; just reached over and took the last tarpaper shingle from its box, and tacked it in place.

"Hey!" Celia called, when he paused to wipe his forehead. He did not appear to notice her. His lips were moving as though he were singing to himself, though he was not making a sound. He dropped his hammer, climbed briskly down the ladder and walked out of sight behind the house.

"I wonder if he's deaf?" said Celia. "I'll bet that's what it is, Mama. She's hired one of those handicapped guys from St. Vincent de Paul's, huh? Danny would have gotten around to it," she added plaintively. "Gee, now I feel bad."

Her mother did not reply.

"Mama, maybe we should knock on the door, see if Tia Adela's okay," said Celia. "Some of those guys are a little crazy, you know?"

"No," said her mother. "We're going home."

She said it in such a way Celia knew there was no point arguing. They walked back down the hill.

• • •

Once or twice, at night, the hot wind brought the lowing of cattle from the big ranch far up the canyon. By day, the twins and Margaret Mary sweated in their blue woolen school uniforms. Rosalie, miserable in the heat, fled her tiny apartment and walked up the street to sit on the porch swing with her mother. The radio blared from the house behind them.

"Did you throw up every damn morning like this?" she asked querulously, raising her voice to be heard over Perry Como.

"Only with you and Marco," Celia replied. "All I could eat for a month was green grapes and crackers. It'll get better, sweetie."

"I sure hope so," sighed Rosalie. "Were you bothered by smells too? I opened a can of sardines, and I swear I nearly died."

"Good thing Jerry's not in port right now, then," joked her mother, but Rosalie did not smile.

"I miss him already," she said, staring out at the sea in resentment. "I had bad dreams last night. It's too late in the year to go out so far, don't you think?"

"It's still summer," said Celia, waving at the electric fan. "Summer in November, for God's sake. And they have to make money while they can, you know."

"It's not fair," said Rosalie. Her mother looked at her sidelong.

"*You* married him," she said. "I told you, didn't I? Marry a Souza, an Avila or a Machado, and half the year he'll be out there on a trawler. And the other half of the year your house will stink like fish."

"Maybe he can get a job at the boatyard with Daddy," said Rosalie. Celia made a noncommittal noise. Rosalie lifted her head to watch a leaf floating down the wind. Her gaze fell on the house against the skyline.

"Don't tell me you got Danny to paint Tia Adela's house!" she said.

Celia looked unhappy.

"No. She has some boy from St. Vincent de Paul's up there, or maybe the Salvation Army."

"It's looking really nice," Rosalie observed, standing to see better. "See, all those hedges have been cut back. Somebody took down that big dead tree! Jerry was going to do that for her, when he got around to it," she added, a little uncomfortably.

Celia shrugged. Rosalie's face brightened.

"Gee, do you think she's getting it fixed up to sell? Like, maybe she's going to move into a home? Maybe you could talk to her about giving it to Jerry and me instead. We really need the room."

"I don't talk much to Tia Adela," said Celia. "Anyway, sweetie, it's her house."

"But we're *young*," Rosalie groaned. "What does she need with a whole house?"

. . .

That night the wind changed again.

The temperature dropped. A long swell rolled in from the sea, and by midnight the surf was booming on the mole. Mist rolled in, too, white under the stars. It brought the smell of salt, of sea wrack and low tide.

Tia Adela, dozing in her chair, started awake. The young man was sitting up in bed, staring at the window. Without even looking back at the girl, he slipped out of bed and drew on the clothes she had laid out for him, the wool and linen that was yellowed but none the worse for having spent a half-century packed in a trunk. He opened the window and drew in a deep breath of sea air.

Turning, he walked out of the bedroom. Tia Adela followed him as far as the front door. He gave her an apologetic grin as he slipped out, ran lightly down the steps. A pink quarter-moon hung low in the west, sending a faint track across the water. He paced down the walk as far as her front gate. But, extending his hand to open it, he faltered; drew back. Two or three tries he made, and couldn't seem to reach it.

He looked down at the trail of white stuff that crossed his path. He began to walk along it, seeking a way through, and followed its unbroken line all around the house, dodging through her garden, stumbling around behind the woodshed and the blackberry hedge, before he arrived at the front walk again.

He turned to look up, pleading silently with Tia Adela. She shook her head. Shoulders sagging, he came back up the walk and climbed the steps. He collapsed into a chair. She brought the wine and poured out a glass for him. He drank it down. It seemed to make him feel better.

In the morning he went out and spaded up her vegetable garden, whistling to himself in silence. She watched him from the window. Now and again she raised her head to look at the sky, where far to the north a thin silver wall of cloud was advancing. The sea was growing rough; it had turned a milky and ominous green, mottled here and there with purple weed.

• • •

"The glass is falling," stated the other old woman. Nobody paid any attention to her except Margaret Mary, who came to look at the barometer. Margaret Mary wore glasses, braces, had frizzy hair and freckles. She was the sort of girl who would be genuinely interested in barometer readings.

"Somebody ought to go," Rosalie was insisting. "She could be lying dead up there, for all anybody knows. Maybe she's had a stroke or something, and the man is some hobo who's just moved in. Maybe he's stealing from her."

"I guess we ought to be sure she's okay," Celia said, glancing uneasily at her own mother.

"Don't you think somebody needs to check on her, Nana Amelia?" Rosalie demanded. "And if she's okay, well, that gives you an opportunity to talk about leaving the house to Jerry and me."

Nana Amelia gave her a dark look. "It's not a lucky house," she said.

"Why don't we all go?" suggested Celia. "That way, if he's trouble, we can send Margaret Mary for the cops."

"Okay!" said Margaret Mary.

Nana Amelia sighed, but she drew on her shawl.

They set off up the street. The three women walked in close formation, arms crossed tightly under their breasts. Margaret Mary followed behind, hands thrust into the pockets of her school sweater, staring up at the clouds and therefore stumbling occasionally.

"Those are cumulonimbuses," she said. "And, uh, stratocumuluses. I think we're going to get a heck of a storm."

Nana Amelia nodded grimly.

They came to the front gate and looked up. The house was tidy, trim as a ship, with its new coat of paint. The doorknob and the brass lamp had been polished until they gleamed. The weeds had been cleared from either side of the walkway and the chrysanthemums staked up, watered, all swelling buds and yellow stars.

The women stared. As they stood there, Tia Adela came around the side of the house, carrying a basketful of apples. She halted when she saw them; but the young man who followed her did not seem to see. He simply stepped around her, and proceeded up the steps. He was carrying a dusty box full of mason jars and lids. He went into the house.

"What do you want?" said Tia Adela.

"We came up to see if you were all right," said Celia reproachfully. "Tia Adela, who's that boy?"

Tia Adela looked at her sister.

"You really shouldn't have strangers up here, Tia Adela," said Rosalie. "We were thinking, maybe you shouldn't live all alone nowadays, you know what I mean?"

"Yes," said Tia Adela. "I thought so too."

"And I was looking in the phone book, and there's this nice place called Wyndham Manor in San Luis, where they'd take—"

"You have offended God!" shouted Nana Amelia hoarsely. She was trembling.

Celia and Rosalie turned to gape at her.

"I don't care," said Tia Adela. "And He has said nothing. But *she's* angry, oh, yes." And she nodded out at the sea, wild and sullen under slaty cloud.

"Mama, what's going on?" said Celia.

Nana Amelia pointed up at the window. The young man was standing behind it, gazing out at the dark sea with an expression of heartbreaking longing.

"That is her husband," she said.

There was a moment's stunned silence, and then Celia said, very gently: "Mama, Tio Benedito has been dead since before I was born. Remember? I think we'd better go home now, okay?"

Her mother gave her such a look of outrage that she drew back involuntarily.

"Don't be stupid," said Nana Amelia. She stormed forward and up the steps, and Celia and Rosalie ran after her, protesting. Tia Adela shrugged and followed slowly. Margaret Mary came with her.

The young man at the window didn't seem to notice the women bursting into the room. Nana Amelia went straight to the wedding photograph on the wall, grabbed it down and thrust it in Celia's face.

"There! Her Bento. See? Dead as a stone. He went out past Cortes Shoals after rockfish, too late in the year. A lot of fools went out. The *Adelita,* the *Meiga,* the *Luisa* all went down in the gale, even the big *Dunbarton*! So many dead washed up on the beach, they loaded them on a mule wagon. Bento, they didn't find. The sea kept him. And *she* never forgave God!" Nana Amelia turned in wrath to her sister, who had come in now and set her basket of apples on the table.

Celia, who had taken up the photograph, looked from it to the young man by the window. Rosalie peered over her shoulder.

"Mama, this is crazy," said Celia. "Things like this don't happen."

"So... he's a ghost?" said Margaret Mary, peering at Bento. "And he's come back to her? Just like he was? Wow! Only..." She looked sadly at her great-aunt. "Only, you're *old*, Tia Adela."

Tia Adela folded her arms defiantly. "I know," she said. "But I have him back. She can call him, she can beat herself white on the rocks, but she can't climb up here. He and I will stay safe in my house, let her gale blow hard as it will."

"Who is this other lady she's talking about?" Rosalie murmured to her mother.

"Adela, don't be stupid!" said Nana Amelia. "You know what will happen."

"This Wyndham Manor you called, how much does it cost?" Celia inquired of her daughter *sotto voce*.

"Look, whoever you are, you'd better go now," Rosalie said, turning to Bento. "Do you hear me? Go back to St. Vincent's or wherever she hired you from."

He made no reply. She strode across the room to him. "Hey! Can you hear me?"

She grabbed him by the arm and then she screamed, and staggered back. Celia was beside her at once, catching her before she fell. Bento had not moved, had not even turned his head.

"Honey, sweetie, what is it?" Celia cried.

Rosalie was gulping for breath, her eyes wide with horror. She was holding her hand out stiffly. Her mother closed her own hand around it and recoiled; for Rosalie's hand was as cold as though she'd been holding a block of ice, and as wet, and gritty with sand.

· · ·

"Should I go get Father Halloway?" asked Margaret Mary.

"No," said the women in unison.

"I don't see why you're all so mad, anyhow," said Margaret Mary. "I think it's neat. If we can really bring the dead back, so we won't be lonely—well—wouldn't that be great? You could still have Grandpa to talk to, Nana! How'd you do it, Tia Adela?"

Tia Adela said nothing, watching Bento. He was pacing back and forth before the window.

"She made a Soul Feast," said Nana Amelia. "Didn't you, Adela?"

"You mean she just cooked some food?" Margaret Mary cried. "Is that all it takes? Can anybody do that?"

"Not everybody," said Tia Adela, curling her lip. "And food is not enough. There must be love that is stronger than death."

"Oh," said Margaret Mary.

"It's *wrong*, child," said Nana Amelia. "The dead don't belong to us! And they want their rest. Look at him, Adela, does he look happy? You have to let him go."

"How are you keeping him here?" asked Rosalie in a little voice, the first time she had spoken since she'd learned the truth. Celia, sitting with her arm around her, shook her head.

"Sweetie, don't ask—"

"Borax," said Tia Adela.

"What?"

"Borax," Tia Adela repeated, with a certain satisfaction. "I poured a line of it all along the fence, and he can't cross it."

"Jesus Christ, Tia Adela, you put down borax powder for *ants,* not ghosts!" yelled Celia.

"It's alkali, isn't it?" said Tia Adela. "The opposite of salt. So it breaks the spell of the sea."

"Um… but alkali isn't the opposite of salt, Tia Adela," said Margaret Mary, wringing her hands. "It's the opposite of acid. We learned that in Chemistry class."

Tia Adela shrugged. "It still works, doesn't it?"

A gust of wind hit the windows, whirling brown leaves. A gull swept in close, hung for a moment motionless at eye level before gliding away downwind. Rosalie shivered.

"No, I'm not letting him go," Tia Adela went on, in a harder voice. "Fifty years I've sat up here, and I got old, yes, and she's still beautiful. Is that fair?"

"There will be a price to pay," said Nana Amelia.

Tia Adela did not reply. Bento sighed, making no sound, but far out and high up a gull mourned.

"Go away now," said Tia Adela. "I've got his dinner to fix."

• • •

Rain advanced like a white curtain. The leaden sea turned silver before it vanished in the squall. One by one the trawlers came in, fleeing for their lives, ramming the pier in their haste to moor. The crews scrambled ashore dripping, dodging the waves that were breaking over the pier. A police cruiser pulled up to the mole with its red light flashing, and cops in black slickers set sawhorses across the walkway.

Nobody was fool enough to go out there, though. The harbormaster sighed, looking at the moored sailboats; half of them would be on the beach, or matchwood, by morning.

The cars were pulling up now to the foot of the pier, and women and old men were getting out, squinting into the flying rain, leaning over as they walked into the wind. Soaked before they reached the harbormaster's office, they came one after another and asked: Was there news of the *Medford*? Was there news of the *Virginia Marie*?

They came away with faces like stone, and went back to their cars and sat, steaming up the windows, except for a couple of the old men, who splashed away through puddles to the Mahogany Bar and could be glimpsed thereafter at the window, looking like fish in a lit aquarium, drinking steadily as they waited.

Night closed down. One by one the headlights came on, pointed out to sea. When the waves began to break over the edge of the parking lot, the cops came and made the cars move back; but they did not leave, and they did not turn out the headlights.

Then there was a confusion of shouting, of horns and red lights, and Margaret Mary started awake as the car doors were flung open. She had to wipe her steamed glasses clear before she could see her mother and father hurrying through the rain, splashing through the long beams of light, calling after Rosalie who was sprinting ahead as fast as she had ever gone in her life.

And beyond her—Margaret Mary took her glasses off, wiped them again and stared openmouthed. Impossibly huge, bizarrely out of context with her prow almost on the asphalt, the *Virginia Marie* lay beached and rolling. Men clung to her, shouting, staring at the solid world of automobiles and houses and warmth, just within reach and terrible yards away, as the black water, the white water kept breaking over them, and the rain glittered and ran.

Sirens howled; a big ambulance pulled up, and another police car. People were crowding too close for Margaret Mary to see much, until the ropes were rigged and the rescued began to arrive on shore, huddled at once in blankets.

The crowd parted. Mary Margaret saw a blanketed man with his wet hair plastered down, and he was talking earnestly to Rosalie. She put her hands to her face and screamed. She just kept screaming, until at last John lifted her in his arms and dragged her back to the car, with Celia running after, weeping. Margaret Mary wept too, withdrawing into her seat. Through her tears she mumbled the Our Father; though a cold, adult voice in her head told her it was a little late for that.

"Daddy, what happened?" she begged, as he thrust Rosalie into the back seat beside her and slammed the door. For all anybody noticed her or answered, she might have been a ghost. Celia reached into the back and gripped Rosalie's hands, and held on to them all the way up the hill to the house.

It was an hour later before she heard the story from her father, as he sat in the kitchen in his bathrobe, over strong coffee with whiskey in it: how the *Virginia Marie*'s radio mast had gone by the board, how she had been making her way back, how they had come upon the *Medford* taking on water and listing, how they had managed to take her crew off; and how Jerry had just gotten the last man aboard and was pulling in the lifeline when he had fallen, and dropped between the two hulls like a stone.

There had been no sign of him, in the rain and the night, and he might have answered their calls—one crewman swore he had heard him answer, and thrown out a life preserver in that direction—but the wind was so loud they couldn't be certain. Then suddenly the *Virginia Marie* had her own problems, and no man aboard had thought to come home again. Yet—

"Only Jerry was lost," said her father, and had a gulp of his coffee. "Can you beat that?"

"But he might have made it," Margaret Mary protested. "Maybe he caught the life preserver. Maybe they'll find him tomorrow when it's light!"

"Yeah," said John wearily. "Sure, honey."

Margaret Mary looked out between the curtains, up through the night at the warm light glowing in Tia Adela's window.

• • •

She slept on the couch in her clothes, because they had put Rosalie to sleep in her bed. Just after seven she rose, put on her glasses and stood at the front window, blinking out at the day. The rain had stopped, the wind dropped, though it was still gusting cold fitfully. The *Virginia Marie* was breaking apart fast, and there was a big crack in the parking lot where her prow had acted like a wedge on the asphalt. More yellow sawhorses blocked it off. Sailboats were lying all along the tideline, and one actually had come to rest on the boardwalk.

Turning, slipping off her glasses to rub her gritty eyes, she heard sudden footsteps from the hall.

Rosalie was up and dressed, pulling on one of her father's coats. Nana Amelia was right behind her, looking unstoppable. After them Celia came, hopping as she tried to put on her shoes while following.

"Sweetie, you need to stay here and rest—" she entreated, but Rosalie ignored her mother.

"Where are you going?" asked Margaret Mary.

"Where do you think?" said Rosalie, in a furious voice, flinging open the door and marching out, as Nana Amelia pulled on her shawl.

Margaret Mary stuck her feet in her saddle oxfords and clumped hurriedly along after them, running to catch up.

The rain had packed down the line of borax before Tia Adela's gate, but had not washed it away. Tia Adela and her husband were out in the garden. She had filled another basket with windfall apples, and he was sawing loose a bough that had been broken by the storm. He did not look up as Rosalie threw the gate wide and shrieked:

"Let him go!"

Tia Adela lifted her head, gazed at them. She looked down at the harbor, where the *Virginia Marie* wallowed broken in the surf.

"This has come of your wickedness, you see?" Nana Amelia told her sternly. "And her child needs a father, Adela."

"Please, Tia Adela! For the baby's sake!" Celia implored.

Tia Adela looked hard at Rosalie, who was scuffing through the line of borax with all her might. She grimaced, looking for a long moment as though she'd tasted poison.

"That won't do it," she sighed. She went to the shed and got a broom. Casting a long regretful look over her shoulder at Bento, she walked to the front gate.

"Stand back," she said. They shuffled out of her way and she swept the borax aside, in a white fan like a bird's wing.

The sun broke through, a long beam brilliant and white, whiter still for the seabirds that rose in a circling cloud through it, crying and calling.

"Look at the rainbow!" cried Margaret Mary, and they all looked up at the great arch that spanned the harbor, in colors so intense they nearly hurt the eye.

When they looked down again, they saw the car pulling up.

It was black, and long, and so, so expensive. The dashboard was inlaid with patterns in mother-of-pearl, all shells and mermaids and scalloped waves; the upholstery was sea-green brocade. The chrome gleamed as though it were wet.

And she who sat at the wheel was exquisitely dressed, tapping with her ivory fingers on the wheel, just a little impatient. Though her face was that of a skull, her very bones were so beautiful, so elegant, as to inspire self-loathing in any woman with a face of flesh (too *fat!*).

She hit the horn. It sounded like a foghorn.

The mortal women heard the quick footsteps behind them, felt the ice-cold touch as Bento shoved through them in his haste to go. He was smiling wide as he got into the car, didn't so much as look back once. He closed the door. The car glided away down the hill without making a sound. The women stood there, looking after it.

"Bitch," they said in unison, and with feeling.

• • •

But before noon the Coast Guard had picked up Jerry from the swamped and drifting derelict *Medford*, which he had been able to scramble aboard somehow, and they brought him home to Rosalie's waiting arms.

• • •

Seven years later, though, in another November, his luck ran out. The *Star of Lisbon* was lost with all hands. The Old Woman of the Sea is a poor loser, but she is a worse winner.

• • •

Rosalie wore black, and once or twice a week climbed the long street to Tia Adela's house, carrying baby Maria and tugging little Jerry by the hand. Jerry sat in the middle of the faded rug with his toy tractors and trucks, running them to and fro while Maria napped, and Rosalie learned how to make the old dishes: *Caldo Verde* with bacon, linguica with sweet peppers, garlic pork roast.

And she waited for the wind to change.

PORTRAIT, WITH FLAMES

Shadow saw the fire from the Hollywood Freeway, and realized it must be near her apartment. Her heart beat faster all the way down the exit at Odin Street, and all along Highland Avenue, until she saw that it wasn't her place after all. One of the apartment complex's garages had caught, instead.

Leaping flames made the predawn gloom darker. The revolving lights of the fire engines strobed out across Highland and flashed on the windows of the apartments above. She had to park all the way up on Woodland Court, threading her way down the narrow winding steps between bamboo thickets to get to her door. She sniffed the air appreciatively: jungle perfumes of copa de oro and night-blooming jasmine mingled with smoke. It smelled like exotic danger.

Letting herself in, she checked the room with a glance. No intruders in her furnished studio sanctuary. A red light hit her like a splash of blood, flicked away. She went to the window and looked down.

She didn't know whose garage was on fire, because she knew none of the other tenants. The firemen were mostly standing around watching it burn, playing water on the adjoining garages to keep them from catching too. These were all of clapboard, built in the 1920s and consequently accommodating nothing wider than a Model A. Fifty years on most of the tenants used them for storage, with the exception of one or two who drove Volkswagen Beetles.

Shadow lost interest. She went to her tiny refrigerator, crouched before it, and pulled out a half gallon of lowfat milk. Thirstily she drank from the carton, in long, sensual swallows. When she put it back, she was pleased that she didn't feel hungrier. She was trying to avoid solid food. Shadow must always be lean.

Prior to reinventing herself as Shadow, her name had been Samantha, and she had lived with her accountant mother in a tiny, courtyard apartment over on Gramercy. Three years ago, when she'd turned eighteen, they had had a terrific fight over—well, everything, really—and parted company for keeps.

She'd dyed her mousy hair black, bought an all-black wardrobe at thrift stores, and lived for a while rent-free over on Franklin Avenue in a basement, in a sort of commune called Mohawk Manor by its members. She'd hung out at Oki Dog, wandered up and down the Strip, and danced at the clubs. But she made it a point never to join any crowd, never to need anyone. People weren't worth the trouble.

Then one night a couple of large girls and a boy with a spiked collar got very drunk, and broke into her room and tried to get her to form a vampire coven with them. She had excused herself to go to the toilet, where she'd crawled out the bathroom window and run down the hill to the all-night market a block away. There she'd stayed until dawn, flipping through magazines.

And Shadow had given the stockroom clerk there a hand job, and secured for herself a job on the night shift bagging groceries. For a few other favors, he'd loaned her the money for a rental deposit on this place. Now she'd moved on to clerking at a bigger all-night market, much better pay. She'd been able to buy a cavernous old Chevy Impala, painted matte black over primer. It had an eight-track music system and the floor of the passenger's side was littered with tapes of the Clash, of the Sex Pistols, of Siouxsie and the Banshees and Buzzcocks. Now she owned the night.

Stretching luxuriously, she threw herself down on her bed without getting undressed. The fire must be out; she heard the big engines rumbling away, like dinosaurs honking and bellowing in the dawn.

• • •

Shadow woke in the early afternoon. Remembering the fire, she sat up and groped under her bed for her camera. She took pictures, mostly images of building demolition or car wrecks, with the vague intention of becoming a freelance photographer. There were a couple of exposures left on the current roll. She put on sunglasses and slipped out with the camera, through the ivy and down the hill behind the building. She emerged behind the trash cans and stepped out in the glare of winter sunlight, and there before her was the blackened shell of the garage.

Someone had already raked out most of the charred contents, and piled them in a heap. The remains of a mattress, a wooden bed frame, a chest of drawers, a bookcase: someone's old life, all gone to charcoal and ash. She squinted at the pile and walked closer.

The cinders must still be warm. A kitten was perched on top of them, a tiny, orange tom like a live coal, blinking sleepily. Shadow, struck by the juxtaposition, lifted her camera. For a moment she hesitated; photographing a kitten seemed such a *Samantha* thing to do. She decided the irony inherent in the image made it okay, though, and took a picture.

The click of the shutter startled the kitten; it leaped from its nest and vanished in the weeds at the edge of the parking lot. She thought of following it, but that was definitely a Samantha thing to do. She used up the last exposure, going around to the front of the garage, to frame a shot with burnt beams and dangling wires against the pitiless white sky.

• • •

A week later Shadow picked up the developed pictures from the drugstore on the corner of Hollywood and Highland. Sitting in the Impala, she flipped through them. A car wreck, a dead dog with its intestines spread over two lanes of traffic, the bulldozers just closing in on the old Hollywood Motor Hotel… and here was the last shot, the burnt remains of the garage. She didn't see the shot with the kitten, and went through the envelope again.

Here was the black pile of cinders: How had she missed it?

She frowned at the picture and held it up to the light. She had missed it because there was no sign of the kitten. There was, in approximately the same place in which it had been lying, a baby. No; a baby doll, must be. The kitten must have fled just before the shutter clicked. Yet, how could she have missed an image so wonderfully grim as a charred baby doll?

But there it was, unmistakable, the figure of a baby baked red by its bed of coals. Disturbing on so many levels. Maybe one of the free papers would buy it. She shrugged, putting the envelope in the Impala's glove box, and drove to work.

• • •

The following afternoon, Shadow lost a little of the night.

She had risen early—maybe noon—and gone down to a poster shop in Artisan's Patio that did enlargements. She dropped off the best pictures and their negatives, including the one with the doll, and ordered a set of eight by ten glossies. Then she drove out to Studio City and bought groceries at the Ralphs market: hair dye, lowfat milk, Flintstones vitamins. As she pulled out of the parking lot onto Ventura Boulevard she noticed the Impala was making a whining noise.

"Shit," she muttered, and when the light changed she pulled into a 76 station on the other side of the intersection. The whine got louder.

"Sounds like you need transmission fluid," said a man at the self-serve island. She shrugged, but went inside and bought a bottle.

She got on the freeway and for a while thought the problem was going to go away, but the minute she exited at Odin the whine returned. It was worse; it became a groaning scream as she turned onto Highland, and now the Impala refused to change gears. Somehow she swung around the corner onto Camrose, but barely made it thirty feet uphill before the shrieking Impala slowed to a crawl and then lost any forward momentum.

"Shit!" She managed to steer to the curb as she coasted backward, and put on the emergency brake. She got out and walked around the car, bewildered and furious. The Impala was bleeding red syrup. Was that the transmission fluid she'd just added?

"Shit!" She kicked one of the Impala's tires. The nearest gas station with a mechanic was all the way down on Highland and Franklin.

The mechanic wasn't interested in helping her. She had to convince him she found him really, really attractive and would do anything, no really *anything* if he'd tow her car off the street and have a look at it. He made her prove it. She never minded hand jobs so much, because at least she was in control, and it was better than him touching her with his black-rimmed fingernails.

He roared with laughter when he saw the transmission fluid running down, and informed her, without even opening the hood, that she'd need a new transmission. He told Shadow what it would cost, and her heart sank; she hadn't paid that much for the Impala in the first place. But she went with him when he towed it back to the gas station, and told him she'd be in to talk to him as soon as she'd gotten her groceries out of the back seat.

Hastily she threw her eight-track tapes into the grocery bag, rummaged around under the seats and found a sweater and thirty cents in change; she put the sweater on, pocketed the change, and was out of the car with her bag and over the wall behind the gas station in under a minute.

Fuming, Shadow took an indirect route home, along the alleys behind buildings, along back fences, and crossed over to Camrose behind the American Legion Hall. As she cut across the lot by the garages, she saw a little kid staring at her from the weeds, a boy, red-haired, maybe five or six. Was he lost? She ignored him and scrambled up the hill to her apartment.

• • •

Now Shadow had to walk down the hill every evening and catch the 81 bus, which ran to no schedule. If the driver felt like arriving early, he did, and made no effort to wait if Shadow hadn't reached the bus stop yet. If he ran late, he might blow through the Camrose and Highland stop, leaving Shadow screaming obscenities from the bus bench.

"Doesn't do any good," said a man who gave her a ride out to the valley. "Anybody who matters has a car, honey. They figure only losers need the bus to go places, and if they don't like it, who cares?"

She was worn out, with the long walks to and from the bus stop. She bought a box of Instant Breakfast, thinking it might give her more energy; but she worried about it putting weight on her, once she read its ingredients, and so about one night in three she went into the employees' restroom at work and made herself puke it up again. Finally she bought a thermos and filled it with black coffee, and took it with her instead. It got her through the last couple of hours of her shift.

• • •

The photo enlargements came in and were impressive enough to be encouraging. Shadow bought a portfolio at the art supply store and spent a long day waiting in the outer offices of the art directors of the two local free weeklies. She was told she might want to look into getting a union card; she was told she needed to invest in professional equipment. Everyone agreed, though, that the shot with the baby doll in the ashes was striking.

"Because, you know why? It's an illusion," said the art director at the *Hollywood Free Voice*. She held it up to the light. "There's no baby there at all, if you look at it closely. It's just flames, or smoke or something. Really, that's a hundred-to-one shot."

But she didn't offer to buy it.

By the time Shadow got out of the *Hollywood Free Voice* office, which was all the way down Santa Monica at Western, there seemed little point in going home to sleep for an hour. There was a coffeehouse by the bus stop; she went in and got an espresso, and sat at one of the tables with her portfolio, flipping once more through the pictures.

Was it a baby doll? It was blurred and soft-edged, but you could see the face and the arms, and at least one leg.

"Damn," said someone, leaning over her. A hand reached down and pulled out the other shot, the one she'd taken of the burned-out garage. "Nice work. You an adjustor too?"

"What?" Shadow looked up at him. He was a little older than she, wore glasses, was smoking a cigarette.

"Are you a claims adjustor?"

"No," she said.

"So, this is just, like, your hobby?" He sat down at her table uninvited. She sized him up: nice clothes. Long-sleeved shirt, narrow tie. He was coked up. He used the same black hair dye she did; she could smell it, under his aftershave.

"I'm breaking in," she informed him.

"Good!" He stuck the cigarette in the corner of his mouth and held out his hand. "Jon Horton. How's it going?"

"Shadow," she said, shaking his hand warily. He put both elbows on the table, took his cigarette out again and had a deep drag on it.

"See, I'm an insurance adjustor. I take a lot of shots like that but I can't use them, isn't that a bitch?"

"Use them for what?" she asked, wondering if he was gay.

"I'm publishing a magazine," he said. "*Negative Pulse.* You've heard of it?"

"Maybe, yeah," she lied.

"Poetry. Stories. Artwork. It's, like, this necessary corrective for fucking hippie fantasy shit. We want stark images. Bitter truths, okay? We're reminding the complacent bourgeois assholes out there that *this* is real life, okay?"

"Okay," she said.

He talked a lot more. He told her all about his life, what a rebel he was, how he'd run his high school paper and how angry he'd made the principal when he'd done an article exposing something—Shadow couldn't quite tell what—but that was just the way he was, he was driven to challenge authority anywhere.

Eventually he came around to talking about *Negative Pulse* again, and how great it was going to be when they got an issue out.

"And, see, here's the thing, Sandra: I think your picture would look great on the cover." He leaned back, stubbed out his cigarette and raised his eyebrows at her.

"How much?" she said.

"What?"

"How much do you pay?"

"Well, eventually, I mean, we're just getting started. It's a communal effort on the part of all the artists involved, see? We're all investing in *Negative Pulse* because we believe in it, we believe it's like this spirit of the times, right? So we're all making sacrifices to get it up and running."

"Shit, look at the time," said Shadow. "Josh, you know, that sounds great and everything but I really have to go catch a bus now, okay? Got a business card? I'll call you sometime."

• • •

Two nights later, as she walked up the hill from the bus stop, she thought saw the little boy again. He was standing back by the garages, staring at her. No; this must be his older brother. He had the same red hair, but appeared to be about ten. She looked in disbelief at her watch. It was 5 in the morning, and freezing cold. She almost spoke to him, but something in his stare creeped her out.

Shadow kept walking, wondering why he hadn't figured out about cutting screens and breaking in through back windows; it had always worked for her, when she'd been locked out.

She went up to Woodland Court to avoid cutting past the garages, meaning to come down the front steps. Near the top, a dark figure stepped out of the bamboo.

"We meet again, little one."

"Shit." Shadow stopped. It was Julie, the queen of the coven from Mohawk Manor, in her white makeup and vampire cape. She must have gained thirty pounds since Shadow had seen her last. A figure moved out from behind a parked car, off to her left: Darlene, the other vampire girl. Shadow heard footsteps running up the hill behind her and turned to see Todd, the boy with the spiked collar, holding his cape out to either side as he ran.

"Yes; we have our ways of tracking you down. We really feel you ought to reconsider *ooof* ohjesuschrist!" said Julie, as Shadow hit her in the stomach with a well-placed Doc Marten. Julie collapsed, clutching her fat gut. Shadow whirled around and bashed Todd right between the eyes with her thermos, but didn't wait to see the result; she dove under his cape and ran down the hill, then skidded around the corner and raced uphill on Camrose. She had to stop for a minute at Hightower to catch her breath, but they didn't seem to be following her.

It was an old neighborhood, never planned; it had evolved as houses had been built up into the hillside. No streets connected with the upper homes. They were reached only by the elevator in the tower that had given the street its name, or by a series of high, narrow flights of stairs and walkways that zigzagged back and forth across the hill. Shadow had explored it all, when she'd first moved into the neighborhood.

She went to the tower and took its elevator up. At the top she got out and doubled back down toward Woodland Court, walking along in a sort of tunnel formed by bougainvillea branches that overhung the public walk, with white trumpet-vine, plumeria, honeysuckle and jasmine. The night air was like paradise.

She could see over back fences as she crept along, now and then getting a glimpse into somebody's lit kitchen: an ancient lady in a bathrobe, sitting hunched over a cup of coffee. A woman in a nightgown, ironing a pair of striped trousers. A young man with all his hair standing up, walking to and fro as a tiny baby screamed on his shoulder.

Shadow flitted past them, unseen and unknown.

Here was the house with the unlocked iron gate; she had learned that if she ran down the steps at the side of the house, crossed the lower garden and ducked through a hedge, she emerged just above the tallest of the bamboo thickets. Now she dropped down the steps in three bounds, silent, and crept into the darkness on the other side of the hedge.

There she stopped, listening, until it began to grow light. She felt her way forward, taking infinite care. A voice spoke from the other side of the bamboo thicket.

"I don't think she's coming back tonight." That was Darlene.

"She has to come back sometime," said Julie. "Little bitch."

"But it'll be daylight soon," said Darlene, with a trace of whimper in her voice.

"I don't give a shit, okay?" said Todd. "She broke my fucking nose. I'm going to kick her ass."

Shadow grinned. She found a comfortable position and settled back to wait. The sky paled; the roar of the waking city rose from down on Highland. Finally she heard Darlene again, crying.

"Look, who needs her anyway? We have to get back."

"It's not like we're *really* going to die if the sun hits us," said Todd.

Julie, sounding outraged, said, "We're creatures of darkness. It's the principle of the thing, you know? She affronted the Kindred!"

"Whatever," said Todd.

About ten more minutes passed before he exhaled loudly, said, "This is crap," and got up. Shadow peered through the bamboo and watched the three of them trudging sadly down the street, in their white pancake makeup and black polyester cloaks.

• • •

Shadow had Sunday and Monday nights off. When she'd had the Impala, she'd gone driving. She'd head out Santa Monica as far as the beach, where she'd walk beside the dark water, or go to some of the clubs out there.

She didn't feel like staying home that Sunday night. The nearest club was down on the Boulevard, just off Orchid; she left early, before sunset, and instead of going straight down Highland took the back way, all the way up and over the hill on the other side, emerging behind Grauman's Chinese Theatre. Once or twice, through the quiet residential section, she thought she heard footsteps echoing her own. When she turned and looked, though, there were no coven members swirling their capes; only a man, indistinct in the twilight, walking along without drama.

The club, The Pearl Diver, had been there since the 1940s and had originally had a South Seas theme. All the tuck-and-roll banquettes had been torn out, though, and now it looked vaguely industrial. There was a bar, there was a platform for the DJ's equipment, there were a few chromed steel tables and folding chairs; all the rest was dance floor.

It was usually pretty quiet on a Sunday. Shadow liked it that way. She didn't go to meet people. She liked to dance, but by herself; she liked to drink, and that was safest done alone too. But it was good to do these things in a public place, in a pool of colored light, to music so loud she felt its vibration in her bones.

Shadow ordered a vodka on the rocks, on the grounds that it had fewer calories than other drinks. It was pure, it was volatile; one drink and her exhaustion drained away, and she was out on the floor and jumping to the music. Her hair flew, her knees and elbows pumped, and she didn't give a rat's ass who might be lurking in the darkness at the edge of the dance floor. She was *moving*.

At some point she was in a bright warm place and the DJ had just put on Buzzcocks' *Ever Fallen in Love*? There was someone dancing beside her, suddenly. She looked up at him, snarling, but her shout of anger died in her throat.

He was as caught up in the dance as she was, he wasn't even looking at her. He was fast, he was sinuous, he was in perfect control. He needed nothing.

She thought he might be a surfer. What was a surfer doing in a punk hangout? His skin was tanned dark amber, with a red flush under it, and his forearms were tattooed. There were bright glints in his red hair. He wore ragged jeans, a torn shirt, but a fire opal winked from his ear.

Shadow felt all her breath going out of her. She staggered away from him, got another drink at the bar, found a vacant table and sat down. Her legs were trembling. Other people were staring at the guy now. Two older girls sitting at the table next to hers watched him with avid expressions.

"Damn," said one of them, in awe.

"Who is *that*?" said the other. "The God of the Beach?"

The music ended, and the dancer looked around. He spotted Shadow, walked to her table and loomed over her. He looked familiar. Where had she seen him before?

"Can I buy you a drink?" he said.

"Hell yes!" said the nearer of the girls at the next table, as she leaned forward to catch his eye. His unmoving gaze rested on Shadow.

"Okay," said Shadow.

He went to the bar and returned a moment later with a pair of vodkas on the rocks. He put them down and seated himself next to her.

"Okay if I sit with you?" he said. He didn't smile as he said it, and that lowered her defenses a little. Smiling people always wanted something more.

"Yeah, okay," she said.

She waited for him to say the stupid things non-punks said when they came into a place like this. Most men, looking at her Doc Martens and black ensemble, assumed she was a lesbian and did something idiotic like jovially telling her they were lesbians, too, trapped in the bodies of men. She'd never known what that was supposed to make her feel, other than contempt.

But he said nothing. He just sat there, watching her.

"You can really dance, you know?" she blurted, and felt like a fool.

He seemed to think about that, watching her as he took a sip of his drink. "Thanks," he said at last. "I liked your dancing too."

Eyeing him sidelong, she tried to define what it was about him that was making her heart contract so painfully. He looked a little like Scott Rosenthal back in eighth grade, the boy she'd dreamed of marrying someday. He looked a little like Rick, the nice guy her mother had dated for a while.

No; *Samantha* had fantasized about a white wedding, without ever actually getting up the courage to even say hello to Scott Rosenthal. *Samantha* had hidden in her room, crying, while her mother had had a drunken quarrel with Rick and ended up throwing him out.

Shadow never wept over anybody.

The guy was talking to her in a low soothing voice, and she realized that he wasn't nearly as inarticulate as he had seemed at first. He spoke quietly, patiently, yes, a lot like Rick. What had Rick's last name been?

"...But I don't really think you're into this?" he was saying. He put his hand over hers. His hand was warm. It startled her a little.

"What?"

"All this," he said, nodding toward the couples at the bar. "All these desperate people."

"No," she said. "I just come here to dance."

"I could tell," he said. "Me too."

"You burn up the floor, man," said Shadow. "Not like the rest of these posers. They're *needy*. That's why I like my space, you know?"

He nodded solemnly. Shadow looked down and saw that her glass was empty. Without a word he got up and brought her another drink.

She found herself talking to him about her life. He listened without comment, without smiling. What was there to smile about? But now and then he squeezed her hand.

It made her feel lightheaded. It made her want to do something stupid.

Someone was standing beside their table. It was the bartender, the older one, looking surly.

"What's this Kiki says about putting drinks on your tab? You ain't got no damn tab," said the bartender.

Rick (No, that wasn't his name. Had he told her his name?) looked up at the bartender and smiled. His smile was all light and warmth; Shadow leaned toward him involuntarily.

"You didn't recognize me, did you?" he said pleasantly. The bartender peered at him, confused. Then he laughed.

"Jesus, what's wrong with my eyes? Never mind! Can I get you another round?"

"Yes," said the guy.

Shadow drank, but was no longer relaxed. She was shaking. Where was her self-control? *She didn't need this guy.* But, she told herself, she could *use* him, couldn't she? Of course she could. Samantha would be going all dewy-eyed and dreaming of a future right about now, but Shadow knew better than that. He was somebody, he was an actor or in a band or something, obviously. He must have money.

If nothing else, she might talk him into walking her home. She could tell him about the vampire covens, and they'd have a good laugh.

Her glass was empty. The music had stopped, the lights gone down; the DJ was taking a break. People at the tables around them seemed to be half asleep. When had she stopped talking?

He closed his hand on hers and rose from his seat. "Come on," he said. "Let's get out of here."

Shadow followed him outside. The night was dank, chilly, smelled tired. He led her along the Walk of Stars, under the glittering lights, and they turned up Orchid into the darkness. She looked around as they got to Franklin.

"Where's your car?" she stammered, suddenly wary.

"We're going back to your place, remember?" he said, sounding amused. "And watching out for vampires."

"Right," she said, and now she remembered telling him, and felt so relieved she took his hand again and gave him a little-lost-girl look. "Vampires are scary."

He put his arm around her as they crossed Franklin. God, he was warm. Maybe he'd loan her enough money to get the Impala repaired. Maybe he'd move in with her. Maybe she'd move in with him. But she wouldn't love him, because only the Samanthas of the world were stupid enough to do that. Shadows kept control, kept their distance.

But she had to admit she wanted the strength of his big body, its heat, its hardness. Well, why not? It was there to be used. All the way up the hill and down the other side, she clung to him. Who wouldn't? Who wouldn't come up with any excuse just to be with him?

They were at her door. No vampires. She let him in.

She switched on the light in the bathroom, which was a dim little bulb with a pink shade. In the half-light he peeled off his shirt, and she saw that his tattoos swirled up his arms and across his broad chest, coiling patterns like Chinese dragons. Nowhere stark white unsunned, even when he stepped out of his jeans. Nothing to repel her, nothing on which she could look in scorn. If Samantha had gone down on her knees and prayed for a lover, he'd look like this.

But she was Shadow.

She got up and skinned out of her clothes, summoning all her arrogance, and if he was repelled by her pallid skin or those five pounds she couldn't shear off no matter how she starved herself, if he regretted being here, well, it was too damn late now. She gave him a push toward the bed.

"Come on, stud," she said. "Do you do anything else as nice as you dance?"

She kept control, at first. She rode him, hard and careless, and he performed like a big, stolid horse. It was only when she collapsed on him, when he put his arms around her and rolled over onto her, that Samantha, dumb bitch, began crying and telling him how beautiful he was.

She couldn't get out of his arms. She was too weak to get out of his arms, even when the sheets blackened and the flames rose in a great burst, lighting up the room like sunrise. Unsmiling, he looked into her eyes. His muscles rippled, the dragons on his body went writhing over her flesh. He put his face close to hers and her hair flared up, all the chemicals from the dye erupting in rainbow sparks, and there was pain but a kind of ecstasy too. The fire was paring away her ugly, overweight body.

And Samantha was gone at last and she was Shadow.

• • •

The landlord was so old his skin was going transparent, but he wore a sporty cap and had no trouble hobbling around with a cane. He led Jon into the parking lot and waved a hand at the incinerated ruin of Unit D.

"That's it," he said. Jon shook his head, looking at the police tape around the wreckage. He leaned back to look up at the overhanging trees whose branches had shriveled from the heat, the stands of bamboo with their leaves seared away. Then he glanced across at the bulldozed space on the other side of the parking lot.

"This is your second fire in a month, isn't it?" he said, with suspicion in his voice.

"Yep," said the landlord. "No connection, though. This one, tenant fell asleep smoking in bed. Near as the cops could tell."

"Yeah?" Jon stepped back, raised his camera and took three quick shots in succession. "That's too bad."

The landlord shrugged. "Good excuse to sell the place. Some young guy like you could tear all these units out, put in a nice big condo building, make a lot of money. You know anybody who's interested?"

Jon shook his head. He walked up to the edge of the police tape and leaned in to get a closer shot of the tumbled ashes, the twisted bed frame with its paint blistered, its rubber casters melted off. He saw no sign of the mattress; the police must have carted it away.

Something caught his attention, moving back in among the cinders. Jon reached forward gingerly and lifted back what was left of a coffee table.

A kitten backed away on unsteady legs. It was black as the cinders themselves, and so young its eyes were pearly.

"Oh, cool," said Jon, wishing he could use the image for *Negative Pulse*. He raised his camera anyway, and took a photograph.

MONKEY DAY

The faithful came in pickup trucks, setting out in the dark hours of the morning. Some came down the highway in old sedans, from other fishing towns. Some simply rose, as Father Souza had risen, and drove five blocks to the parking lot where the parade was assembling, under sea-fog and the curious stares of surfers getting into wetsuits. It was the day of the Grand Festival of St. Anthony of Padua.

Father Souza parked his elderly Toyota and got out, looking around.

All the panoply was unpacked and assembled. Here was the statue of the Saint himself, on a platform decked with lilies, hoisted into the air on two long poles by daddies and uncles and brothers-in-law, carried in state on their shoulders. Here was the ox in its harness, its horns tipped with gleaming brass knobs. A man hitched it to the two-wheeled carreta while various members of the Apostolic Association filled the cart with St. Anthony's bread. This year, the Saint was providing turf club rolls out of big plastic bags from Ralphs market.

Here were the Queens and their Courts, teenaged girls in ballgowns, bearing flowers. Here were the Little Queens, first graders restless in scratchy tulle. Here were their mothers and aunts, bringing out the trailing capes and trains to grace their daughters. Grandmothers, now quiet and expectant dust, had embroidered the Holy Spirit doves, the roses, the Madonnas, the sacred hearts bleeding diamonds and fire in gold and silver thread on heavy, red velvet. Each cape bore the emblem of its particular group, winking in crystal: TAFT ALTAR ASSOCIATION, 1908. PORTERVILLE ROSARY SOCIETY, 1882. MCKITTRICK CHI-RHO CLUB, 1938.

Father Souza opened the Toyota's hatchback and took out his own vestments, slipping them on over his black shirt and trousers. They were a little threadbare and nowhere near medieval in their splendor.

"Hey, Father Mark, I have an outfit too. See?" The voice floated up from elbow level.

"Good morning, Patrick," said Father Souza, as his head emerged from the chasuble. He looked down at Patrick Avila.

Patrick turned proudly to display himself. He was playing Francisco, one of the three little shepherds who witnessed the miraculous visitation of Our Lady of Fatima. There was a red sash threaded through the belt loops of his jeans. He wore a red tasseled stocking cap.

"See? Isn't the hat great? My daddy loaned it to me. It's part of his French trapper clothes."

Father Souza was mystified for a moment, and then remembered that Patrick's father did historical re-enactments.

"Right. Yes. Very nice, Patrick."

"Because I couldn't wear my Super-P outfit," Patrick continued. "Because I'm supposed to be Francisco today."

Father Souza blinked. "Super-P?"

"That's me when I'm going to have my superpowers," explained Patrick. "Actually I won't have them until I turn eighteen. But I have the outfit already. It has a cape and everything."

"Good morning, Father Mark." Kali Silva, who was six, like Patrick, wandered up with a tall fifth grader named Brittany Machado. The girls wore bandanas on their heads and carried rosaries. They were playing the other two Children of Fatima.

"Mrs. Okura says we're supposed to walk in front of you," Kali informed Father Souza.

"Are you?" Father Souza looked around in a helpless kind of way. "I guess so."

"It's on the schedule," said Brittany. She looked at Patrick severely. "Where's Our Lady?"

Patrick looked blank a moment and then shouted, "Oh my God, she's still sitting in my mom's car!" He tore off through the crowd.

"You're going to go to Hell," Kali shouted after him.

"You're not supposed to say Hell," Brittany told her.

"But he took the name of the Lord thy God in vain," said Kali.

"Cool it, kids," said Father Souza. "Six-year-olds don't go to Hell."

Both girls turned bright, speculative faces up to him.

"Really?" said Kali. "Not even if—"

"Here she is," bellowed Patrick, charging up with Our Lady of Fatima, who resided that day in a ten-inch-tall plastic statue glued to a white pillow representing a cloud.

The schoolbuses bringing the bands arrived at about the same time as the van bearing the news crew from KCLM *(K-CLAM News at Six!)*. The Knights of Columbus arrived shortly thereafter, with their swords and plumed hats. Patrick attempted to sidle over and get a better look at the swords.

"You're supposed to stay here," said Kali.

"Everybody else is moving around," grumbled Patrick.

"Let's just stay together, okay, kids?" said Father Souza.

"So, Father Mark?" Brittany tapped his elbow. "My grandma told me about this little girl, who took Communion only she spit the Host out into a Kleenex and took it outside and cut it open with a knife to see if it did anything, and it started really bleeding, and *she* went to Hell."

"I heard that story, when I was your age," said Father Souza. "But I think—"

At that moment the PA system was switched on, with a deafening squeal of feedback, and a DJ named Ron introduced himself at high volume. He led everyone in singing the national anthem, followed by the Portuguese national anthem. After that he called out the marching order of each group, as the fog burned off abruptly and everyone began to sweat.

Father Souza led the children to their place in line, just in front of the ox cart. There they waited, shifting from foot to foot on hot asphalt, until the parade stepped off.

The ox behind them started forward, and the cart began an ominous shrieking that grew louder as it moved slowly down Addie Street. By the time they rounded the corner onto Cypress Street, it was painful to hear. Brittany and Kali walked with their hands over their ears, rosaries held in their teeth. Patrick ignored it all, marching along cheerfully, happy to be moving. He spotted one set of his grandparents taking photos and raised Our Lady in a high sign for them, being unable to wave. "*Cut it out!*" hissed Brittany.

Patrick ignored her too. He spotted his parents and the other grandparents with them, video cameras whirring, and he shifted Our Lady to one hand and did the Macarena as he marched.

"You're going to Hell," said Brittany.

"Nuh uh," said Patrick.

"Kids, that's enough sending each other to Hell," muttered Father Souza.

Someone came running out of the Lions Club kitchen with a bottle of Mazola and poured it over the cart's screaming axle, and that helped a little.

"Thank you, God," said Patrick

"You're going to—" began Brittany, and then all three little faces turned up to Father Souza, as to a referee.

"If he said 'Thank you, God,' as a prayer of thanks from his heart, then it wasn't a sin," said Father Souza patiently. "Brittany, don't get so angry about—"

"Yaay!" said Patrick.

"But my *grandma* says—"

"Kali, look, it's Ms. Washburn," exclaimed Patrick, pointing.

"Hi, Ms. Washburn," said Kali, waving with her rosary.

Ms. Washburn, who taught second grade at Cornelia Harloe Elementary, was seated at an outdoor table in front of the Surf Coffee Shop. She was watching the parade with a cool and amused smile, sipping her coffee, but there was a frown line between her eyes.

"My grandma says *she's* going to Hell too," said Brittany, unexpectedly. Both Patrick and Kali turned to stare at her.

"She can't be going to Hell," said Kali, "we're going to be in her class this year."

"Didn't you know? She's an—" said Brittany, but then the band behind them struck up "Louie, Louie" and drowned out further conversation. Father Souza wondered what Ms. Washburn might be, to have gotten on old Mrs. Machado's comprehensive list of the damned.

The parade turned the corner and wound its way up the long hill. At the highway intersection, two cops stopped traffic in installments as the parade came across to the vast parking lot of the church. Father Souza moved in front to lead the children through, watching the highway traffic with his pale, worried face.

Someone parked the ox and got it a bucket of water, as the rest of the parade filed into St. Catherine of Alexandria's. The band members crowded upright in red and blue rows. There were so many of them they had to leave their instruments in the garden, in gleaming piles. The trains of the Queens were gathered up awkwardly, layered over the backs of pews. Elevating the Host, Father Souza looked out over the packed house and sighed. Today, he had a congregation. Next Sunday's attendance would drop back to the usual single row of grandmothers and three families.

After Mass, Father Souza administered a general blessing, invoked St. Anthony, and said a few hopeful words about donations for the Earthquake Retrofitting Fund for St. Catherine's School. Nobody pulled out their wallets, though.

The teenagers changed out of their band uniforms or Queen ensembles, grabbed surfboards, and raced back down the hill to the beach. Mothers and aunts collected the abandoned robes and packed them carefully away. The other adults and children went into St. Anthony's carnival, which had been set up on the empty schoolground, and threw beanbags through holes or ping-pong balls into fish bowls. They won goldfish, black eyepatches, rolls of Smarties candy and tiny pink plastic cars.

· · ·

School started a month later, though not at St. Catherine's Elementary. No ABC cards were tacked up above the first grade blackboard. At Halloween there were no drawings of pumpkins; at Thanksgiving, no turkeys made from paper plates and construction paper, nor drawings of Indians and Pilgrims. The day on which Christmas vacation had begun came and went without hysteria, cheers or the janitor dressing up as Santa Claus. Mr. Espinoza had been dead for five years, anyway. Valentine's Day approached, and there were no red construction paper hearts.

The rituals of life went on, or they didn't; when they ceased, it was astonishing how quickly they were forgotten. St. Anthony still had his day, but for how many more years?

Father Souza sat in his office and looked out at the vacant school building, at the rows of empty windows. His gaze settled inevitably on the jagged cracks that had shot up through the old brickwork, like black lightning out of the earth, on the morning the earthquake had hit. He had long since learned to accept acts of God, but this one had rather surprised him.

Phantom children moved on the weedy playground, in the plaid woolen uniforms or salt-and-pepper corduroy of a generation past. A tetherball swung listlessly against its post, as the fog blew by.

A real child was coming up the walkway to his office, followed by a woman. Startled, Father Souza rose and opened the door.

"Hi, Father Mark," said Patrick. "We have to talk."

"Patrick," said his mother, in tones of reproof.

"Mrs. Avila?" Father Souza guessed, extending his hand.

"Hi," she said. "Do you have a minute to talk to us?"

"Okay," said Father Souza. He let them in and they settled in the two chairs that faced his desk. He returned to his chair, wondering why Patrick was wearing gardening gloves fastened over his sneakers with duct tape.

"I, ah, I've met Patrick's father at Mass, of course," he said.

"Oh, I don't come because I'm Lutheran," she said, amiably enough. "Well, not *Lutheran* Lutheran, but… you know."

"Sure," said Father Souza.

"My dad is away on Campaign," said Patrick.

"Campaign is where he and the other re-enactors go up to Lassen Campground in full costume and pretend they're sixteenth-century Italian troops fighting battles," Mrs. Avila explained patiently. "Which is why I had to take the afternoon off to deal with this."

"I have this really big problem, Father," said Patrick.

"What kind of problem?"

"Well…" said Patrick, "we were supposed to make holidays, right? And so I had this really great idea, and—"

"Ms. Washburn gave them this creative assignment at the beginning of the semester," said Mrs. Avila. "They were supposed to invent holidays. Come up with a reason for the holiday and make up customs for it, and pick a day of the year, and that kind of thing. So Patrick came up with Monkey Day."

"Which is this really cool holiday all about monkeys?" said Patrick. "Like everybody wears monkey shoes, and eats monkey food like bananas and banana bread and banana milkshakes? And chicken strips only you call them monkey fingers? And—" He jumped to his feet and waved his arms. "Just do everything monkey! Like playing Monkey Island on your dad's computer and watching monkey DVDs and stuff. King Kong. Mojo Jojo. Tarzan. You know."

"He put a lot of work into it," said Mrs. Avila.

"And I got an A and a gold star!" said Patrick, husky with fresh anger.

"He did too," said Mrs. Avila. "But, this morning, he asked me for permission to take his Tarzan DVD to school."

"Because today *is* Monkey Day," said Patrick. "And I even put on monkey feet and we stopped at the store and bought bananas for everybody in my class—"

"And I asked him if he had permission to bring a cartoon to school," said Mrs. Avila, looking at Patrick sternly.

"Well, it's Monkey Day!" shouted Patrick, "So I said yes, okay? But then when I got to school I was giving everybody bananas—and Ms. Washburn said there was no eating in class—and I said it was Monkey Day, and she—"

"She laughed at him," said Mrs. Avila.

"So then I said I was going to go to Audiovisual to get the DVD player, and *she* said no, and I said but it was Monkey Day, and *she* said, Patrick, don't be silly, that was five months ago, and I said no it wasn't, Monkey Day is on February 12—"

"Because it's Darwin's birthday," explained Mrs. Avila, looking a little embarrassed. "His father came up with that."

"No, that's okay," Father Souza said. "Catholics don't have a problem with Evolution."

"And *she* said, Monkey Day was only made up, so we couldn't have it! And then she said, 'Take those rid—ridic—ridiculous things off your feet'!"

"And *he* called her a Work Destroyer," said Mrs. Avila dryly. "And a few other things. I got quite an e-mail from her. I had to leave work to go pick him up from the principal's office."

"Oh, dear."

"They have a behavior chart at his school," said Mrs. Avila. "It's set up by colors. You get a green ticket in the morning, and if you're good, you get to keep it all day. If you misbehave, you lose the green ticket and get a yellow one. If you act worse, the Yellow gets taken away and you get an orange one. Patrick went all the way down the chart over a period of three minutes and wound up with five red tickets."

"Oh, dear," said Father Souza.

"I hate her!" said Patrick.

"No, no, Patrick, you can't do that," said Father Souza. "It sounds as though it was just a misunderstanding."

"She laughed at me," said Patrick.

"I plan on talking to the principal about that," said Mrs. Avila. "But what has him really upset is that she said—"

"*All* holidays are just made up," said Patrick, in a terrible voice. "Even Christmas. She said they're all imaginary, that people just make things up!" He folded his arms, and glared at Father Souza in righteous indignation.

"Ah. Okay," said Father Souza. He took off his glasses and rubbed the bridge of his nose. Up from his memory floated a scrap about Ms. Washburn: Brittany Machado's grandmother said she was going to Hell. "I guess she's a militant atheist?"

"And I have to say I'm a little annoyed at her agenda," said Mrs. Avila. "I'd like to choose my own time to tell my kids there isn't any Santa Claus, thank you very much."

"Except Santa Claus *is* real," said Patrick. "Right, Father Mark?"

Father Souza looked uncertainly from Patrick to his mother. "Saint Nicholas is real, yes. And children get presents at Christmas for the sake of Baby Jesus, of course. Some people don't believe that, Patrick. It's a shame, but we shouldn't hate them for it."

"Can we hate people because they're mean?" asked Patrick.

"No," said Father Souza. "But you can hate meanness."

"Well, I really really really hate meanness," said Patrick. "And I think what you ought to do is go over to her house with a Bible like that guy in that exercise movie and say a spell so her head turns around. Because then people will laugh at her and not listen to what she says."

Father Souza and Mrs. Avila stared at him in mutual incomprehension. Then Mrs. Avila said, "Did you watch *The Exorcist,* after your father and I told you not to?"

Patrick winced.

"Um, just a little. Because it happened to be on. Because I was over at Kyla's house. And it was way back at Halloween. So *anyway* Father, you need to use your powers on Ms. Washburn, okay?"

"Patrick," said Mrs. Avila, "we're going to have a long talk with Daddy when he gets back. And priests don't do magic spells. Is that what you made me bring you all the way up here to ask?"

"They do spells in Theo's Dragon Gamer Module," muttered Patrick, not meeting her eyes.

Sensing an explosion immanent, Father Souza said hastily: "I'll try to talk to your teacher, okay, Patrick?"

"And we're going to have a long talk with your brother too," said Mrs. Avila to Patrick, rising to her feet. "I'm sorry, Father Mark. It looks as though Patrick wasn't really interested in spiritual advice."

She led Patrick out the door by his upper arm. Patrick turned in the doorway and winked broadly, twice, so Father Souza wouldn't miss it.

• • •

Father Souza had used to play ping-pong with Father Connolly, until the old man had passed away. Now he got his exercise most afternoons by walking down the hill and out onto the pier, as far as the end, and back.

He never power-walked. He idled. Sometimes he chatted with the fishermen; today he leaned on the rail and watched the surfers riding the long white combers into land or more often idling themselves, floating on the swell, resting on their boards. Some of the surfers were girls. The black neoprene suits made them look like seal-women out of Celtic legend, strangely arousing. Father Souza watched them regretfully, and lifted his head to stare far down the beach. Just visible at the edge of the dunes was a grove of dead trees, with silvered and twisted trunks. It was a white and silent place. When he had been a child, he had thought that God lived there.

Sighing, he put his hands in his jacket pockets and moved on. Salt mist was beading on his clothes, chilly and damp.

The arcade that used to be at the foot of the pier was gone, had been gone since a long-ago winter storm sent waves over the seawall and collapsed its roof. There was a doughnut shop there now. Father Souza stopped in and bought a latte, and settled into a vacant booth.

He warmed his hands on the cup and watched the early twilight falling. Something came rolling down the sidewalk, on a wobbly trajectory: a cocoanut. It came to rest against a planter containing a skimpy date palm, as though huddling with a fellow exile from tropical climes. Father Souza wondered how it had got there.

A woman was sitting in the booth across from him, sipping coffee and making notes on something with a red pen. Grading papers? Yes. He recognized Ms. Washburn.

He cleared his throat. "Excuse me," he said. "You teach at the public school, don't you?"

She lifted her eyes to his, and he had a mental image of a figure in armor going on guard. Her eyes were gray as steel.

"I do, yes."

"You're Patrick Avila's teacher?"

"Ah," she said. "I imagine I know what this is about."

He smiled awkwardly and extended a hand. "I'm Father Souza. I guess you did me a favor; one of my parishioners actually got upset enough about something to ask my advice. Can I hear your side of the story?"

But he could tell his attempt at self-depreciating charm was wasted. It was plain, from the look on her face, that she saw a host of blood-drinking popes and Inquisitors in phantom form standing at his shoulder.

"I don't particularly see any need to defend my actions to you," she said. Her accent was patrician, with a certain New England starch.

"Defend, no, no. I just thought you could enlighten me a little," said Father Souza. "Patrick was pretty upset."

"Patrick had a violent episode in class," said Ms. Washburn.

"So I gathered."

"I've made a recommendation that he should be tested for Attention Deficit Disorder."

Father Souza winced. "I wouldn't have said Patrick's problem was paying attention, would you? Just the other way around. He was able to keep focused on the monkey thing for five months."

"Are you an educator, Father Souza?" inquired Ms. Washburn.

"No," he admitted. "But I know it's not a good idea to be in a hurry to pin a label on a child."

"Neither is it a good idea to let a condition go undiagnosed," said Ms. Washburn. "The sooner Patrick can undergo corrective counseling, the better."

Father Souza sat back and stared at her, baffled. "What exactly did he do that was so bad? Did he hit you?"

"Not physically, no. He resorted to verbal abuse. He kicked a chair across the room. He disrupted class to the extent that a full hour of the school day was lost," said Ms. Washburn.

"Sounds like a pretty angry young man," said Father Souza. Ms. Washburn flushed and took a sip of her coffee.

"Patrick was clearly acting out," she said. "His home life, possibly. I understand his father is in some kind of paramilitary cult. If his parents encourage violence as a means of accomplishing goals—"

"I don't think they do," said Father Souza. "I think Patrick was angry about getting laughed at, when he thought he'd invented this wonderful holiday. Patrick's mom thinks you were trying to demolish belief in Santa Claus."

"*Demolish* is a loaded word, don't you think?" said Ms. Washburn. "I would have said that, as a teacher, I have an obligation to teach what is true. I will not teach lies. If I can encourage my students to see through lies, I owe it to them to do so."

"So the point of the made-up holidays assignment was…?"

"To teach my students the truth about social rituals," said Ms. Washburn, looking Father Souza in the eye. "People simply make them up. Patrick made up Monkey Day. These events are only as real as we make them. They have no significance, otherwise. If people are ever to be free, they need to understand that. All that absurd... *panoply*, all that pageantry and symbolism, is a trap."

Father Souza remembered her frown lines, as she'd watched the parade go by.

"It's folk art," he said. "It's the celebration of people's faith, it's their identity. You ought to at least respect cultural tradition."

"It's a trap," she repeated. "An impressive spectacle that keeps people from thinking."

"Okay... and how do you feel about respecting other people's beliefs?"

"I tend to favor truth over illusions. 'Wine is strong, a king is stronger, women are stronger still, but Truth is the strongest of all,'" Ms. Washburn quoted. "That's in your Bible, isn't it?"

"Third book of Esdras, actually," he said.

"There you are. And the truth shall make you free."

"Gospel of John. Look, you know that Patrick's parents are pulling him out of Harloe," he said. "They're going to send him to Saint Rose's, all the way out in San Luis Obispo. That's a twelve-mile commute every morning and afternoon, and the tuition isn't free. You've lost a bright student, and I know they made a formal complaint against you. Nobody's winning, here."

"It's a shame, isn't it?" said Ms. Washburn. "Perhaps you ought to convince them to reconsider."

Father Souza bit back a retort and stared at the wall above her head, trying to summon patience. The wall was covered in bright yellow vinyl, with a pattern of green monkeys linked together by their tails. They seemed to writhe and blur, under the fluorescent light, vaguely menacing.

"Look," he said, "we shouldn't be at odds, here. We're both in the same business, aren't we? We're working for the common good. You get their brains working, and I look after their souls."

Ms. Washburn shook her head. "Between Reason and Unreason there can be only war," she said with certainty. He looked sadly at her, realizing that he envied her. She was young, and beautiful in a severe kind of way, and had endless strength to marshal for her argument.

"The thing is," he said, "the pageantry doesn't matter. It's just something they do because it's fun, because it's always been done, because they want to see their kids dressed up. About God, they're apathetic. The Unreason isn't there, don't you see? The, the direct, bolt-of-lightning, burning-bush moment when they *know* He exists—isn't there for them. You think religion holds people in chains... Ma'am, I barely have a congregation. What harm can a few parades and statues do?"

Mrs. Washburn gave him a shrewd look, not entirely without sympathy.

"You've lost your faith," she said.

"No," he said. "I never had any. I *knew.* That knowledge, that's what I've lost."

"No, you haven't," she said, leaning forward and almost—but not quite—putting her hand on his. "You're free of illusions, that's all. And, once you move past that—"

"Then what is there?" he said. "You think there's some kind of utilitarian political paradise awaiting us all? Some future where we're all rational and accept seventy-five years of consciousness as all there is and all there'll ever be?"

"You'll learn to accept that."

"Then what was the point of leaving the jungle?" said Father Souza. "We'd have been better off as monkeys. Why become creatures that can imagine a Heaven with a God in it, and want Him there?"

"Because we're engineered to progress by outgrowing our primitive selves," said Ms. Washburn. "And that means we must leave our fantasies behind, and our need for them. We're leaving them already."

"Patrick isn't," said Father Souza, sighing as he got to his feet.

• • •

Saint Rose's, as it happened, had a waiting list, and its principal was unwilling to bend the rules for Patrick's parents, since they were not members of St. Rose's parish. There was also the matter of Patrick's First Communion, which ought to have happened when he was six, but due to one thing and another had been postponed several times.

It was suggested that Patrick might be homeschooled for a few months. It was suggested that Mr. and Mrs. Avila might want to resolve that little matter of the holy sacrament before the start of the next school year, when (if they were truly committed to a Catholic lifestyle for their son) Patrick's case might be reconsidered.

Patrick did not especially want a Catholic lifestyle. He did not at all want to be pulled out of class with the children he had known since kindergarten and sent to a distant school full of strangers. Nor was he particularly happy about being enrolled in a catechism class on Tuesday evenings with two teenagers, three recovering alcoholics and one aggressively friendly lady who called him Sparky.

"This isn't fair," he complained. He and Father Souza were sitting out on the rectory steps after class, waiting for Mrs. Avila to come pick him up. The early summer sun was low, throwing long shadows across the parking lot.

"Unfair things happen, Patrick," said Father Souza. "To everybody. What we have to do is choose whether we'll do the right thing anyway, or sit around feeling sorry for ourselves."

"What do you do when bad stuff happens to you?" asked Patrick, pulling himself up on the handrail of the steps.

Father Souza glanced over at the old school, where a new crop of weeds was greening the empty playground. "I say to God, 'This is a test, right? Things only look bad. I'm going to go on as though things are going to get better, and trust in You that they will, and... and that'll be to Your greater glory.'"

"And what does God say back?"

He never says a damn thing anymore, thought Father Souza miserably. "See, you have to believe He's listening—and that there's a point to all this, even if you can't see it—"

"There's Ms. Washburn!" Patrick flung out his arm accusatorily, pointing.

"What?" Father Souza peered across the parking lot. The library was just closing for the day; it had no parking spaces of its own, so people using the library parked in the St. Catherine's lot. Ms. Washburn had indeed emerged from the library, and was even now making her way to her solitary silver Volvo. She walked upright as a soldier, holding her keys like a weapon.

"She's so mean," said Patrick in a choked voice. "I thought she was nice at first. She laughed at me!"

"I know," said Father Souza. "But you have to learn—"

There was a shimmer in the air. All the leaves in the rectory garden fluttered, the big, glossy leaves of ivy and acanthus, the red leaves of ornamental plum, the broad and pointed maple leaves. There was a gust of heat; there was a wave of overpowering smell, like a banana-scented car freshener overlaid with crushed and steaming vegetation, and a certain mammal stench.

They burst out of the ivy like brown cannon balls, screaming.

"Monkeys!" yelled Patrick in delight. "*Get* her, monkeys!"

But they were already racing across the asphalt toward Ms. Washburn, two dozen howling monkeys, with pink-rimmed fuzzy ears and streaming, curly tails, like Curious George on crack, beating the ground with their knuckles as they came, baring their fangs. Behind him Father Souza heard thumps and the swaying of tree branches. Black hairy bodies hurtled past him, chimpanzees as real as any on an *Animal Planet* special. They, too, converged on Ms. Washburn, shrieking threats.

"Holy God," cried Father Souza. "Get into your car! Get in and lock the door, Ms. Washburn!"

She lifted her head and looked out at him, across the advancing tide of simian rage. "I beg your pardon?" she said coldly.

"Look out for the damn monkeys!" shouted Father Souza, leaping to his feet.

"What monkeys?" she said, just as they reached her.

He braced himself, expecting to see her torn apart; but she made a negligent gesture with the hand holding her car keys, and the sharp silver keys glittered in the afternoon light, and the foremost monkeys in the pack burst like bubbles, vanishing without a trace. The others pulled back angrily and swarmed around to either side, circling, and some produced cocoanuts from thin air and hurled them at the Volvo. Its windows began to crack and star, but Ms. Washburn didn't seem to notice.

"Come on, monkeys!" ordered Patrick, leaping up and down. From the shadows under the big eucalyptus trees vaulted baboons, with long, gray bodies like jungle wolves and hideous red and blue muzzles, and white manes, and long, white teeth. They roared forward in a second assault, but Ms. Washburn looked right through them. By this time the chimpanzees had found something else to throw at her car, and it splatted and stank, but nothing seemed to touch her.

"Ms. Washburn, for God's sake!" Father Souza started down the steps to her, his heart in his mouth. The first of the baboons to reach her vanished in midleap, though foam from its jaws flecked her dress. "Don't you see them?"

"There are no monkeys," she said, raising her handful of keys. The little monkeys cowered back and then sprang again, hooting, beating her car with bananas, and the baboons bit savagely at its tires. With a hiss, the left rear tire flattened.

"Yes, there are!" shouted Patrick gleefully, as ten silverback gorillas pushed up out of the cracks in the asphalt, throwing flat chunks of it aside like tombstones, and lumbered forward. They stood upright, rocked from hind foot to hind foot and beat their chests, grunting menace. One after another they worked themselves into frenzies and rushed Ms. Washburn, who stood her ground and stared through them defiantly.

She refused to acknowledge when they veered away at the last possible moment, merely gripped her bright keys. Her unbelief was a silver helmet, her refusal an Aegis. Three of them exploded into powder, but the others attacked the poor Volvo. They put their fists through the windows, they leaped up and down on the roof.

"Go, monkeys, go!" said Patrick, running forward. Father Souza ran after him and pulled him back.

"Patrick, you have to make them stop—" he said, just as a roar shook the earth. He looked around and saw nothing new emerging from the bushes, from anywhere in the parking lot; then something moved at the edge of his vision and he tilted his head back to see—

"Oh, no," he murmured. Patrick looked up and fell silent, cowering against him.

For something black was lifting itself above the hilltop behind them. A monstrous face moved jerkily up from the reservoir fence, stared down with living eyes out of what was patently so much rabbit fur and rubber skin, but it was still Kong, the Eighth Wonder of the World, and it was *ten stories tall.* Its grunts sent gusts of hot wind rushing down the long grass. Up and over the hill it came, moving unevenly but with appalling speed, trampling everything in its path, making straight for Ms. Washburn.

Ms. Washburn turned pale, but did not flinch. She raised her little fistful of keys. "There are no monkeys," she repeated.

Over the past thirty seconds Father Souza had felt something growing in him, inappropriate joy mingled with entirely appropriate terror mingled with something else, something he couldn't quite put a name to but which seemed obvious, something that burned through him and lit him up like neon.

These events are only as real as we make them.

He saw the boy, brilliant innocent of terrifying faith; he saw Ms. Washburn in all her harsh bravery and steely resolve. Monkeys who could envision a heaven full of glorious divinity, or a crystalline rational universe of ice and stars. Wonderful monkeys! Who could have made such creatures?

"Enough," he said, in a voice not his own, and a blast of blue-white light and shockwave force moved out from him at high speed. It caught the little generic monkeys and blew them into oblivion like so many autumn leaves. The chimpanzees, the baboons and gorillas puffed out like smoke; and Kong itself became no more than a towering shadow, before dropping in a rain of black sand across the parking lot.

"Dude," said Patrick, awed.

Father Souza looked at himself in disbelief. Little residual white flames were running down him like water, sinking into him as though he were so much spiritual blotting paper.

Only as real as we make them.

"Ms. Washburn, can I call you a tow truck?" he heard himself saying.

"No, thank you," she replied, in a voice nearly as firm as was her accustomed wont. "Why would I need one?"

He looked up and watched as she got into her car. She ignored the broken glass and the fact that she had to crouch forward because the roof had been so badly dented. The engine started up and the Volvo limped away on three wheels, shedding cocoanuts and banana peels as it went. Ms. Washburn did not look back.

Real as we make them.

"That was *so* cool," said Patrick. "Except, um, King Kong. He was too scary. But, see? You can, too, do spells. I would have stopped him myself, except he was so big. When I get my superpowers, though, it'll be different."

Father Souza stretched his shoulders, rolled his neck, felt all the little stresses and tensions of years of everyday life melting away.

"You know," he said, "you're going to have to swear to use your powers for good, right?"

"Okay," said Patrick happily. "Does this mean I don't have to take catechism classes anymore?"

"Oh, no way." Father Souza leaned down and grinned, putting a hand on his shoulder. "They're more important than ever, now." His grin widened. "You belong to God, Patrick."

"Okay," said Patrick, grinning back. "I can pretend I'm taking secret ninja lessons, all right?"

A car rounded the corner and came up the hill into the parking lot. Mrs. Avila waved and honked the car's horn, steering around the potholes left by the gorillas. Patrick ran to her and climbed into the car.

"Was he good?" Mrs. Avila called.

Father Souza smiled and nodded. He waved after them as they drove away down the hill. Then he went inside to have a long talk with the Almighty.

CALAMARI CURLS

The town had seen better days.

Its best year had probably been 1906, when displaced San Franciscans, fleeing south to find slightly less unstable real estate, discovered a bit of undeveloped coastline an inconvenient distance from the nearest train station.

No tracks ran past Nunas Beach. There wasn't even a road to its golden sand dunes, and what few locals there were didn't know why. There were rumors of long-ago pirates. There was a story that the fathers from the local mission had forbidden their parishioners to go there, back in the days of Spanish rule.

Enterprising Yankee developers laughed and built a road, and laid out lots for three little beach towns, and sold them like hotcakes. Two of the towns vanished like hotcakes at a Grange Breakfast, too; one was buried in a sandstorm and the other washed out to sea during the first winter flood.

But Nunas Beach remained, somehow, and for a brief season there were ice cream parlors and photographers' studios, clam stands, Ferris wheels, drug stores and holiday cottages. Then, for no single reason, people began to leave. Some of the shops burned down; some of the cottages dwindled into shanties. Willow thickets and sand encroached on the edges. What was left rusted where it stood, with sand drifting along its three streets, yet somehow did not die.

People found their way there, now and then, especially after the wars. It was a cheap place to lie in the sun while your wounds healed and your shell-shock faded away. Some people stayed.

Pegasus Bright, who had had both his legs blown off by a land mine, had stayed, and opened the Chowder Palace. He was unpleasant when

49

he drank and, for that matter, when he didn't, but he could cook. The Chowder Palace was a long, low place on a street corner. It wasn't well lit, its linoleum tiles were cracked and grubby, its windows dim with grease. Still, it was the only restaurant in town. Therefore all the locals ate at the Chowder Palace, and so, too, did those few vacationers who came to Nunas Beach.

Mr. Bright bullied a staff of illegal immigrants who worked for him as waiters and busboys; at closing time they faded like ghosts back to homeless camps in the willow thickets behind the dunes, and he rolled himself back to his cot in the rear of the Palace, and slept with a tire iron under his pillow.

• • •

One Monday morning the regulars were lined up on the row of stools at the counter, and Mr. Bright was pushing himself along the row topping up their mugs of coffee, when Charlie Cansanary said:

"I hear somebody's bought the Hi-Ho Lounge."

"No they ain't, you stupid bastard," said Mr. Bright. He disliked Charlie because Charlie had lost his right leg to a shark while surfing, instead of in service to his country.

"That's what I heard too," said Tom Avila, who was the town's mayor.

"Why would anybody buy that place?" demanded Mr. Bright. "*Look* at it!"

They all swiveled on their stools and looked out the window at the Hi-Ho Lounge, which sat right across the street on the opposite corner. It was a windowless stucco place painted gray, with martini glasses picked out in mosaic tile on either side of the blind slab of a door. On the roof was a rusting neon sign portraying another martini glass whose neon olive had once glowed like a green star against the sunset. But not in years; the Hi-Ho Lounge had never been open in living memory.

"Maybe somebody wants to open a bar," said Leon Silva, wiping egg yolk out of his mustache. "It might be kind of nice to have a place to drink."

"You can get drinks here," said Mr. Bright quickly, stung.

"Yeah, but I mean legally. And in glasses and all," said Leon.

"Well, if you want to go to *those* kinds of places and spend an arm and a leg—" said Mr. Bright contemptuously, and then stopped himself, for Leon, having had an accident on a fishing trawler, only had one arm. Since he'd lost it while earning a paycheck rather than in pursuit of frivolous sport, however, he was less a target for Mr. Bright's scorn. Mr. Bright continued: "Anyway it'll never happen. Who's going to buy an old firetrap like that place?"

"Those guys," said Charlie smugly, pointing to the pair of business-suited men who had just stepped out of a new car and were standing on the sidewalk in front of the Hi-Ho Lounge.

Mr. Bright set down the coffee pot. Scowling, he wheeled himself from behind the counter and up to the window.

"Developers," he said. He watched as they walked around the Hi-Ho Lounge, talking to each other and shaking their heads. One took a key from an envelope and tried it in the padlock on the front door; the lock was a chunk of rust, however, and after a few minutes he drew back and shook his head.

"You ain't never getting in that way, buddy," said Tom. "You don't know beach winters."

The developer went back to his car and, opening the trunk, took out a hammer. He struck ineffectually at the lock.

"Look at the sissy way he's doing it," jeered Mr. Bright. "Hit it *hard,* you dumb son of a bitch."

The padlock broke, however, and the chain dropped; it took three kicks to get the door open, to reveal inky blackness beyond. The developers stood looking in, uncertain. The spectators in the Chowder Palace all shuddered.

"There has got to be serious mildew in there," said Charlie.

"And pipes rusted all to hell and gone," said Mr. Bright, with a certain satisfaction. "Good luck, suckers."

• • •

But the developers seemed to have luck. They certainly had money.

Work crews with protective masks came and stripped out the inside of the Hi-Ho Lounge. There were enough rusting fixtures to fill a dumpster; there were ancient red vinyl banquettes, so blackened with mold they looked charred, and clumped rats' nests of horsehair and cotton batting spilled from their entrails.

When the inside had been thoroughly gutted, the outside was tackled. The ancient stucco cracked away to reveal a surprise: graceful arched windows all along both street walls, and a shell-shaped fanlight over the front door. Stripped to its framing, the place had a promise of airy charm.

Mr. Bright watched from behind the counter of the Chowder Palace, and wondered if there was any way he could sue the developers. No excuses presented themselves, however. He waited for rats to stream from their disturbed havens and attack his customers; none came. When the workmen went up on ladders and pried off the old HI-HO LOUNGE sign from the roof, he was disappointed, for no one fell through the rotting lath, nor did sharp edges of rusted tin cut through any workmen's arteries, and they managed to get the sign down to the sidewalk without dropping it on any passers-by. Worse; they left the neon martini glass up there.

"It *is* going to be a bar," said Leon in satisfaction, crumbling crackers into his chowder.

"Shut up," said Mr. Bright.

"And a restaurant," said Charlie. "My brother-in-law works at McGregor's Restaurant Supply over in San Emidio. The developers set up this account, see. He says they're buying lots of stuff. All top of the line. Going to be a seafood place."

Mr. Bright felt tendrils of fear wrap about his heart and squeeze experimentally. He rolled himself back to his cubicle, took two aspirins washed down with a shot of bourbon, and rolled back out to make life hell for Julio, who had yet to clear the dirty dishes from booth three.

· · ·

The place opened in time for the summer season, despite several anonymous threatening calls to the County Planning Department.

The new sign said CALAMARI CURLS, all in pink and turquoise neon, with a whimsical octopus writhing around the letters. The neon martini glass was repiped a dazzling scarlet, with its olive once again winking green.

Inside was all pink and turquoise too: the tuck-and-roll banquettes, the napkins, the linoleum tiles. The staff, all bright young people working their way through Cal State San Emidio, wore pink and turquoise Hawaiian shirts.

Calamari Curls was fresh, jazzy and fun.

Mr. Bright rolled himself across the street, well after closing hours, to peer at the menus posted by the front door. He returned cackling with laughter.

"They got a *wine list!*" he told Jesus, the dishwasher. "And you should see their *prices!* Boy, have they ever made a mistake opening *here!* Who the hell in Nunas Beach is going to pay that kind of money for a basket of fish and chips?"

Everyone, apparently.

The locals began to go there; true, they paid a little more, but the food was so much better! Everything was so bright and hopeful at Calamari Curls! And the polished bar was an altar to all the mysteries of the perfect cocktail. Worse still, the great radiant sign could be seen from the highway, and passers-by who would never before have even considered stopping to fix a flat tire in Nunas Beach, now streamed in like moths to a porch light.

Calamari Curls had a glowing jukebox. Calamari Curls had karaoke on Saturday nights, and a clown who made balloon animals. Calamari Curls had a special tray with artfully made wax replicas of the mouth-watering desserts on their menu.

And the ghostly little businesses along Alder Street sanded the rust off their signs, spruced up a bit and got some of the overflow customers. After dining at Calamari Curls, visitors began to stop into Nunas Book and News to buy magazines and cigarettes. Visitors peered into the dark window of Edna's Collectibles, at dusty furniture, carnival glass and farm implements undisturbed in twenty years. Visitors poked around for bargains at the USO Thrift Shop. Visitors priced arrowheads and fossils at Jack's Rocks.

But Mr. Bright sat behind his counter and served chowder to an ever-dwindling clientele.

• • •

The last straw was the Calamari Curls Award Winning Chowder.

Ashen-faced, Mr. Bright rolled himself across the street in broad daylight to see if it was really true. He faced down the signboard, with its playful lettering in pink-and-turquoise marker. Yes; Award-Winning Chowder, containing not only fresh-killed clams but conch and shrimp too.

And in bread bowls. Fresh-baked on the premises.

And for a lower price than at the Chowder Palace.

Mr. Bright rolled himself home, into the Chowder Palace, all the way back to his cubicle. Julio caught a glimpse of the look on Bright's face as he passed, and hung up his apron and just walked out, never to return. Mr. Bright closed the place early. Mr. Bright took another two aspirin with bourbon.

He put the bourbon bottle back in its drawer, and then changed his mind and took it with him to the front window. There he sat through the waning hours, as the stars emerged and the green neon olive across the street shone among them, and the music and laughter echoed across the street pitilessly.

• • •

On the following morning, Mr. Bright did not even bother to open the Chowder Palace. He rolled himself down to the pier instead, and looked for Betty Step-in-Time.

Betty Step-in-Time had a pink bicycle with a basket, and could be found on the pier most mornings, doing a dance routine with the bicycle. Betty wore a pink middy top, a little white sailor cap, tap shorts and white tap shoes. Betty's mouth was made up in a red cupid's bow. Betty looked like the depraved older sister of the boy on the Cracker Jack box.

At the conclusion of the dance routine, which involved marching in place, balletic pirouettes and a mimed sea battle, Betty handed out business cards to anyone who had stayed to watch. Printed on the cards was:

ELIZABETH MARQUES
performance artist
interpretive dancer
transgender shaman

Mr. Bright had said a number of uncomplimentary things about Betty Step-in-Time over the years, and had even sent an empty bottle flying toward his curly head on one or two occasions. Now, though, he rolled up and waited in silence as Betty trained an imaginary spyglass on a passing squid trawler.

Betty appeared to recognize someone he knew on board. He waved excitedly and blew kisses. Then he began to dance a dainty sailor's hornpipe.

"Ahem," said Mr. Bright.

Betty mimed climbing hand over hand through imaginary rigging, pretended to balance on a spar, and looked down at Mr. Bright.

"Look," said Mr. Bright, "I know I never seen eye to eye with you—"

Betty went into convulsions of silent laughter, holding his sides.

"Yeah, okay, but I figure you and I got something in common," said Mr. Bright. "Which would be, we like this town just the way it is. It's a good place for anybody down on his luck. Am I right?

"But *that* place," and Mr. Bright waved an arm at Calamari Curls, "that's the beginning of the end. All that pink and blue stuff—Jesus, where do they think they are, Florida?—that's, whatchacallit, gentrification. More people start coming here, building places like that, and pretty soon people like you and me will be squeezed out. I bet you don't pay hardly any rent for that little shack over on the slough, huh? But once those big spenders start coming in, rents'll go through the roof. You mark my words!"

He looked up into Betty's face for some sign of comprehension, but the bright, blank doll-eyes remained fixed on him, nor did the painted smile waver. Mr. Bright cleared his throat.

"Well, I heard some stories about you being a shaman and all. I was hoping there was something you could do about it."

Betty leaped astride his pink bicycle. He thrust his left hand down before Mr. Bright's face, making a circular motion with the tip of his left thumb over the tips of his first and second fingers.

"You want to get *paid*?" said Mr. Bright, outraged. "Ain't I just explained how you got a stake in this too?"

Betty began to pedal, riding around and around Mr. Bright in a tight circle, waving bye-bye. On the third circuit he veered away, pulling out a piece of pink Kleenex and waving it as he went.

"All right, God damn it!" shouted Mr. Bright. "Let's do a deal."

Betty circled back, stopped and looked at him expectantly. Glum and grudging, Mr. Bright dug into an inner coat pocket and pulled out a roll of greasy twenties. He began to count them off, slowly and then more slowly, as Betty looked on. When he stopped, Betty mimed laughing again, throwing his head back, pointing in disbelief. Mr. Bright gritted his teeth and peeled away more twenties, until there was quite a pile of rancid cabbage in his lap. He threw the last bill down in disgust.

"That's every damn cent I got with me," he said. "You better be worth it."

Betty swept up the money and went through a routine of counting it himself, licking his thumb between each bill and sweeping his hands out in wide elaborate gestures. Apparently satisfied, he drew a tiny, pink vinyl purse from his bicycle's basket and tucked away the money. Leaning down, he winked broadly at Mr. Bright.

Then he pushed his little sailor cap forward on his brow and pedaled off into the fog.

● ● ●

Three days later, Mr. Bright was presiding over a poker game at the front table with Charlie, Leon and Elmore Souza, who had lost both hands in an accident at the fish cannery but was a master at manipulating cards in his prostheses, to such an extent that he won frequently because his opponents couldn't stop staring. Since they were only playing for starlight mints, though, nobody minded much.

Mr. Bright was in a foul mood all the same, having concluded that he'd been shaman-suckered out of a hundred and eighty dollars. He had just anted up five mints with a dip into the box from Iris Fancy Foods Restaurant Supply when he looked up to see Betty Step-in-Time sashaying into the Chowder Palace. His friends looked up to see what he was snarling at, and quickly looked away. A peculiar silence fell.

Betty was carrying a Pee Chee folder. He walked straight up to Mr. Bright, opened the folder with a flourish, and presented it to him. Mr. Bright stared down at it, dumfounded.

"We should maybe go," said Leon, pushing away from the table. Charlie scuttled out the door ahead of him, and Elmore paused only to sweep the starlight mints into his windbreaker pocket before following them in haste.

Betty ignored them, leaning down like a helpful maitre d' to remove a mass of photocopied paper from the folder and arrange it on the table before Mr. Bright.

The first image was evidently from a book on local history. It was a very old photograph, to judge from the three-masted ship on the horizon; waves breaking in the background, one or two bathers in old-fashioned costume, and a couple of little board and batten shacks in the foreground. White slanted letters across the lower right-hand corner read: *Nunas Beach, corner of Alder and Stanford.* Squinting at it, Mr. Bright realized that he was seeing the view from his own front window, a hundred years or more in the past.

Silently Betty drew his attention to the fact that the future site of Calamari Curls was a bare and blasted lot, though evening primrose grew thickly up to its edge.

"Well, so what?" he said. In reply, Betty whisked the picture away to reveal another, taken a generation later but from the same point of view. A building stood on the spot now—and there were the same arched windows, the same fanlight door, above which was a sign in letters solemn and slightly staggering: ALDER STREET NATATORIUM.

"A nata-what?" said Mr. Bright. Betty placed his hands together and mimed diving. Then he gripped his nose, squeezed his eyes shut and sank down, waving his other hand above his head.

"Oh. Okay, it was a swimming pool? What about it?"

Betty lifted the picture. Under it was a photocopied microfilm enlargement, from the *San Emidio Mission Bell* for May 2, 1922. Mr. Bright's reading skills were not strong, but he was able to make out enough to tell that the article was about the Alder Street Natatorium in Nunas Beach, which had closed indefinitely due to a horrifying incident two days previous. Possible ergot poisoning—mass hallucinations—sea-creature—prank by the boys of San Emidio Polytechnic?—where is Mr. Tognazzini and his staff?

"Huh," said Mr. Bright. "Could we, like, blackmail somebody with this stuff?"

Betty pursed his cupid's bow and shook a reproving finger at Mr. Bright. He drew out the next paper, which was a photocopied page from the *Weekly Dune Crier* for April 25, 1950. There were three young men standing in front of the Hi-Ho Lounge, looking arch. The brief caption underneath implied that the Hi-Ho Lounge would bring a welcome touch of sophistication and gray-flannel elegance to Nunas Beach.

"So I guess they boarded the pool over," said Mr. Bright. "Well?"

Quickly, Betty presented the next photocopy. It was an undated article from the *San Emidio Telegraph* noting briefly that the Hi-Ho Lounge was still closed pending the police investigation, that no marihuana cigarettes had been found despite first reports, and that anyone who had attended the poetry reading was asked to come forward with any information that might throw some light on what had happened, since Mr. LaRue was not expected to recover consciousness and Mr. Binghamton and Mr. Cayuga had not been located.

Mr. Bright shook his head. "I don't get it."

Betty rolled his eyes and batted his lashes in exasperation. He shuffled the last paper to the fore, and this was not a photocopy but some kind of astronomical chart showing moon phases. It had been marked all over with pink ink, scrawled notations and alchemical signs, as well as other symbols resembling things Mr. Bright had only seen after a three-day weekend with a case of Ten High.

"What the hell's all this supposed to be?" demanded Mr. Bright. "Oh!...

I guess this is… some kind of shamanic thing?"

Betty leaped into the air and crossed his ankles as he came down, then mimed grabbing someone by the hand and shaking it in wildly enthusiastic congratulation. Mr. Bright pulled his hands in close.

"Okay," he said in a husky whisper. He looked nervously around at his empty restaurant. "Maybe you shouldn't ought to show me anything else."

But Betty leaned forward and tapped one image on the paper. It was a smiling full moon symbol. He winked again, and backed toward the door. He gave Mr. Bright a thumbs-up, then made an OK symbol with thumb and forefinger, and then saluted.

"Okay, thanks," said Mr. Bright. "I get the picture."

He watched Betty walking primly away, trundling the pink bicycle. Looking down at the table, he gathered together the papers and stuffed them back in the Pee Chee folder. He wheeled himself off to his cubicle and hid the folder under his pillow, with the tire iron.

Then he rolled around to his desk, and consulted the calendar from Nunas Billy's Hardware Circus. There was a full moon in three days' time.

• • •

It was Saturday, and the full moon was just heaving itself up from the eastern horizon, like a pink pearl. Blue dusk lay on Nunas Beach. The tide was far out; salt mist flowed inland, white vapor at ankle level. Mr. Bright sat inside the darkened Chowder Palace, and watched, and hated, as people lined up on the sidewalk outside Calamari Curls.

Calamari Curls was having Talent Nite. The Early Bird specials were served, and senior diners went shuffling back to their singlewides, eager to leave before the Goddamned rock and roll started. Young families with toddlers dined and hurried back to their motels, unwilling to expose little ears to amplified sound.

Five pimply boys set up their sound equipment on the dais in the corner. They were the sons of tractor salesmen and propane magnates; let their names be forgotten. The front man tossed his hair back from his eyes, looked around at the tables crowded with chattering diners, and said in all adolescent sullenness:

"Hi. We're the Maggots, and we're here to shake you up a little."

His bassman leaped out and played the opening of "(I Can't Get No)

Satisfaction" with painful slowness, the drummer boy joined in clunk-clunk-clunk, and the front man leaned forward to the mike and in a hoarse scream told the audience about his woes. The audience continued biting the tails off shrimp, sucking down frozen strawberry margaritas and picking at Kona Coffee California Cheesecake.

When the music ended, they applauded politely. The front man looked as though he'd like to kill them all. He wiped sweat from his brow, had a gulp of water.

Betty Step-in-Time wheeled his bicycle up to the door.

"We're going to do another classic," said the front man. "Okay?"

Ka-*chunk!* went the drums. The keyboardist and the lead guitarist started very nearly in sync: Da da da. *Dada. DA DA DA. Dada.*

"*Oh Lou-ah Lou-ah-eh, ohhhh baby nagatcha go waygadda go!*" shouted the front man.

Betty Step-in-Time dismounted. Just outside the restaurant's threshold, he began to dance. It began in time with the music, a modest little kickstep. A few diners looked, pointed and laughed.

"*Nah nah nah nah asaya Lou-ah Lou-ah eh, whooa babeh saya whaygachago!*"

Betty's kickstep increased its arc, to something approaching can-can immodesty. He threw his arms up as he kicked, rolling his head, closing his eyes in abandon. A diner sitting near the door fished around in pockets for a dollar bill, but saw no hat in which to put it.

"*Ah-nye, ah-dah, ah ron withchoo, ah dinkabobsa gonstalee!*" cried the front man. Betty began to undulate, and it seemed a tremor ran through the floor of the building. A tableful of German tourists jumped to their feet, alarmed, but their native companion didn't even stop eating.

"Just an aftershock," he said calmly. "No big deal."

"*Ah rag saga leely, badoom badoom, wha wah badoo, jaga babee!*"

Betty began to dance what looked like the Swim, but so fast his arms and legs blurred the air. The lights dimmed, took on a greenish cast.

"Who's playing with the damn rheostat?" the manager wanted to know.

"*Ayah ha Lou-ah Lou-ah eh, whoa ba-bah shongo waygatchago!*"

Sweat began to pour from Betty's face and limbs, as his body began to churn in a manner that evoked ancient bacchanals, feverish and suggestive. The green quality of the light intensified. Several diners looked down at their plates of clam strips or chimichangas and stopped eating, suddenly nauseous.

"Ya ya ya ya ah-sha-da Lou-ah Lou-ah he, Nyarlathotep bay-bah wey-gago!" sang the front man, and he was sweating too, an—so it seemed—dwindling under the green light, and the carefully torn edges of his black raiment began to fray into rags, patterned with shining mold.

Betty's hips gyrated, his little sailor hat flew off, and every curl on his head was dripping with St. Elmo's fire. Several diners vomited where they sat. Others rose in a half-crouch, desperate to find the lavatory doors marked *Beach Bums* and *Beach Bunnies.* Half of them collapsed before they made it. They slipped, stumbled and fell in the pools of seawater that were condensing out of the air, running down the walls.

"Ah Lou-ah Lou-ah eh, ph'nglui mglw'nafh Cthulhu R'lyeh wgah'nagl fhtagn!" wailed the white-eyed thing the front man had become, and his band raised reed flutes to their gills and piped a melody to make human ears bleed, and the mortal diners rose and fought to get out the windows, for Betty was flinging handfuls of seaweed in toward them, and black incense.

The pink and turquoise linoleum tiles by the bandstand popped upward, scattered like hellish confetti, as a green-glowing gas of all corruption hissed forth, lighting in blue flames when it met the air, followed by a gush of black water from the forgotten pool below. The first of the black tentacles probed up through the widening crack in the floor.

Betty sprang backward, grabbed up his sailor hat, leaped on his pink bicycle and pedaled away as fast as he could go, vanishing down the misty darkness of Alder Street.

The neon olive had become an eye, swiveling uncertainly but with malevolence, in a narrow scarlet face.

Watching from across the street, Mr. Bright laughed until the tears poured from his eyes, and slapped the arms of his wheelchair. He raised his bourbon bottle in salute as Calamari Curls began its warping, strobing, moist descent through the dimensions.

• • •

He was opening a new bottle by the time gray dawn came, as the last of the fire engines and ambulances pulled away. Tom Avila stood in the middle of the street, in gloomy conference with the pastor of St. Mark's, the priest from Mission San Emidio, and even the rabbi from Temple Beth-El, who had driven in his pajamas all the way over from Hooper City.

Holy water, prayer and police tape had done all they could do; the glowing green miasma was dissipating at last, and the walls and windows of Calamari Curls had begun to appear again in ghostly outline. Even now, however, it was obvious that their proper geometry could never be restored.

Tom shook hands with the gentlemen of God and they departed to their respective cars. He stood alone in the street a while, regarding the mess; then he noticed Mr. Bright, who waved cheerfully from behind his window. Tom's eyes narrowed. He came stalking over. Mr. Bright let him in.

"You didn't have anything to do with this, did you, Peg?" the mayor demanded.

"Me? How the hell could I of? I just been sitting here watching the show," said Mr. Bright. "I ain't going to say I didn't enjoy it, neither. Guess nobody's going to raise no rents around *here* for a while!"

"God damn it, Peg! Now we've got us *another* vortex into a lost dimension, smack in the middle of town this time!" said the mayor in exasperation. "What are we going to do?"

"Beats me," said Mr. Bright, grinning as he offered him the bourbon bottle.

· · ·

But the present became the past, as it will, and people never forget so easily as when they want to forget. The wreck of Calamari Curls became invisible, as passers-by tuned it out of their consciousness. The green olive blinked no more.

Mr. Bright found that the black things that mewled and gibbered around the garbage cans at night could be easily dispatched with a cast-iron skillet well aimed. His customers came back, hesitant and shamefaced. He was content.

And mellowing in his world view too; for he no longer scowled nor spat in the direction of Betty Step-in-Time when he passed him on the pier, but nodded affably, and once was even heard to remark that it took all kinds of folks to make a world, and you really shouldn't judge folks without you get to know them.

KATHERINE'S STORY

1937

She knew the marriage had been a mistake by the time they stepped off the train.

All the same, she smiled and waited patiently as Bert got their suitcases from the porter. She had determined to make a life as different from her mother's as was possible; that meant making the marriage work, whether or not Bert was the man she had envisioned him to be when she gave up college for him.

This was a pretty place, at least. There were big, green mountains and trees, and the little train station was quite rustic if not exactly charming. Lean men in overalls, red clay thick on their workboots, waited in a silent line as goods were unloaded: sacks of feed, sacks of fertilizer, wire cages full of baby chicks. The chicks peeped and poked their tiny beaks through the mesh. The heat was shimmering, sticky.

Bert approached with the luggage. She turned to smile at him but he was looking past her, grinning and hefting one suitcase in a wave.

"Pop!"

One of the lean men was loading cages into the back of an old truck. He turned and saw Bert, and nodded in acknowledgment. Bert ran toward him and she followed.

"Hey, Pop!"

"Hey," the man responded, looking them up and down. "You're early."

"I got the train times wrong," Bert said.

"Well, that's you." Mr. Loveland shook his head. His gaze moved briefly to Katherine. "This the wife?"

"Yes—"

"Pleased to meet you, Mr. Loveland, I've heard so much about you," said Katherine, smiling as she twisted the strap of her handbag. He just nodded, considering her.

"We got your room ready, anyways," he said.

"Oh, thank you—"

"You may's well put those in the back," he told Bert, gesturing at the suitcases. Bert stepped close and hoisted the suitcases into the truck bed. As he did so he kicked one of the wire cages and there was a pitiable cheeping from the chicks inside.

"Oh, Bert, you've hurt one of them," Katherine cried, stooping down. "It's this black one, look! I think his little foot is squashed. There's blood—"

"Oh! Sorry—"

"Things happen," said Mr. Loveland.

. . .

The ride to their new home was silent and uncomfortable. Literally; she rode perched on Bert's lap, which would have been funny and romantic under other circumstances. They bumped along unpaved roads for miles, up into the mountains, far out of town, before turning down a gravel drive to a frame house set back among trees. There was an enclosed porch running the length of the front.

Katherine hopped out and waited, clutching her handbag, as the men unloaded the cages and carried them around to the chicken pen in the side yard. Mr. Loveland remained with the chicks, opening the cages and dumping their contents into the pen. Bert got their suitcases again and she followed him into the silent house.

To her dismay, she saw two cots set up on the porch and an old chiffonier, clearly intended for them.

"Are we living out here?" she whispered.

Bert looked down at the cots. "Oh," he said. "I guess so. Well, it's hot, ain't it? We'll be all right." He dropped the suitcases and pushed through the door into the house. She followed him, wondering where she was going to put her things when they arrived.

"Ma!"

The kitchen was small and dark, and the woman kneading biscuit dough at the table filled it effectively. She looked up at them. She had Bert's strong jaw. She did not smile as she said: "Oh."

"Hey!" Bert edged forward and embraced her.

"You'll get your good clothes floured," Mrs. Loveland told him, looking over his shoulder at Katherine. "You're Kathy, I guess."

"Yes, Mother Loveland, Katherine," she said, smiling and nodding. "I'm awfully glad to meet you—though I guess we're a little early. I hope that's not an inconvenience."

"*Katherine*, huh?" Mrs. Loveland looked coldly amused. "Now, that's funny. Bert told me you were born in Chapel Hill, but you sure don't talk like it."

"Well, I was," Katherine stammered, "but I grew up in New York, you know. I studied at the Metropolitan Museum of Art, did Bert tell you?"

"No," said Mrs. Loveland.

• • •

She was miserably homesick, through the weeks of Indian summer. Without his football sweater Bert no longer looked much like Nelson Eddy; and he'd changed, as a son will change in his mother's house. The other illusion, about coming home to the South and having a big, loving family instead of living in boarding houses with Mother and Anne—that was fading too.

She saw clearly enough that she'd better make Mrs. Loveland like her, but her attempts to help out were dismissed—she didn't know how to cook. She and Mother and Anne had eaten in restaurants, or heated Campbell's soup over Sterno cans in their rooms. She took on the task of feeding the chicks, but her decision to make a pet of the crippled black one earned her contempt even from Bert. She persisted; made it a separate pen, gave it special care, named it. It lived and grew, to Mrs. Loveland's disgust.

Her things came, in far too many crates, and Bert and Mr. Loveland grumbled as they stacked them in the barn. With them came the letter from Mother, and she cried as she read it. She could hear the stern, quiet voice so clearly, she could see Mother looking up at her over her steel spectacles, as term papers waited for grading.

Beloved daughter,

I hope this finds you well and settling in. It may be difficult at first, as the life is not one to which you are accustomed. "I slept, and dreamed that life was Beauty; I woke, and found that life was Duty." Please believe, however, that I wish you happiness with all my heart.

I have sent all your books, and some of the things from the Goldsborough house that you loved, as well as the rest of your trousseau. If there is anything else you require, I will send it along at the first opportunity as soon as you let me know what you lack.

Your sister and I continue well. Anne is now understudy for the ingénue as well as in the chorus. I had occasion to meet Kurt Weill, the composer, who was dining at the table next to mine. His music is considered quite avant-garde but I found him to be a very nice little man, quite shy. What I have heard of his work so far impresses me mightily.

I must go now, but send sincerest wishes for your continuing joy, and the earnest hope that you will find with Bert the domestic happiness for which I know you have always longed. It is not given to all of us, but may it be given to you.

Your loving
Mother

So she couldn't write to Mother about how miserable she was, not without seeming like a worthless failure. Mother would send another gloomy letter that talked around the shame and scandal of The Divorce while never actually bringing it up. She had never discussed it, never once in all the years Katherine and her little sister had been growing up, rattling around in the back of the Ford as Mother drove from teaching job to teaching job.

All that Katherine knew about The Divorce, she had learned from the servants, when they stayed at Grandfather's house in those intervals in which Mother was broke. *Philanderer... Miss Kate had her pride, she wouldn't stand for it... threw him out... never gave him a second chance, never spoke of him again...*

And once a neighbor's little girl had asked Katherine if it was true her mamma and daddy had had a Divorce, and she'd run home crying to ask Mother, who was taking tea with Grandmother. Mother's face had seemed to turn to stone; she stood and towered over Katherine, and she had looked like the statue of the Goddess Athena on the library steps. She'd swept out of the room without a word. Grandmother had set down her teacup and held out her arms, but all she'd told Katherine in the end was: *Some things are best not spoken of, child.*

In the present, Katherine endured. Most of her clothing was inappropriate for daily life on a farm. Under Mrs. Loveland's blank stare she was stupidly inept, burnt clothes while ironing them, broke dishes while washing them.

The warm weather ended and it rained, and in the leaking barn her books got soaked. She carried them into the house frantically, armloads spread and opened before the stove to dry, weeping as she peeled back wet pages from the color plates: *A Child's Garden of Verses* with its Maxfield Parrish illustrations, Kay Nielsen's *East of the Sun and West of the Moon*, *Myths and Enchantment Tales*, the *Volland Mother Goose*, *Lamb's Tales from Shakespeare*. When Mrs. Loveland saw them her jaw dropped.

"You still look at *picture books?*" she said.

1938

The winter was mild, so she and Bert continued to sleep on the enclosed porch.

One night she dreamed that she was back at college, that Mother had left her at the entrance to the dormitory and she'd gone in to find that the building was dark, deserted. Everyone had gone home for Christmas. She turned in panic and hurried outside again, and to her horror saw Mother driving away.

She ran after the car, after its red winking taillights. She chased it for miles. There was brilliant moonlight, blue-white, so bright it hurt her eyes. She lost the car at last and stood there alone, sobbing, and then a strange little girl came to her and told her everything would be all right.

Then she woke, and found herself alone on a country road in her thin nightgown, in the terrifying silence of the night. Had she been sleepwalking? She was more than half a mile from the house. Teeth chattering, she hobbled back, and Bert did not wake when she crawled back into bed.

She was unable to get warm again, and lay awake for hours. She hadn't walked in her sleep since the winter she'd been twelve, in New York, when the letter came informing Mother that Daddy had died of pneumonia. He'd been living in a hotel only the other side of Central Park, all that time; she might have stolen away and visited him, if she'd only known.

And in her dreams, for months afterward, she kept trying to cross the skating pond to reach him. She could see Daddy so clearly, standing under a lamp on the other side, but she knew he didn't know she was there, and she knew if she didn't run to him he'd never know. She never managed to cross the ice, somehow; and once she started awake on the sidewalk, with Fifth Avenue roaring before her like a river and a horrified doorman clutching her arm to stop her plunging into the traffic.

• • •

By April she knew without doubt that the baby was on the way. Bert took the news stolidly, no least sign of happiness at the prospect of a little child of their own.

Mrs. Loveland shook her head. "You're going to be sorry you didn't wait," she said. Katherine very nearly retorted, *Tell that to Bert,* but turned away and went to go feed the black chicken.

She gave up any attempt to be a good farm wife, and nobody seemed to care. She luxuriated in her freedom; took long walks alone, now that spring had come and the dogwoods were flowering. Where the red clay road cut across the hills she imagined she'd walked into a Thomas Hart Benton painting. This was the only part of the South that was the way she'd dreamed it would be.

One afternoon she was passing a house set close to the road, and heard music: Tchaikovsky's Piano Concerto no.1, to her astonishment, sounding scratched and tinny as though it were coming out of the horn of an old Victrola but still flowing magnificently on. She leaned against the split rail fence, listening, rapt. Someone was moving inside the house, through the window she saw someone dancing. Wild, free-form, arms flung out. A second later the woman pirouetted close to the window and saw her. She stopped dancing immediately.

"Oh, I'm sorry," said Katherine, blushing. "I just—the music was so beautiful. I love Tchaikovsky, but there aren't any classical radio stations here—"

"I know," said the woman, pushing up the window the rest of the way and leaning out. Her face was pale and sharp, her gaze fixed. "It is an absolute purgatory for anyone of any culture. Or decent breeding. Tell me, are you a devotee of Beethoven?"

"Well, yes—"

"Please, come in. Will you come in?" said the woman. She ducked inside and slammed the window. By the time Katherine had come reluctantly up the path, the woman was standing at the open door.

"I am Amelia DuPlessis Hickey," she said, inclining in a queenly sort of way. "I would introduce my dear husband, but he is currently traveling abroad on necessary business. Please, do come in! And you would be?"

"Katherine MacQuarrie," she replied, and then added, "Loveland."

"I see," said the woman, as the music behind her wound down to hissing silence. "Would that be of the Greenville MacQuarries? With the DeLafayette MacQuarrie who perished at Gettysburg?"

"I don't think so," said Katherine, stepping across the threshold. "I'm afraid I don't know a lot about my father's people—"

"Ah! Well, things happen," said Mrs. Hickey graciously. "Won't you stay for tea?"

"Why, thank you," said Katherine, and recoiled as something sprang up out of a packing box beside her and screamed.

"Now, Peaseblossom, that won't do!" said Mrs. Hickey. "I really must apologize, Mrs. Loveland. Pray allow me to introduce my beautiful little geniuses: Peaseblossom, Cobweb, Moth and the baby, Mustardseed!"

She was referring to the pale and sullen children who crouched together in the corner. The two boys wore only overalls, rolled up thickly at the ankles; the girl wore a flour-sack dress. They had retreated behind what appeared to be a wooden model of the Brooklyn Bridge. From the pieces scattered on the bare floor, it seemed that they themselves had been constructing it. They were fox-faced, emaciated, staring with enormous dark eyes. A whimper from the floor drew her attention to an ashen baby waving its skinny arms from an apple box.

After a moment of appalled silence Katherine said:

"How clever. You named them after the fairies in *Midsummer Night's Dream*, I guess?"

"I adore Shakespeare. Another passion of mine. My grandfather, Zadoc DuPlessis (for we are of the Chaney County DuPlessises, you see) had the good fortune to see the immortal Junius Booth in Charleston where, I believe, he was portraying Hamlet," said Mrs. Hickey, stoking up the stove. She put a saucepan of water on the burner. Katherine looked around. The room was as filthy as a bare room can be. There were ancient books stacked everywhere, piled against the walls, and three crates of phonograph records. In the corner by the window was, yes, a Victrola with its morning-glory trumpet.

"Gosh, how lucky," said Katherine. There were no chairs, so she wandered over to the children. "How are you all today?"

They shrank back. The little girl bared her teeth.

"I do beg your pardon," said Mrs. Hickey, coming swiftly to her side. "They are terribly shy with strangers. We have, alas, nearly no social life. Now, you come out here and be ladies and gentlemen for our caller! Perhaps then we'll go out for a Co-colee."

The children blinked and scrambled out, lining up awkwardly against the wall.

"They do love Coca-Cola," said Mrs. Hickey.

It was two hours before Katherine could get away. Mrs. Hickey told her life story: her family had once owned most of three counties, but of course The War had altered their circumstances, though not so grievously she hadn't been raised with the best of everything and taught to appreciate all that was exquisite in the arts.

And she'd given it all up for love; so now she rusticated here, teaching her brilliant offspring herself. The boys were clearly destined to be engineers. Why, they'd made that bridge themselves from nothing more than slatwood, all you had to do was show them a picture and they'd build anything! And little Peaseblossom had inherited a love of great literature, she just devoured books. The children listened to all this silent and expressionless.

Later, back at the Lovelands', Katherine went out to feed the chickens. She picked up the little black hen and buried her face in its feathers, feeling her hot tears spilling, and prayed that she wouldn't turn out like Mrs. DuPlessis-Hickey.

· · ·

Summer came and went, and autumn arrived with cornshocks and pumpkins. In the early hours of October 30, Katherine went into labor. Bert joked about the baby being a little Halloween goblin as he drove her to the hospital in town. She wasn't laughing by the time they got to the hospital. The pains were terrible.

The nurses got her into a room and Bert told her he had to get back, that he'd come see her that evening. She begged him to tell the nurses to give her something for the pain. The head nurse came in and told her they were having difficulty locating Dr. Jackson; as soon as they heard from him they'd give her something.

All the interminable morning and afternoon, they were unable to find him, had no idea where he might be, and at last they gave Katherine drugs anyway. The relief was blissful, unbelievable, and she received with floaty equanimity the news that the baby was turned wrong. "Well, just turn it around," she told them, smiling.

The bright window darkened and it was night. She floated in and out of a dream about Halloween, big yellow pumpkins on gateposts, little children scurrying in the dark with papier-mâché faces. But that wouldn't be until tomorrow night, would it? They gave her more drugs. Trick or treat!

Suddenly there was a nurse screaming and crying, praying to Jesus. Her sister had called from New Jersey. She'd been listening to Charlie McCarthy and when Nelson Eddy came on she'd switched away. (Katherine felt mildly outraged. How could anyone switch off Nelson Eddy?) The man on the radio had said Earth was being invaded by Martians! They'd come in a big cylinder and were burning people up! State troopers too! It was the end of the world!

The baby was turned around now but the head was too big. The head was stuck. There was a colored lady talking to her soothingly, wiping her face with a cold cloth. *You have to work, honey,* she kept saying. Nobody could find news of the invasion on the little radio in the cafeteria, but a man ran in and said he'd heard strange lights had begun to appear in the sky, were swooping and circling the town, had they landed yet? There was one. It was right outside the hospital. It looked like a soup plate on fire. The colored lady was crying now too but she stayed right there.

Sometime in the night the doctor came at last. Not Dr. Jackson. It was a strange doctor.

. . .

It was afternoon before Katherine woke up. Nobody said anything about Martians, and she assumed it had all been a crazy nightmare. Her little girl was fine, just fine, they assured her; but she had to ask and ask before anybody would bring the baby for her to hold.

When they did bring her in, Katherine's first thought was: *Why, she looks like Mickey Mouse.* Both her eyes were blacked and all the dome of her head was one black-purple bruise.

"Oh, that's normal, sugar," a nurse told her, too quickly. "She just had a big head, that was all. The bruises'll go away." The baby lay quiet and waxen in her arms, barely moving, but they told her that was normal too.

1939

It wasn't normal. Bette Jean was an exquisite baby, with delicate white skin, with perfect little features, with enormous solemn eyes the color of aquamarines. Her hair was black and wavy. She looked like a doll, but by her first birthday she was still unable to sit up.

When it became impossible to deny that something was wrong, Katherine wrote to Mother. Mother sent money—Anne had the lead in a Broadway show now, she could afford to—and told her to take the baby to a specialist.

There was a doctor in Chapel Hill who saw "slow" children. It was most of a day's drive in the old truck but Bert took them, tight-lipped and miserable. Bette Jean stared at the trees, the sky, the mountains, and exclaimed in her funny little unformed voice, a liquid sound like a child playing with panpipes.

In the waiting room were retarded children, spastic children, children blank and focused inward on private and inexplicable games, gaunt listless children sprawling across their parents' laps. Overalled fathers silent, shirtwaisted mothers staring like wounded tigers. Bert took one look and murmured that he had to see the man about the mortgage, and he left. "It's all right," Katherine whispered to Bette Jean, who wobbled her head and looked astonished.

Through the transom she heard a man's voice raised. "She's still not thriving. You can't be following my orders! I told you she needs lots of green and yellow vegetables. What on earth have you been feeding her?"

"Corn bread," replied the raw cracker voice, defensively. "Corn's yellow, ain't it?"

Katherine shuddered.

The doctor was tired, and perhaps not as kind as he might have been. He listened to Katherine's story, interrupting frequently as he examined Bette Jean. When he had finished he leaned back against a cabinet and took off his glasses to rub his eyes.

"Well, Mrs. Loveland—your baby has spastic paralysis. I'd conclude she was brain-damaged at birth, either by the forceps or the fact that birth was delayed so long. There is no cure for her condition, unfortunately. Given that the family is of limited means—I'd recommend you put her in a home."

"Oh, I couldn't!" Tears welled in Katherine's eyes, but the doctor raised his hand.

"She'd receive decent care. Do you understand that her illness is only the result of an accident? You're young; there is no reason why you can't have healthy, normal children after this. When you do, you'll find yourself increasingly hard-pressed to give this abnormal child the attention she'll require every day of her life. You owe it to the child, to your prospective children—and, I need hardly say, your husband—to put this unfortunate occurrence behind you."

Katherine wept and refused. The doctor wanted to speak to Bert, too, but he never put in an appearance. He was nowhere in sight when Katherine carried Bette Jean out to the truck. They waited another half-hour before he came up the street, unsteady, and climbed into the cab. He'd had a drink or two. It was a long ride back, in the dark.

· · ·

When they understood the diagnosis, Bert and his parents argued at once that the only sensible thing to do would be to follow the doctor's advice and place Bette Jean in an institution. Katherine screamed her refusal, wrote a tearful letter to Mother. Mother received the news with her customary stoicism and responded by inviting Katherine to bring Bette Jean to New York for Christmas, thoughtfully sending money for the train fare.

· · ·

It was almost Heaven. No boarding houses anymore: a fashionable apartment nowadays, because Anne's name was in lights on Broadway, and there was talk about Hollywood. And, oh, the Metropolitan Museum! The bookstores! The music! The shows! Katherine took Bette Jean to Central Park to watch the ice skaters, and Bette Jean stared and stared from her arms in wonder, never cried at all.

But there were telephone calls, there were letters and visits from all her aunts and uncles, who'd loaned Mother money over the lean years, who'd shaken their heads over The Divorce. Every one of them told her to put Bette Jean in an institution, for the sake of her marriage if nothing else. After the latest such call she put down the phone and wandered disconsolately out to the sitting room, where Anne had Bette Jean on her lap at the big Steinway piano and was pretending to play a duet with her. Bette Jean was whooping in delight. Mother looked up from her book, peering at her over her glasses.

"And what did your Uncle James have to say?"

"Just—more of the same." Katherine glared at Mother. She wanted to seize Mother by the shoulders and scream at her, but what could she say? *If you hadn't gotten The Divorce, I'd never have been in such a hurry to get married to the first handsome boy I met. You never once explained it to us. You never once apologized. Not you. Why should you apologize, when you were entirely the offended party?*

Oh, when will I ever escape from your life?

Instead, Katherine sank down by Mother's chair. She drooped forward and leaned her head on Mother's arm, wanting to cry.

"They want me to put her away and let strangers care for her," she said. "They say it'll be more convenient. They say I'll forget about her when I have another baby."

Mother stared straight forward.

"Don't do it, child," she said at last. "The human heart doesn't work that way."

Katherine raised her head, thinking: *What would you know about human hearts?*

"You'd regret it the rest of your life," Mother said. "Believe me, daughter. Our emotions don't answer to reason."

• • •

Bette Jean caught a cold on the train going back; she was feverish and wailing when Bert picked them up at the train station. Katherine sat with her in the rocking chair beside the kerosene heater, rubbed her tiny chest with Vicks VapoRub, desperately fought off pneumonia. She slept sitting up with the child's head cradled on her shoulder. Bert bought a steam vaporizer and set it up beside them, with the pan of water and eucalyptus oil simmering over its little flame. It was a week before she felt safe leaving Bette Jean long enough to attend to any chores.

Scattering feed for the chickens, she looked across at the pen where she'd kept the black one and saw that it was empty. When she questioned Bert he looked away, and said at last:

"Ma had me kill it. It couldn't hardly walk, Katherine, you know that."

She wouldn't let him see her cry. She went into the house. Bette Jean was awake, and her eyes tracked to follow Katherine as she came close and sat down on the edge of the bed.

Ma-ma.

Katherine was so shocked she just sat staring. After a moment the voice came again, odd and artificial-sounding as a doll's but with a note of pleading. Bette Jean's mouth was slack, did not move, but her eyes were intent.

Mama.

Trembling, Katherine reached out and took Bette Jean's hand. Her little fingers, long and white, were ice cold. Katherine raised them to her lips and kissed them.

• • •

It was so strange she wouldn't think about it, but it kept happening; little silent greetings, complaints, questions, observations. Nobody else heard them.

It's the stress, Katherine told herself. *It's being shut up here with the Lovelands. I'm going mad like Mrs. DuPlessis-Hickey.*

• • •

She found herself wandering in the direction of Mrs. DuPlessis-Hickey's residence one morning, hoping for comfort, hoping the visit would reassure her of her own normalcy. She carried Bette Jean with her; she never left her alone with Mrs. Loveland anymore.

The music this time was Rimsky-Korsakov's *Scheherazade,* rolling out like clouds of attar of roses or patchouli, wildly out of place in this country of red clay roads and split rail fences. As Katherine came up on the front porch, the music stopped and she heard Mrs. DuPlessis-Hickey shriek: "Mustardseed! *Hide!*"

"It's only me, ma'am. Katherine Loveland," she said cautiously, raising her voice. A moment later and Mrs. DuPlessis-Hickey opened the door. She looked paler, thinner, crazier.

"Why, Mrs. Loveland, how delightful to see you! All is well, Mustardseed. Do come in! And who is this charming young lady?"

"This is my daughter, Bette Jean." Katherine stepped inside. There was no sign of the older children; the new baby in the apple box might have been Mustardseed, except for the fact that Katherine could see a wraithlike toddler crouching behind the Victrola.

"Oh, what exquisite eyes she has!" said Mrs. DuPlessis-Hickey, holding out her arms. Reluctantly, Katherine let her hold Bette Jean, who went to her without complaint. Katherine swallowed hard.

"She's…"

"Unique, yes, I can see that," said Mrs. DuPlessis-Hickey, smiling at Bette Jean. Bette Jean stared at her and then smiled back.

"It's all right," said Katherine, waving at the child behind the Victrola. "Are the others out playing?"

Mrs. DuPlessis-Hickey's face twisted for a moment. "Why, no," she said. "They are, in fact, attending a special school now. For remarkable children. The county is providing their scholarships. I do feel the void, of course, but… I haven't introduced my youngest! Little Ariel. He was an unexpected blessing. Yet they are all blessings, are they not?"

"Of course," Katherine murmured.

"What glorious hair, as well," remarked Mrs. DuPlessis-Hickey, stroking Bette Jean's curls. "Mustardseed's might as well be dandelion down, mightn't it, Mustardseed? Do come out and be sociable, now; we are amongst friends."

Mustardseed stood up and trotted over. He leaned on Katherine's knee, startling her, but she patted his head. He looked up at her out of pale eyes sharply focused.

"Has she tried to speak yet?" said Mrs. DuPlessis-Hickey.

"Only to me," said Katherine. "I mean… I understand her…she sort of…"

"Oh, I comprehend," said Mrs. DuPlessis-Hickey. "What a rare gift! *Communication de pensées,* they call it, you know. Thought transference. The mind, unfettered by the demands of the body, refines and expands itself beyond the abilities of the common mortal intellect. As they say the blind develop extraordinary musical gifts. Nature compensates, you see."

"I've heard that said," said Katherine. Her own mind shoved the idea away reflexively—clairvoyance, for heaven's sake!—and then, with hesitance, considered again. What if there *were* some truth to it? Why should it be sane and rational to believe in angels in Heaven, and not in something like this?

"Indeed. 'There are more things in heaven and earth, Horatio, than are dreamt of in your philosophy,'" said Mrs. DuPlessis-Hickey. "Angels and ministers of grace do defend us, or so I truly believe." She leaned forward and patted Katherine's hand. "It keeps one from despair."

• • •

She got a book on clairvoyance out of the library, on one of their trips into town, but it had been written by a fairground charlatan. Its claims were ridiculous. Still, Sigmund Freud seemed to have believed that something like mind-reading had existed, or so the charlatan stated. Katherine tried to research the matter further, but the little town library had no books by Freud at all.

• • •

"Looks like it'll be another hard winter," said Bert, at the breakfast table. He watched Katherine spooning grits into Bette Jean's mouth. She had outgrown the high chair, and Katherine had converted one of the kitchen chairs with cushions and clothesline.

"Better hope that baby doesn't get another cold," said Mrs. Loveland, setting a plate of ham on the table. "You'll be up all night wiping snot out of her nose. And if you don't keep her setting up, it'll turn into double pneumonia."

"She's much stronger," said Katherine. Mrs. Loveland grunted, shaking her head.

"Some night, she's just going to stop breathing," she said.

Mama, careful. Careful.

1940

A long letter from Mother: Anne had been offered a contract at RKO studios in Hollywood. Mother had quit teaching and was going out on the train to look for an apartment for them. It promised, she said, to be quite an adventure for a lady her age.

Katherine sat reading the letter over, uncertain how she ought to feel. She had a momentary vision of red taillights winking, receding, leaving her in darkness.

Mama. Bette Jean was staring at her, and one little white hand beat against the blanket with a motion like a leaf fluttering. *Mama!*

Katherine went into one of her trunks for writing paper and a pen. She began to write, hesitantly at first and then swiftly, with decision.

· · ·

Mother sent the money. Katherine made it easy on Bert; it was only for the child's health, after all. She needed a warmer climate. They both knew it would end in a divorce, but the word had lost its power over Katherine. Bert was so relieved he became kind, attentive, made the last days almost nice.

· · ·

The journey was interminable on the train, but her heart was singing the whole way. Bette Jean sat propped beside her, in her best dress. With her tiny feet stuck out before her in their patent leather shoes, she looked more like a doll than ever. She whooped and moaned in excitement, staring at everything, fascinated; and the silent voice kept up its running commentary too. *Mama, nice! Mama happy now?*

They came into California and Katherine felt as though she'd escaped into her books at last, because it all looked like a Maxfield Parrish illustration: the smooth golden hills crowned with stately oak trees, the glimpses of Spanish-style houses with their red tiled roofs and white walls, the green acres of orange trees in blossom. The fragrance came through the windows of the train for miles.

"We're going to Hollywood, Bette Jean!" Katherine told her. "We'll see all the movie stars. We'll be together, and we'll never be cold anymore, and this is such a beautiful place, don't you think? Are we about to have adventures?"

There was a wordless sense of affirmation. Bette Jean's little face was slack, her limbs useless; but her thoughtful soul looked out and wondered. What was so strange in the idea that she might have found some way to communicate? In a world so full of heartbreak and disappointments, why not indulge in a little irrational hope?

As they neared the station, the porter came to see if she'd need any help getting Bette Jean down to the platform.

"Well, hello, Miss Big Eyes!" he said, bending to look into Bette Jean's face. "My goodness, that baby's got pretty eyes."

"Thank you," said Katherine, smiling.

"My sister's boy was born like her," he said, standing straight and pulling down Katherine's suitcase.

Katherine started to say, *Oh, I'm so sorry*. She paused and said: "They're a blessing from God, aren't they?"

"Yes, ma'am, they surely are," the porter replied. "And I surely believe they're sent down here to Earth for a good reason."

Katherine stepped down from the train, with her daughter and her suitcase. She had come to the land where miracles happened to ordinary people. She lifted Bette Jean to her shoulder and walked away down the platform, into the sunlight.

OH, FALSE YOUNG MAN!

"Push that lighter over here, will you, Dick?" said Madame Rigby, out of the corner of her mouth.

"Right away, ma'am," said her assistant, hopping up from his workbench. Four paces from Madame Rigby's chair stood a squat column on casters, the top of which was surmounted by the little tin figure of a grinning devil, standing amid a heap of painted coals. "May I wind him for you?"

"Sure," said Madame Rigby, not looking up from her task.

Dick pushed the column within her easy reach and, fitting a crank into its socket just under the devil's left hoof, wound it three or four times. The devil shivered briskly, as though waking; then, tilting its head and winking once, it thrust its pitchfork out. There was an audible *click* and a tiny jet of flame danced on the centermost tine of the fork.

Dick, who had not worked for Madame Rigby very long, applauded in delight. Madame Rigby scarcely noticed; she merely leaned over until the tip of her cigarette touched the flame. Two or three puffs obscured her in smoke; when it cleared, Dick saw that she was once again preoccupied with the work before her.

"It's looking very nice, ma'am," he said. "Makes you wonder how so much dust could get into a sealed glass case, though, doesn't it?"

"Mm," she said.

The object of his admiration was a glass-fronted box, fully six feet long and eighteen inches high, resting on a wooden case of roughly the same size. It was a mechanical diorama, a set of six miniature tableaux. The style of clothing worn by the tiny manikins within made it plain the thing had been built some twenty years earlier; that, and the dust, and the faded paint.

However, all was being made new by Madame Rigby. Scene by scene, the dust was being cleaned away with diminutive sponges; the wax faces of the dolls given fresh and lifelike tints with a delicate brush. Already the first scene in the little play, *He Comes A-Courting,* glowed like an immortal memory.

It depicted a clock shop, with its walls lined with clocks of all descriptions, and when the scene was in motion all the little hands must have spun round and round on the dial faces, and pendulums rocked to and fro. A tiny calendar gave the month and year as January 1880. Through a rear doorway was represented an horologist's workbench, at which a lean, old man sat, peering through a jeweler's loupe at a gold watch. His neck was clearly jointed to permit his head to nod.

In the showroom, however, a petite beauty stood behind the counter. She wore midnight blue satin with a bustle and train, and her upswept chignon and ringlets were a glossy black, rather as Madame Rigby's might have once been. The object of her smiling attention was the handsome young man before the counter, whose jointed arm was raised to his hat; clearly he was meant to sweep it from his head and bow to her.

Beneath the second scene was painted *He Vows To Be True.* Here the same little man stood in a painted representation of a front parlor, and by the action of a pin and lever in his jointed leg might well be made to kneel before the little beauty, whose hand was placed in his. His neck was cleverly jointed as well, and perhaps enabled the head to drop forward upon the beloved's hand when he knelt, in imitation of a kiss.

It was plain that the painted furnishings behind this demonstration of affection were meant to represent a certain threadbare gentility. And what could the artist have meant to imply, by showing a lady's boudoir so plainly through the painted arch to the rear of the room? And was that a gentleman's waistcoat, finely embroidered, draped over the foot of the bed?

The third scene was *Upon Reflection He Grows Cold,* and here was another public location: an expanse of painted lawn, and in the background an admirable representation of the Conservatory of Flowers in Golden Gate Park, with the delicate tracery of its spires and glittering dome. Charming; less so was the action in the foreground, where the young man stood stiffly upright. His face was turned from the young lady, his left hand extended in a gesture of repulsion that would become more emphatic when the forearm rose and dropped, as its jointed elbow clearly permitted it to do.

The young lady's arms were jointed too; they must permit her to raise them in a beseeching motion. She clutched a handkerchief no bigger than a postage stamp. Infinitesimal tears were painted on her pale cheeks. And could the dollmaker have really meant to present the young lady in a gown cut so loosely about the waist? What a shocking implication!

The next scene, *He Seeks a Wealthy Bride,* showed the little gentleman at the seaside; he wore a straw hat, and the flush of sunburn on his cheeks was very well rendered. He stood with his hands in his pockets on the gray sand, apparently one of a party. Here, seated upon a checkered cloth, were three dolls, two meant to represent a well-to-do older couple; or so one might assume from the expanse of the old man's waistcoat with its gleaming golden watch chain, and the ostentation of the old woman's hat, and the richness of the painted wine, cake and roast chicken in the miniature picnic basket between them. The third doll was clearly their golden-haired daughter, smiling up at the young man without expression in her great, flat blue eyes.

In the distance behind them rose Cliff House, not Sutro's splendid castle, but the little boxy structure that had been there before it; and if one looked very carefully one might spot the tiny, woeful figure in midnight blue, standing poised on its parapet as though she were about to jump into the saw-edged wooden waves—a proceeding sure to grind her to a pinch of sad dust, were they moving back and forth on their respective tracks, as presently they were not. The artificial perspective made it difficult to ascertain the young lady's condition, but managed to suggest a reason for her desperation.

The fifth scene was titled *Oh, False Young Man!* Here was the interior of a grand church, seen through its open door; perhaps Grace Church. Real painted glass had been used in the windows, and perhaps there was an electric lamp behind them when the mechanism was switched on. If so, this would backlight the tiny, tiny figures of the groom and his golden-haired bride, standing one step below the tinier minister all in black, holding an open prayerbook.

All this through the door; without, on the church steps, sat the wretched doll in midnight blue, bowed forward in a transport of grief. Her body was jointed at its unmistakable waist; when she rocked back and forward, as she must, and raised her handkerchief and lowered it, there could be no question of her particular sorrow.

The sixth and final scene was titled *She Meditates upon Her Vengeance,* but was represented at present by a bare and dusty void, into which gears and wires protruded. Madame Rigby had removed the little scene which once occupied the space, and it sat unrestored to her left: a graveyard by night, with a solemn moon casting blue radiance over the doll in mourning black. She stood beside an infant's grave, with her clasped hands lifted as in prayer. A black cat, perched on one of the tombstones, arched its jointed back when in motion; perhaps its glass eyes were lit from within too. Hinges on certain of the tomb lids suggested that the spectral occupants might emerge to regard the young lady's anguish.

All this was being replaced, however, by a new final scene: the shabby front parlor once again, and the doll in midnight blue seated by a cradle containing a peanut-sized bundle in swaddling clothes. The doll held in her hand the finely embroidered waistcoat, last seen forgotten on the foot of the bed. Her face had been painted with a distinct expression of bitter regret. Madame Rigby, reaching in with a pair of long-nosed pliers, threaded a wire between the doll's foot and the cradle's front rocker and twisted its end to fasten it in place.

"That'll do it," she muttered, and felt under the scene's floor for the wire's other end. She tugged experimentally; the doll's foot tapped, and the cradle rocked to and fro.

"I hope you don't mind my saying so, ma'am, but I'm awfully glad you're taking out the old ending," said Dick. "It's just too unbearably sad."

Madame Rigby cocked an eye at him. "You think so, do you?" she said, as she slid the new scene into place. "What a lot you men find unbearable."

"I guess that's true, ma'am," said Dick, abashed. He opened the front of the lower case for her, in order that she might connect the wires into the greater mechanism. A second's careful work with the pliers, and it was done. Madame Rigby leaned back; Dick closed up the case, felt in his pocket for a slug nickel, and dropped it in the coin slot on the left side.

Six little curtains dropped, like window shades. Then each one rose in succession, revealing the respective scenes properly lit and animated. The tiny drama played out to its tragic end. The lamps extinguished themselves; the curtains dropped once more.

"You men," repeated Madame Rigby, with a hoarse chuckle, and added a word seldom heard in polite society. Dick blushed and hung his head; then attempted a witticism to restore his composure.

"Why, it's true we're not perfect creatures. Maybe you'll improve on the original design with Mr. Waxwork, over there."

"Ahhh! You bet," said Madame Rigby. She smiled, and pushed herself up from the bench, and went to a cabinet at the far end of the workroom. It was plain that if she had ever once resembled the doll in midnight blue, the years had made alterations; she was thickset now, bespectacled, gray-haired. But there was a certain vigorous pleasure in her step as she approached the cabinet and threw it open. She beamed with pride at what was disclosed within, and Dick caught his breath.

Anyone seeing the occupant of the cabinet for the first time might be excused for thinking they beheld a living youth, interrupted perhaps on his way to the bath, for he was loosely draped in a sheet. Every limb, every hair and eyelash, were perfect counterfeits; the human form was here presented with a degree of perfection unknown since Praxiteles. Yet this was no marble image of snow. The bloom of robust health was in the image's cheeks, his thick hair was black and glossy as a raven's wing. His eyes were a dark blue—one might almost say a midnight blue—and gleamed as though with intelligence and ready wit.

"Gracious, ma'am! When did you put in those eyes? He had 'em closed, last time I peeped in the cabinet!" said Dick.

"So you peeped, did you?" Madame Rigby scowled at him. "You're a regular Pandora! The eyes are lenses, you see? There're little shutters in his head, on timers. You must have stolen your look at night."

"Yes, ma'am. It was when I'd come up to turn off the lights, before going out to dinner."

"Well, mind I don't catch you prying where you're not asked again; or I'll fire you, and I mean business, mister! That young wise-ass from the Polytechnic College thought he knew a trick or two Eudora Rigby didn't; but I guess I showed *him*," she said. She took a last pull on her cigarette, dropped it to the floor and crushed it out with her foot.

"Oh, no, ma'am, I'd never presume!" Dick protested. "It was only that I felt such an admiration of your work! I've never seen anything to beat this fellow."

"Haven't you?" Madame Rigby looked at him sidelong. "Well, here's an eyeful for you!"

She pulled the sheet away, and laughed heartily when Dick turned scarlet with embarrassment.

"Oh, my hat!" Dick averted his gaze; then, unable to resist, looked again on the figure's generous perfection with a certain horrified envy.

"The human form improved," said Madame Rigby, in complacent satisfaction. There came a rap on the door, and she swiftly covered the figure once more and shut the cabinet. "That'll be the moving van fellows! Let 'em in."

Dick obeyed, and two hulking men in overalls and brogans stepped into the room, removing their caps.

"'Morning, ma'am. We're here to see Mr. Rigby, about his exhibition?" said the elder of the two.

"That's *Madame* Rigby, and it's my exhibition, my good man," said she, tapping her foot briskly. She waved her hand at the crates piled against the wall. "This all goes to Cliff House. Fourth floor, Gallery Hall, see? I'll want you today and Thursday too. Make it snappy!"

• • •

Thursday evening Madame Rigby returned to the hotel where her workshop was presently housed. She was followed by Dick, who was drooping with exhaustion, having worked all day at setting up the exhibits. She unlocked the door, entered, and stood looking around her in satisfaction at the absence of packing crates.

"Now we'll see, by God," she said. She went to the table and rolled herself a cigarette, and the obliging little devil lit it for her.

"Oh, no!" said Dick. "We've gone and forgotten Mr. Waxwork!"

He went cautiously to the cabinet and opened it. There stood the figure as before, but with its eyes closed. As Dick watched, however, some inner mechanism reacted to the light of the street lamp falling upon the face; the eyes flew open, and appeared to view Dick's consternation with gentle amusement.

"I haven't either forgotten him," said Madame Rigby. "Why, he's the main attraction, boy!"

"But we'll have to hire another van to get him out to Cliff House," said Dick.

"Tut-tut! A cab will do perfectly well," said Madame Rigby, smiling as she exhaled smoke through her nose.

"I suppose. Still… that'll be some job for you and me, carrying him up all those stairs. He must weigh a couple of hundred pounds," said Dick.

"Two hundred and nine," said Madame Rigby. "But we won't be carrying him, you fool. He'll walk up on his own, as easily as you or I."

"Walk!" cried Dick, delighted and astonished. "Why, you don't mean he's an automaton too? Like your spinet-playing girl, or the two little boys that write and draw? Or the old Turk who deals cards?"

"Ah! Those? Toys, all of them," said Madame Rigby, with a dismissive wave of her hand. "Early lessons. No more complicated than clocks. This fellow's the real goods. My masterwork, and no fooling. And he'll do the job—you'll see."

"Holy Moses," said Dick. "What will he do, ma'am?"

"Let's start him up, and I'll show you," said Madame Rigby. She went to a side table, where there stood a decanter of some colorless liquid. Drawing a long funnel from a drawer, she took it with the decanter to her creation, and tapped gently at his mouth. He parted his lips; Dick had a glimpse of white teeth and pink tongue, rather than the hollow of steel frame and silk lining he had expected. Madame Rigby thrust the funnel in, and poured the liquid down the automaton's gurgling throat—or down a pipe, Dick supposed, into some unseen tank.

"Invented this fuel myself," said Madame Rigby proudly. "One part cod-liver oil, one part Paris Lilacs *parfum*, and eight parts gin. He'll run a week on a bellyful of this."

"I should say he would," said Dick. "I think I would too."

"There now, my darling; that'll set you up," said Madame Rigby, with a tenderness in her voice Dick had never before heard. "Your day has come at last! Time to make Mama proud of you."

She withdrew a curious long key from her reticule, and thrust it up the automaton's left nostril. She turned it smartly. There was a *click,* and she withdrew the key. Dick half-expected to see the figure shiver with disgust, and clutch his nose; but he only began to breathe, or rather to go through the motions of breathing.

"Watch this, now," said Madame Rigby, extending her hand in front of the automaton. She waved it from side to side; the figure turned its head as though following her movement with its eyes. Loudly and distinctly she said: "Your name, sir?"

The automaton blinked once, and when it opened its mouth Dick clearly heard the hiss of air being drawn in; the next moment a voice sounded, proceeding presumably from some bellows and reed mechanism in the chest.

"Jack Rigby, at your service," said the thing, moving its lips in flawless imitation of the motions of speech. For all his delight, Dick felt a chill run down his spine. The more so when Madame Rigby laughed, triumphant, and the automaton drew its lips back from its teeth in a smile, as though politely sharing in the jest.

"Ha, ha, ha!" it said. "Very good."

"Now, my boy," said Madame Rigby, "step down!"

Jack Rigby, to use his own name, bent his head as though to judge the distance from the cabinet to the floor. Then with only the slightest unsteadiness, he stepped down from the cabinet.

Dick staggered backward, and collapsed in a dead faint.

When he came to himself again, Madame Rigby was forcing a stinging liquid down his throat. For a moment he had the dreadful fancy she had transformed him into an automaton, and was filling him with fuel; but it was only brandy. Madame Rigby was laughing again, and Jack was smiling and nodding along.

"Well, aren't you the delicate lily!" she said. "Does my boy frighten you?"

"Nothing of the kind!" insisted Dick, sitting up hastily. "I-it's a shock, that's all; I never expected him to do anything like that. Why, it's like witchcraft!"

"Witchcraft?" Madame Rigby looked scornful. "Well, I should think not! This is the year 1900, after all, young man. There's no hocus-pocus nonsense to my Jack; just hard work and practical engineering. Haven't I labored at my trade these twenty years, and learned from all the clockmakers and dollmakers and mechanics in Bavaria and Paris? Jacky proceeds out of all they've done, only I've gone them all one better. *Me!* Eudora Rigby."

"But… this isn't like a clock," said Dick, shivering. "You've made a thing that thinks like a man."

"Not a bit of it," said Madame Rigby. "Any more than a music box really sings, or a loom makes up its pattern as it goes along. He's got leaves of metal in him, you see, thousands of 'em, tiny, and each one has a pattern of holes in it that tells him something to do. And inside those ears there's mechanism that takes sounds and reads 'em as patterns. When it picks up a pattern it knows, why, it matches it up to one of its own, and gives him something to do in reply."

"I think I see," said Dick. "Didn't it take a long while for you to punch all those little patterns, though?"

"Ages," Madame Rigby admitted. "That was why I hired on that boy from the Polytechnic; I had too much to do. He sat there for two solid years, working out all the commands."

"Well, this beats anything I've ever seen," said Dick. "Yes, *sir*! That is to say, yes, ma'am."

"Mind him a moment," said Madame Rigby, going into her private chambers. "I'll go fetch him some britches."

Dick, much to his consternation, was left alone with Jack. He put on as bold a face as he could muster, and said loudly:

"Say! Think we'll get any rain?"

Jack turned his head slightly when Dick spoke, as though to better hear him. He drew breath, smiled and said:

"Perhaps."

"But there isn't a cloud in the sky!"

"That's true."

"I might as well have said, do you reckon we'll get ice and snow in July!"

"Tell me what you think."

"He's got an empty phrase to suit any occasion," said Madame Rigby, returning with a suit of men's clothing under her arm. "Help me get him dressed, now."

This proved much easier than dressing the other automata in the exhibit, for Jack, while unable to respond to an order as complex as *Dress yourself*, was nonetheless able to lift or extend his limbs when told to, and could follow a specific order such as *Button your shirt*. Presently he stood, fully clothed, in a suit of smart modern cut; the waistcoat he wore with the suit, however, was out of fashion. Twenty years ago it had been the latest thing, to be sure, and its fancy embroidery was still bright.

"Ma'am, if you don't mind my saying so, this fellow's going to make you millions," said Dick in awe.

"Think so? Maybe," said Madame Rigby. "Say, did you mail those invitations to the exhibition, like I told you?"

"I sure did, ma'am," said Dick. "Did that first thing Monday morning."

"Including the one to Congressman Gookin?"

"Yes indeed, ma'am. I think he's already replied; it came in the morning post, but I haven't had time to look through your correspondence today—"

Madame Rigby hurried to the table by the door, where her unopened mail sat in a basket. She picked up the letters and shuffled through them. One in particular she pulled out, and held up to the gaslight.

"That's not his hand," she said, frowning.

"I guess he has a secretary, ma'am," said Dick.

"Oh! Sure he would, nowadays," said Madame Rigby. She tore open the envelope and held up the letter, peering at it. Then she whooped with laughter. Jack smiled again and said, "Ha, ha ha!"

"What's he say, ma'am?" said Dick, edging away from Jack.

"He says he'll come!" cried Madame Rigby. "I knew he would. I asked him whether he might oblige us by saying a few words when the exhibition's opened. He wouldn't pass up a chance to stump for votes, not Fremont T. Gookin. The old son of a bitch is running for re-election, see?"

Dick winced at her language. "Yes, ma'am. I saw plenty of his banners up in Portsmouth Square, when I was posting handbills."

Jack said, "You don't say!"

"Listen to my pretty boy!" Madame Rigby said. "Well, this calls for a celebration. Come on, Dick; I'll treat you to dinner at the Poodle Dog." She grabbed up her hat and cape once more.

"What about *him*?" inquired Dick, turning out the lights.

"Why, he'll stand guard; he never complains, my Jacky," said Madame Rigby.

• • •

On Saturday morning, the long, sandy drive below Cliff House was crowded with buckboards and carriages. Above, a steady stream of people was dismounting from the streetcars that came and went. They milled about before the main entrance, where a sign had been strung up before the door:

RIGBY'S AUTOMATA AND SCENES MECANIQUES
GRAND EXHIBITION

Shortly before noon an impressive object came rattling up the Great Ocean Highway. It resembled a stagecoach, but was notable in that no horses galloped before it. The coachman, wearing goggles and a cap, drove from a small compartment in the front of the carriage; two men perched on the upper seats at the back, clutching their hats as the automobile accelerated to take the hill at a run. Within could be seen an imposing-looking gentleman of middle age, with a young lady seated beside him.

Many in the assembled crowd assumed this to be Mr. Rigby, and applauded at his grand arrival. No sooner had the automobile pulled up before the entrance, however, than they were disabused of this notion; for the two men behind the coach leaped down, bawling:

"Re-elect Congressman Fremont T. Gookin!"

One of them reached down and withdrew a bundle of painted canvas, and they hurried in through the arches; a moment later they could be glimpsed above on the outer deck, where they spread out a banner reading:

FREMONT T. GOOKIN FOR RE-ELECTION!

Congressman Gookin himself had meanwhile dismounted from the automobile, and extended his hand to the young lady, who stepped down, looking around her rather sullenly.

"Honestly, Papa!" she murmured. "That really is the height of bad manners."

"Hush, Evangeline," said her father. "There's a reporter for the *Morning Call!* Smile; and pray don't say anything objectionable." He drew off his hat and waved it at the throng. "Well met, citizens!"

There were scattered cheers. With his daughter on his arm he strode within, smiling and nodding to one and all. Just to the left of the entrance was a reception room with a bar, where more members of the press were assembled. Congressman Gookin flashed them a broad smile.

"Gentlemen! What a grand day, is it not? I wonder if you could tell me whether Mr. Rigby has arrived?"

The reporter for the *Examiner* coughed meaningfully.

"*Madame* Rigby," said she, stepping forward. Congressman Gookin turned to regard her.

"Oh! Like Madame Tussaud? Oh, I see! I hope you'll pardon me, madame; entirely unintentional oversight," he said. "Fremont T. Gookin, your servant. May I introduce my daughter, Evangeline?"

"What a pretty child," said Madame Rigby. "You know, my dear, your papa's quite forgotten me! Haven't you, Congressman? Or is it possible the name Eudora Rigby has not quite faded from memory?"

Congressman Gookin opened his mouth to make some gracious rejoinder, and halted. He looked at Madame Rigby with recognition; horror came into his face. Before he could recover himself, Madame Rigby grinned, and urged forward the young man whose arm she held.

"And do let me present my son, Jack Rigby."

"How do you do, young man," stammered Congressman Gookin. Jack cocked his head slightly, smiled and said:

"Very pleased to meet you, I'm sure."

Congressman Gookin's distracted gaze traveled over the youth's features, which bore a certain resemblance to his own; then he noticed the embroidered waistcoat, and the color quite fled from his cheeks. He pulled out a handkerchief and mopped away cold sweat.

"Madame—please—"

"I think you had a few words to say to the gentlemen of the press?" said Madame Rigby.

"Why—yes, I have—" Congressman Gookin fumbled in his coat pocket and brought out a paper containing the notes for the speech he had prepared. In doing so he disengaged his arm from that of his daughter, and Madame Rigby was quick to lean forward and take her hand.

"Miss Evangeline, wouldn't you like a private tour of the exhibition, before we let in the public? Jack! Take her arm, there's a good boy. Dick, you go with 'em, show Jack the way."

"Yes, ma'am," Dick said, stepping away from the bar.

"But—" said Congressman Gookin, looking around wildly. Madame Rigby took his arm.

"Now, now, Congressman dear, I'm sure we're all anxious to hear what you have to say," she said, looking around at the reporters. "Aren't you, boys?"

And in fact Congressman Gookin had prepared a fine speech, full of references to the New Century, and Progress, and American Capability. He had hired his automobile especially for the occasion, and had meant to laud American inventors in several clever references to it; he had even done a little research on the history of clockwork automata, and worked up an elaborate metaphor involving the American industrial worker as a proud engine propelling forward the American economy. This was designed to lead to an impassioned appeal for re-election, on the grounds that Progress would cease unless he, Congressman Gookin, were permitted to continue his efforts on its behalf.

It was a rather long speech, and this was unfortunate, for several journalists present noticed that Congressman Gookin stuttered on not a few occasions throughout. He seemed to have difficulty concentrating; several times his eyes tracked nervously to the door through which his daughter had vanished with the two young gentlemen. Madame Rigby stood by the door with her arms crossed, smiling at him the entire time.

Meanwhile, a floor above, Jack Rigby strolled along with Miss Evangeline on his arm, and Dick followed behind them, scarcely able to contain his mirth.

"These are the tableaux, miss," said Dick, pointing to a row of cases. "They're mostly her older pieces. This, here, is the Visit to the Circus; allow me to demonstrate."

He dropped a slug nickel into the coin slot, whereupon Miss Evangeline was treated to the sight of a three-ring circus in miniature coming to life. Little trapeze artists swung to and fro, a lion tamer raised his whip before a snarling beast that lifted and dropped its head, and a magician made a crystal ball appear and disappear.

"Oh, everything *moves*," exclaimed Evangeline, and gazed up at Jack. "Isn't that clever!"

"Charming," agreed Jack.

"And this one's the Message from the Sea," said Dick, trying to catch Evangeline's eye, for he thought she was quite a pretty girl. She glanced at the tableau instead, as it whirred into motion. It depicted a ballroom. On a dais on one corner, musicians sat, and rocked to and fro as though playing their various instruments. Real beveled mirrors were set in the wall, the better to reflect the naval officers and their ladies who waltzed round and round, on a circular track, to a music-box waltz. Beyond, in a painted harbor lit by a white moon, great warships rode the sea surge, going slowly up and down; in the foreground a ship's boat rocked too, full of sailors who rested on their oars. A tiny midshipman bearing a sword no longer than a toothpick was halfway up the terrace steps, waving; in his raised hand was a sealed dispatch.

"That is too, too romantic," said Evangeline to Jack, with a sigh. "Whatever do you suppose is in the message?"

"Tell me what you think," said Jack.

"Oh, I suppose—perhaps war's been declared, and all those gallant seamen must leave their sweethearts broken hearted," said Evangeline. "And yet, their love shall burn the more fiercely for being cruelly separated."

"Indeed," said Jack.

"Do you want to see the automatons?" said Dick, a trifle sulkily. "There's a peach over here—Professor Honorius. He'll write you out a personal message."

"Yes, thank you," said Evangeline. "I declare, Mr. Rigby, your mama is a woman of most remarkable talents!"

"Ah, well," said Jack.

"You don't think so? But then I find that parents and children seldom appreciate one another as they ought," said Evangeline. "My papa, for example, seems incapable of regarding me as anything other than an ornament to his arm during election time. *My* thoughts and feelings are quite inconsequential to him."

"Dear, dear," said Jack.

"Here," said Dick, stopping beside a glass case wherein sat, large as life, a whimsical old gentleman in the robe and mortarboard of a schoolmaster. His right arm, pen in hand, rested on a small writing-table. "You have to stand in front of him for it to work."

He took Evangeline's elbow and steered her to a spot directly in front of the case. He had assumed she would let go of Jack's arm in the process, but she held tight and Jack followed like an obliging fellow, close at her side.

"Not sure he'll get the message right, if there's two of you," grumbled Dick, but he felt in his pocket for another slug and dropped it in the coin slot.

Professor Honorius raised his head and turned it from side to side, as though peering before him. Then his left hand lifted a pair of spectacles to his eyes, and he looked straight ahead at Evangeline and Jack. He nodded, smiling. As he did so, a card dropped into a small tray on the writing-table.

Professor Honorius lowered his spectacles and turned his face to the writing-table, seeming to look down on the card. His right arm lifted, reached across to an inkwell, whose cap opened for him; he dipped the pen and then, slowly but with perfect articulation of his fingers, wrote upon the card.

"Well, I never!" said Evangeline.

"Very true," said Jack.

The message having been written, Professor Honorius raised his hand. A peg rose under one side of the tray, tilting the card outward and down a chute; it dropped through the front of the case, and fell to the floor. Jack's head lowered, and his eyes seemed to focus on the white pasteboard.

"Allow me," said Jack. With a graceful motion he bent at the waist, and picked up the card. He presented it to Evangeline with a slight bow. She read the card. She blushed, her eyes sparkling with excitement. Dick, leaning past Jack to see what was on the card, read:

True Love is Within Your Grasp

"My goodness, what a delightful thought!" said Evangeline to Jack.

"Please," said Jack. "Tell me about yourself."

Which Evangeline proceeded to do, as Dick led them along the row of automata, past the Turk who dealt cards and the other Turk who smoked a hookah, past the clown whose little dog balanced on a ball, and they might have been blank walls for all that Evangeline paid the slightest attention to them. She spared not even a glance at the remarkable replica of Vaucanson's Excreting Duck. When Dick set the Grand Orchestrion playing, blaring out "Wellington's Victory" so loudly the glass cases all rattled, she merely raised her voice to be heard. The whole while, Jack seemed to follow her words with interest and sympathy. "Ah," and "Well, well," and "Do tell!" and "How very interesting," in no way exhausted his vast repertory of responses.

Presently applause downstairs indicated that Congressman Gookin had staggered to the end of his speech, and a moment later the waiting crowd was let in to climb the stairs to the exhibit hall. Madame Rigby walked at the forefront, firmly clasping Congressman Gookin's arm. The congressman looked sick and faint, as though he would rather be anywhere else. Madame Rigby had the air of a smiling tigress.

"Well, Jack, have you entertained the young lady properly?"

"I'll have to think about that," said Jack.

"Oh, Jack dear, don't be silly! Madame, he's too modest; I'm having the most wonderful time!" said Evangeline.

"How very nice. Now, Congressman, I've something special to show you," said Madame Rigby. "The oldest piece in the exhibit, the first one I ever built."

She pulled him with her to the lovers' tragedy in six acts. Dick slouched after them, having given up any attempt to draw Evangeline's notice. Dutifully he dropped a slug in the coin slot, and the first little curtain rose on the scene in the clockmaker's shop. Congressman Gookin regarded it with a face as waxen as the manikin's.

Dick, well used to the little play by now, found himself watching its audience instead. He observed Congressman Gookin's pallor, and the light of baleful joy on Madame Rigby's face. Suddenly the full import of what Dick beheld dawned on him. He looked uncertainly from one face to the other, and then at the tableau.

"Oh!" he exclaimed under his breath. Shaken with disgust, he left the exhibit hall and went downstairs to the bar, where he fortified himself with a whiskey. In doing so, he missed the congressman's rapid exit, pulling a protesting Evangeline with him.

• • •

"Well, well, listen to this," said Madame Rigby, tipping ash from her cigarette. She read from a sheet of scented letter-paper:

My very dear Jack, I am scarcely able to express my pleasure at meeting you Saturday, but even less able to express my indignation and outrage. You may well wonder why! In the Automobile I expressed to Papa my intention to invite you to my Birthday Soiree, and to my shock and horror he positively forbid it! We had quite a Row and the Consequence is, I have canceled the entire affair. Which will end up costing a Great Deal I am sure, as the caterer's deposit cannot be refunded at such short notice, but as it is my fortune anyhow, or will be, I do not care.

"In any case I shall certainly not let such an Unfair Prejudice as Papa's stand in the way of my further acquaintance with your gracious self. He is all Affability when there is a Reporter anywhere nearby, but quite another person in Private. Be that as it may, we are not in Ancient Rome and I am free to take the streetcar anywhere I like. It is my intention to visit you at the Exhibition tomorrow, and indeed any day that I am able, when we may continue our Interesting Conversations.

"Unless—perhaps I am too Forward? But surely you do not think so. Do reply by return post and tell me that you share my Enthusiasm for our continued friendship. Yours Affectionately, Miss Evangeline Gookin.

Madame Rigby tossed the letter down on her workbench and took a long pull on her cigarette.

"*Her* fortune anyhow, is it? 'Or will be'. Now, I wonder if the family fortune wasn't settled on the child? How unfortunate for the congressman! Where's my writing-case, Dick? Jack's got to write her straight back, just as she asked him to."

"You don't mean he writes, too?" said Dick, fetching her the case.

"Oh, I reckon I could modify him to do it; but what need, when his own dear mama knows exactly what he'll say?" said Madame Rigby. She took out a sheet of paper and a reservoir pen of her own design, and paused.

"Now, let's see. 'My dear little girl—' Just so old Fremont Gookin used to begin! But, no; this is Jacky's first letter, and he's a gentleman. *He* wouldn't make so bold." Madame Rigby began to write, reading aloud as she went.

" 'My very dear Miss Gookin; painful as I find the report of your father's unreasoning dislike, it is difficult to express my corresponding joy at your kind regard and your desire to continue our acquaintance.' "

"Ma'am, don't you think—" said Dick.

"Hush, boy. 'Especially since it will, sadly, be of such a brief duration; for, you know, we will be returning to Paris when the Exhibition closes at the end of the month.' "

"Ah," said Dick.

" 'So I will be delighted to spend my brief interlude here as much in your fair company as possible. Please do meet me at the Exhibition tomorrow, the Twelfth; I shall linger amongst the cases, disconsolate until you come.' There!" Madame Rigby signed for Jack with a flourish. "Just you run this out to the post box, Dick."

"Yes, ma'am," said Dick, smiling uneasily. "You know, it's a fine joke; but do you think you can keep it up for a month? What if Jack's exposed for what he really is?"

"Exposed! Why, let him be," said Madame Rigby. "Can you think of better publicity for us? It's the grandest joke that's ever been played; and the longer we can keep it going, the bigger the story will break. *Then* we'll see the money rolling in. I've planned this hoax for twenty years, sonny; no matter what may befall, I'll come out of it a winner. And you'll stick with me and win too, if you've any brains."

Dick saw before him the prospect of a trip to Paris, France, with all he might learn from Madame Rigby there, and the mansion on Nob Hill that might one day be his if he became a master mechanic. He swallowed hard and said:

"It does seem a little hard on Miss Evangeline, is all."

Madame Rigby's eyes glinted. "Hard? Well, she'll survive it. A few rude shocks are liable to do such a spoiled beauty good."

• • •

The exhibition was a success. It was favorably written up in the *Examiner*, the *Chronicle* and the *Morning Call*. Only the *Examiner* quoted from Congressman Gookin's speech at any length, so it is unlikely his efforts did much to sway the forthcoming election.

But San Franciscans took the streetcar out to Cliff House in great numbers. There they stood in line to file up the stairs to the gallery, and gladly spent their bright nickels to make the acquaintance of Professor Honorius, or to marvel at the detail and perfection of the Excreting Duck. Not a few of the gentler sex shed a tear over the sorrows of the little black-haired doll in midnight blue. Dick worked for two hours each evening after the gallery closed, emptying the machines; he never failed to retrieve at least two buckets' worth of nickels, which were satisfyingly heavy when rolled up in brown paper and taken to the bank next morning.

Though Miss Evangeline Gookin visited the exhibition on very nearly a daily basis, she spent no coin, and scarcely looked again at the *scenes mecaniques*. All her time was spent with Jack, walking round and round the fourth-floor porch outside the exhibition. The sun shone, the salt-gray sea roared and surged around Seal Rock, the booming wind streamed her hair out and brought her the squeals of bathers far down Ocean Beach; it is unlikely Evangeline noticed any of this, so caught up was she in her conversations with Jack.

She thought him quite the kindest and most thoughtful youth she'd ever met. He never interrupted her, as every other boy of her acquaintance did; never told her that her opinions were silly, never scoffed at her tastes in Literature or Art, never boasted, never grew impatient, never attempted to change the topic under discussion to Sports, and never, never in word or deed suggested anything immoral.

Indeed, Jack seemed to like nothing more than to listen to her, chastely holding her hand all the while. Evangeline supposed that this was because he was a pure and chivalrous person, though she had to admit to herself that Jack's behavior might have been a little more ardent, had Madame Rigby not loitered continually in the near distance. But this too was entirely proper; and Madame Rigby played the smiling chaperone on the several occasions they took tea in the ladies' parlor next to the Gallery Hall. And if Jack's hands were a little cold, Evangeline never wondered at it; for the porch at Cliff House, exposed as it was to the full force of the wind off the Golden Gate, ranked just above Alaska in January on any list of the world's chilliest places to court a lover.

It must be admitted that sometimes Evangeline found Jack's conversation a little vague and absent-minded. His letters to her (for they wrote each other often) were another matter, however. He wrote in a witty, dashing style, and used the courtliest expressions of love she had ever heard. Had Evangeline known that their source and origin was a bundle of yellowed deception written by Congressman Gookin himself, harbored in the bottom of Madame Rigby's trunk these twenty years, she would have recoiled in horror; but she didn't know, and so continued to treasure Jack's correspondence.

The closing day of the exhibition drew inexorably nearer. If Jack's letters and manner remained serene, Evangeline was increasingly wretched to contemplate that she might shortly be deprived of his company forever.

• • •

"Whew! I want a brandy," said Madame Rigby, throwing down her hat and gloves. "I'd forgotten how cold the wind blows out there. Dick, take Jack to the water closet; he drank three cups of tea today. I wonder he hasn't leaked."

Dick rose, shuddering, and guided Jack to the lavatory. Fortunately, he was not obliged to assist Jack further at this point; as he slouched in the doorway, he blessed his predecessor, the nameless fellow from the Polytechnic who had worked out all Jack's more detailed masculine commands. One terse phrase was all that was required for Jack to make the necessary adjustments to his trousers before draining off approximately twenty-four ounces of stale tea, after which he buttoned himself once more and turned with a beaming face to receive his next order. Taking Jack by the shoulder, Dick walked him to his cabinet and thrust the key up his nose before shutting him away for the night.

"Lordy! Here's another letter from Miss Evangeline," said Madame Rigby. "Well, well! Are these tear-stains I see? Jack, you rogue, what have you been up to?"

She poured herself a brandy and lit another cigarette before settling down to read the latest letter. Dick sat down wearily and unwrapped a ham sandwich bought from a pushcart vendor, for he had yet to dine. He was not to enjoy his meal in peace, however. Madame Rigby perused but a few lines before she leaped to her feet and began to pace as she read, puffing out furious clouds of smoke.

"Listen to this!" she said, from the corner of her mouth. " 'Oh, my Beloved! You may well wonder at my Tears, or maybe the fact that my writing is so Tremulous. I am a Prisoner in my Own Room! You shall not wonder long, for here is the whole Dreadful Truth!

" 'Papa has found one of your Letters and for Heaven's Sake I thought he was going to Drop Down Dead right there on the Floor from Apoplexy! Never have I heard Such Language! He has called you all kinds of Dreadful Things I will not repeat, and (Which is Worse to my Way of Thinking) your dear Mother also.

" 'I am Forbidden to see or speak to you Ever Again!!! And am presently Locked In on the Third Floor!!!!

" 'Yet, Despair Not, for the man doesn't live who can keep Evangeline Gookin from her True Love. Hear me Patiently a Little While, for I think I see a Way we may yet be Happy.

" 'I am Certain the Servants will let me out To-Morrow whilst Papa goes to his Odious Campaign Meeting, for they all Detest him as much as I do, especially Daisy, whom he has Treated in a Beastly Manner I will not soil my pen with Describing. And even were they not to be bribed, what Papa does not know is that one can quite Easily climb from my Window to the little Porch above the Breakfast Room and so down the Drainpipe to the Garden, and then you know the Streetcar Tracks run right past the Corner.

" 'But all of this Availeth us Not but to a Temporary Reunion, unless your Passion is the Equal of mine. Darling, I really think we must Elope. You surely have seen plenty of folks do it over in France where people are less Cold-Blooded than Over Here and I bet you would have no trouble making the Arrangements. And then, what Bliss & Ecstasy awaits us!!

" 'Though I hope you will not come to Smoke or Drink, Jack, for I find those to be Intolerable vices. Nor go to the races. Nor take up with a lot of Objectionable fellows and stay out late much. And I do expect you will Permit me to Manage the Household Accounts. I feel my poor Mama's Health was Considerably Wrecked by Quarreling and I don't much think you ought to oppose a dear and loving Wife who only seeks your Happiness.

" 'Lest you have any Fearful Considerations—you know I am of Age, and that my late Mama's whole Fortune was settled on me to inherit at my Marriage. So I am sure Papa Dreads any such Happy Day for me on account of he is Heavily in Debt and after the way he Carried On just now I am Determined to cut him off without one Red Cent and serve him right.

" 'Daisy is waiting to take this down to the Post Office so it goes right out. She always collects the mail too so she will Intercept your Reply and bring it right up. Write back Immediately, Jack Dearest, and tell me our Hearts will soon Beat as One. Your own adoring Evangeline Rigby (or so I fondly anticipate).' "

Dick sat appalled, his sandwich half-eaten, as Madame Rigby finished the letter and folded it carefully. Her eyes glowed with a hellish light. She dropped the end of her cigarette, stepped on it, and took a hearty drink of brandy. Setting the glass down, she said:

"Dick, I want you to go over to the Palace right now, and reserve a suite of rooms for tomorrow night. Here's a pair of twenty-dollar gold pieces. Get the best you can."

"Good God!" cried Dick. "You can't mean to—"

"Why, Dick, whatever do you take me for?" said Madame Rigby. "Weren't you listening to that poor child's letter? She's in deadly peril! When she's an heiress, and her wicked father's in debt? I imagine he's planning her destruction even now. You don't know him as I do! We must convey her to safety, and she can't come here; it wouldn't be proper."

"Forgive me," said Dick, abashed. He pocketed the money and ran out, and an hour later had secured a fine suite of rooms for the following evening.

Madame Rigby was not there when he returned. Suffused with feelings of dread, he peered into Jack's cabinet. Jack opened his eyes and looked at him, as though inquiringly. Dick heard the door opening behind him, and, closing the cabinet with an air of guilt, turned to see Madame Rigby entering the room.

"Where have you been?" said Dick.

"Mailing a letter," she replied. "Did you do as I told you?"

"Yes, ma'am," said Dick. He dug in his pocket and found the receipt, which he handed to her. Madame Rigby took it eagerly, studied it a moment, and then tucked it away in her reticule.

"Now, Dick," she said, "I'm going to be busy all day tomorrow, so you'll have to mind the exhibition yourself. See that you telephone the moving men and engage a van for Monday."

"Yes, ma'am," said Dick. "Shall I take Jack with me tomorrow?"

"No," said Madame Rigby.

This filled Dick with suspicions so horrible he was scarcely able to name them even to himself; how much less, then, was he able to utter them to the composed and masterful woman who stood before him?

Long he lay awake that night in shameful torments, before falling into uneasy slumbers full of dreams of Evangeline: as a dainty and gossamer-winged butterfly trapped in the net of a squat spider, or as a tiny, jointed doll waltzing round and round in the arms of Professor Honorius, or bound in a straitjacket as she screamed, and screamed again without cease.

During the long streetcar ride the next morning, Dick was so dogged by the fantastic horrors of the previous night that he felt obliged to go straight to the bar, upon his arrival at Cliff House, and fortify himself with a stiff drink.

The whiskey braced him enough to enable him to open the exhibition for the day, but did not quiet his misgivings. As soon as the doors had been opened and visitors were filing through, Dick went back down to the bar and had another whiskey, and then another. By noon, the accumulated effects of four whiskies with a breakfast of stale pretzels had reduced Dick to a sorry condition indeed.

Unable to bear his apprehension any longer, Dick then pulled out a memorandum book and, tearing out its blank back pages, wrote in pencil a long and somewhat incoherent letter. In it he revealed as much as he understood of Madame Rigby's melancholy history, as well as the truth of Jack's extraordinary origins, in some detail. He ended with the earnest assurance that he disclosed these things only to spare Evangeline greater shock and humiliation.

Having acquired an envelope from the proprietor of the souvenir stand, Dick ventured out and caught a streetcar, and spent an unsteady eternity rattling across town. At last he spotted the Palace Hotel and leaped off in mid-block, under the nose of an affronted draft horse. Leaving chaos in his wake, he lurched into the vast hotel lobby and slid the envelope over the desk, with a slurred request that it might be delivered to suite 507, when the party for whom it had been reserved should check in.

Dick meant to return then to his duties at Cliff House. He may have done so; he certainly got as far as the bar there, but his next clear memory was of being at Sutro's Baths, struggling into a woolen bathing costume that seemed to have been made for a one-legged man. The clearest memory after that was of being held upright in an ice-cold shower bath by a pair of muscular attendants.

At some point after that Dick found himself on the floor of the work-shop, and made his way on hands and knees to the far wall. There he meant to pull down the window-drapes to serve as blankets, but somehow failed to do so. He attempted to get Jack to help him, but the doors of the cabinet were standing ajar; nothing was in there but the long, brass key, which seemed to have fallen to the floor and been overlooked. Dick put the key in his pocket and, weeping for the sorrow and the pity of it all, curled up and went to sleep.

• • •

"Well! You're some pretty picture, aren't you?" said a voice, high-up and distant and yet shockingly loud. Dick groaned and opened his eyes. He was greeted by the spectacle of a giantess looming above him, arms akimbo, smiling widely.

He lay there, stupefied, until Madame Rigby flung open the drapes and let in the light of broad noon. He flung up an arm to shield himself from its poisonous brilliance, and as he did so realized that he had failed to close down the exhibition, or to empty the coin boxes either, on the previous night.

"Oh, ma'am—I'm so awfully sorry— It won't ever happen again!" he said.

"Why, that's all right," said Madame Rigby, lighting a cigarette. "By rights I ought to fire you, but I'm feeling the most extraordinary peace today. Take your time getting up, Dick; no need to hurry. We don't sail until this afternoon."

Dick sat up. As he did so a newsboy screamed out, very nearly under the window:

"EXTRA! Congressman Gookin dead! Fremont T. Gookin suicide suspected!"

"What?" said Dick, as the floor seemed to roll like the breakers at Ocean Beach. Madame Rigby laughed quietly.

" '*Suspected?*'" she said scornfully. "Why, he had the gun in his hand. They found him stretched out in front of his dressing-room mirror. At least, that's what the morning edition says." She held it up for Dick to see. "Care to read for yourself? There's no mention of anyone finding my letter, though; so I suppose he had the good sense to burn it first."

"What letter?"

"The one I left for him, when I called in a cab for Miss Evangeline," Madame Rigby replied. "Don't you remember? We were going to assist her in her escape. We drove straight to the chapel."

Dick scrambled to his feet, as memory overtook him. He cast a swift glance at Jack's cabinet; its doors still stood open, revealing its emptiness.

"Where's Jack?" he shouted.

Madame Rigby's smile widened further still, giving her something of the air of a happy crocodile.

"On his honeymoon," she said, and roared with laughter as Dick staggered backward.

"Oh—oh, heaven! You old witch! Oh, how could you?" Dick gasped. "I'll go to the police!"

"Oh, no, you won't," said Madame Rigby. "Just you think for a moment about your future, mister. I can teach you all I know; the world will be your oyster. I've booked us a pair of berths on the *Belle Etoile,* and we'll be sailing off to Paris long before that girl stops screaming.

"You *can* stay here, if you like; but you'll have a real hard time convincing anyone you weren't my accomplice. Didn't I tell you that, whatever happened, I'd come out the winner? Well, I have."

Jack stared at her, breathing hard. At last he said:

"But—the exhibition—Jack—"

Madame Rigby waved her hand impatiently. "Trash. I built 'em for one purpose; well, that purpose is served." She cast a glance at the newspaper, and smiled again. "And well served too. I'll build something new and better next time—"

The door was thrown open.

Evangeline stood on the threshold, looking pale but determined. Madame Rigby glared at her like a startled cat; but smiled nonetheless, after a moment's silence, and drew on her cigarette.

"Why, Evangeline dear," she said. "So sorry to hear about your papa."

"It was scarcely a surprise," said Evangeline coolly. "He was being blackmailed by at least three women, and with the re-election coming up their demands were becoming importunate. Or so I should judge from his bank withdrawals. I really do fear you cannot take all the credit for his untimely death."

Madame Rigby's smile froze.

"Miss Gookin— I had nothing to do with—" Dick began, but she stopped him with a raised hand.

"*Mrs. Rigby*, if you please. You haven't asked after Jack, dear mother-in-law! And may I say I cannot thank you enough for your kindness yesterday? I confess to being a little astonished on my wedding night, but what married woman is not? I soon came to realize my good fortune. For, you see, Jack is so perfectly the sort of husband I had wanted; so patient, and understanding, and obedient. And *untiring*," added Evangeline, as a lovely flush came into her cheeks.

Madame Rigby gaped at her, until the sense of her last word sank in, and dropped the cigarette. Her face empurpled with fury.

"You—he—oh—oh, that damned boy from the Polytechnic!" she shrieked.

"I haven't the slightest idea what you mean," said Evangeline. "And I'll thank you not to use such language. In any case, I did not come here to speak to you." She turned to Dick. "Admirable as my darling husband is in so many ways, he is nonetheless a trifle forgetful. I should like to engage your services as his valet. You will be handsomely remunerated."

Dick blinked at her.

"Don't you dare go, you little crawling bastard!" said Madame Rigby. Evangeline spared her only a pained glance. She smiled enchantingly at Dick as she extended a hand to him.

"Recall that I am now in possession of a fortune which, if not quite as splendid as it once was, is still considerably more than it might have been had poor dear papa lived to continue stealing from it. *Handsomely* remunerated, sir."

Dick seemed to wake up. He stood straight, shook his hair out of his eyes, adjusted his coat and lapels, and shook Evangeline's hand most energetically. "Yes, ma'am!" he said.

He grabbed his hat and followed her out the door.

Madame Rigby was left alone. At length she noticed the curl of smoke rising from her forgotten cigarette. She stamped it out, cursing, and rolled herself a new one. Looking around, she spotted the little devil and wound him up. He winked and offered her a jet of flame. She leaned down to him.

"I can count on you, anyhow, Lucifer," she murmured, sucking her smoke alight. "Can't I?"

She went to the window and stood looking out, smoking. The smoke tasted sour. She coughed, and coughed again.

SO THIS GUY WALKS INTO A LIGHTHOUSE

Jan 1—1796. This day—my first on the light-house—I make this entry in my Diary. As regularly as I can keep the journal, I will—but there is no telling what may happen to a man all alone as I am—I may get sick, or worse... The cutter had a narrow escape—but why dwell on that, since I am here, all safe?

My spirits are beginning to revive already, at the mere thought of being—for once in my life at least—thoroughly alone; for, of course, Neptune, large as he is, is not to be taken into consideration as "society".

What most surprises me, is the difficulty De Grät had in getting me the appointment—and I a noble of the realm! It could not be that the Consistory had any doubt of my ability to manage the light. The duty is a mere nothing; and the printed instructions are as plain as possible.

It never would have done to let Orndoff accompany me, with his intolerable gossip—not to mention that everlasting meerschaum. Besides, I wish to be alone... Now for a scramble to the lantern and a good look around to "see what I can see"...

To see what I can see indeed!—not very much. The swell is subsiding a little, I think—but the cutter will have a rough passage home, nevertheless. She will hardly get within sight of the Norland before noon to-morrow—and yet it can hardly be more than 190 or 200 miles.

Jan 2. I have passed this day in a species of ecstasy that I find impossible to describe. My passion for solitude could scarcely have been more thoroughly gratified. I do not say satisfied; for I believe I should never be satiated with such delight as I have experienced to-day... Nothing to be seen but ocean and sky, with an occasional gull.

• • •

Jan 3. A dead calm all day. Occupied myself in exploring the light-house...
It is not quite 160 feet, I should say, from the low-water mark to the top
of the lantern. From the bottom inside the shaft, however, the distance to
the summit is 180 feet at least:—thus the floor is 20 feet below the surface
of the sea, even at low-tide...

It seems to me that the hollow interior at the bottom should have been
filled in with solid masonry. Undoubtedly the whole would have been
thus rendered more safe:—I have heard seamen say occasionally, with
a wind at South-West, the sea has been known to run higher here than
anywhere with the single exception of the Western opening of the Straits
of Magellan.

No mere sea, though, could accomplish anything with this solid iron-
riveted wall—which, at 50 feet from high-water mark, is 4 feet thick, if
one inch...

• • •

Jan 4. Wind out of the South-West—I am uneasy in my mind. Swell very
high, and though the sky is a bright and mild blue, there are prodigious
streaks of foam on the wide surge. More—a moaning, at times a muffled
howling in the long hollow throat of this tower. I have twice descended
to the floor of the shaft, but can find no source for the sound, other than
conduction of the walls themselves, reverberating with the blast. I will
just go down once more to be certain...

Though the sunken floor is quite dry—some comfort at least—I was
appalled to discover, on opening the door, that the tide has risen nearly
to the threshold, and I now observe, as I did not in the excitement on my
arrival, that the hand-rails are deeply eaten with rust. All the same—no
rust on the *inside,* and the patent lock is well greased. So I am quite safe.

I shall master myself. Will I exist here perpetually under the fear of horrible danger? Let lesser races quail...

I will just move this table to the far wall...

• • •

Jan 5. Wind has not shifted—in 24 hours no falling off of the sea. The
tower shrieks now like a damned creature.

The waves rise in absolute mountains, to break in a fury of shattered
water well over the door now, as I discovered when I went up to the lan-
tern-walk and peered down. The wind is a roaring physical *force,* no less

than the sea—only by clutching my woolen cap with both hands was I able to prevent it from being torn away and whirled a sickening distance out on the vast face of the waters.

I will go down just this once more. All is secure, I know, and yet—that chalk foundation…

• • •

Jan 6. I still live—yet the tempest has truly come. I watched it advance like a host armored in copper, spreading implacably from the South-West, boiling and hissing over the sea. I have retreated with this journal to the topmost chamber—tried to write a while in the lantern room but soon regretted it—gigantic seas! Frenzied, heaving, headlong seas rushing with monstrous velocity! Such high, black, mountainous ridges of water—

The tower shakes with each blow. The ghastly crests break, higher with each successive wave—*something is out there!* That cannot be what it seems. 4 feet thick. 4 feet thick. 4 feet thick. 4 feet—

There is a *boat*—

• • •

Jan 7. Oh, intolerable!

My solitude has been violated. They have at least now withdrawn to the lowest chamber, with interminable protestations of thanks, with endless apologies—the voluble Italian servant particularly offends, with his grating and presumptive familiarity. The mute is hardly less irritating, with his absurd antic gestures…

I see that I will be obliged to endure their company, if the boat is ever to be dislodged from the lantern room. It cannot be left as it is, protruding out like a wave-thrown dart—a full 8 feet and 7 inches.

Some sort of hauling tackle must be improvised—and rope must be found to lower it to the rock below, before any effort can be made to get the damned thing seaworthy again—and my unwelcome guests sent on their way. The broken glass must be repaired as well—I trust they do not expect *me* to replace the panes. This has made the draught worse—and I am certain I caught a chill when my clothing was soaked. What shall I do if it develops into something more dangerous? At any other time I should have been glad of the presence of a doctor…

On the whole I do not place much faith in Herr Doctor Treibholz, or in his story. His rapid and insinuating flow of speech—his sly, sidelong glances—above all that villainous bottle-green tailcoat, and the disgraceful condition of his wig—all argue the mountebank rather than the respectable physician, much less holder of the Chair of Splanchology at the University of Bohemia, as he claims. His vile cheroot produces clouds of fume at least as offensive as Orndoff's meerschaum—my eyes are red and watering yet. And his young assistant Luftschiff is altogether too smooth and urbane to be trusted—a thoroughgoing courtier in his manners. Exactly the sort I fled to this hermitage to escape!

That their ship unaccountably sank I find suspicious—I hardly think castaways would have found the time to pack such a vast quantity of trunks and barrels as my uninvited guests have brought with them—it is far more likely they were set adrift on purpose, whether for stealing from their fellow passengers or merely annoying them with disgusting chatter...

Yet I cannot imagine that the woman is party to whatever villainy they perpetrated.

"The woman"—how ungallant a phrase! These interlopers have provoked me to incivility. *She* is Frau Von Berg, a widow of a certain age yet still fair, Junoesque in her beauty, clearly of purest descent—I am reminded of my dear mother. She appears quite bewildered by her unlikely companions. I must find some way of conveying to her that she, and she alone, is free to come and go as she pleases here—I shall not mind *her* gentle company...

$$\cdots$$

Jan 8. My suspicions are confirmed—Herr Doctor is the basest kind of charlatan!

I descended as far as the storeroom this morning for oil for the lantern, and encountered Frau Von Berg on the stair. I greeted her cordially, wishing to correct the perhaps unfavorable impression of me she may have formed on the evening of the wreck—asked her if there were anything I might do to make her enforced stay more pleasant—she replied there was—

It transpired that she had been sent to borrow a cup of sugar—*she*, a lady, meekly running errands for Doctor Treibholz! Concealed my outrage and invited her to the upper room for tea. She accepted my offer without reluctance, rather with that air of bemusement I had previously noted in her...

Prepared tea at the stove and used the opportunity to "draw her out" a little—spoke lightly of the curious fortune that brought a nobleman and a gentlewoman together under barbarous conditions—she asked, and was told my lineage—I warmed to her even more, seeing she was obviously impressed. Frau Von Berg related a little of her own history—widow of the younger brother of Baron Rittenhaus, her late husband a shrewd investor—*very* well provided for in his will—such a sum named that an involuntary tremor caused me to spill tea in my lap. Fortunately she did not notice...

She then volunteered the most fantastic story...

That Doctor Treibholz, having taken a sabbatical from his duties at the University, had traveled to certain regions in Africa. There, exploring an uncharted wilderness, he discovered a tribe of Pygmies worshipping an idol of ancient manufacture—clearly Greek, from the inscription, which I take to have read παρτηενογενεσισ—most likely the Goddess Athena—perhaps left by some pupil of Archimedes. The idol proving, upon examination, to be in fact a *device*—Doctor Treibholz saw with his own eyes its remarkable properties...

For the Pygmies (he claims) are generated not as other races, but are rather formed from "a coalescence of atomies"—which I gather are particles floating in the air—focused like light through a burning glass—the operative mechanism an ingenious system of lenses mounted in a bronze ring above the head of Pallas!

Utter nonsense! And yet—with what sweet solemnity did Frau Von Berg relate this tale—clearly she believes every word. She must have led a sheltered life—as is only fitting for a lady of her rank—I cannot think less of her, though I instantly despised *him*.

The conclusion—that, owing to some misunderstanding, Herr Doctor was obliged by the Pygmies to flee for his life without further study of the fantastic device. Nonetheless he had observed it closely enough to attempt a copy. Money was wanted—he persuaded dear, trusting Frau Von Berg to invest her fortune—the copy made and now in working order—he *claims*.

And he *claims* to have improved on the original machine! For the one in Africa produced, naturally enough, half-scale African Negroes; but Doctor Treibholz purports to be able to produce half-scale white Europeans with his device. Nor is this all—each diminutive specimen steps forth from the mechanism a fully grown adult, complete in reason and understanding!

And so—Frau Von Berg informs me—this preposterous liar coaxed her to arrange passage to the late American colonies, with the intention of presenting his fraudulent contraption to the President there. For, since the Americans are presently in the process of domesticating a savage and empty wilderness—what, after all, would be more useful there than an army of sturdy homunculi, fit to cut wood and draw water?

I was assured by the poor, innocent woman that these Improved Pygmies had many advantages over colonists of the usual kind—for example, being smaller, they were more economical to feed, and required less room—moreover, were engendered without the necessity of an immoral act, unlike the rest of society...

Could see it was no use remonstrating with her—her trusting nature is too pure. But it is plain to me the scoundrel must have employed a troupe of itinerant dwarves to masquerade as specimens—for, she assures me, the device worked perfectly well on board the ship in which they were bound for America—indeed, produced a number of Improved Pygmies who were quite useful—though regrettably they all perished in the shipwreck...

It would be laughable were it not the basest confidence trick. Felt such ire on Frau Von Berg's behalf, I had palpitations for upwards of two hours afterward. Checked my pulse just now—still unsteady. Perhaps Treibholz has Mesmerized her! That must be the case...

For, she says, the mechanism itself was rescued, and will now be used to produce a crew of little workmen who will salvage and repair the boat, to enable Treibholz to return to the mainland and charter another ship—however, the necessary atomic particles are in short supply in this remote place—something about the air—but the device may be primed with *sugar,* which makes a tolerable substitute!

Absurd...

• • •

Jan 9. My head swims. I cling to this rational act of ordering my thoughts on paper—Perhaps I have become a raving lunatic—perhaps hallucinations have paraded before my eyes. Or—can it be—I too have been somehow Mesmerized?

I was sitting over my solitary breakfast in blessed silence when there came a peremptory knock at my chamber door. Before I could respond, the door was opened—the Italian servant, Beppo, put his head in. I leapt to my feet in indignation at his audacity, but he smiled broadly—assured me he was only there to take care of the boat.

Reluctantly I bid him enter, then—he flung wide the door and ushered in not only his mute and grinning companion, as I had expected, but a half-dozen dwarves!!!

They wore the blue uniform of some engineering corps and, stranger still, carried with them several fathom of rope—blocks and sheaves—all necessary tools. They were all so alike as to have been brothers. As I gazed in stupefaction, they mounted the stair to the lantern room without a word to me—busily set to work up there, clearing the broken glass from the frame, lashing pulleys in place, readying the boat for its removal.

I turned back as the last of them vanished through the door, only to see the mute lurking near my breakfast. I ordered him away at once—he scrambled aside, miming innocence, rolling his eyes to heaven. The Italian intervened, scolding him, and apologized—I demanded to know whence the little workmen had come.

He then related a story that agreed substantially with that of Frau Von Berg—though there were some sordid details, concerning the erstwhile African explorer's adventures amongst the Pygmies, of which I am sure Frau Von Berg knew nothing. Yes, the dwarves had come out of the re-markable machine—had coalesced not only fully formed, but clothed and equipped, rope, blocks, tackle and all!

My expressions of disbelief were met with a smile and a wave of the hand—what I had just seen was nothing compared to what *il Dottore* could do. When they reached America, he said, everyone would want Improved Pygmies. Improved Pygmies, he said, loved to work—why, they were rest-less and unhappy if they couldn't work—and *il Dottore* was going to be a wealthy man, I would see…

All the while he spoke, a constant din of thumps and creaks above our heads suggested that the dwarves were indeed working like demons—pres-ently a dark shape dropped by the window, descending in steady jerks as the boat was winched to the rock below. As I observed this, there was a knock at the door—the mute opened with a flourish—and in came yet another dwarf, bearing a file of panes of glass bound to his back, for all the world like monstrous insect wings—as well as carrying a bucketful of putty and a glazier's knife!

The little creature would have gone straight up without a word and set to work— I persuaded the Italian to stop him a moment, while I took his measurement—He was exactly 3 feet tall, and—with the exception of the panes of glass—all his tools, clothing and other gear seemed to be to scale as well. I was unable to get precise measurements on these, because he shook himself free with some irritation and proceeded with his task.

They have all departed now. When the door had at last closed behind them, I raced up to the lantern room—beheld it empty and serene, the boat gone, the twisted window leads repaired—Were it not that the new panes have a greenish cast compared to the other glass, I should have thought the whole fantastic episode a dream…

And yet—can I be certain it is *not?* Though I hear even now the brisk work of hammers on the boat, echoing up through this tower—the whole tale is too grotesque to be real. Even my fair visitor may be a creature of the imagination. Perhaps my nerves—what if my stores of salt beef or flour have been contaminated? I may be slowly dying of some subtle poison that affects the mind…

And all my silverware seems to be missing…

• • •

Jan 10. How laughable my fears now seem! I have "seen through" Doctor Treibholz.

Last night as I paced this room, feverish and despondent, lit intermittently by the circling flash of the lantern above—for its brightness strikes down like lightning—I was transfixed by illumination no less blazing.

The barrels and trunks! Did I not remark on the vast amount of luggage my visitors had loaded into their boat?

Of course the dwarves were secreted in the luggage. They must have been. Some circus troupe, hired by Treibholz to impersonate his creations, nothing more.

To think I believed a word of that story!

I must make careful note of all particulars of Doctor Treibholz and his accomplices—height, age, complexion, moles or tattoos—and will forward a detailed report to the mainland authorities with the next supply cutter. Prison is the only fitting—

There is a tiny shepherdess on the stairs.

I heard a plaintive knock—a soft voice—I set down my pen and rose in haste, thinking it was Frau Von Berg. Opened the door and beheld what appeared to be a little girl in the costume of a shepherdess, complete with crook and three diminutive sheep—like nothing so much as a Dresden figurine come to life. She inquired, in a high, clear voice, whether I knew where the rest of her flock had got to.

I shut the door hastily and retreated to the far side of the room. She has been knocking and calling out for a quarter of an hour. Ashamed to say I have gone into the private drawer in my trunk for the medicine—Nerves are much steadier now, however.

After all it is not so unlikely the circus troupe have a sister or wife—I understand dwarfism runs in families—doubtless she was sent up here as a prank. I will just—

She has been joined by a little man...

He seems to be a gardener, from his costume—He bore a potted geranium in his arms and asked me, with some petulance, whether he ought to mow the lawn—I told him I haven't got a lawn—he asked whether I had any fruit trees to be espaliered then—and responded with remarkable high-pitched profanity when I once again shut the door.

But it is silent out there now—perhaps they have gone away?

This is all a malicious trick. I am too visibly a sensitive man—and I was scarcely able to conceal my distaste for Doctor Treibholz—likewise the mute—and though the Italian, Beppo, professed amiability, he has doubtless all the cunning and vengefulness of his race—They are colluding to shatter my nerves...

Well, I have merely to ignore them, and wait. I can hear the intermittent hammering and sawing, far below—soon the boat shall be seaworthy once again and they will leave me in blessed silence. Why demean myself by responding...

• • •

Jan 11. Peace—of a sort—at last...

I have turned my back to them all—I can shut them out, here, with the wind screaming in my ears—how curious, that in the teeth of the gale I find tranquility.

Another wretched night of disturbed sleep—appalling dreams—Doctor Treibholz pursued me through them with his odd crablike gait—then dreamed I was at the hunting lodge, and shot a duck—it dropped at my feet—I bent to pick it up and it sprang upward again as though on a rope—leered at me with Treibholz's eyes, rolling behind their spectacles. Dreamed I had entered the gates of Heaven, welcomed by my dearest mother—led by deferential angels to that section reserved for nobility—then—mother transformed somehow to Frau Von Berg—and the nearest angel, unaccountably playing some vulgar beer-hall song on his golden harp—lifted his face and I saw it was the mute!

Woke screaming—became conscious there was a tapping at my chamber door. Had fortunately thrown myself down fully clothed to sleep—therefore no impropriety when I hurried to open the door to Frau Von Berg. I scarcely heard her tremulous plea for sanctuary, so transfixed was I by the spectacle behind and below her on the stair.

On every step, crowding and fighting, were tiny men and women. They were dressed in the costumes of every conceivable profession—soldiers, shopkeepers, milkmaids, demimondaines, cooks, butchers, fishermen, nursemaids, coachmen, musicians, clerks! I saw a little king, in robes of ermine—I saw a ballet dancer in ribboned slippers. The full spectrum of humanity, the pulsing quarreling shrieking *crowd* from whom I had fled to this tower, swarmed here below me, the whole world at half scale.

My gaze was arrested, in its descent into the microcosm, by the glimpse of a taller figure struggling upward through the mass—practically swimming—the detested Doctor Treibholz! And further down the stair, young Luftschiff and the servants, scrambling over the squeaking, protesting army of minimi…

In haste, I pulled Frau Von Berg into my room, and shut the door.

"What has happened?" I cried.

She wept that it was too dreadful—that something had gone wrong with Treibholz's device, and it had begun to generate Improved Pygmies continuously—could not be shut off—out they came, like sausage from a grinder, at a rate of about one every minute. It was now so crowded in the cellar-chamber there was no room to move—and the uproar from the Pygmies' quarreling was fit to wake the dead—for they were all disoriented, and each demanding to commence his or her proper occupation…

Indeed their noise hummed and echoed in the tower. We might have been standing atop an immense beehive. I comforted the poor creature as best I could—assured her that she had found safe refuge with me. I would simply keep my door locked—the vile mass of homunculi must in time go away, spilling out through the tower door at sea-level—some must drown, but that was nothing to either of *us*—I had enough provisions on this floor to last easily 6 months.

She thanked me profusely—the radiance of gratitude in her eyes made my heart beat the faster—but asked what would become of "poor Doctor Treibholz and the men?"

I saw it was time for firmness. Taking her hands, I led her to a chair—seated her, knelt before her—explained to her how our very survival required stern measures. How the Doctor had clearly been foolish in copying a monstrous engine whose workings he did not understand—how it was regrettable he must suffer the consequences, but he had brought this on himself—how he could probably contrive to escape in the boat, in any case—how it was my sacred duty to protect a lady…

And somehow I found myself speaking my heart…though let me state here and now that I never once thought of dear Frau Von Berg's *fortune*.

She was gazing down into my eyes with a lovely mixture of bewilderment and—perhaps dawning affection—and all would have gone so well…

The door opened. In strode Doctor Treibholz, puffing furiously at his cheroot, and fixed us with an ironical and knowing leer. I leapt to my feet in outrage.

"That door was locked, sir!" I said. He replied that it was fortunate he'd had a Pygmy burglar at hand—I turned and saw a dwarfish knave in a black domino, in the act of putting away a set of lockpicks! Thrust the little beggar out bodily and shut the door again—turned and demanded to know what Treibholz meant by this intrusion—*he* in turn demanded to know what I meant by making love to his intended—dear Frau Von Berg looked as shocked at this as I was—whereupon he flung himself down on his knees before her, and declared passionate adoration!

Stood there speechless with rage—oh, for my dueling saber, or a pistol! Then a knock upon the door behind me—I turned and flung it open—a rash mistake, for into the room tumbled a miniature bishop, a barrel-organ player and his tiny monkey, and a greengrocer with a basket of onions. Luftschiff stepped over them smoothly, pitched the intruders back out into the stairway, and informed Doctor Treibholz that all was not lost—the mechanism had slowed its rate of production down to one Improved Pygmy every 5 minutes—Not a word of apology to me for his intrusion!

So—I ignored him in turn—stepped forward to seize Treibholz by his collar and pull him to his feet—told him to desist with his unwanted attentions to Frau Von Berg—he writhed free, skipped back nimbly and asked Luftschiff to provide him with a glove. Luftschiff provided one, after feeling about in his pockets—a rather cheap item of lisle thread—whereupon Treibholz took it and had the effrontery to strike me in the face—

How my blood boiled! The more so as I would be unable, by any laws of decency agreed upon by gentlemen, to accept a challenge from a creature so far beneath me—informed him I would never so sully my blade—and that in any case we had no blades…

Whereupon he ordered Luftschiff to fetch him a pair of Heidelberg students—the youth obediently dove down the stair, admitting as he went a circus acrobat and a diminutive chancery advocate. I collared each and dragged them to the door to pitch them out again, but was struck and thrown backward as the door flew open once more—in came Beppo and the mute, each bearing an Improved Pygmy under either arm—others fell in after them—it was all I could do to fasten the door again, and the new intruders—a group of madrigal singers, apparently—ran and crouched under my writing-table, where they promptly began a chorus of shrill song.

Beppo meanwhile greeted his master with the news that he need not worry—at least we should not perish from hunger, for he and his companion had found an Improved Pygmy poultry farmer, as well as two agriculturalists and a pork butcher—set the little creatures down and displayed the one with a small pair of chickens clutched in his arms, while the others carried each a fruit tree in a pot and a basket of cold cuts respectively—they should provide us with all the hard boiled eggs we needed, and more…

Treibholz responded that he had no time to concern himself with such matters—he was attempting to fight a duel. Beppo, with every evidence of glee, asked whether his master wanted them to fight for him—Frau Von Berg, gentle soul, cried out in protest at this—but the grimacing mute thrust aside a welter of Improved Pygmies and stepped forward to face me, striking the attitude of a pugilist!

My wrath could no longer be contained, and this at least the laws of chivalry permitted me to do—rain blows upon an impertinent lackey! I raised my own fists and squared off with the mute, who feinted a blow with his right fist—but as he did so, danced sideways, and a kick came flashing up from the depths of his ragged coat—his left boot struck my posterior with painful force—the coward!

I howled with rage and struck at him with all my strength, but he evaded me and feinted—pulled the same trick again! And yet again! We circled in the steadily narrowing floor space, for the chancery advocate had begun to hold a trial and the acrobat was turning hand-stands—the mute swung again, but this time as he did so there was a metallic clatter, and a torrent of silverware fell from his sleeve. *My* missing silverware!

"You thief!" I roared. And such was my incandescent fury that I would have obliterated him—but that out of my eye's corner I saw a shadowy figure raising a weapon—turned to catch the treacherous Beppo in the act of raising a dry salami, doubtless stolen from the pork butcher, like a club—Frau Von Berg shouted a warning—the mute wasted no opportunity to push me from behind, and I fell amid tiny chickens, mulberry trees and spoons.

But I sprang upright swift as a tiger, only to see the door open once again, admitting another tide of Improved Pygmies. Luftschiff came wading in foremost, clutching under either arm a pair of scowling duelists, bearing half-sized scars and sabers.

"Ha!" cried Doctor Treibholz, and seized their weapons. He tossed one to me—flexed the blade of his own—cried, "En garde!" and lunged—which was preposterous, for the blades were no more than 15 inches long...

Goaded beyond all endurance, I raised the little blade like a dagger and struck wildly—missed, and felt it stab harmlessly into the lining of his tailcoat under his arm. For a heartbeat's space I beheld my own reflection in Treibholz's spectacle lenses—my face red with exasperation—eyes starting from my head—the ludicrous mask of a fool!

Treibholz—the dog—dropped his own blade at once and clutched his side, groaning that he'd been mortally wounded. He collapsed backward, to be grudgingly caught by the Improved Pygmy agriculturalists. Then— oh, frailty! Frau Von Berg descended upon him with cries of dismay, lifting him to her bosom—begging him not to die...

I was half-mad with disgust and heartbreak—turned and fled up to the lantern room, seizing my book, my inkwell and a bottle as I passed. Have shut the door and write now with my back pressed against it, though it strains outward with the pressure of lesser creatures. Here at last I have been able to calm myself... My hand is steady—see how neatly I form the letters now!

They cannot force me to endure their society—I have spied a rope that was left by the workmen, fastened to the outer rail—will let myself down and take the boat—or, if the little people guard it, will *swim* for the mainland—bearing an odometer of my own design, with which to measure the precise distance to the Norland.

But will first tear out these pages and seal them within the bottle—if I am lost, 'twill serve as witness against Treibholz and his ruffians...

They beat against the door. I hear their cries. I must be going...

SILENT LEONARDO

1505

The inn is dark, low and uninviting. Its ale is not good, nor are its rooms cozy. The locals give it a wide berth. Even travelers benighted in English rain generally prefer to ride on to the next village, rather than stop at such an unpromising spot.

This is precisely why it stays in business.

The inn, as it happens, is subsidized by certain shadowy men. They made themselves so useful to the late king that their services have been retained by his usurper. Royal paranoia keeps them on the move, listening, spying, collecting evidence; and this remote country tavern has proven a great place to meet unseen, to interview witnesses, exchange information. Or to sequester those whose status is somewhere between political prisoner and guest…

The man entering the inn has no name, at least none that will ever make it into history books. He hangs his cloak of night on its accustomed peg. He climbs the stair without a word to the innkeeper. He has no need to give orders.

Two men are seated at a table in an upper room. He sits down across from them, studying their faces by the light of one candle.

They are both men of middle age, in travel-worn garments. The one leans forward, elbows on the table, staring into the eyes of his visitor. He has a shrewd, coarse, sensual countenance, like an intelligent satyr. The other sags back against the wall, gazing sadly into space. He has the majesty of a Biblical prophet, with his noble brow and milk-white beard, but also an inexpressible air of defeat. The visitor notes that his left arm, tucked into a fold of cloak, is withered.

Preliminary courtesies are exchanged. The satyr speaks easily, with

119

ingratiating gestures and smiles, congratulating the visitor on his precise Italian. Ale is brought; the satyr seizes up his tankard, drinks a toast to their enterprise and wipes his mouth with the back of his hand. He begins to speak. Unseen behind a panel, a clerk takes down every word.

• • •

No, he don't talk. That's what I'm for!

Is he my master? No, no, signore, we're more sort of partners. Almost like brothers, you see? His mama and mine, they lived on the same farm. But Leo's a gentleman, yes. Father was from a good old family. Much too good to marry his poor mama, but Ser Piero couldn't get no sons by any other girl, so he kept his boy and brought him up, with a tutor and everything.

And, was the boy smart? Why, Leo was writing with his left hand (and, you know, that's hard to do) by the time he was four! But then, one fine day, we boys were playing out in the orchard, and there was this big apple out on a high branch. Leo climbed out after it. And the branch fell! Boom, down he came and broke his left arm. Broke it so bad, the bones stuck out and the Doctor thought it might have to come off. Even when he saved the arm, it didn't work so good anymore. It'd been shattered. Never grew right, after.

So then, Leo had to learn to do everything with his right hand. And I guess maybe it threw his humors out of balance, because he started to stutter. Stammered so bad nobody understood one word he was saying. Except me! I *listened* to him, you see, signore? And I could, uh, interpret for him. He got so he wouldn't say nothing to nobody, except when I was around. We got such a, what's the word, such a rapport, Leo and me, that I know what he wants to say before he says it.

And his papa said, "Say, Giovanni, you're such a smart boy, my Leo needs you around to do his talking for him. You come live with us. I'll pay you a nice salary." Which was a big opportunity for me, I don't mind telling you. When Leo was studying in books, I got to play in the street and learn a little something of the ways of the world, you understand? And I learned how to fight, which was good, because nobody dared call Leo a dummy or steal from him, while I was around.

I said, "Don't feel bad, Leo, you're plenty smart! One of these days we'll get rich off your cleverness, wait and see!" And we did, signore. Plenty of times, we've been rolling in scudi. We just had bad luck. It could happen to anybody.

Ah! Well, let me tell you about Florence. Leo's papa sent us to Andrea del Verrocchio, that was a big rich painter there. I said, "How are you today, signore? I'm Giovanni Barelli and this is Leonardo da Vinci, and he's the greatest painter you're ever going to teach, and I'm his manager".

Signore Andrea didn't take that too well, he must have been thinking, "Who are these kids?" But he looked over Leo's little pictures that he done, like this rotten monster head he painted on a shield, with dead snakes and flies so real you could practically smell it, and he agreed to take Leo as an apprentice.

It probably didn't hurt that Leo was good-looking as the Angel Gabriel himself, in those days. Those artistic types, they like the boys, eh? Saving your grace's presence, but that's how it is in the Art World.

So we settled into that studio, with all those other boys there, and Leo painted better than any of them. He painted so good, pretty soon he was better than Signore Andrea. Signore Andrea painted this big picture of Jesus getting baptized, but Leo helped him some. And, I'm telling you, there were these two holy angels standing side by side in the picture, and the one Signore Andrea painted looked grubby and sneaky as a pickpocket, but the angel Leo painted was just beautiful, shining so bright you'd think he had a candle stuck up his, uh, hidden under his robe or something.

I watched Signore Andrea and I could tell he wasn't so happy about this. The little boys were crazy jealous, and I knew sooner or later somebody would slip poison into Leo's dinner. So I went to Signore Andrea, I said, "Thanks a lot for the training, signore, but it's time my Leo opened his own studio someplace else, don't you agree?"

But he didn't agree. He said Leo had to work for him a certain number of years and a day, or he wouldn't get into San Luca's Guild, blah blah blah. I saw Signore Andrea didn't want no competition. So I knew it was time to get us some leverage.

Any rich man has secrets, eh, signore? You know what I mean, I can tell. And I could climb drainpipes real good, and open windows too, and get locked cabinets open with one of Leo's palette knives. Pretty soon, I knew some things about Signore Andrea I'm sure he wouldn't want the Pope to hear about. You'd be amazed how fast he changed his mind about Leo getting his own studio, after I put a little word in his ear! Even threw in a nice parting gift of money.

And, signore, the commissions poured in! Big murals for churches. Painted shields and armor. Portraits of little, rich girls. Half those little girls fell in love with Leo, good-looking as he was. Of course, to talk to him they had to go through *me*, and I wasn't so bad-looking either, in those days. Life was sweet, signore.

The only problem we had, and I'm only telling you this because it turned out to be a blessing in disguise, was, if I left Leo alone in his studio while I was out with Ginevra or Isabella or Catarina, I'd come back and find he'd been, uh, distracted by his little drawings. Just filling up page after page with pictures of his hands, or water, or clouds or dead mice or anything. "Leo," I said, "think of that nice bishop, waiting for his painting of the three wizards adoring Baby Jesus! You got to concentrate, Leo!" I told him.

I thought if I took his pens and paper away and locked him in, he'd have to paint. And it worked. But then one night I came in late, and I was a little, maybe, upset, because I was having troubles with Isabella, and I went to let Leo out so he could eat. There was this big canvas he was supposed to have been working on, still white as Isabella's—well—he hadn't painted one brushstroke on it, signore. What he done was *drawn all over the walls.* I was so mad I socked him, boom, and he went flying. The candle fell and set fire to his straw mattress. What I saw, with the room all lit up, was that these were all drawings of *machines.*

Which was something new for him, see? Instead of useless things, here were pictures of gears and blades and ratchets, with soldiers and horses getting cut to little pieces by them. "Giovanni," I said to myself, "you're looking at a fortune here!"

So I beat out the fire, and I gave Leo all the pens and paper he wanted. I went off to the kitchen and made him a nice dish of fried cheese. And while I cooked I figured, figured, all the time figured the angles.

Well. You heard of Galeazzo Sforza, eh? Duke of Milan, Lord of Genoa, the one they call *il orrendo*? Yes, him.

He was crazy mean. The kind of little boy who liked to pull wings off flies, and worse when he grew up. No beauty, either; eyes too close together and a weak chin. But he respected artists, signore.

The duke had only been on the throne a couple of years then, but people already knew the way his tastes ran, which is why I thought of him when I saw Leo's pictures. So Leo wrote this beautiful letter to him, about what he could design for his dungeons and armies. I told him what to write. Such a letter we sent, signore! Such a lot of promises we made. I knew it was our necks in the halter if we couldn't deliver, but I had faith in Leo.

Pretty soon the duke sent a letter back, too, mostly saying, "Why don't you boys come to my palace in Milan so we can have a nice little talk?" It came at a good time, because Isabella's papa was about to send over a couple of *his* boys for a little talk with me, you follow, signore? So I bundled up Leo and his books and papers and pens on one fast horse, and me on another, and away we went.

Now, one book Leo had with him was by this old Greek named Hero, full of clockwork and infernal machines. Leo studied the whole time we traveled. First, he copied the pictures. Then he made new drawings, taking all the old machines apart on paper and mixing up the pieces. Every inn we stopped at, he'd sit there at a table, drawing, while I got the drinks and talked to girls. We had to buy another horse to carry all the ideas Leo had.

We went to see the duke, in Milan. You know what he was doing, when we were shown in? He was gambling with a pretty girl. He'd bet her she couldn't keep an egg in her open mouth from the stroke of noon until midnight. Her father's life was the stake. She was standing there the whole time with tears in her sweet eyes, her mouth stretched wide around this goose egg, and I knew her jaws must have been aching bad. He was just ignoring her. If I didn't know what kind of man he was before, I knew then.

But I acted big, I told him about the great machines Leo invented, that would make him powerful as Caesar, Alexander, Charlemagne! And, maybe I'm a little crude when I express myself, and I was only a country boy then and didn't know much about impressing people. I could see the duke smiling, like he was going to enjoy sending us to the dungeon for wasting his time.

Lucky for us both, Leo had his papers with the drawings all ready, and his beautiful clear handwriting that anybody could read. Leo bowed before him and offered the sketchbook. The duke looked at the pages, and he couldn't take his eyes away after he'd seen the picture on top. He started reading, saying nothing, turning pages. After a while he called for some wine. He didn't give us any. We stood there, and the girl stood there too with the egg still in her mouth, staring at us. The sun slanted across the tiles on the floor and the fountain outside splashed the whole time.

Finally the duke closed the sketchbook. He asked Leo if he could really build all these devices, and I told him of course we could! Only, we'd need some of his best armorers and blacksmiths, not to mention money. "Well," said the duke, "Smart boys like you, you'll have everything you want!"

I thought to myself, "Giovanni, your fortune's made!"

So you can imagine, signore, how I nearly wet myself when Leo walked over to the girl and took the egg out of her mouth. Who were we, to criticize a rich man's fun? But the duke, he took it all right. He just laughed and said we could have the girl too.

Her name was Fiammetta. She was crazy in love with Leo from that moment. Waited on him hand and foot, in the nice rooms the duke gave us. Cooked and cleaned and brushed his clothes, which was nice for me, because I was too busy for that now.

But, signore, you should know that Leo is chaste. Eh? No, no, not like that at all. It's all *up here* with him, see? So you can be sure there wasn't nothing sinful going on. Which I'm telling you in case your king has any question about his morals.

So, I got busy. We had a whole kind of blacksmith-studio to build, and workers to hire. I got a clerk to copy Leo's drawings and pass them out to the workers, so everybody understood what we were making. There was iron and coal to buy. Getting it all up and running was like making a big machine, too, but I'm good at that. I can run around, yell at people to get going. I push things, you see? And I pushed Leo on the job, so his mind didn't wander. He kept wanting to change the design once he'd finished, kept having new ideas. "Leo," I told him, "get *organized!* One thing at a time!"

But, once all the workmen understood Leo's designs, he could afford to draw his little pictures. The big machine started rolling. The master smith, smart man named Marulli, such a pity he's dead now, he really caught fire with the idea of Leo's steam engine. He even pointed out one or two ways it could work better. Pretty soon the forges were going day and night. The workers were coming in all hours and forgetting to eat, they were so excited.

The duke himself came in to watch. I showed him all the models, and the work going on. He had the brains to appreciate good ideas. He was happy with our work, I tell you. There was a look in his nasty little eyes that was almost pure. You know what I mean? Bad men don't love God or other men, but sometimes they love *things,* and that's the closest they ever get to being human.

So what happened? The duke got himself armed for war and, sure enough, one started. The Ligurians sent in condottieri to take Pavia.

Yes, Pavia, you know the name? Famous siege. Changed the way wars were going to be fought forever after, and I should know, because I was there. You want to hear what really happened?

Pavia was defended pretty good. *Il orrendo* had built new walls only a little while before. The condottieri got there and saw they had one tough nut to crack. Then up came this Pavian traitor named Lazzaro Doria, and he said to them: "Say, there's this big place called the Mirabello over there, it's the duke's own hunting estate with walls and a castle, and he ain't home. If you camp there, you can starve out the Pavians from a nice defensible position."

"Good," said the condottieri. Pretty soon they were living high, eating venison from the duke's own park while the Pavians were rationing food, marching out in the morning to make big threats and fire off a gun or two. At night they slept in the duke's feather beds. One soft campaign!

Until the duke heard about it. I was there when he got the news and I saw him smile. *Uh-oh,* I said to myself, *I sure wouldn't want to be those condottieri.*

"Barelli," he said, "I think we'll give our new toys a test. Load the engines; we're going to Mirabello."

Well, *that* was easier said than done, because of what-you-callems, logistics. But I'm good at pulling things together, see? All we had ready was the Horse, but I pulled Leo from playing with his models and got him to make a few changes. We finished a few other little surprises too. And on the day the wagons rolled for Mirabello, Fiammetta begged to come along. Just like a woman, eh? Crazy in love. We took her with us, in the baggage train.

You should have seen us marching along, signore. Soldiers with their steel armor shining in the sun. The duke with his pretty armor and the Sforza banner streaming, such bright colors! What a day that was, the sky so blue and the hills so green! Leo rode next to me on a white horse and half the soldiers thought he was an angel, with his golden hair, sent from God to work miracles for us. The war-wagons were all loaded, so heavy their axles creaked, with bad news for Mirabello…

You a soldier, signore? No, that's none of my business, you're right. But anybody, soldier or not, would have admired the duke's strategy.

When we got to Pavia, the duke ordered his men in without any of the special stuff we brought. Just like they were an ordinary army come to relieve Pavia, see? The condottieri were caught with their pants down, saving your presence, but they beat his men back and ran to Mirabello.

So there they were, safe behind the wall of the park. The game was turned on its head, a siege to break a siege. The duke brought his army up and occupied the land north and east of the park. He sent his herald to the Porta Pescarina to say, "Hey! You! Genovesi big shots! Come out here right now, or I'll send your heads home to your mamas in a bunch of fruit baskets!"

The condottieri didn't know *il orrendo* like we did, or they'd never have said what they did in reply, which was something real rude, saving your presence. He got their answer and he smiled, and spat out a fig he was eating and said: "Barelli, let's have some fun with them."

So I grabbed Leo and we ran back to the wagons. I ordered the Horse to be unloaded.

The duke sent troops in a feint attack, as though they were going to breach the wall at the Porta Pescarina. He did it so slow, and so obvious, the condottieri laughed and whooped from their places on the wall. But in a few minutes they stopped and got real quiet, looking east, where our wagons were.

What they saw, signore, were teams of men pulling on ropes, raising with pulleys and tackle a big monster, an iron Horse. We'd brought it lying on its side, lashed to three flat wagon-beds. It rose up slow. When it stood at last, tall as a church tower, it looked like Sin and Death.

It stood there maybe a half hour, while we made it ready. All the time the condottieri were staring at it, trying to figure it out. We could hear their officers telling them it was just a Trojan Horse. "That's the oldest trick in the book!" they said. "Dumb Sforzas!"

But then it began to roll forward, all by itself, belching steam. The rumbling and clattering it made was the only sound for miles. The condottieri were frozen like rabbits. We hardly drew breath ourselves, watching it. The duke looked like he was in church, seeing something holy. Leo was biting his lips to blood, praying I guess that everything would work. Fiammetta was crying, but that's what women do, eh?

And the condottieri were so busy looking east, they didn't think to look north, which they should have done.

Because, there was the duke's cavalry, racing along like they were at full charge. But they weren't charging the walls, signore. They were pulling the Flying Machines. Yes, that was the first place they were ever used. You didn't know? Leo's invention! Oh, he sweated blood over those, his little clockwork bird models, no use to anybody until I slapped him and said: "Not flapping, gliding! Look at how vultures fly, dummy!"

Fast and faster the horses ran, and men ran behind holding up the big machines with their spread canvas, bouncing, looking foolish until they lifted off—one, two, three, ten angels of death rising up on black wings! And such big shadows they cast, crossing the bright face of the sun that day. You had to look hard to see the tiny man in each one, clinging tight to the framework, but I could make them out, and, I'll tell you, signore, every one of them had wet himself.

Some crashed right away, ran into trees or only got across a few fields before coming down, but there were three that remembered to work the controls. They circled and soared. Only one or two archers on the wall noticed them—nobody else could tear their eyes away from the Horse, that was coming on faster now, but it didn't matter. By the time they got a few shots off, the Flying Machines were high up out of range. Still they circled, just like vultures. Then—ha, ha!—they laid their eggs, signore.

Yes, they dropped grenades of Greek Fire, on the army camped in the park behind the wall. Dropped from so high, how far it splattered! What screams we could hear! Smoke began to rise, and you could see the men on the wall thinking: "We've been tricked! They sent this stupid Trojan Horse to make us look the other way while they attacked from the sky!"

But they were wrong, signore.

Because, while half of them were running from their positions on the wall to try to put the fires out, the Horse just kept rolling closer. The ones who were smart enough to stay at their posts, you could see them wondering: "What's it doing? Do they think we'll let it through the Porta Pescarina?" Because, see, they expected a Trojan Horse to be full of soldiers. That's called, ah, what's that big word, Leo? *Misdirection.*

Only when it got right to the base of the wall did they figure out it must be some kind of siege engine. They started peppering it with crossbow bolts, which only tinkled off like rain. The Horse just stood there a minute, smoke coming from its nostrils like a real horse breathing out steam on a cold morning.

Then it began to rise up, rearing from its wheeled platform, and the gears ratcheting echoed loud over the field. I was keeping my fingers crossed, because I didn't know if we'd made it able to extend high enough. But up it went, and pretty soon it brought its big iron forefeet down, *clang*, on the battlements. Men on the wall were hitting the feet with axes; no good. Up above, the Horse turned its head slow, like it was looking at them. Smoke twined out of its nostrils, past the flames dancing there, from the little oil-lamps we'd built in.

Now, in the head there was a little room, with one gunner in there. He worked a pump. Nasty stuff—worse than Greek Fire, Leo's own invention—came spraying out of the head, igniting as it passed the flames in the nostrils, splashing all over the men on the wall. *Then* we heard screams! Some of them died right there, cooked like lobsters in their own armor. Some jumped down and ran, trying to get to the little Vernavola stream that ran through the park, but it was already full of men trying to wash off the Greek Fire.

And so they left the wall undefended.

Now, signore, the Horse's head opened right up, like one of Leo's pictures of cadavers opened out, and from his platform the gunner opened fire over the wall, but not with a cannon! No, this was a machine with rotating chambers, fired hundreds of little grenades, looked like bright confetti flying, but where they came down there wasn't no carnival, you see? *Boom boom boom,* black smoke and red flame, men flying to pieces, little pieces, arms and legs blown everywhere! We found them for days afterward, all over the park.

But that ain't the best part.

The Horse's behind had a room in it too, and three men in there got busy, cranking the reciprocating gears, and the Horse's prick—is that the word in English, not too rude? Well, saving your presence, but that's what came out of the Horse, an iron prick turning as it came, with a burin on the end all sharp points. It bit into the wall. Oh, we laughed like hell! Round and round it went, boring at the wall, one big screw!

When the screw had gone in deep, the men set the Horse in motion, thrusting and pounding at the wall like it was a mare. I thought the duke was going to rupture himself; he laughed so hard the tears were streaming down his face.

But when the wall broke, when it fell in with a crash like thunder, he was all business: he gave the order and his men charged the breach, shrieking. They poured through, looking like silver ants below the horse. Not that there was much work for them to do, when they got inside. You never saw such a sight in your life, signore. Most of the condottieri burned black, or blown to bits, or both. It was fantastic. Magnificent. You wouldn't believe ordinary men could do it, but we did.

What happened afterward?

Well, Ingratitude is a terrible sin. The duke got to thinking, I guess, that he could conquer the world, as long as he was the only one with these machines. He figured the only way to be sure nobody else got them was to see Leo and me didn't go nowhere, and the only way to be sure of that was a nice unmarked grave for us. Marulli put a word in my ear. Me and Leo were out of Pavia on fast horses the same night, you can bet.

…The girl? Oh, Fiammetta. Funny thing about that… she hanged herself, after the battle. Women! Eh?

But we went other places, made stupendous things. We never made another Horse, but *il orrendo* got what was coming to him when it blew up the next time he tried to use it. That's how God punishes bad men. Plenty of other great princes were happy to see us! War ain't like the old days, signore, oh, no. You don't need hundreds of peasants to send in waves against your enemy's walls; all you need is a few smart guys with a good machine or two.

And you don't need hundreds of peasants to work your fields, either, if you got the steam-powered plows and mowers Leo invented.

But that didn't go so good, with the riots and all; maybe you heard about that? Well, it's all quiet over there now. After the work we did for Cesare Borgia, Machiavelli called us in. He said, so nice and polite: "What do we do with all these useless, disobedient peasants? Nobody needs them anymore. Please, Ser Leonardo, with your brilliance in solving logistical problems, with your unparalleled talent for orderly arrangement and innovative thinking—could you not propose a final solution to this problem?"

And, you bet, I kept Leo's nose to the grindstone until we had one.

But, can you believe it? Even with us being big shots with defense contracts, there's always some rich man after Leo's valuable time, trying to get Leo to paint his wife's portrait or some other foolishness. And that's the reason—well, that and a few other things, like Cesare Borgia getting murdered—that Leo and me thought we needed a nice vacation someplace besides Europe. So, we try our luck here in England, eh?

• • •

The satyr falls silent, gazing intently at his host. The melancholy man for whom he speaks appears disinterested in the conversation; he has watched the shadows on the wall the whole time.

The nameless man smiles, sips his ale, refills the satyr's tankard. With a slightly apologetic air, he explains that all this is most impressive; it is certainly an honor to converse with the men who fathered modern warfare. His master found the Flying Machines, in particular, of great use in the late civil strife. And it is a shame, before God, that such artistry of invention has not been suitably rewarded. However—

England has no need of the redundancy camps nor the crematoria. Two generations of dynastic war have left it with a shortage of peasantry, if anything; and in any case, it is a country of smallholdings. Steam plows, able to subdue vast acreage in Europe, might prove impractical in a country of lanes and hedgerows. Even if that were not the case, it has of late been rumored abroad that in Europe corn is so plentiful now, as a result of the new devices, there is even a glut on the market. His master is a thrifty man; it would scarcely be in his interest, therefore, to invest in steam-farming.

Perhaps his guests have another proposition?

The satyr narrows his eyes. He is silent a long moment, pulling thoughtfully on his lower lip. He glances at his silent friend, who does not respond. At last he smacks the table with the flat of his hand, laughing heartily.

• • •

Well, sure, we have lots of ideas!

And it's a good thing for your master we're here, and I'll tell you why.

You had those Roses Wars over here, right? First the Red Rose up, then the White, then Red, then White. Now your Henry Tudor's on top, but for how long?

England's confused. That makes the crown slippery on the head. I heard about those two little boys in your Tower, eh? Pretty convenient for you that they just disappeared like that. Who done it? Nobody knows what to think. What you need, signore, is to *tell them what to think*.

Leo and me, we're old men now, and we know something about human nature. You got to tell your story like it was the truth. Make it such an exciting story everybody wants to hear it, and make sure your version is the only one they get to hear. Then everybody will believe it. So, what do you do?

You get some smart poet to write a play, and you send actors to every village in England. Not just one troupe of actors, but a hundred, a thousand, and Leo will build steam-coaches to get them everywhere fast. Not in threadbare old costumes but in scarlet and purple silks, cloth of gold! Leo will make it so gorgeous the people have to look. He'll make it a spectacle, with fireworks, music, dancing! All to show how Henry Tudor is the best thing that ever happened to England.

You got to get your message out, signore. That's how you'll win wars, in the future.

THE MAID ON THE SHORE

PROLOGUE

Kidd wasn't more than a lad, back then; Teach himself wasn't even a gleam in the Devil's eye, not yet.

Thirty-six captains anchored together at Cape Tiburon, summoned by Harry Morgan, bound on gold and revenge. There never was such an assembly of the Brethren before, nor ever afterward until that last wild party Teach held at Okracoke; and that was a sad business, at the end of it all.

But when Morgan was in his prime, a man might muster the ships and men to go looting the Spanish Main, and gentlemen called it *privateering*. That was, if a man's commission was in order.

That was the trick, you see; for the British ministers of state, off in London, blew hot and cold on the question of peace with Spain. A man might set off on an expedition legal as you please, and come home to find the rules had changed, with some Madrid grandee in Whitehall screaming to have him clapped in irons. So it required a fine and careful hand, that game.

Nobody played it better than Harry Morgan.

He came out to Barbados in old Cromwell's time, a young ensign from a family of hard men, mercenaries who'd served with distinction. You mark that; Morgan was no bond-slave boy. Hendrik Smeeks started that story out of spite, and paid dearly for it later, because Morgan sued him. Oh, Ned Teach roared and blazed, and Kidd was a mean hand with a bucket, but a Welshman with an attorney—there's a thing to frighten you!

• • •

What was Morgan doing in Barbados?

It started because Spain had the New World and its gold all to itself, like a boy locked in a room with the biggest fruitcake you ever saw. England

131

and France, and the Dutch too, all knocked on the door politely, asking if they mightn't come in and share a slice or two; but no, Spain kept that door locked, and gobbled away at the rich stuff until it was so sick it was pissing sugar.

Sooner or later there were pinprick outposts of other nations on all the little leeward islands in the Caribbean anyway, looking enviously over at Hispaniola and the mainland where the gold was. Oliver Cromwell planned an expedition to take Hispaniola. Sir Francis Drake had taken it, a long generation before; why shouldn't the New Model Army do it too?

Ah, but Drake hadn't *kept* it; Drake was out for loot and revenge, not settlements and plantations and careful account-books. He'd come and gone from Hispaniola. Cromwell intended England should invest in the Caribbean. So he sent his generals out to Barbados to muster an expedition. That was in 1655. Young Harry Morgan went with those generals, and served in their ranks, and watched as they made a hash of the job. And learned from their mistakes.

Having failed to take Hispaniola (and what a failure it was: supplies held up, messages crossed, storms, fever, cowardice, infighting...), the generals looked around for some sop, any sop, to offer Cromwell, so as to keep their heads on their shoulders when they got home.

What about Jamaica, they must have said. It was an easy grab; had some arable land, didn't it? Nice harbor too. Not much of a defense force stationed there, either.

They took it in a day. The Spanish governor surrendered, packed his bags and got out. He likely caught hell when he got home to his king; the English generals Venables and Penn fared not much better, for they both of them wound up in the Tower at Cromwell's displeasure.

But Jamaica was in the hands of the Commonwealth now. And if the presidentes, gobernadors and alcaldes of the Spanish Main weren't waking up with night terrors and forebodings of doom, if their rosaries weren't squirting out of their sweaty hands whilst they prayed for deliverance from evil—they should have been.

• • •

It was a merry time! Spain demanded Jamaica back, and Cromwell recovered his temper enough to see clear that his generals had grabbed a plum for him. So, a fig for the dons and the Pope; the Commonwealth went to war with Spain. Cromwell's navy had a secure base in Jamaica from which to prey on the Spanish plate fleet. All those timid galleons beating to windward with their holds stuffed with gold and emeralds... why, the Commonwealth could make a fortune.

And anyone could play! Private gentlemen who could outfit a ship had but to apply for a commission from Jamaica's governor, and they became privateers, duly licensed to attack enemy shipping.

And if a man wasn't a gentleman, or if his crew had too much the look of thieves and murderers for the governor's taste, it was no matter. Privateering commissions were also being handed out by the somewhat-less-discriminating governor of Tortuga. The French issued them. The Dutch issued them. Anyone could play...

And then the news came that Cromwell was dead, and King Charles had come out of exile to be welcomed back to England. The new Privy Council, bless their peace-loving little hearts, desired to negotiate a treaty with Spain. Think how many black slaves could be sold to the Spanish, if only there wasn't a war on!

So negotiations began, and England called its navy home. Jamaica was left out in the Caribbean with no defenses but what she could think up for herself, and all those Spanish presidentes, gobernadors and alcaldes were stroking their beards, and grinning at her thoughtful-like.

Jamaica did what any prudent innkeeper would do, with her man away and Spanish thieves peering round the shutters; she woke up the English thieves that had passed out on her own hearth, fired them up with more rum, and bid them prey for her.

They were the Brethren of the Coast.

• • •

So much is history, for anyone to read in books.

This, now, is rumor:

There were once two young officers come out from London with Venables, and they wandered through the streets of Barbados with their mouths open, falling under the spell of the West Indies. One thought it looked like a good place to earn a name of his own; one had only known paved streets all his life, and couldn't get over such flowers, such fireflies, such blue water. One was blackavised as the Devil himself, and the other had a pale countenance like a poet.

One had luck, and the other hadn't.

They learned to drink rum together in a grog shop kept by an old seaman. The seaman had a pretty daughter. The blackavised fellow fancied her, but the pale fellow became infatuated with her, went so far as to write her a poem. Then they both shipped out to conquer Hispaniola, and you know how that went.

The dark fellow's luck stood by him. He stamped, he swore, he beat the Newgate scum he'd been given into fighting troops, he rallied his men to charge when others fled, he survived starvation and storm and the haplessness of his superior officers.

The poet caught fever and died, and was buried on Jamaica.

Well, so the dark one was left in charge of a regiment when Venables departed Jamaica. He sailed over to Barbados for fresh troops and supplies, and as his friend had just been laid in the ground, he took himself to the grog shop for old time's sake, and had a stiff drink *in memoriam.*

The girl waited on him and wept at the unwelcome news, for she had loved her poet. The dark one comforted her.

He was climbing from her bed next morning when he looked out and saw the sail coming in, the cutter that must have been just hull-down behind him the whole way from Jamaica, following him hard. He swore, thinking it was some message of disaster that had befallen as soon as he'd been over the horizon. Pulling on his breeches and his boots, he rushed down, to learn that it was only last-minute messages about things forgotten until after he'd sailed. Oh, and a miracle.

His friend had come back from the dead.

It had been known to happen. Overworked, incompetent army doctors failing to notice little details like pulses. Hasty burials under cold, cold clay that brought a man's fever down wonderfully. Clawing his wild-eyed way out of a shallow grave, the poet had seen his life pass before his eyes and found only one thing of value therein: his love for the girl in Barbados.

He'd staggered back down into camp, filthy, half-naked, and the black men muttered and the white men flinched. Altogether it was thought best to let him have a bath, a suit of clothes and passage back to Barbados, because no one wanted him in camp. It was thought he'd bring bad luck…

What tears of joy the girl wept at her true love's return! What nervous glances she cast at his dark friend, who bowed gravely, kissed her hand and kept his silence. He was best man at their wedding. He stood godfather to the little girl, born nine months to the day after the joyful reunion.

It's only a rumor, you see.

• • •

Jamaica flourished. Sugar cane was planted, planters grew prosperous. Merchants established themselves. The sandy point that thrust out into the harbor was fortified and a little town built there, a lure to welcome in privateer captains and their crews and keep them happy. Taverns and brothels in plenty, gambling dens, eating-houses, pipe-shops with good tobacco, other shops with anything a drunken sailor on a spree might look for: gowns of silk for whores, maybe, or pretty things that had belonged to some great lady of Spain, just what was wanted to reward a wife who welcomed you home from sea and didn't ask questions.

Oh, the Brethren of the Coast might take their prizes to Tortuga now and then, if the diplomatic wind from London was foul, if infighting politicians decided to hang a poor captain or two as a gesture of good will toward the Spanish. For the most part, though, Port Royal was their own city.

Its governors came and went, but Harry Morgan ruled there.

He'd learned the privateering trade under little Commodore Mings, as legal as you please, before the navy was withdrawn. They took Santiago de Cuba and sailed home in triumph, leaving the King of Spain the poorer by six fine prize ships and no end of silver plate, cannons, bales of hides, barrels of wine and church bells. If it hadn't been nailed down, it was stolen; the rest was blown up or set afire. Campeche fell next, with her little, stone houses. She yielded up fourteen prizes, and plunder enough for a celebration that lasted days and days.

Morgan wasn't the best seaman in the world—in fact he wasn't especially good at sailing at all, he was always more of a soldier. But he could command, by God, with those coal-black eyes of his. You looked into them and the idea of crossing him never once entered your head, no matter how drunk or cowardly or depraved you were.

Somewhere in all the blood and flame and smoke, Morgan picked up the knack for *inspiring* men too, as opposed to just scaring them into obeying. He learned all the actor's craft of putting a throb in his singsong Welsh voice and a flash in his eye, he learned how to stand six inches taller than he really was, and he learned the words that fired men up like hot rum.

Men listened to his voice and followed him through the swamps of the Mosquito Coast, three thousand miles to sack Villahermosa, and Trujillo, and Gran Granada with its seven churches. The Spanish said he was Drake come again, or the Devil, which was nearly as bad.

He came home with his ships stuffed with loot. There he found that his uncle was the new lieutenant-governor, and had moreover arrived in Jamaica with honor, glory, a household of pretty daughters and scarcely anything else. Bravery hadn't made Colonel Edward Morgan wealthy. It was hoped one of his girls might manage to win the heart of her cousin Henry.

Mary Elizabeth saw him first from her window as he came ashore—wild and handsome as the Devil with his pointed, black beard, and in his train grinning buccaneers throwing Spanish doubloons to the whores all along Queen's Street.

She met him in a quiet drawing-room with shades over the windows to keep out the tropical heat, and him cleaned up and dressed in his elegant best, curled hair, lace collar, emeralds glinting on his fingers as he took her hand and bowed to kiss it, murmuring something polite the whiles she caught his scent: something subtle and expensive, just failing to mask the tang of rum and male sweat.

They fell in love. They must have. Harry took her as she was, without a penny's worth of dowry. They settled down on his fine new estate with the intention of starting a dynasty.

Which didn't happen, somehow.

Oh, there was passion and desire enough. There was good blood: Mary Elizabeth's sisters married Harry's friends, and proceeded to raise great broods of babies. There was opportunity: Harry stayed home from the taverns for a great while after the honeymoon, and slept in most mornings.

But no son came to bless his grand new house, nor any little girl.

Still, folk shrugged and said it would be only a matter of time. Hadn't Harry Morgan more luck than any other man in the West Indies?

• • •

Here's something else you'll find in the history books.

Around the time that the first *Mayflower* sailed for New England, her sister ship the *Seaflower* set sail too, but took her cargo of sour-faced Puritans south and west. They ended up on a tiny speck of land, far out by itself in the Caribbean, which suited them fine. They sang psalms, tilled the soil, and named the place Providence. It came to be called Old Providence, to distinguish it from a place in the Bahamas called Providence too.

Some years later the Spanish reached out from the Main and flicked them away like so many righteous flies, and put a garrison there, and called the place Providencia.

Around the time that Mary Elizabeth was watching her calendar and counting days off in a hopeful kind of way, Governor Modyford of Jamaica sent an expedition to take Curacao. It was headed by Captain Edward Mansfield, who was an experienced old buccaneer, though not the persuasive devil Harry Morgan could be.

Halfway there, his men mutinied. They didn't want to try for Curaçao, they said; it was defended by the Dutch, who were nasty fighters, and the plunder was bound to be skimpy pickings. Cartago, they said, was rich and undefended, another Gran Granada for sure! So away they sailed to sack Cartago, and bungled it royally. Too much rum, too much quarreling, too much greedy anticipation.

The survivors were lucky to sail away again, with Mansfield—like Venables and Penn before him—wondering how he was going to explain his little failure to the governor. What could he offer up to excuse himself?

He decided to recapture Old Providence. It might make a good base for the Brethren of the Coast, when things got too hot in Port Royal; there was only one little troop of Spaniards to guard it. About half his forces had deserted him and sailed off, as drunken cutthroats will, but there remained enough men for a modest assault.

A modest assault was all it took. The Spanish surrendered to a man, and were put on a ship and let off at Portobelo, according to the terms of truce. Mansfield left a garrison to secure the place and sailed back to Port Royal.

Governor Modyford was not as angry as he might have been, but by no means as pleased either. Old Providence had tactical value, true, but where was he to get the men to hold it? Buccaneers couldn't be trusted not to desert their posts.

A call for volunteers went out, and two ships were made ready. Thirty-three solid citizens put their marks on paper and took the first ship for New Providence, under command of Major Samuel Smith. The second ship was delayed, waiting for more volunteers, but sailed in its time.

• • •

It's said that on the night before the second ship sailed, a man crept from a Port Royal cellar and made his way to the interior, to a fine grand house owned by a wealthy planter. Here he knocked, and begged leave to speak with the master of the house. It's said he gave a password that brought the planter downstairs in his dressing gown. They spoke alone together in the drawing room, late at night behind closed doors, but you know how servants are; something was heard through a keyhole, it seems.

The stranger was lately come from Barbados, he said, with his wife and little daughter, one step ahead of his creditors. You wouldn't think it would be possible to go bankrupt selling grog to seamen, but the stranger had done just that. His luck was as bad as ever it had been.

Yet now Governor Modyford was calling for volunteers to re-settle Old Providence. It lay better than a thousand miles to windward of the stranger's misfortunes—no one would ever find him there, if he started again under an assumed name—he and his wife and child might make a new life for themselves, and breathe easy, if they were allowed to go.

All that was wanting was a recommendation to the governor. And money, of course.

The master of the house heard him out. Then he called for paper and pen, and wrote out a recommendation in his steep slanting hand, and signed it; then he went from the room, and returned bearing a purse heavy with gold. They embraced. The stranger took money and paper, and crept from the house, and disappeared into the night.

The ship sailed the following day. Two years passed, without a word from New Providence.

· · ·

One August day in 1668, two men stepped onto the quay at Port Royal. Maybe they sank to their knees in prayer, and kissed the ground; maybe they simply fell, for they were weak as ghosts, mere skeletons under scarred and scabbed skin. One was the British master of a merchant ship. The other was Major Samuel Smith, who'd been sent out to command the garrison at New Providence. They had been released from a dungeon, where they'd spent the last twenty-three months.

The Spanish had retaken the island, landing a force outnumbering the English by ten to one. The English fought with all they had; when they ran out of shot they sawed the pipes out of the church organ and fired those off too. When they saw there was no hope, they surrendered, and were bound in irons.

Then, as the Spanish were mopping up, the second ship from Jamaica sailed into the harbor. Only fourteen men, one woman and her daughter aboard. They were tricked into walking ashore by a ruse, and so were taken prisoner too.

And did the Spanish abide by the terms of the truce, and send them packing back to Port Royal? No indeed.

The Spanish carried them in chains to Portobelo, and staked them to the ground in a dungeon ten feet by twelve. They were made to work at building the port's defenses, waist-deep in water from sunrise to sunset, naked, ill-fed, beaten, their hands worn raw with stones and mortar, and hectored and abused by priests into the bargain. Many died. Some few were taken out and sent to work on other defenses on the Spanish Main. Major Smith was released at last, sent back to let Jamaica know what pirates might expect who trespassed on the dominion of Spain.

He did not know what had become of the woman and her child.

• • •

The loss of Old Providence was bad enough; worse still was the rumor of the treaty that England was negotiating with Spain. Under its terms, it was said, the Spanish were to be left to do as they pleased in the West Indies, and the English must issue no more privateering commissions to those naughty pirates. Jamaica must just look out for herself as best she might.

In vain did Governor Modyford protest that the Spanish, pleased with their success at Old Providence, were arming a fleet for a new expedition to take back Jamaica herself. The King's ministers wrote back that if any such attack took place, why then England would of course avenge it—maybe six months later. Maybe later still, depending on the amount of time it took for the news to reach home, and the wind, and the tide, and the dance-steps of the diplomats in London and Madrid...

To hell with all this, thought the governor, and he called in Colonel Henry Morgan.

• • •

Harry Morgan was now thirty-three, head of the family since his father-in-law's death, uncle and godfather to many little Morgans, but father to none of his own. He it was who'd organized Port Royal's militia, and commanded it now.

It was only of an evening he might be taken for a pirate, drinking in the tavern on Cannon Street or the one over on Thames Street, carousing into the late hours. He could drink any other man under the table, and remain upright and coherent a surprising while after too.

Sometimes, though, late at night, when the lamps had burned low and the other drinkers had fallen silent, he'd get a puzzled look in his black eyes. He could be seen putting out his hand cautiously, touching a glass or an onion bottle as though he expected it to vanish at his touch, like a soap bubble. Once he was seen to put his hand into the flame of a candle, as though to learn whether it would burn him.

On the day the bad news came about Old Providence, he went into the Cannon Street tavern at sundown and remained there till dawn, taking on board enough rum to make any other man paralytic drunk; but all he did was stare into a pool of spilled drink for hours, and answer in few words or not at all when approached.

Still, Harry was stone-cold sober when Governor Modyford called him in for advice. He walked out of the governor's mansion Admiral Morgan, and sent word through the taverns of Port Royal that any member of the Brethren with a ship and a crew might want to get himself to the South Cays, where he would undoubtedly learn something to his advantage.

• • •

They came from all the winds' quarters, did the Brethren of the Coast, to rendezvous with Harry Morgan. It was understood that the object was to strike where it might do the most harm, to prevent an attack on Jamaica, even as Sir Francis Drake had struck the shipyards of Cadiz. It was further understood that no man in the fleet would lift a finger, even to save Jamaica, unless there was plunder to be had. But there was always loot when you sailed with Harry Morgan!

They raided Camaguey first; then Portobelo, with its Iron Fort and Castillo de San Gerónimo and the battlements of Triana. Here there was rare butchery, and no wonder; for here Morgan found eleven English-men, chained together in a tiny space, covered with sores, blinking up at the torchlight from their own shite and piss to a foot's depth. They were from the Old Providence colony.

When they could be made to understand they were free, Morgan heard again the tale of Spanish betrayal, with new particulars he had not heard before. He looked into their faces keenly and saw not one he knew, though never so changed. He inquired whether there were any other survivors. No, he was told, none at all.

He held the place for a month, and what he did there you may well imagine.

The viceroy of Panama ransomed Portobelo at last, for a sum that would take your breath away and one gold ring set with an emerald. Morgan sailed home with more loot than any privateer since Drake. He dipped his ensign as he passed over Drake's grave, sailing back to Jamaica in triumph.

His luck held, and mad luck it was. Even when his own flagship was blown to hell—some fool with a lighted candle in the powder magazine—Morgan and all who drank with him on his side of the table were thrown clear, whilst all the men who'd sat across the table were killed.

Now, it was claimed afterward that Morgan's men tortured prisoners to get information from them, and that may well be so; for in every Spanish town they found racks, brands and thumbscrews, thoughtfully provided by the Holy Inquisition for their New World outposts. And what would you expect of filthy English heretics, but that they should use these sacred instruments for profane purposes?

Treasure was taken; treasure was spent in Port Royal brothels, or used to engross estates with yet more acreage of sugar cane. Treasure was pissed against the wall in week-long drinking bouts, or carefully invested with prudent firms. But when it was all spent—why, to sea they'd go again, to get more.

1670: PORT ROYAL

There was once a young fool, and his name was John. He was big and he was strong and reasonably good-looking. His people weren't rich—he was one of eleven children—but he was apprenticed to a bricklayer in Hackney, and his future was assured.

Then he went and killed a man.

Mind you, the man had been trying to kill him, and both of them in a low tavern, and he'd been drunk and the other man sober. The dead man had been a right bastard, himself up before the magistrate many a time for one kind of viciousness or other. And John's mother had wept and wrung her hands so piteous at the trial, that the magistrate let her boy off with a sentence of transportation to the West Indies.

So Farewell Mother Dear and away went John, to sweat in the sun as a redleg bond-slave on a plantation in Barbados. It didn't kill him. When he'd been there two years he escaped, in a dugout canoe he'd made with two other men. They thought they could paddle their way to some other island and shift for themselves there.

It didn't fall out so. The canoe capsized the first day, and though they righted her again they'd lost their victuals and drink in the sea. They were in a bad way by the time they sighted a passing ship and got taken aboard. The captain was a sometime merchant, a pirate without even the least pretensions to being a privateer, and half his crew had been lost to yellow fever. He put a mug of water in John's hand and made him take an oath to serve on board his ship. John gulped and reckoned he may as well take it, if it was a question of him living or getting tossed back overboard, which it seemed to be.

He learned the ropes, he learned how to reef a sail without getting himself or anyone else killed. But he did learn to kill when required.

He'd been raised to be polite to ladies and respectful to his superiors, and to sit in a pew of a Sunday and keep his mouth shut except when it was time to sing a hymn; that was morality. Still, the first time somebody came at John with a pike, he reacted just as he had in the tavern in Hackney, only faster.

He reasoned it out that a man may be forgiven for murder; why, if his country is at war it isn't even murder, but duty. On the other hand, if a man stands like a stock and lets himself be slain, that amounts to suicide, which will send him straight to eternal damnation. Why take a chance with the eternal part of himself, when he was adrift in a land where it was so easy to lose the earthly part?

So John was a pirate, and a good one, and followed his luck from ship to ship. Now and then he heard his mother's ghost telling him he could get work as a bricklayer, if only he'd try; and he assured her he would try, next time the opportunity presented itself.

He liked looting, if he was taking loot from foreigners. He liked lying on a beach of white sand by night, watching the stars slide down toward the mangrove trees. He liked fiery rum, though not so much after the first time he woke up naked in an alley in Tortuga. He only wanted luck, he thought, to make enough to buy a plantation somewhere and live like a gentleman.

That was why he listened avidly to the stories, whether they were told beside a driftwood fire or on deck under a tropic moon, or beside a guttering candle at a filthy table. The stories were all about Harry Morgan, king of privateers, luckiest man in the West Indies. His luck rubbed off on any man so happy as to set sail with him, or so they said.

They said at the lake of Maracaibo, Morgan took a fortune, and then found his way back to the sea blocked by a Spanish fleet. He sent a dummy fleet among them, loaded with powderkegs, with logs of wood dressed as men on the decks, and the Spanish never realized the trick until the fireships blew up in their faces.

They said he'd got past the high castle guarding the harbor by seeming to land five hundred men in the mangroves, and the Spanish garrison grew fearful and trained their great guns on the trees, expecting an attack from that side; and all the while it was only the same ten men going back and forth in one longboat, sitting up on the way out and lying flat in the bottom of the boat on the way back. Night fell and the Spaniards kept watch on the land, while Morgan's fleet sailed out under their noses, and they never realized they'd missed him until he was well out to sea. There was no predicament so dire Morgan's luck couldn't get him out of it.

John's luck, on the other hand, came and went.

He was sitting on a wharf one summer evening, watching the yellow moon sparkle on the sea, when he heard the rumor: *Morgan's drinking with his captains, and they're going out for plunder!*

John's hair fairly stood on the back of his neck. He jumped to his feet and ran to the tavern, praying he had the right one and thinking surely he had; for there were three or four skulkers outside, peering in through the window and looking as though they were getting their nerve up. Timing is all, John had learned that much. He shouldered through the lot of them and, ducking his head, stepped inside.

He blinked in the smoky gloom. The tavern was crowded, each table and settle occupied by men with tankards and jacks, and long-stemmed pipes, and cards, and dice. The rum went untasted, though, and the cards might have been blank and the dice spotless as souls in Paradise for all anyone noticed them. Every man in the place had his head turned, staring at one particular table lit by a hanging lantern.

Harry Morgan sat there in the pool of light with four others, prosperous captains all. They spoke together in low voices. John walked up to the table and took off his hat. "I do beg your pardon, gentlemen," he said, with a dry mouth. "But I did hear there was an expedition toward, and take the liberty of inquiring whether you might need an able-bodied seaman. Sirs."

Morgan looked up at him.

"An expedition toward, is it?" he said, and his Monmouthshire voice was sharp as a needle. "And who says so?"

John swallowed hard. He mustered all the boldness he could and grinned. "Why, sir, even the chimney-pots have heard by now. Sure, Fame follows you like a shadow."

"Flattery, too," said Morgan, eyeing him. He stroked his beard. "It may be, sir, that we are contemplating certain business. It may be that we need a man or two. Bradley!" He tapped his finger on the table before one of the other captains, and indicated John with a jerk of his head. "There is perhaps a berth wants filling on the *Mayflower*, is there not?"

Captain Bradley looked around swiftly, but with elaborate casualness yawned, and said: "Perhaps. Who's this great side of beef? Are you much of a fighter, sir?"

"Please you, sir, a powerful fighter," said John, showing the size of his fist. "And a gunner too, by God."

"Not a delicate one, are you?" Morgan demanded. "No trick knees? No weak backs? No fainting in the heat of the sun, eh?"

"No, sir," said John. "And I've had the fever and lived to tell the tale. I'm your man, sir, for a forced march or boarding a ship, either one. Nor blood don't give me no swooning fits, neither."

"Well, that is a good thing," said Morgan dryly. "And how much ready cash have you to hand? For, look you, you'll want plenty of powder and shot. I should say three muskets and a brace of pistols, in good condition, and cutlasses too. Shall you have all these by the fourteenth? As we sail then, you know."

"Why—sure, I have them," said John. "Or will have, by the fourteenth."

"See that you do," said Bradley. "And if you are a true gunner, so much the better; you'll get a double share."

"Always assuming there is any profit," said Morgan, setting his finger to the side of his nose. "For we go out on the old terms, you know. No purchase, no pay."

"Aye, sir," said John. "The fourteenth, is it?"

"From King's Wharf," said Captain Bradley. "Mind you be there by the evening before, so as to sign on. Sooner, if you can; lest the berths be all full then."

"Aye, Captain," said John. "I will, indeed."

They went back to their drinking, so he bowed and backed away. Emboldened by what he'd done, a crowd of men rushed to fill the place he'd just left, and John heard their voices raised in supplication to Morgan. He found his way out alone, and the relative cool of the night wind was sweet on his face.

The plain truth of it was, John hadn't a penny to his name. He owned a sea-chest, a cutlass, one pistol, a hammock and a pair of blankets, plus the clothes on his back; and he was reckoned pretty well-to-do for a sailor, at that.

He lived, just then, in a camp on the beach some two miles along the sand spit, with some of his shipmates from the old *Clapham*. It was an easy life, living on fish and turtles, so long as a man had no thirst and wasn't too particular about sand flies; but his mates were drifting away one by one, and pretty soon the camp would fill up with strangers. It was time to move on anyhow.

Pity about the money, John thought to himself. He wandered away up Lime Street, half-hoping some thief would have a go at him; for he had turned the tables more than once, beating an assailant into unconsciousness and possessing himself of whatever he found in the man's pockets. No one came near him tonight, however. The only other figure he could spot, all along the street, was a drunken man staggering along some thirty paces ahead of him.

John being sober, pretty soon he came upon the other man, and was about to pass him when the fellow gave a sort of gasping cry and dropped as though he'd been clubbed. John stood back, aghast. He stepped into the shadow of a wall and watched for a long moment, as the cold starlight glittered down. The other fellow never moved again.

So, John came and knelt by him, and turned him over. This took some doing, for the man was exceedingly fat, and soaked with sweat besides. He stared up at the stars unblinking, though sand was in his face and dusted on the lashes of his eyes. Dead as mutton; of apoplexy maybe, for he didn't stink of fever, but only wine. And maybe his tonnage killed him, for it was all John could do to take him by his soft hands and haul him into Pelican Alley, so heavy he was.

What John had his eyes on was the dead man's boots, for they were grand things, new, by the look of them, high to the knee, and just John's size too. John's ankles stung with sand-fly bites, and his worthless rawhide shoes had worn through to the point where he could feel every broken shell in the lane.

"After all, it ain't like you'll need them where you're bound," he muttered to the corpse, as he pulled the boots off. Oh, they were new: thick and stiff, fancy-stitched with colored stuff, and they went on John as though they'd been made for him. John was so happy he nearly walked away from the dead man there and then, which would have changed the way his life went considerably.

But as an afterthought he turned back and went through the dead man's coat. It was a heavy great coat. No wonder the man had dropped dead, if he didn't know better than to wear something like that in this sticky heat. Then John encountered the bulge of the purse, and hauled it up as eagerly as though he were pulling in a netful of cod.

It was a well-lined purse. John looked down at the dead man and grew thoughtful. This was somebody; this was no nameless redleg like him.

People came asking questions after a corpse like this one. It seemed wisest to leave the dead man far in his wake. John took the purse and ran off, in the salvaged boots. Though they kept his feet from harm they were a little hot, and pretty clammy with the dead man's sweat, and when he saw what sharp, clear prints they left in the sand behind him, John went down to the tideline and walked there, so the sea would wash out his track.

When he got to the camp at last, it was deserted. Some nameless bastard had gone through his trunk and taken his weapons. Much he cared; he rolled up in a blanket and caught what sleep he could until morning, when he broke camp and hauled everything he had left back to town. Come sunrise John was sitting on his sea-chest outside the armorers', whistling a cheery tune as he waited for them to open shop.

• • •

Three hours later John went swaggering up to King's Wharf where the *Mayflower* was anchored, carrying a bundle of black doglock muskets over his shoulder as though they were new brooms, and a porter panting after him with his sea-chest and the kegs of powder and shot. Aboard he came, under the gaze of a sour-faced little man with the look of a clerk.

"What's your business, man?" he said to John.

John tipped the porter, removed his hat and said grandly, "Reporting for duty, sir. As Captain Bradley said I ought, when I spoke to him personal yestereen."

The clerk took in all that shiny new gear, and his tone was a little more pleasant as he said: "Like enough. Why, then, you must be read in. Step over here, if you please."

He had a ship's muster laid out on top of an empty water barrel, with ink and pen to hand. Here he seated himself on a nail-keg, took up the pen and said:

"Your name, sir?"

"John James," said John, which was half a lie.

"*Very* likely," said the clerk with a sniff, but he wrote it down. "Your age, sir, and place of birth?"

John told him, and they were lies too.

"Able-bodied seaman, yes?"

"Please you, sir, and I'm a gunner," said John.

"We'll see about that," said the clerk. "If the captain rates you so. Here-with the articles: Mariner sails conditionally at Captain Bradley's pleasure, share to be determined according to worth. Venture to be determined at the Admiral's pleasure. Terms are, no purchase, no pay.

"Mariner provides his own weapons, amounting to no less than two muskets, two pistols, two cutlasses, and powder and ball sufficient for the endeavor. All weapons to be kept clean and fit for service at all times.

"Mariner shall not steal, nor quarrel, nor murder in the course of quarreling, nor dice, nor game at cards. Default in this at thy peril. Mariner shall not desert or turn coward under fire. Default in this at thy peril. Mariner shall not mutiny or propose venture other than ventures heretofore duly determined by the Admiral. Default in this at thy peril."

"This is hard straits," protested John.

"This is Harry Morgan's way," said the clerk. "We're none of your pirates here. You may sign articles or you may go back on the beach, as you please."

"I was just saying," said John, but he stood down. The clerk cleared his throat and went on:

"Mariner entitled to free use of any garments taken in the course of venture, for his own proper wear. Mariner entitled likewise to victuals and drink so taken, with daily allotment from the ship's stores, save upon occasion of short commons, when allotment to be determined at Captain's pleasure.

"In the matter of recompense for injuries: mariner to receive value of six hundred pieces of eight for loss of *either* right or left leg. Mariner to receive value of six hundred pieces of eight in recompense for loss of right hand. In recompense for the loss of right hand *and* left hand, mariner to receive eighteen hundred pieces of eight. In recompense for sight of one eye, mariner to receive one hundred pieces of eight. In recompense for the loss of the sight of *both* his eyes, mariner to receive six hundred pieces of eight." John was nodding impatiently by the time the clerk had reached the end of the recitation. The clerk ignored him and read:

"In the matter of recompense for singular bravery, if any man shall distinguish himself under fire, or be first to enter any stronghold under fire, or to lower the Spanish colors and raise those of England: that man shall receive fifty pieces of eight, to be paid directly upon division of spoils and the attestation of witnesses.

"Mariner agrees to all articles herein and signs-or-makes-his-mark," said the clerk, and offered John the pen and a paper. John signed his first name, started to write his last name, caught himself in time and scratched it out, blotting somewhat, at which the clerk pursed his lips. John hurriedly wrote *JAMES* after and underscored it with a flourish, and the clerk shook sand on the lot, and that was that.

. . .

The *Mayflower* sailed with the rest of the fleet on the day, certain as clockwork, following Morgan in the *Satisfaction*. Yet they went no further than up the coast a little to Blewfield's Bay, there to put the ships in trim and take on stores and water. John heard mutterings that Morgan wanted to avoid losing his crews to the entertainments of Port Royal, nor have them talk overmuch while ashore.

"Not that any one of us knows enough where we're bound to tell," said the old man with whom John had been set to work. They stood in the shadow of the *Mayflower*'s hull, vast above them as a dead whale, while they smashed and chipped off barnacles.

"Well, we can't be going out for Portobelo again, can we?" said John. "That well's dry. And it won't be Maracaibo again, neither."

"I hear it's to be Vera Cruz," said the old man dreamily, descending his ladder. He moved it over a pace and squinted upward. "Or Santiago de Cuba, the which I hope is wrong. That's a hard place to take. Unless rumor's true and Prince Rupert comes along with us. They say he could crack a fortress like a nut."

"Prince Rupert?" John turned, staring through the salt sweat that trickled down. He mopped his face with a rag. "What's he?"

"Only the king's kinsman," said the old man. "Fought for the old king against the Roundheads, you know. When they won, Prince Rupert took to sea and privateered. They say he was a right devil! I never sailed with him; but they do say he took Cromwell's ships along with the Spanish, never mind whose blood he shed. I heard he had a familiar spirit like a dog, that sniffed out treasure fleets for him.

"They say he came out here to try what he could get in the way of good fortune; but I reckon he lost his dog, for half his fleet went down in a storm, and his own brother with it. Gave it up for a bad job and sailed home again."

"He'd be old now, though, wouldn't he?" said John. The other man winced.

"That was only in '52," he said defensively. "Not so long ago as all that! He was a young devil then; he'd be a prime cunning devil now, you mark me."

"Aye, but—" said John.

"He was burning Spanish ships when you was puking on your nurse," said the old man, and dug with particular vehemence at a knotted gob of weed and shell. John shrugged and held his tongue.

However good a privateer he might have been, no Prince Rupert came out of retirement to join them, when they'd all refitted and sailed off to Tortuga. Still it was a great host of the Brethren, French and English, that met with Morgan in the lee of Cape Tiburon. Morgan played the lord, with his brother captains sipping rum aboard his flagship, the great *Satisfaction*.

Things weren't nearly so grand for John.

He was learning that he needn't have hurried so to get aboard the *Mayflower*; she had plenty of berths free, for it turned out that Captain Bradley was no great shakes as a privateer. He had a reputation for being, you might say, unenterprising. No sooner had the *Mayflower* put in at Cape Tiburon than half its crew was over the side under cover of darkness, signing on with other captains. John would have deserted, himself, but that Bradley offered him position as chief gunner at three whole shares to stay.

Worse, Bradley discovered John could read and write, and so offered him a fourth share to serve as mate to the pinch-faced purser, Felham. It was surely a better bargain than serving as a plain hand before the mast; and John's mother started up her doleful crying in his head, and told him all about the respectable little shop he might set up in, if he made his pile on this expedition. So John stayed on, to his regret.

He discovered that there was a deal of a lot of clerking to do, which might surprise those thinking a pirate's life is all carouse. There were terms and articles, there were ships and their captains to be commissioned, there were shares to be reckoned and set aside for the King and the Duke of York. All of it so much inky nothing, as the fleet hadn't taken in a penny yet. John climbed into his hammock at night with stained fingers, and heard shuffling paper in all his dreams.

All the while, the steady desertion bled from Bradley's ship. It wouldn't do; Bradley wasn't much of a man for taking prizes, but he was Morgan's friend, and so Morgan put the order out that berths on the *Mayflower* would be filled before they sailed.

• • •

"They must have scoured the bilges for this lot," muttered Felham. John, seated beside him at the plank table, felt inclined to agree. He cast a dubious eye over the stragglers lined up before them, and sneaked a glance at Captain Bradley, to see what he thought of it all. Bradley was looking pretty bleak.

"Step up, you lot," said John. "Who's for a berth on the *Mayflower*, and riches?"

Someone far back in the line cackled with laughter. There were cripples, and dazed-looking men far gone in drink, and thin, sickly fellows, and one or two clear lunatics. "Read them in, for the love of God," said Captain Bradley, and stalked off to the wood's edge to sit in the shade.

"Name?" John inquired of the first to step up. He tilted his head back to see a tall man in shabby black, skeletally gaunt, white-faced, looking down at him. The man gave what must have been intended as a friendly smile. On a wolf, it would have been.

"His name is the Reverend Mr. Elias Hackbrace," piped a sharp voice, nothing like what John would have expected to come out of that narrow chest, and that was because it hadn't. A small man stepped around Reverend Hackbrace. He was a pale, mouselike individual, but his glare was flinty.

"Reverend, is it, now?" John looked from one to the other. "Why, sir, with all respect, we ain't likely to need sermons."

"We are perfectly aware of that," said the little man. "It is our intention to pursue the vicious Spaniard, to the greater glory of the Almighty God, trusting in His monetary recompense by way of spoils of victory."

John and Felham looked at each other. John rubbed his chin.

"To be sure," said John. "But this is likely to be dirty work, see. I wonder whether the Reverend mightn't feel a bit faint about killing a man?"

"I assure you, sir, that is not the case," said the other. "Mr. Hackbrace has a quite ungovernable temper when it is aroused."

"I have broken the Sixth Commandment on several occasions," said the Reverend Mr. Hackbrace, in a rusty-sounding voice.

John counted off the commandments on his fingers, and his eyes widened. "Murder?" he said.

"Only Papists," said Reverend Hackbrace. His hands twitched.

"No worse than what any soldier would do, sir, in defense of his country," said the little man. "Or, in this case, the true faith."

"Well, see, some of our mates here is Frenchmen, and they're Papists too," said Felham. "If he's going to go killing just any Papists when his temper's up, that won't answer, will it?"

"Oh, no; but the dear Reverend has discovered an unfailing means to check his wrath," said the little man. "Allow us to demonstrate."

He pointed to a young palm tree that grew some ten yards away.

"Mr. Hackbrace, regard that tree. Think of it as a *sinful* tree, Mr. Hackbrace! It is the very lair of the Old Serpent! It is the throne of the Woman Dressed in Purple and Scarlet, Mr. Hackbrace! It is the Pope's own tree, Mr. Hackbrace!"

The Reverend Mr. Hackbrace obediently regarded the tree, and the tremor in his hands grew markedly worse. He developed a facial tic. A thin flow of spittle started from the left corner of his mouth. His eyes reddened with an indescribable light; his head jerked back, as though he were about to fall in convulsions. Instead he hurled himself screaming at the palm tree.

Such was the force of his assault that the tree snapped clean off at its base, and he rolled with it in the sand, screaming still, stabbing at it with a knife he had pulled from his left boot and biting savagely at the green fronds that lashed his face.

John and Felham looked on, open-mouthed. So did the rest of the queue of men, who had fallen quite silent.

"Mr. Hackbrace!" said a new voice, one high and clear and sweet. John turned and saw the speaker, a short man so fat as to be nearly spherical. He had a beardless face like a painted doll's. He linked arms with the mousy man and the pair of them lifted their voices in shrill song:

"The little white lamb in the meadow so green
Looks out on the wood where the wolf he is seen
I'll not be afraid, says the lambkin so dear
For Jesus, sweet Jesus, sweet Jesus is near!"

The song had an immediate effect on the Reverend Mr. Hackbrace. The flailing about and frenzied stabbing stopped. He lay limp, gasping, and lifted his sandy face to croak the last line with them.

"Sweet Jesus," echoed John.

The two singers turned to face him.

"You see?" said the thin one, with an air of triumph. "What mastiff was ever so vicious in the service of his lord and master? Or so obedient? Of course, we must accompany him."

"You might sign on," said Felham, "but—the other one's a castrato, ain't he? What the hell use is *that* going to be on board a ship?"

"I am a deadly fighter, poltroon!" said the fat one, narrowing his eyes.

"Are you insulting my cousin?" said the Reverend Mr. Hackbrace, getting unsteadily to his feet.

"No, not at all!" said John. "Sure, it'd be an honor to sign him on. What's your name, friend?"

"Dick Pettibone," said the eunuch, setting his hand on his hip in a challenging sort of way.

"And I am Bob Plum," said the mouse-man.

"Right," said Felham, and read them in. They signed, all three, and waded out to take their places in the longboat.

"Christ," sighed Felham, and wiped his face with a handkerchief. "Who's next? Step up, you lot!"

They were two who stepped up next, hand in hand. They were *boucaniers,* rogue men who lived by hunting wild cows and curing the beef over smoke-pits.

Both carried long muskets and wore tunics of rawhide; no brocade for these gentlemen, no plumes nor gold lace. Their limbs were bare, save for leather leggings below the knee, and their naked feet looked hard as horn. Both reeked of the barbecue. Both smoked clay pipes, wreathing themselves in yet more fume, as though to provide their natural element while they were away from it. In this much they were identical.

The differences were, that one was tall and the other was short and squat; one was black, and the other was white; one was clean-shaven, with a mass of knotted and beaded hair on his head, while the other's face was so heavily bearded only his red eyes and the tip of a little, red nose were visible.

The fact that they were holding hands didn't weigh much. There weren't any women amongst the cow-killers and maroons, so they got up to certain practical vices to compensate for it. The gleaming muskets counted for a great deal more, as *boucaniers* were deadly marksmen and the toughest of fighters. John and Felham exchanged glances, hardly able to believe their luck.

"Names?" said Felham.

"I am Jago and this is Jacques," said the black. He had lived amongst both Spanish and French, to judge from his accent. The white man merely nodded in confirmation. "We hate the Spanish *cochons*. We will sail with you."

"Two shares each, if you're able marksmen," said Felham.

Jago's lip curled in disdain. He loaded his musket, with his pipe drooping over his powder horn—John and Felham drew back involuntarily—and then turned and took aim at the shattered palm tree.

"See the centipede on the trunk?"

"No," chorused John and Felham.

"I take off his head," said Jago, and fired. A spurt of sand was kicked up a little way beyond the palm trunk. John got up and went to the trunk, crouching over, squinting to see. There was a centipede there, or most of one anyway, writhing and scrabbling. John squashed it and turned to shout:

"He done it, by God."

"*Three* shares," cried Felham, and grinning broadly he reached out and shook Jago by the shoulder. "Well done, mate!"

Jacques scowled—at least it looked as though he was scowling, under all that beard—and seized Felham's wrist so hard John heard the bones crack. He began to bellow abuse, in French so far as John could tell, shaking his fist under Felham's nose. Jago turned round and shrieked more French at Jacques; Jacques let go of Felham but rounded on Jago, thundering away death and destruction. Jago rolled his eyes, threw his hands in the air and screamed something impatient. Jacques wept, tears starting from his little, red furious eyes, and he began to slap Jago. Jago got a double handful of Jacques' hair and pulled on it. Jacques caught Jago by the wrist and bit him.

John pulled out his pistol and fired it in the air. They stopped quarreling at once and stood apart.

"He very jealous," said Jago.

"You ain't going to do that on board ship, I hope," muttered Felham, rubbing at his wrist. He read them in and they went splashing out to the boat, holding hands once more.

"Next," John called. The next man stepped up to the table, and John blinked at him suspiciously. He seemed familiar, and not just in that he looked like any one of the down-at-heel cavaliers who'd come out to Jamaica one step ahead of their creditors. No; John had seen him here on Tortuga, three or four times in the past few days. He'd stuck in John's mind because, each time he'd passed by, he'd *looked into John's eyes*. He gave John a smile now, in which there seemed something a little sinister.

John, mindful of the two *boucaniers* just read in, felt a blush burning up from his collar and glared at the table. "Name?" said Felham.

"Tom Blackstone," said the cavalier.

"Indeed, my lord?" said Felham. "Age and place of birth?"

"Thirty-one. Waddon Hill, Dorset."

"Of course," said Felham, in the politest possible tones of disbelief. John wrote it down, refusing to look up.

"I suppose you ain't an able-bodied seaman, my lord?"

Clear across the water came the sound of violent quarreling from the longboat, where Jago seemed to have affronted Bob Plum in some way. Felham sighed, drew his pistol and fired a shot in their direction.

"Stand to!" he bawled. Lowering his voice he went on: "Sorry, my lord. You was saying—"

"I was upon point of saying that I am an indifferent sailor, but a damned good fighting man," said Blackstone. "And well armed, I might add." He waved a lace handkerchief, and from behind him two shaky old drunks stepped to the fore, each one setting down the chests they'd been bearing for him. They opened the chests to reveal kegs of powder, bars of lead for casting, and what looked to be the ready stock of an armorer's shop.

"Oh, yes," said Felham, and read him in. Tom Blackstone stepped up and signed to the register in a bold scrawl. The drunks were paid off with gold and backed out of Blackstone's presence, knuckling their forelocks.

"If you'll just walk out to the boat, my lord?" said Felham. "Haul them boxes, John, and see them stowed directly."

"Aye aye," said John, feeling surly. He hoisted the chests to either shoulder—for John was strong as a bull in those days—and waded out to the boat, with Blackstone prowling along beside him.

"Shame to get those fine boots wet," said Blackstone.

"They're sea-boots. They'll do," said John.

"Ah, but I think they're a little more than sea-boots, aren't they? All that fine cutwork," said Blackstone. And then he stopped right there, with the sea foaming around their ankles, and looking straight at John said: "Cumberland."

"Beg pardon?" John replied.

"Cumberland," Blackstone repeated. When John just stared at him by way of answer, he narrowed his eyes. "Pray tell me, sir: Where might I buy such boots, if I were so minded? In whose shop?"

"Don't know, mate," said John. "I had them off a dead man, didn't I?" As who should say, *I'm a killer, friend, and you don't want to cross me!*

"Did you indeed," said Blackstone thoughtfully, and said nothing more.

They got to the boat, where the *boucaniers* and the Reverend and his mates were now chattering away and laughing like old friends. John stowed the chests, scrambled in after Blackstone, and watched him sidelong as they rowed out to the *Mayflower.*

. . .

Well, so the captains decided to take Panama. Morgan argued for it, shrewdly, in that way he had of making it seem as though it was somebody else's idea. Wasn't Panama the great clearing-house of the world, the place where all the silver and gold of Peru was brought down to be shipped away to Spain? She was open and undefended, she had never been sacked at all!

And no wonder, argued some of the captains: for she lay clear on the other side of the Main, facing into the South Sea, with sixty miles of jungle at her back, steep mountains and a winding river. Morgan pointed out that the perfumed grandees of Panama couldn't imagine anyone attacking them from the west; they themselves would never risk mud on their fancy shoes, or work up a sweat slashing through the jungle.

Then Morgan mentioned, in an offhand kind of way, those great cities he'd taken on his first ventures: Villahermosa and the rest. He'd led his men *hundreds* of miles through that stinking, mosquito-haunted wilderness, and out again. Child's play, he said.

But he didn't press the point. Morgan was too clever for that. He let the images work for him: the bar silver from the mines of Potosi, the long emeralds and beaten gold, the silks and porcelains and pearls. When the captains had all agreed on taking Panama, he got them to sign a paper to that effect, the wily devil, giving sane and serious reasons relating to the safety of the realm. It stood him in good stead later too.

There was one other suggestion Morgan made, one to which all the captains agreed readily enough. Why not take themselves a base on the Main first, a place near to the business at hand, some island where they could refit and revictual at need? Old Providence ought to do nicely, he said. Recapture it, and get a little revenge into the bargain.

THE ISLAND

The fleet raised anchor and sailed, with a fair wind behind them all the way. Six days it took. On Christmas Eve—as the Papists amongst them reckoned it by the new calendar, which was ten days out from the right one—there were the three mountain peaks of Old Providence, red in the sunrise. By midmorning the Brethren sailed up to the anchorage and saw the battery guarding the harbor, and the black mouths of four silent guns. Morgan had a good look at the place with his glass.

No little figures moved along the parapets; no Spanish banners waved. Nobody moving inland, either; no sight of a living soul.

Morgan closed his glass and, cool as ice, bid his captains enter the anchorage. The *Satisfaction* first; he stood tall on her quarterdeck as they slipped in, right in range of the guns, but never a shot was fired. Had the Spanish deserted the place, after breaking so many hearts to take it? Morgan landed a thousand armed men, and went ashore to find out.

• • •

John led the little party of his messmates that Captain Bradley sent: Reverend Hackbrace with his cousin Pettibone and Bob Plum, who seemed some sort of relation too, and the two *boucaniers*; at the last moment Tom Blackstone jumped down into the boat too, much to John's discomfort. He made no trouble, though; he merely bent to the oar like a common hand and kept his mouth shut, though once John noticed him studying John's boots again.

They splashed ashore and drew the boats up, and John had a long look around. Eerie silence. Inland he could just glimpse a few roofs, bare beams gaping and thatching rotted away. There were wide weedy places that had been fields, maybe. Only, a flock of wood-pigeons rose suddenly in flight, wheeled and circled once, and vanished.

"Do you see, Elias?" Bob Plum pointed to the desolation. "This is the work of the Pope."

"Here, now, don't you go setting him off yet," said John in alarm.

"If you please, I require the proper frame of mind," said the Reverend. He raised his hands and began to pray; Plum and Pettibone knelt in the sand beside him and joined in. Blackstone watched them with a smirk. The *boucaniers* were composedly loading their muskets, puffing away at their lit pipes. John shuddered and looked around.

A few yards down the beach, Morgan's own boat was coming ashore. John thought he'd draw a bit of notice for himself, so he splashed out and helped them pull the boat up. He did his best to catch Morgan's eye, but the Admiral was staring inland at the ruins, looking grim. So John stood to his full height and saluted smartly, and with him being so big Morgan couldn't help but see.

"Please you, sir, this plantation ain't been worked in years," said John. "Not a sign of a living soul here."

Morgan looked at him, and John thought he saw a flash of recognition in Morgan's black eyes.

"Perhaps not," he said. "Look you, take six men and reconnoiter down the coast." He pointed, and John set off smart; as he hurried away he heard Morgan ordering other parties out to have a look round.

Well, John led his little party down the beach and saw never a footprint, not so much as a goat's track; Jago and Jacques cast inshore a ways as they went, and though they walked silent as cats they found nothing either. They met all together at the end of the beach, under the rock cliff, and John splashed out with them to look around into the next little bay.

"Fresh water," said Jago, pointing. There were some dark wet rocks, with a runnel of clear water flowing down over gravel and shells from the trees to the beach, and white mist blowing along it.

"That's something, anyway, water," said John. He blundered forward through the surf and walked up on the glass-smooth sand. He looked again at the mist, and caught his breath.

There was a girl standing there by the water, pale as the mist, still and slender as an egret. She lifted her head and looked at him. John felt a stab of something go right through his heart and lodge there, like the barbed head of a spear. He had never seen anything so beautiful in his life, nor would he ever again: nothing like that girl by the water, with her long, wet hair and her gray eyes gazing so quiet.

Jago and Jacques and the rest came up the beach after him and John put out his hand, trying to make them be quiet. He was sure she'd vanish like a ghost; he was half sure she *was* a ghost. But she didn't vanish, and then Pettibone had seen her and cried, "There's a spirit!"

John was sure she'd turn and run, then, but she didn't. She stood there, watching them; slow and cautious they walked toward her.

Close to, and she was real enough. She looked young, only a maid of fourteen or so, clad in rags faded and stained. Her hair was a tangled mat, pale as ashes.

John was talking low all the time he came near her, like he was talking to a skittish horse, telling her what a pretty little thing she was and how she needn't be afraid. He never took his eyes from the girl, but Jago and Jacques were watching the scrub pretty sharp. Nothing moved. She was alone.

Ever so careful, John reached out and took her hand. It felt like ice.

"What's your name, dearie?" he said.

She never drew back from him, but looked at her hand in a sort of wonder, it seemed, and said, "Anguish."

"She means English!" exclaimed Bob Plum. "Merciful God! She's one of the Righteous. She must have escaped the Spanish, and been hiding here all this while."

"It is a miracle," said Pettibone. "Oh, the poor child!"

Jacques said something, and Jago translated: "Ask her, where have the Spanish gone?"

But she didn't seem to know. She just looked at them, mute, though she didn't resist when John pulled at her hand.

"You come with us, sweeting," he said, and felt her hand warm a little in his grasp.

"Listen to me, girl," said Blackstone. "Are there others here? Other English, like you? Any men?"

"She's mad," said Jago, shaking his head. Pettibone shrugged out of his coat, that was big enough to go round the girl three times, and wrapped it around her shoulders.

They led her away and around the cliff, back to the boats. Morgan was gazing through his glass at the interior, and so did not see them until they were just at his elbow, so to speak.

"Here's a thing, sir," said Blackstone. "A young lady."

Morgan lowered his glass and turned. He saw the girl, and his dark face went clay-color in shock.

"Oh Christ," he said. He just stood there staring at her, so John, trying to be helpful, said:

"She's said she's English, sir."

Morgan spoke as though his mouth was dry. "What's your name, child?"

She said nothing. He reached out a hand and brushed back her hair, looked into her eyes.

"Are you alone?" he asked. "Is your mother here? Your father?"

Not a word from her, though tears formed in her gray eyes. Morgan was breathing hard, like a man that's run upstairs.

"You're safe now," he told her. "Safe, and going home. She can't stay here," he added, looking around as though he'd only just noticed John and the rest standing there. "Some of you, row her out to the *Satisfaction*. To my cabin. She's not to be touched, do you understand? I'll kill the man who touches her. She needs tending—she must be clothed and fed—" His voice trailed off in a helpless kind of way, as he looked around him and realized he hadn't exactly the most trustworthy lads to minister to a virgin pure, like.

So John, ever a thoughtful lad, put in his oar. "Please you, sir, Pettibone here's a eunuch."

Pettibone shot him an evil look, but stepped forward and bowed.

"In Jesus' name, you may rely on me. I will minister to the poor child, sir."

"You were best," said Morgan harshly. "Go, now."

So John led the girl into the boat, and Pettibone stepped in after them and Blackstone followed quick to get in too, which John didn't much care for. The others pushed the boat off, and John and Blackstone rowed back to the Admiral's flagship. Pettibone hauled his fat, little bum aboard, and the girl ascended easy as though she'd done it a hundred times, with John giving her a lift up. He didn't peep up her rags, but he couldn't help seeing her fair white ankles and her naked feet as she went over the side. Then Blackstone headed the boat around, and they were rowing back to shore.

John looked out at the *Satisfaction* and watched Pettibone, like a mother hen, guiding the girl to the great cabin, and heard Pettibone snapping out short words to the deck hands. He fancied the girl looked for him, as he rowed away.

"I wonder what you'd take for those boots," said Blackstone, as they rowed.

"Eh?" said John, startled from his dream.

"I've conceived a desire for boots of Spanish make, with curious stitchery," said Blackstone. "Such as those red noughts and crosses on your own boots. Unusual, those. Distinctive. Never seen such a pair, God's my life."

"I'd have thought you'd owned plenty of fancy boots in your time, a rich boy like you," said John, giving him a hard stare.

"Oh, once upon a time, I might have done. My father was a prudent, old devil; bent the knee to Cromwell, and kept his fortune and his lands. He was obliging enough to die untimely and leave me with the lot. Off to court I went, when the king returned, to try my hand at being a courtier. Do you know, it can ruin a man? I'd no notion of the cost of silks, and carriages, and fine sherries. Not to mention the gambling one is required to do!" Blackstone shivered, as though in disgust. "I wasted my substance in a year, who'd credit it?"

"Imagine that," said John, watching him close.

"The only advantage to ruining oneself so speedily," said Blackstone, "is that the news doesn't travel apace, and one can, if one is prompt, find a creditor or two who'll still advance enough money for a passage to the West Indies. And out here, as you've doubtless learned, a man may vastly improve his lot with but an hour's dirty work."

"I reckon so," said John.

"Indeed. I may, therefore, indulge my whims once again, not to my former extent, of course, but handsomely nevertheless. To return, then, to the issue at hand: How much for the boots, my man?"

"I ain't selling," said John. "Besides, they ain't your size."

"They are," said Blackstone, setting his foot beside John's. John, glancing down, saw it was true. "Remarkable, isn't it? So hard to find ready-mades in my size, as a rule. Why, we might be brothers. And brothers to the man you killed to get them."

"I didn't kill nobody," said John, wondering whether he could club Blackstone with an oar and have it look like an accident. "The bastard dropped dead in the public street, on my life and honor. Look here, the cobbler don't look likely to set up his stall on this Goddamned ghost island any time soon, thank you very much. What would I do for shoon, if I sold them? What are you after, anyhow? *Was* it your brother, as died?"

Blackstone looked at him at long moment, as though he was taking his measure.

"No," he said. "Merely a man with whom I was to exchange boots."

John stared, dumb as a codfish. Blackstone sighed.

"Oars inboard a moment. Your knife, if you please."

They shipped oars and John drew his knife, ready to cut Blackstone's gullet and shove him over the side, if he had to. But Blackstone only reached out with his finger and tapped the fancy-work at the top of John's boot.

"Oblige me by opening that seam, will you? You have my word of honor I'll repair it with my own lily-white hands."

John was a fool in those days, but not so dull as all that. He thought he understood, in a flash as it were, what the man had been driving at. He felt out the seam and cut along it. Neat as a wallet, it opened, and he caught a glimpse of oiled paper that had been tucked flat in there behind the cutwork, before Blackstone reached down, quick as a snake striking, and extracted the paper between finger and thumb.

"Thank you," said Blackstone.

"Love letter, is it?" said John, grinning.

"Something of the sort," said Blackstone, opening the paper and reading with difficulty, for the writing was much blurred.

"Well, now, that's as good as a play!" said John. "You been looking for that poor dead son of a whore, ain't you? And you was arranged to know him by his boots!"

"As you say."

"That ain't half-clever!"

"Mm-hm."

"And here was me wearing them quite by chance!"

"Astonishing."

"What's it say, eh?"

"I've no intention of telling you."

"Oh. Right. Lady's honor concerned, aye?" John lay his finger beside his nose.

Blackstone stuck the paper inside his coat. He looked at John once more, with that same measuring gaze.

"A man's life is in the balance," he said. "One of your own Brethren of the Coast, you might say. And that will have to suffice you."

The tide ran them up on the beach, then, so no more was said.

• • •

The island was secured before two in the afternoon, empty as it was, and it would have been quicker if there hadn't been so damn many mountains. Morgan found out where the Spaniards were: all holed up in the fortifications atop the little sister islet that lay at Old Providence's north end, across a stretch of seawater serving as a moat. But the drawbridge had been hauled in, and the first parties who came in sight of the guns met with concerted fire.

"No ghosts in there," said John, panting as he ducked behind a rock.

"The cowards," said Bob Plum, glaring as he bandaged the Reverend's ear, which had stopped a splinter of shattered rock sent flying by a four-pound ball. That had been on their third attempt to wade across the moat, and even the Reverend's ferocity had begun to flag a little. A tear trickled down his gaunt cheek.

"I have failed the Almighty," he said.

"Ah, no you ain't," said John. "It'd take God Almighty himself to get us in there this side of a six-month. I reckon it'll come to starving them out."

"I doubt our Admiral has the time to spare for a siege," said Blackstone. He turned and squinted back at their own forces, dispersed behind hillocks and clumps of trees, under a lowering sky of black cloud. "Where *is* our Admiral?"

"He gone back on board the *Satisfaction*," Jago informed them, scrambling down into their shelter. "Captain Bradley giving orders out there. We to wait."

"That's Bradley, by God," John muttered. "Wait and see."

"What's he gone back aboard for?" demanded Blackstone. Jago shrugged, and Blackstone grinned. "Oh ho. Interrogating the fair prisoner, I dare say."

"Our Admiral is a married and a God-fearing man," said Bob Plum. "I'm quite sure he would never do anything improper."

A cannon ball smacked into the rock behind their redoubt. It sounded like a hammer hitting an anvil under a thundercrack, sending up a smoke of dust and shards of rock. They cursed and fell flat, waiting for the rain of splinters to end. But the pattering did not cease, and John felt the splash on his outstretched hand.

"*Il pleut*," said Jago, and spat.

Jacques began to sing mournfully, "*Un flambeau, Jeanette, Isabella…*"

• • •

They lay out there in the rain getting soaked until nightfall, before Bradley called them back. Under cover of darkness they retreated, swearing and hating Bradley, and some found shelter in a few ruined stables. No rations were served out; Bradley sent his apologies, and assurances they'd be along any time now. None arrived that night. Jacques shot an old spavined horse, which they butchered and cut into gobbets, and attempted to cook over a smoking little tongue of blue flame. Hungry men appeared out of the darkness and snatched for raw shares, and fights broke out.

By the time the dawn came, it was a mutinous crew that slogged back through the wet grass, and the usual sea-lawyers from every ship stood around Bradley haranguing him about their rights. The French amongst them weren't for fighting at all, but for going back to the ships and celebrating Christmas in dry clothes. This seemed like a good idea to the English and to the blacks and Indians too, mince-pies or no. Bradley was upon point of giving in when Morgan returned.

He gave a fine speech then, eloquent enough to make the night just past seem like a little inconvenience. Men were sent back to the ships posthaste for provisions, and great fires were built in the deserted village (a right scrubby place), and rum served round. The slow-match coils were hung out to dry like garlands. The *boucaniers* scared up a few flights of pigeons and dropped them with quick shot, so there was Christmas squab and jerked beef, cheer for one and all.

Though a fight did break out when Jacques fancied one of the English was eyeing Jago's charms, and there was screams and slaps and a knife-fight, but it was broken up before anybody got killed to spoil the holiday.

The Spanish were still firing off a few rounds, just to let it be known they weren't sleeping. Morgan went out to see their defenses, and came back looking haggard. John put himself in Morgan's way with another sharp salute.

"We done our best, sir, but they ain't budging," he said. Morgan turned and looked at John blankly. John wanted to ask how the girl was, but he couldn't think of a way, and all Morgan said to him was:

"Rig a coracle. I'll not waste a boat on this."

"A coracle, sir," said John stupidly, but there was an Irish *boucanier* who knew how to make one of the little basket-boats, and he stepped up and said so. In a half-day he had framed a coracle of green wood, and covered it in pitched canvas. All the while, Morgan had retired to one of the deserted shacks to compose a letter, and then rendered a translation into Spanish.

He had the Irishman given a clean white shirt, and a white flag made to fly from the coracle, and gave the Irishman his letter to deliver too.

The man hoisted his little boat and carried it down under the battlements, bold as brass, while the Spanish watched like hawks. He paddled about, with the wind whipping the white flag to and fro, until they made up their minds and sent a black down, carrying another white flag, to see what was wanted. The Irishman handed off Morgan's letter and the black carried it up.

What the letter said, was that if the Spanish governor there did not surrender pretty quick, Morgan swore to him and his that he'd put them all to the sword, no quarter given. A fine threat, with Morgan sitting there in the drizzle with his muskets and pikes and near-mutiny, and the Spanish garrison bristling with big guns.

But Morgan's luck held.

Two hours afterward the Spanish sent over a canoe of their own, with two emissaries bearing a letter from the governor. John was standing by Morgan when he read it. The funny off-color that had been in Morgan's face since he'd seen the girl, fled clean away; Morgan laughed heartily. He strode out grinning white as a new moon, and called in his chief captains, Bradley and Morris and Collier.

Bradley came out grinning too.

"What's toward, Captain sir?" said John.

"Christmas mummery," said Bradley. He gave orders, and they were followed smart, with sniggers and blank-loaded muskets.

The Spanish governor had sent word that he'd like to surrender cruel bad, but there was the little matter of him getting sent back to Spain in irons and garrotted for cowardice if he did so. To get round this painful chance, he proposed that a mock battle be staged: Morgan's men would storm the islet and the governor's men would defend it as fiercely as they might, with everyone shooting blanks. The governor would leave the main fort and rush "to the defense" of a lesser one; Morgan's men could "capture" him then.

And so it fell out. The sham battle began at nightfall, with a great deal of noise, as men on both sides pretended to take fatal wounds and died most theatrical, and lay giggling amongst their comrades. By midnight the whole thing was over, and not a drop of blood spilt.

Next day all was mutual congratulation, and no few surprises. It turned out the Spanish had been armed to the teeth up there—more than thirteen ton of gunpowder, over a thousand muskets, forty-nine cannon, pistols and slow-match in barrels. They might have kept it up for weeks, if they'd been so minded. But, as the Spanish governor explained to Morgan, they weren't so fond of the place as to die for it; most of them had been sent there as punishment anyhow. Besides, the island was haunted, and they would be happy to see the last of it.

There were upwards of four hundred people came filing out of the fortresses, with their livestock: soldiers, married settlers and their children, slaves and their children too. Morgan watched them come out, his mood something shadowed and his dark face somber. He had given orders that the men were to be set to work and the women and children sent to the village's church, when out of the line of slaves one old beldame tottered, calling out to him in Welsh.

Morgan turned on his heel and stared. The old lady fell on her knees, begging him for succor; John heard later she was from some Welsh town, come out to the West Indies as a nurse for somebody's daughter, but the ship had wrecked. She'd survived but fallen into the hands of the Spanish, who had used her hard twenty years or more.

Morgan took her into the house he was using, and questioned her close. John didn't know about what, for it was all in Welsh, and anyhow he was trying not to listen too openly, where he stood on duty outside the open door, with another big fellow. But the old lady wept, and carried on no end, and sang sometimes; and John could hear Morgan beginning to sound impatient, and his fingers drumming at last on the tabletop. At last he said something short and sharp, and came outside.

"You; John, your name is?"

"Aye, sir!" said John, ever so pleased his name was sticking in Morgan's memory.

"Row the woman out to the *Satisfaction*. She's been a nurse. Likely she can be some help to Pettibone, looking after the girl."

"Aye aye!" said John, wondering if he'd get to see the girl, and feeling that spear-point in his heart again. Morgan stepped back inside and led the old creature out. Seeing her close to was no treat; for she was bent and whitehaired, with a nutcracker face and rolling eyes, and she curtsied and simpered for Morgan most unseemly. John thought she was more likely to need a nurse than to be one, but he kept his mouth shut and did his duty.

He had to walk the length of the island with her to get back to the boats, with her singing the whole way, poor old drab, seen by everybody, and that must have been how the story got started that Morgan had brought a Welsh witch with him. All talk. Morgan never needed anyone to conjure trouble for his enemies. He was close enough to the Devil to do it for himself, and in any case there were plenty of conjure-wives in the Caribbean if he'd wanted one.

• • •

Pettibone opened at John's knock, and pursed his little cupid's bow mouth in disapproval.

"What are you doing here?" he demanded. Seen close to with his jacket off, it was evident he had breasts like a woman, the way fat men will. John shuddered.

"Captain's orders; here's a goodwife, to be serving-woman for the girl," he said, and led the old lady into the great cabin. The girl was sitting quiet, in a dressing-gown of purple silk that must have been Morgan's own. She'd been having her hair tended, to judge from the brush and combs on the table. She looked up at John with that clear-as-water gaze, and John smiled foolishly.

Pettibone took the old lady in charge and clucked over her. John made so bold as to sit at the table across from the girl, and stretch out a hand.

"You remember me, sweeting?" he said, scarce able to get his breath for the words. "Happy to be rescued, are you?"

The girl smiled at him. He smiled back, a grin so wide he must have looked like a Hallowe'en face carved on a turnip, and there might have been a candle burning in his empty head too, so bright he felt.

"None of that," said Pettibone. "You take your great boots out of here, and leave the poor child alone."

"Aye aye, *ma'am*," said John, feeling like the cock of the walk. He got up to leave, but smiled again at the girl before he went, and whistled as he rowed himself back to shore.

• • •

John reported back to Morgan personal and smart, where the Admiral was busy with his captains; Morgan gave order for a party to be got together to move all that powder and shot down to the beach, so it might be parceled out amongst the fleet. John had been without sleep a day and a night, but he was young then, and fearful ambitious of Morgan's good notice, so he said, "Aye aye, *sir!*" and went off straightaway.

By this time the Brethren were disporting themselves with rum, or roasting slaughtered livestock, or sprawling out for a good sleep; so the first few times John bawled for volunteers, he was told (and roundly too) what he might do with himself. Thinking his own messmates might be more agreeable, John walked about looking for any of the *Mayflower's* crew.

He crossed one of the rubbishy little fields, and there was one of the Spanish prisoners who'd been sent out to forage, with a basket of maize in his arms, and there was Tom Blackstone, as if he were escorting the prisoner under guard. But they were standing still, heads bent, talking serious together. As John drew close he heard Blackstone speaking Spanish, as easy as kiss your hand.

Now John remembered the slip of paper that had been hidden in his boot, and once again the flash of understanding lit up the inside of his thick head, and he reckoned he'd had it all wrong before. Maybe Blackstone was no intriguer ladies' man, said John to himself; maybe Blackstone was a *spy!*

But he kept his face bland, resolving to play a deep game and watch Blackstone. He was mild as a May morn greeting him, and gave no sign he'd the least suspicion of anything amiss. Blackstone went readily with him, and on the way they collected the Reverend and Bob Plum, and all that afternoon until dark hauled powderkegs down from the fortress to the camp.

And John did his best not to drop off asleep by the fire, where he'd cannily positioned himself near Blackstone as night fell. All the same, he opened his eyes with a start to find the stars had sunk far west, and the fire gone down to red embers without his knowing anything about it. All around him, men lay snoring something prodigious.

John sat up, grimacing to feel how the cold dew had soaked through his clothes, and in his ear his mother told him he'd catch his death of cold. He looked over at where Tom Blackstone had lain; but the man was gone. So John turned his head this way and that, peering through the night. It seemed to him he heard a murmuring, away out in the dark. It wasn't the surf, and it wasn't the ape-bellowing of wakeful drunks. It sounded like someone talking quiet on purpose.

It was coming from the direction of the village church. That was where most of the prisoners had been shut up. John could see the light of a fire still kept blazing before its door, for sober men stood guard there. Round by the back, though, a figure crouched at a little window. Its back was to John.

John got to his feet and walked close, soft-footed as he was able, drawing his pistol as he went. He got to within ten paces and heard for certain the soft hiss of Spanish being spoken, and knew for certain the speaker there in the dark was Tom Blackstone.

He could move quiet when he was young, could John, and so he did now, and came up behind Blackstone and set his pistol to the back of Blackstone's neck and cocked it. Blackstone fell silent a moment; then he said something in Spanish cool as you please, maybe, "Pardon me, sir, I must be going," and he stood up slow.

"If you blow my brains out, you'll never know what I was doing," he said. "I believe our Admiral might be rather vexed with you on that account. Whereas, if you'll allow me to make a full confession, you can take it to the Admiral. Glory for John, eh?"

Which shows that he was a shrewd judge of character. John felt his face grow hot for shame, to be so easily read. He grabbed Tom's shoulder and marched him away a few yards, never lifting the pistol.

"Where are we bound?" said Blackstone, as easy as though they were chatting over two pints.

The truth of it was, having caught Tom Blackstone, John couldn't think what to do with him next, short of marching him all the way to Morgan's tent and waking up the Admiral.

"Just you shut your damned mouth," he said.

"I thought you wanted to hear my confession," said Blackstone. "See here, my back is like to break after all that crouching by the window. Would you make any objection to my sitting down whilst we have our chat?"

"Sit, then," said John, and as Blackstone sat John sidled around quick to face him, keeping the pistol-muzzle close the whole while. Cautious, he hunkered himself down. There they sat, in the middle of someone's weedy vegetable patch, under the winking stars.

"I am in the employ of a certain gentleman," said Blackstone composedly, "and you should know that he is a loyal subject of King Charles Stuart, God save him, and of no mean birth himself besides. Some years ago, this good gentleman lost his beloved brother at sea.

"A twelvemonth since, my gentleman received a message from persons unknown, bearing the news that his dear brother was alive, but a captive here in the West Indies. Certain tokens were enclosed with the letter, as proof thereof.

"The sum of his ransom was named. The unknown correspondent stated further that circumstances called for the greatest secrecy in effecting the release. Should he wish to pursue the matter further, therefore, my gentleman was informed that he must send an emissary of a certain shoe size to Port Royal. This person must bring with him four thousand pounds in gold.

"Once in Port Royal, he must look for a man wearing boots of a particular curious design, with red noughts and crosses worked into the leather."

"Oh, bugger," said John, as the truth began to glimmer through.

"Bugger indeed. Had the emissary been able to find the man in question, he was to have approached him and given a certain password, on the pronouncement of which the other party would collect the ransom money and exchange boots with him. The boots were purported to contain information as to the whereabouts of His Royal Highness' brother."

"Oh."

"I am that emissary, sir," said Blackstone. "I arrived in Port Royal, only to see the very boots I sought on the legs of some ruffian lounging at the rail of the departing *Mayflower.* By the time I had arranged passage to follow the *Mayflower* to Blewfield's, she had departed for Tortuga. I coursed thence and so tracked you down."

"Well, but," stammered John, "I told you what happened. And you got the bit of paper, didn't you?"

"For all the good it did me," said Blackstone. "The paper instructs me to proceed to Chagres with another payment of four thousand pounds. I begin to suspect His Royal Highness is being played for a fool."

"His Royal Highness?"

"No less. I suppose you've never heard of Prince Rupert, Duke of Cumberland; he hardly frequents the same bawdy-houses you would."

"'Course I've heard of him, hasn't everybody?" said John. "The king's own kinsman who turned pirate. And he lost his brother in a storm, didn't he? Is that the one you're after?"

"Prince Maurice," said Blackstone. He turned his head to look at the east, which was glimmering pale. "Learning that this island has been used as a sort of oubliette by the Spanish, I thought it prudent to enquire amongst its inhabitants as to whether there had ever been a prince in residence."

"Was that what you were doing?" John lowered the pistol. "There ain't no princes here, that's certain."

"But there were, apparently," said Blackstone. Against the dying night, his profile looked sharp and grim. "I am informed there was an English prisoner of high rank but lately here, held in great secrecy; a year since he was removed, to Chagres as they believe, but do not know."

"By hell, that's bad luck," said John. "And here's me crossing your hawse time and again. What'll you do now?"

"Proceed to Chagres, what d'you think?" said Blackstone.

• • •

Had John been an older and wiser man, he'd never have believed such a tale, or trusted a man like Blackstone; so it was just as well all this happened when he was young. He scrambled to his feet, and helped Blackstone up with a hearty apology, and went off to build up a fire and see what might be had for breakfast.

• • •

Morgan kept his men busy, now, as he sat in council with the captains. There were the island's stores to be raided, and the fortifications to be pulled down, the big guns spiked and thrown into the sea. Most of this was done by the prisoners, working under armed guard, but they didn't seem to mind it much. Most of them were overjoyed at the thought of getting off Old Providence and back to the mainland, and a few even went over to Morgan's side and joined as fighters. Morgan left standing only the fort, which he garrisoned, and the church; hedging his bets, maybe.

The decision was to go for Chagres next; small wonder too. Given the choice between hacking their way overland across mountains to Panama, or going by boat on the river Chagres, all parties present agreed that the river route was the thing. There was only the matter of a bloody big castle guarding the river's mouth on the Caribbean side, that would have to be got past before the Brethren could proceed any further. And there was no sneaking past this one under cover of night; it would have to be taken, or Morgan would have the enemy at his back all the way up the river, and a gauntlet to run again on his return.

So John and his messmates got ready.

After a few days Pettibone returned from the *Satisfaction*, with the news that the girl seemed to be mute, but that the old lady had recovered her wits enough to make a passable serving-woman. John longed to row out and see her, but Pettibone told him the Admiral kept her under lock and key.

"And no wonder, in a fleet of brigands and cutthroats," he said.

"Of which you're one, ain't you?" said John

Pettibone looked indignant. "Only in the service of his king," said Bob Plum.

"She's an admiral's plaything, you great oaf," said Blackstone to John, as he set an edge on his cutlass, running the stone carefully along the blade. "How should the likes of you compass such a dainty?"

"And you're mistaken too," said Pettibone. "I'll have you know our Admiral has treated her as any true gentleman would treat a lady in distress!"

"Praise God," said the Reverend.

"Bollocks," said Tom Blackstone. The Reverend drew on him and he blocked, whereat both Bob Plum and Pettibone screamed, and it took three choruses of "The Little White Lamb" to get the Reverend to calm down, and both Jago and Jacques to get his blade out of his hand.

"I merely meant," said Blackstone, when things were calmer, "that our Admiral locks up the rum, and being a wise man, locks up the women too."

"And he no fool," said Jago. "There is no camaraderie with the ladies present. Scheming like Eve, like Delilah, leading the boys to cut each other throats."

"Be that as it may," said Pettibone, "he is sending her back to Jamaica, dispatching a cutter and a trustworthy crew. She is to be put into the care of his own dear wife; so a fig for your lewd thoughts."

"That *is* a patient wife!" said Blackstone.

John thought his messmates all a sour and unromantic lot, and he didn't much like the way Blackstone could read what he was thinking in his face. He resolved to keep his own counsel on the girl henceforth.

• • •

Morgan sent three ships to go clear the way at Chagres. There were some quiet groans when it was announced that Bradley would command. There was no arguing, though; away they went, and Bradley's luck was with them almost from the first, as they ran into southeasterly gales. For a week the *Mayflower* and her consorts fought their way toward the Main. Her timbers worked so in the crossing seas that she leaked no end, and the pumps were manned watch and watch.

So one evening Captain Bradley sent John down to the powder magazine, to feel if all was dry there. *Feel,* because he couldn't see; Morgan had given strictest orders (as you might imagine) about what would happen to any fool caught groping around near powderkegs with a light.

It was all John could do to find the lock, clinging to the cage-door in the dark. He got it open at last and stepped through, groping forward. There—waist height, there were stacked kegs. He turned his head in the darkness. He could smell rats, and bilge, and mold, and all manner of filth; he could hear the groaning of the ship's timbers, and the muffled shrieking and knocking that was rats fighting somewhere. But did he hear water trickling? He couldn't tell.

He crouched down and felt around his feet. It seemed dry enough. He stood, and reached out until he encountered something: more stacked kegs. How far back? Three rows? Four? What about the bulkhead beyond them, was that dry?

That was when John put his hand down on another hand. He sucked in breath for a great yell; with the breath came a scent he knew. The hand twisted and took hold of his own, and it was a little hand, and soft. John steadied himself. A voice spoke out of the darkness.

"John," it said. He hadn't heard but one other word spoken in that voice, yet John recognized it. It was his girl from the beach.

"Lass!" he cried. "What—"

She sidled close to him, squeezing his hand tight. "Please," she said, "you must help me."

John's heart was jumping like a big, happy dog, yet his head kept some rule. "I'd walk over coals for you, dearie," he said. "Only, you didn't ought to be here! This ain't no place for a little maid. Wasn't our Admiral himself sending you safe back home? How'd you—"

"I plied the old woman with rum," said the voice in the darkness, sounding just a little sullen. "When she slept, and it was dark, I went over the side and swam to this ship. The watch were drunk too; they never noticed me come up the cable, or slip down here. I won't go back to Jamaica. Not until I've had my revenge."

"What revenge would that be?" asked John, fancying he could almost make out her white flesh glimmering like the Pleiades.

"On Spain," she said. "You're bound for Panama; I know your Admiral's intent, I listened to his councils. I'll go too, and cut Spanish throats if I can."

"Ain't you the brave girl!" said John. "But it's no work for a lady, sweeting. It'll be hard marching, and worse fighting, cruel bad."

"You don't know what's cruel," said the girl. "I know; I saw what happened when we were betrayed. I escaped. I lived, stealing to feed myself, creeping out by night. The Spanish came to be afraid of me. Do you think I can't kill? Do you think I haven't dreamed of killing, every night these five years?"

"Whyn't you talk before? I thought you was a mute."

"Trust comes hard," said the girl, "but I'll trust *you*."

She pressed closer still to John, and lunging up quick she kissed him full on the mouth. Her cold, slender arms slid inside his shirt. What happened then, why, you may guess at, and it may not surprise you; but it surprised John, though he'd been imagining it for some days. They loved, awkward, and constrained crouching there in the pitch dark, and half-painful but white hot all the same.

When they were done he was murmuring that he'd give her anything, anything, he'd storm all the cities in the West Indies and present her with the loot borne on the backs of a thousand chained Spaniards, so she'd only be his girl forever. He didn't hear his mother's voice once.

But the girl said, sharp and clear out of the darkness:

"Just you fetch me a lad's clothes to wear, and a sword and pistol of my own."

"Sweetheart, I will," said John, and staggered away to Felham's slops chest. There he got her loose breeches of canvas and a great coarse-woven shirt, and thoughtfully a roll of bandage to conceal her breasts; for he was all taken with the romance of it, that his little dear should wish to fight beside him. He got her a cutlass and a pistol too, tied with bright ribbon. He got her a red silk scarf to bind up her hair. It fairly broke his heart, then, when he led her up into the starlight, to see that she'd hacked off her long locks somehow.

But John fell in love again, in a twisty kind of way, with the brave, pretty boy who had such fierce eyes. For her sake John gave up his little snug berth forward of the captain's own cabin, and slept as best he could on deck. For her sake John went hungry, and took her his share of dry beef and biscuit. Much he cared for food or sleep, when he crept away to her hiding place and she took him in her arms. She about ravished his soul away to Paradise.

THE CASTLE

It was a week's worth of hard fighting the wind before the *Mayflower* and her consorts came in sight of Chagres Castle on its rock, with the fortress of San Lorenzo firing at them from the biggest guns John had ever seen in his life.

Bradley bid them stand off a safe distance out at sea, while he thought what he might do.

Getting into the Chagres River was treacherous as picking a man's pocket, and the pocket full of broken glass. Bad enough that the castle with its fortress stuck out on a headland into the bay, from which it could hammer anyone passing by; there was a reef placed right at the harbor entrance too, most inconvenient.

"Can we storm them, Captain?" asked John, peering out at Chagres Castle. The ball came long before he heard the cannon's *boom,* and fell short with a fountain of white water. Bradley folded up his spyglass.

"There's no climbing that rock," he said. "And they've the range on us with their guns, damn them. We'll have to go ashore and come at them that way." He took a squint along the coastline. "Pass the word; we'll sail north and look for an anchorage."

Graceful as swans the three ships tacked and glided away, white sails under a mild, blue twilight. John went scrambling down into the stinking darkness, and edged into the tiny cupboard room where he kept his love. The girl was naked, sitting still as an image, with her blade across her knees.

"We're at Chagres," she said.

"Aye," said John. "And I thought up a stratagem, see. If you was to hide in a barrel, we could get you ashore—"

"No," said the girl. "You go ashore. I'll slip over the side when there's none to see, and I'll find you there."

She sounded so cool and certain John never once thought to wonder how in hell she'd manage such a thing. He kissed her, until she laid the blade aside and opened her arms to him. There they kept company together, until the late watch.

Then John parted from her, taking his guns and powder horn, and a cutlass with a keen edge on it. He went above with a heart full of little pink angels, in that black dawn, and no thought to the bloody strife to come.

His messmates were already on deck, watching along the rail as the jungle breathed out its night sounds at them, and the night paled. The *Mayflower* and her consorts had dropped anchor only a league away, in view of San Lorenzo's lookout.

The stars were fading when Bradley gave order for the loading of the boats. Men were rowed ashore. They milled about on the beach, waiting as supplies were brought, shivering to walk on the soft, cold sand, unwilling to go in among the dark trees. Within an hour of sunrise they were sweating, bored with the long wait, as the boats kept going back and forth. Higher the sun rose, glittering on the bright water so it hurt the eyes, and still the boats came and went, and there was a deal of grumbling from the ones who waited in the narrowing strip of shade.

John kept with his messmates, looking out anxious to see if he could spot a little figure dropping from the *Mayflower*. By him, Blackstone and the two *boucaniers* sat, quiet and calm, passing a whetstone back and forth as they put fresh killing edges on their blades. Bob Plum and Pettibone sat either side of the Reverend, on a fallen palm trunk, mopping their faces and complaining of the heat and the flies. The Reverend showed no sign of minding the heat, though he wore his black coat buttoned up high, and a black neck-stock tied tight. He only nodded his head over his big, scarred hands, clasping them together in prayer.

"There's our lieutenant-colonel coming ashore," remarked Blackstone, pointing with his cutlass. John looked out and saw Bradley arriving at last, gazing at the jungle as he stepped from the boat. Someone shouted:

"Columns come to order!" and sand was kicked up in flurries as four hundred men scrambled to their feet and formed ranks, grumbling and muttering.

"How like the army," said Blackstone. "Hardly what one expects of sea-robbers bold and free, eh?"

"Oh, shut your face," said John, looking around for the pennant he had been assigned. He raised it up; it hung fluttering limply in the glare of the tropical sun. He looked down, blinking his dazzled eyes, and when his vision cleared he saw the girl had slipped in beside him, silent, and stood now at his elbow. She had dressed herself, with her bubbies bound down flat, and tied the red silk scarf about her cropped hair, and smudged her fair countenance with soot.

John heard another gasp. He half turned and saw Dick Pettibone regarding the girl in horror.

"*You*—what are you—" began Pettibone. The girl reached out, swift, and seized Pettibone's arm tight, and muttered something into his ear. Pettibone stepped back, looking appalled, but he said nothing more.

At the head of the column, Bradley was consulting with a villainous-looking fellow, a thief they'd pulled from the Spanish dungeon, who'd volunteered to guide them for sheer spite's sake. Bradley's second-in-command, Captain Norman, walked up and joined them, gesturing. They seemed to agree on something; Bradley squinted at the sun, just then dead overhead, and swept his arm up in the signal to march.

Two hours they plodded along, keeping to the beach where they could, fighting uphill and inland through the jungle where the headlands stuck out into deep water. The first column tried to hack their way through with cutlasses, though the *boucaniers* among them frowned and shook their heads; that was no way to do it, they said, it only blunted blades and made a lot of noise. In the end Bradley agreed with them and gave orders to lay off. The *boucaniers* fell out and went ahead, slipping through the branches without noise, and the rest followed. The girl marched by John's side, steadfast, without complaint.

Over the last hill, and there were the bastions of San Lorenzo, peeping between the trees. The column of men fanned out now, moving in a thin line through the jungle, and came to a wide cliff's edge where the land had slid, leaving the trees with their roots hanging out over the air. John parted the leaves with his standard and peered down.

"No more than six or seven feet," he announced. "We can jump it easy."

So the men pushed forward, dropping down one by one through the brush and scrambling to their feet below; and the first wave to land turned and stared about them amazed, and soon horrified.

The forest had been cleared from where they stood to the very walls of San Lorenzo itself, making an open plain where there wasn't so much as a blade of grass to cover them. John could see the Spanish gunners on the near palisade grinning at them, they were that close. He had just time to notice that before he heard the first shots cracking, and a scream from somewhere on his left, and then John was scrambling for his life back up the slope to the cover of the jungle.

"Back! Back!" Bradley was howling, and something big struck the earth right by John's head with a *whap* and traveled deep into the clay.

"Ba—" Bradley's voice broke off. John reached desperately for the creepers, and saw Jacques and Blackstone reaching down to grab for him. He caught their hands and they pulled him to safety. Other men were being hoisted up, here and there among the trees. John saw Bradley being dragged out between two stout fellows, and him bleeding and cursing a blue streak. Down below, though, there lay a score of men who hadn't turned in time, pierced through with shot or the arrows of the Indian archers. Some were crying for their mothers. Some were quiet for ever and aye.

The Spanish indulged themselves in catcalling and threatening no end, or at least that was what John reckoned they were doing. He was too busy binding up Bradley's leg to pay much attention.

"What do we do, Captain?"

Bradley had bitten a dry stick clean in half, in his pain. Now he spat it out and glared at John.

"Bring up the grenades!" he said. "And send one of the *boucaniers* to reconnoiter. Where's that damned thief? I'll cut his heart out—"

"He's down there," said Blackstone, crawling close. "If he betrayed us, he's been well and truly paid for his trouble."

Some men crept up into the trees, and from the screen of leaves took potshots at the Spanish, who kept up an answering fire. In a while, Jago climbed back down.

"Pretty bad," he said. "Other side of the field, deep deep ditch, the palisadoes they go up straight on the other side. He runs across the field alive, get his death falling down the ditch."

"We ain't getting at 'em that way," said John. "We better fall back, sir, whiles we think what to do."

"I'll shoot you dead," said Bradley, baring his teeth. "Come back here, you sons of bitches! Dick Norman! Take two squadrons with grenades and charge again! They're only wooden walls!"

John, peeping out through the leaves, saw what he meant; for instead of being stone, San Lorenzo's bastions were made of wooden planks shored up with posts. Fire might do for them; and John understood why so much trouble had been taken rowing all those barrels of grenades ashore. They were dragged forward now and handed around, and Captain Norman stepped to the fore and led his two squadrons down on that bare ground, where they rushed screaming for the walls.

It was a slaughter. They never got so far as the ditch; half their number were mown down on that field. Though one or two of them managed to hurl their grenades across the ditch and into the dry brush at the base of the palisades, it was no use. The fires caught readily enough, the weather being very dry, but the Spanish soon flung down enough sand to smother them. Bradley, propped up against a tree, watched it all and swore bitterly.

John watched too, and thought he had never seen such a close likeness of Damnation: the dead and dying sprawled across that bare field, frying in the heat and glare of the sun, and here and there a grenade bursting in the dead hand that clutched it, or sputtering down to add its acrid smoke to the smoke coming up out of the ditch.

Captain Norman ordered a retreat, like a sane man, and the survivors regrouped under cover of the trees. There proceeded a fierce debate amongst them, the two opposing points being: that they could not take San Lorenzo, and that they must take San Lorenzo. As these points went back and forth for the next hour, getting louder and more profane with each repetition, John listened close to his mother telling him that there was no sense in him getting himself killed.

He looked round on his messmates with a cool eye. The Reverend and his mates hadn't been out yet; they sat quiet and pale, all three seemingly praying together. Jago and Jacques were enjoying a quiet pipe, passed between them. Blackstone had stretched out with his hat over his face, cold-blooded fellow that he was. The girl sat still, looking through the leaves at the battlements of San Lorenzo. John sidled up to her.

"See, now?" he said, quiet. "See what a nasty business this is? You've had your soldier march; it's time to go back to the beach. Much safer place for a pretty girl. I'll take you; let's just slip away, sweeting, eh?"

She never so much as looked up at him. "I'd not have taken you for a coward," she said. "A big man like you."

John fell all over himself trying to deny he'd meant to desert; he was only afeared for *her*, on his life and honor, and had meant to come straight back and storm the wall himself, single-handed, once he'd seen her to safety. His mother wailed in his ear, asking was he mad, that he'd rather face death than disgust in the eyes of a slip of a girl. John made no answer to that.

The girl shrugged at his fine words anyway. "Not long until sunset now," was all she said.

John walked away feeling like an empty wine-skin, and saw Blackstone sitting up, grinning at him.

"What are you smiling at?" said John, cross as a bear.

"The follies of the heart," said Blackstone. "You may as well rest yourself, man. Unless they've sent out a party to come around and attack from the trees, we're safe enough here; and when night falls it'll be a different game altogether."

And so it was. Bradley bawled and thundered, persuading the men they'd be worse off if they deserted now. Maybe all he'd needed to make him a decent commander had been pain and rage; if he'd shouted like that when he'd been cruising the Main, he'd have had better luck. Word went out that they'd try again come night, and all parties settled down to wait for dark.

The sun dipped low; the shadows slanted away, and the wind rose, and changed, and blew from the jungle out to sea. All around, in the under-brush, men were getting up and priming their muskets, and rummaging in the crates of grenades.

Then the sun was gone. Bob Plum got up in the purple gloom and led Reverend Hackbrace to the edge, and parted the branches to show him the Spanish gunners outlined against the red sunset. He began talking to him in a low voice. John saw the Reverend begin to shake and clench his hands.

Blackstone watched them sidelong as he wound a twist of slow-match through his buttonhole. Jago and Jacques appeared from somewhere—they came and went silent as cats—and waited beside him on the edge, looking through the screen of leaves. John glanced over at Captain Bradley, who was limping along looking up at the musketeers he'd stationed in the trees. Bradley muttered something to Norman; Norman turned and passed the word, and all along the ragged line men grabbed up grenades and poised themselves to drop.

John felt a squeeze on his hand. He started and looked round. The girl pulled him down, kissing his dry mouth. There was a light in her eyes like the green flare before a thunderstorm. He had a moment's unease at what anyone should think, seeing him kissing a pretty boy. Then he decided he didn't give a damn, them being all about to die anyway.

So they dropped, stumbling down the ploughed-up slope, and ran like madmen but without a sound, as they'd been ordered. Meanwhile the musketmen in the trees sent covering fire, picking off the Spanish sentries backlit so nice and sharp as they were. It was what should have been done the first time, and it worked now. Shadows skipping over the bodies of the dead, near invisible in the twilight, the grenadiers were to the ravine and down one side before the Spanish knew what was what.

Their Indians saw what was happening first, and had the presence of mind to start shooting arrows down into the ditch. Even so, John saw the Reverend, frothing at the mouth, going up the side like a spider scaling a web, tearing at the rotten wood with his nails. Bob Plum followed him close, shoving lit grenades all along the base of the wall and scrambling on. *Fifty pieces of eight for them,* thought John.

He lit a grenade whilst running and lobbed it high and far as he could. The Spanish sentries had made themselves a nice palm-thatched sunshade that ran the length of the rampart, for their ease in keeping watch under the noonday sun no doubt; but it made a pretty target for firebombs now. John missed, but heard his grenade burst and voices howling behind the rampart.

Jago dashed past him, a glint of white teeth in the smoke, his knotted hair bristling. John looked up just as the arrow struck home clean through the saddle of Jago's shoulder. The force knocked him back on his heels; Jacques was by him at once crying, *Petite, ma petite,* but Jago's eyes were red and mad. He pulled the arrow out, not seeming to feel it at all, and shoved it down the muzzle of his musket, making to fire it back at the bowman.

"Wait!" The girl appeared out of the smoke, pulling the red silk from her head. "Here!" She tied the silk about the arrow's shaft and held an end of slow-match to it. It kindled up bright straightaway.

"Ah!" Jago was laughing as he took aim. *Bang,* and the arrow flew like a bird and lighted in the palm-thatch sun shade, lighted indeed, for the leaves curled back and the bright fire spread and licked along. The girl was laughing, they were all laughing to hear the shrieks from above as the Spanish tried to put the blaze out, but it seemed all their sand was gone.

By the firelight John could see plenty of arrows scattered along the bottom of the ditch, as could all the other grenadiers. He grabbed up one and tore off a piece of his shirt for kindling; all along the ditch others were doing the same; up went the flight of little phoenixes, and some stuck in the thatch and some in the wooden palisades. The inshore wind, gusting down the ravine, fanned the flames like Hell.

From behind them came a roar as Bradley gave the order for the marksmen to advance, and John heard them dropping from the trees now, charging the field, coming on toward the ravine. They kept up a steady fire the whole time, reloading on the run. John scrambled to and fro, finding dropped grenades, relighting them and pitching them as fast and as far as he could go; for he had a strong right arm then. The girl flitted here and there, bringing him grenades too, and they laughed together to hear the Spanish scream so, when the whole of the burning thatch collapsed on the walls.

Just as the marksmen came to the ditch, something behind the wall exploded, with a crash to tear open the sky and a blaze of light like day come early; John heard later it was the biggest of the Spanish guns. Red-hot bronze shrapnel came out of the air and fell like hail, wounding all men alike. Someone yelled beside him and he turned to see Blackstone on the ground, clutching his head. Someone else yelled above him. John looked up and saw the palisade beginning to collapse, eaten through as it was with flame, and a great wave of earth and stones burst from behind it and came down the slope into the ditch.

When John knew anything again he was clear down the far end of the ditch, toward one of the other bastions, and he and the girl were dragging Blackstone between them. Blackstone was slick all down one side with blood, and he was saying over and over, "My ear, my ear, they've blown off my fucking ear," and there were more explosions sounding.

The palisades had collapsed nearly all the way across, and the earth they had had packed behind them all gone down into the ditch, filling it in in some places, so Captain Bradley's marksmen had a nice open window through which to shoot at the Spanish who ran to and fro, exposed as though they were on a theater stage. Some were trying to put out the fires; some were fighting hand-to-hand with privateers who'd crawled up over the fallen palisade. John caught a glimpse of one unlucky bastard fending off Reverend Hackbrace, who was on him like God's own werewolf.

But the defenders weren't done for yet; some among their officers were rallying to drag over guns from the other batteries, aiming them out at the gap to slay all comers that way and any of the marksmen out there in the night. They loaded the cannon with musket-balls and fired point-blank into the waves of men coming up the hill, and washed them back down in blood. Others of the defenders had run and fetched their own grenades, or even chamber pots, flinging down anything they had to repel the privateers.

John was all for finding a cool place in the dark and waiting for the bullets to do their work up above, once they'd bound up poor dear Blackstone's bloody head; but the girl went sprinting over the fallen earth with her cutlass drawn, screaming like an Irish witch. To John's amazement he found himself scrambling after her, and so was Blackstone, dodging grenades and shite. They all three gained the top at about the same moment, and looked straight into the faces of the Spanish defenders, and then it got nasty for a long while.

Now and again John had a moment to notice things, over the red hours; that he was wet to the elbows like a butcher, and that Dick Pettibone had somehow gotten his fat bulk up the slope and was cutting the throats of the wounded, and that the girl seemed to be everywhere at once, lithe as the flames that spread, and spread, and that the Reverend was roaring out a hymn that wasn't about any little lambs, and that at last the gray dawn was showing up eerie and cold beyond the walls.

The Spanish weren't firing anymore now, whether from a wish to save powder for the last assault or because they'd used it all, John couldn't guess. He slumped down behind a mass of smoldering timbers, trying to get his breath, watching dully as the girl bound up a cut that had laid his upper left arm open. He wondered when that had happened. He could see down the causeway the fallen earth had made, where Captain Bradley was in conference with a group of *boucaniers,* Jago and Jacques amongst them. They were passing their muskets to a couple of Bradley's aides, who collected them like bundles of firewood. Then they drew pistols and cutlasses.

"It'll be close work, now," said the girl, laughing. John looked at her in wonderment. Then he understood: they were readying for the last push, and Bradley must intend for the *boucaniers* to be the spearhead. It seemed like a dream, or a story someone was telling him. If he turned his head he could see down to the green trees and the Chagres River winding gray away between them, and one and then two and three canoes moving up its placid water. *Deserters,* he thought. *Don't blame them.*

The sun came up, red as a wound in all the smoke and stink; the Spanish had retreated to the inner buildings, seemingly, for there was no sign of them but the dead ones on the bastions. There came a shout from below. John looked down and saw the *boucaniers* formed up for the charge. Over they came, yelling, *Victoire! Victoire!*

The Spanish began to fire again, but it was scattered now, and as the Frenchmen rushed over the edge the other privateers followed after them.

Captain Bradley came up and was cut down almost at once by a bullet that broke his shin, so he rolled screaming on the bloody ground. John staggered to him and gripped his leg tight; Dick Pettibone appeared out of the haze and helped him bind and set the leg, and splint it as best they could. So they missed the end of the fight, when the last of the Spanish holed up in the inner castle and their officers died to a man. John and Pettibone dragged Bradley behind a broken wall, into a patch of shade.

John sat beside him, meaning only to wait until the shooting had stopped. When he opened his eyes, the shade had gone clean away. He was all alone. The noonday sun was broiling straight down, and flies were buzzing to celebrate the taking of Chagres Castle.

• • •

John went limping like a ghost among the dead and wounded, hoping to find a bottle of rum somewhere that might ease his pains. The slash on his arm had bled through its bandage; he had taken a couple of arrow-points in the fat of his leg, sometime in the long night, and a musket-ball had creased his scalp, and he'd hit his head on something hard enough to raise a lump like a goose egg.

He didn't know where the girl had gone. He had a sick fear of finding her dead, but could not stop himself searching, wandering to the heap of piled corpses to look into every staring face. He was crying as he tottered along, in an absent-minded way, like a child will do. Ned Cooper was lying there amongst the slain, his old shipmate from the *Clapham,* but nobody else he knew.

None of the living paid him any mind. Privateers were ordering gangs of slaves and prisoners about; the wreckage of battle was being cleared away and the defenses already being repaired. The Spanish dead were being pitched down the cliff into the sea by their weeping fellows.

Tom Blackstone came blinking out of one of the doorways, shielding his eyes from the sunlight. His head was bandaged, his arm in a sling; he was pale and filthy and looked to be in a savage temper.

"Looking for your little friend?" he said to John. "I shouldn't fear for—*him*. *He* preserved *his* life through the fray. Pettibone tried to get *him* to tend the wounded, but the, ah, *boy* went off with a gang to round up slaves."

"Oh, bugger off," said John, ever so grateful.

"I ask myself: 'Has this pirate swain any wits at all? For surely a certain vicious little fury will do for him when she's weary of his embrace, or else our dear Admiral will have him hanged for debauching a maiden fair.'"

"It wasn't like that," said John.

"Oh, no, of course not." Blackstone stared down at the heap of dead men. He picked at the dried blood in his beard. "I'll keep your secret for you; none of my concern, after all. What will you do for me in return?"

"I don't know," said John.

"Well, I'll tell you. Should I get my death-wound on this wretched venture, perhaps you might get word of it back to a certain lady in Port Royal." Blackstone squinted at John, then leaned down and took hold of the arrow-stump protruding from John's thigh. One quick jerk and he had it out, taking a flap of skin with it. John stared down dumbly at the little gush of blood, too surprised to curse. Blackstone held the arrowhead up, examining it. "Look at that edge! A man could shave with that."

"Did you find your prince?" John groped, pulled away his neckerchief and held it to the wound.

"Haven't had time to look, yet. I hope he wasn't being kept in the inner redoubt; they were all slaughtered, in there."

"Or you been diddled again, I reckon, and he wasn't never here in the first place," said John, spiteful.

"Entirely likely, damn your eyes," said Blackstone, tossing the arrowhead away. He glanced over at the prisoners who were at work on the seaward battlements. "But let's you and I take a walk over yonder, messmate. One never knows who might have had the sense to beg for quarter."

They went shambling to the parapet together, looking like a couple of beggars, and saw Jacques lounging in a shady corner, with his musket trained on the prisoners. The Spaniards were praying at each body before they cast it over the edge, and every time they made the sign of the cross Jacques would too, solemn and respectful, before pointing his musket at them again.

Blackstone led John promenading up and down once or twice before John realized what he was about; that was when one of the Spaniards noticed John's boots, and nearly dropped his end of a dead capitano. His mates swore at him, or at least that was what it sounded like to John, and he seemingly apologized and hauled the body up again. All the while he was praying at the edge, though, he kept his red-rimmed eyes on John's boots. Blackstone grinned.

"*Je v'lui parler*," he said to Jacques, jerking his thumb at the Spaniard. Jacques nodded, crossed himself and took aim at the hapless man. Blackstone pulled him aside.

"You like the boots?" he said. The Spaniard, who was small and thin and wretched-looking, said something in Spanish, not surprisingly. Blackstone talked back to him in the same tongue. The gist of what they said was, as John found out after:

Prisoner: Please, sir, you are too late.

Blackstone: I hope you're not going to disappoint my friend with the fine boots. See what a big man he is? He could flatten you with his fist.

Prisoner: Please, please, señor, I am not to blame. We kept the Englishman here as long as we dared.

Blackstone: Oh, dear, my friend won't be happy to hear that. I might be able to prevent him from hurting you, but you must tell me everything.

Prisoner: If you had come sooner, all had been well. It was the safest place we could think of to keep him. How were we to know your Enrique Morgan would be so mad as to come here? Now the Englishman has been taken to a new hiding-place.

Blackstone: Gone again, is he? Why, damn your soul.

Prisoner: Did you bring the money, senor? I could serve as your guide thence.

Blackstone: Did I bring the money? You impudent little ape, I'll find my own way, with fire and sword. When I tell my friend here what you just said, he'll throw you down the cliff alive.

Prisoner: Oh, in God's name, señor, have mercy! I am only a clerk!

Blackstone: Then tell me this much: Why all this mummery? Unless you have been lying, and the Englishman was never here.

Prisoner: No! No! Look, señor, here's proof!

He drew a leather bag from out of the depths of his shirt, digging in it. He held up something that glinted in the sunlight. Blackstone snatched it from him, and studied it closely. John leaned down and had a look at the thing; it was a seal-ring with a curious device on the shield, such as great folks have painted on the doors of their carriages.

Prisoner: I was bid to give you this, and tell you to come to the river-post called Torna Caballos. That is all I know. Please, señor, I am not to blame, I am a poor creature.

Blackstone turned away in disgust, taking John by the arm.

"Another damned feint," he said. "Let's go see if we can find some wine."

· · ·

You may have heard tales of all the merry times to be had when a city is sacked on the Spanish Main: all the drinking, and looting, and whoring, and happy freebooters lying unconscious in piles of plunder. There was none of that at Chagres Castle, at all.

Captain Bradley lay sweating in a fever, but his shattered leg was cold. If a man were at all inclined to be fanciful, he might almost see the black-robed figure with the scythe waiting patiently in a corner, just passing the time in a game of primero with War and Pestilence. Captain Norman stalked about hollow-eyed and sleepless, seeing to the repair of the defenses; for John hadn't been the only one to notice the canoes escaping up the Chagres, and everyone reckoned it was a race to see who arrived first, Morgan with the rest of the fleet (please God) or Spanish troops come to the relief of their comrades.

The first night's watch fell to John and his messmates, by the open palisade. They'd only a low basket of coals to warm themselves, as a cheery fire would have blazed out through the fallen wall good as an invitation for any snipers who cared to pick them off.

John sat with his head in his hands, feeling low. His skull ached and his wounds stung, but all he cared for was that the girl hadn't come back, and nobody seemed to have seen her.

"It's on your own conscience," said Dick Pettibone, shrill as a fishwife. "You ought to have known better than to have brought that poor child. She was half mad, after what she'd suffered. Then, to think of her being pawed by a great brute like you! And now, I don't doubt she's run mad in the forest, and will perish miserably."

"Run mad maybe, but I doubt very much she'll perish," said Blackstone. "You didn't see her fighting! A more bloodthirsting harpy I never saw." He looked sidelong at John. "She's left you, you great lout, and you ought to be grateful. Can't you see that she kept with you only to serve her purposes? You got her where she wished to go, and then it was hail and farewell. If I were you I'd be grateful I still had my prick."

"So you should," agreed Jago, where he lay with his head in Jacques' lap. "She fight like a devil, but they are heartless, heartless."

"So *you* say," said John.

"Men are more heartless than women," said Bob Plum. "Do they think twice about deserting their faithful wives? Do they care for the helpless infants left to starve? *Oh* no, they go swaggering off to the arms of other women—or to ale houses—or the wars—perfidious, treacherous beasts!"

The others turned their heads to stare at him. Reverend Hackbrace, so bound up from a score of wounds he looked like a great long roll of bandage, shifted uncomfortably where he sat.

"Now, then, Bob, let us keep our tempers," he said. "Scripture tells us—"

"*Oui*, Scripture! What about the sin of Eve, eh?" said Jago. "Slut mother sleep with the Serpent and eat of the fruit, get us all thrown out of Paradise. And Jezebel. And Salome."

"Delilah," said Jacques.

"And Delilah!"

"That's true," said Bob, looking down at his feet. "I must bear in mind the counsels of Saint Paul. Women are of a more natural disposition to sin, alas. After all, there are no male whores."

"I beg your pardon," said Blackstone. "You have never been at Court, or you'd never say such a thing."

"Ain't you never heard of the Grand Turk?" John lifted his head. "'Course there's boy whores."

"There are?" Bob's eyes were wide. The Reverend cleared his throat.

"The sins of the people of the plain, Bob," he said. "The crime of Sodom."

"Buggery," said Blackstone. Bob's eyes got wider.

"You mean people are *still* doing that?" he said. Jago began to snicker.

"Don't be an imbecile, Bob," said Pettibone waspishly.

"But—but why hath not the Lord rained down fire and brimstone upon them?" cried Bob.

"I often ask myself that question, in the still watches of the night," said Blackstone.

"No doubt the Almighty is waiting His vengeance for the Last Trumpet," said the Reverend.

"Yes, that must be the case," Bob agreed. "How dreadful!"

"Perhaps a more edifying topic of conversation might be begun," said the Reverend. John listened in wonder; it was the first time he had ever heard the Reverend say so much at one go, in his ruined-sounding voice. "For example, it might be pleasant to contemplate what we shall do with the riches awaiting us at Panama."

"So it might," said Blackstone. "For my part, I'll set up as a planter. Build myself a grand house, live in style; perhaps in Virginia or Carolina. The weather is more temperate there, so I hear."

"I thought of doing that," said John. "Or setting up in a shop, you know. I was going to settle down with—" He choked back what he had been about to say, and hated himself for the hot tears that welled in his eyes.

"No, you wouldn't have done," said Blackstone, not unkindly. "You'll spend it all on a spree, my friend, and go to sea again."

"I ain't like those poor, stupid bastards you see in the gutter," John protested. "I could have been a bricklayer, you know."

"Well, well perhaps you may yet. What about you gentlemen?" Blackstone looked at the Reverend and his mates. "But why do I even ask? Surely you'll establish a mission for the conversion of the benighted Indian."

"No, sir, we will not," said Dick Pettibone. "The Reverend has humbly acknowledged that he lacks the patience for missionary work."

"I am too great a sinner," said the Reverend mournfully.

"Being as he is no gentle persuader, he is nevertheless a brilliant man of God," said Pettibone. "We have resolved to buy a quiet country retreat where he will complete his great scholarly work, so unfortunately inter-rupted when we were obliged to fly from Yorkshire."

"It is called *One Thousand Canonical Instances Wherein the Claim to Author-ity of the Bishop of Rome Is Refuted*," said Bob proudly. "With appendices."

"Really," said Blackstone. "And what will the two of you do?"

"Why, keep house for him," said Bob. "A-and perhaps engage in small farming."

"I see," said Blackstone. Jago coughed in a pointed sort of way.

"And take ourselves virtuous wives," said Dick Pettibone. "Of course."

"Now, what in hell do you need a wife for?" John asked.

"There is more to a marriage than swiving," said Pettibone, with great dignity.

"Than what?" said Bob.

"Swiving," said John, and called it by another name. Bob reddened and fell silent.

"What about the two of you?" Blackstone inquired of the *boucaniers.*

"We need nothing," said Jago proudly. "Buy ourselves the *tabac,* buy the powder and shot. New muskets, belike, eh, *mon plus cher?* Go back to Tortuga, we got Paradise already."

"Adam avant l'erreur," said Jacques, nodding.

"If you've such a damned Paradise, what are you out of it for?" said John crossly.

"The revenge," said Jago, with a red light in his eyes. Jacques sighed and shook his head.

"On whom, exactly?" inquired Blackstone.

"All of them," said Jago. "Spain specially. When I was little boy in Marseilles, my monsieur, he keep me in the golden cage. I wear the ribbon, like the kitten, eh? He feed me the candies, sweet rice, sweet wines. I sleep on his sheets, wear the perfume. Then he gamble away everything and English lord win me, give me to his lady to wear the turban. She make me stand in the livery by her door. But Sir Robert gamble too, and then Don Pedro win me. I am nothing, me, but the object."

"C'était il y a un longtemps, mon cher," murmured Jacques.

"Don Pedro ship me off to Hispaniola. Poor little me, never before worked in the fields! I am beat half to death. When I get big, I kill him and run away. Steal the boat, go adrift, almost die of the thirst. Wash up on the little island. There was Jacques.

"My Jacques, he's too poor orphan, steal the game on the rich man's land. They catch him, make him row the prison galley. Galley taken by the pirates, Jacques set free, turn pirate. Spanish catch him and take him to be hanged. Beat him bad. But their ship goes on the reef off the little island, they drown, he swim ashore. When he find me, carry me to his refuge with great *tendresse.*

"My Jacques, he is the, the philosopher. He explain to me: the black, the poor, neither one creatures of reason, say the rich men. They make us only the beasts. *Eh bien,* then we are beasts, and free. We prey on them like the lions, like the wolves. What they have, we are free to take, if we can take; or die free. There is no, no *coupable* for the beasts. No sins."

Jacques said something long and earnest in French, which Jago translated to mean that he and Jacques, playing at being animals, had found their way back into Eden: freedom, and true comradeship. Free air, the forest and the sea, all things held in common between true brothers, far from the jealous eyes of other men or wicked whores. He said further, that he hoped as how Jago might slake his thirst for revenge soon and give over his anger, so they could go back to their island.

"It is indeed a noble idyll," said Bob Plum, "but for being Godless."

They all looked at Bob in wonderment, except for Dick Pettibone, who hid his face in his hands, and the Reverend, who was gazing into the coals contentedly, as though he watched the damned burning there.

• • •

For a week they worked on the bastions of San Lorenzo, building them up with as much effort as they'd expended in bringing them down. John, who was reckoned able-bodied compared to some of the others, was sent into the jungle with a gang of prisoners to cut wood and haul logs back through the heat and stink. He searched the green shadows, shading his eyes with his hands, hoping to catch a glimpse of a white leg or a peering face; but he never saw his girl.

He worked with the grave-digging detail too, putting the wounded away in their eternal beds as they died, and he looked closely at each gray face as the dead were sewn into their shrouds; but none of them were the girl.

He wandered amongst the company in the evenings, from watch-fire to watch-fire, questioning all whether they'd seen a young lad in the fighting, no more than fifteen, wearing sailcloth breeches and a blue shirt. He said how the lad was his cousin, run away to the West Indies after listening to pirate tales, and how he'd felt obliged to look out for him for his mother's sake. Some had seen the boy that night, and some hadn't; some had seen him since the fighting, but couldn't recollect where. None could tell him where to find her.

• • •

"The fleet!" roared the lookout. There was a rush to the wall, to stare out at the wide sea. The crowd parted to let Captain Norman through, with his spyglass, but the sharper-eyed had already made them out: the foremost of Morgan's ships, hull-down yet on the horizon. Norman closed his glass with a snap, and looked ever so relieved as he said:

"Bleeding Jesus, not before his time. Run up the colors!"

So the flag was hoisted up, the English colors true and plain. A shot was fired, and in the anchorage below, the *Mayflower* and her sister ships, which had been brought down the coast after the victory, ran up their colors too.

The fleet came on under a following wind, swift as gulls gliding across the sea, and how it gladdened the hearts of them on the walls to see the size of that armada! Morgan's own ship the *Satisfaction* came foremost of them all.

"There's the Admiral himself, by God!" said John, waving his hat. "See him, on the quarterdeck?"

"What a brave fellow he looks!" said Bob Plum.

"Do you suppose he's wondering where his little sweetheart got to?" said Blackstone at John's elbow. John shivered, and it seemed to him that Morgan turned his dark face up just then and looked him in the eye, a sober questioning sort of look.

"What are they about?" said a seaman on John's other side. "They're making dead for the reef!"

"Hard over to starboard!" shouted Captain Norman, waving like a madman.

But the *Satisfaction* came on straight into the harbor, with all her crew whooping and calling from the waist like a pack of merry-andrews, and only Morgan, with sudden alarm in his countenance, reading the faces above him. He turned and shouted an order, and the helmsman seemed to wake up and tried to put her hard over. No use; the *Satisfaction* ploughed into Laja Reef, *smash!* Over went her foremast, yards and shrouds and blocks and all, onto her bowsprit, dangling, as the waving apes on her deck were thrown off their feet.

And while John and his mates were gaping from the castle walls, hardly able to credit what they'd just seen, here came the stately *Port Royal*, and where her helmsman's eyes were was anybody's guess, for she sailed straight into the reef too. Then two more of their number followed close behind, as the sea slewed the *Satisfaction* and the *Port Royal* around, so the newcomers pushed them forward across the reef as across a tabletop, with an almighty grinding of keels. In less time than it takes to tell, the four were one knotted wreck together. There was an appalled silence.

Morgan still stood on his tilted quarterdeck, staring, clutching the rail. He glanced upward at Captain Norman. He bared his white teeth in a grin, though John thought it looked more like a grimace of pain; then, quite deliberately, he threw his head back and shouted with laughter. The sound of his merriment echoed off the great rock, loud, long peals, as who should say it was a prime joke!

Uncertainly at first, the men began to laugh with him.

"Damnation, there's a bold-faced bastard!" said Blackstone. He applauded, and all around the men began to cheer Harry Morgan.

And in cheers and laughter they brought him off the wreck of the *Satisfaction,* as the rest of the fleet steered carefully to safe anchorage, and led him up to see what good work they'd done.

By nightfall it was all transmuted to Morgan's Luck; for hadn't they managed to get all the stores he'd brought them out of the holds of the wrecks, good beef and corn, and rum too? And only one person killed on the reef, think of that! (And that was only the old, mad Welshwoman, who, finding herself unwatched, had crept below to partake of spirits in a quiet corner, and been too drunk or amazed when the water rushed in to save herself.)

And the ships were only ships, after all—soon enough Harry Morgan would take new ones from the Spanish. And if a lot of good fellows had died in the taking of Chagres Castle, well, that was the way of war, and there'd be a greater share of plunder for everyone else. At least Bradley had hung on long enough for Morgan to take his hand, before breathing his last.

John cheered with the rest, even as he labored up the narrow stair cut in the face of the rock, laden down with sacks of dried beef from the *Satisfaction*'s hold. Only one thing made him uncomfortable, and that was that Harry Morgan had spotted him in the crowd, as they'd brought the Admiral into Chagres Castle. He sore regretted now all the effort he'd expended making sure Morgan knew his name and face. His mother's voice told him Morgan knew everything he'd done, and he was for the rope's end. He replied in short words, telling his mother's voice to hush.

So it gave him a shrewd old turn when Captain Norman sought him out, that evening where he sat drinking with his messmates, and told him the Admiral wanted a quiet word with him.

• • •

John was shown into what had been the castellan's rooms, and then Norman's command post. It looked for all the world like the Justice's office in London, with a big table and a Turkey carpet, and Morgan sitting at the table in a big chair just as the Justice had sat, with the lamplight flickering on his lean, dark face, and glinting on his black eyes.

"How might I be of service, Admiral sir?" said John, saluting smartly.

"John James, is it?" said Morgan, looking at him.

"Aye, Admiral sir," said John.

"You were one of the lads found the girl, at Old Providence," stated Morgan.

"Aye, sir," said John.

"I meant to send her to Jamaica, you know," said Morgan, never taking his eyes from John's. "To keep her as far away from harm as I might. I was sending her home in the *Diana*. Wouldn't you have done the same?"

"I reckon I would have, sir," said John.

"I believe she is my goddaughter," said Morgan, and John felt as cold as though Death had clapped him on the shoulder right heartily. "I thought she might recognize me. I couldn't get her to speak; I thought her too frightened to speak, and Christ knows she must have seen enough horrors to take her voice away forever.

"But it seems the girl could speak well enough, when she'd anything to say. I came back to see her, in the evening after Bradley's little fleet sailed; and what should I find but that poor, old, mad bitch, that's dead now, crooning and singing in the empty cabin. *Where's my girl,* quoth I.

"Quoth she: *O, she's gone to fight the Spaniard, that made so great a boast. Revenge, revenge, she'll eat his black heart out. She's told me never to say a word till she was gone. Have I not kept my promise to the letter?*

"And so I lost her again."

John saw well enough that he'd sink himself if he denied anything, so he'd best tell as much of the truth as was to his advantage.

"Admiral sir, she stowed away on the *Mayflower*," he said. "I didn't find her till we was three days out. She said she wanted revenge, right enough; wanted to go cut Spanish throats, on account of what they done at Old Providence."

Morgan kept his dead stare on John, but he nodded ever so slightly.

"And what did you do, John James?"

John took a deep breath. "Why, Admiral sir, I was scared green—a pretty lass like that, amongst the kind of dogs and murderers we had aboard? I knew what you'd said, about killing any man as touched her. So I brought her a lad's clothes, and I talked to her like she was a little child, see, telling her she could march with us when we took Chagres Castle, only she'd have to disguise herself, and stay hid in my cabin until then. And I slept outside on the deck a'nights, Admiral sir, and God strike me down if that ain't the truth."

"And when you came here?"

"I locked her in the cabin, meaning she should stay safe when we went ashore. But damned if she didn't slip out and swim to the beach, and there wasn't nothing for it then but keeping her by me in the fighting."

"Was she wounded in the fray?" Morgan lowered his eyes, at last, to the dagger he was turning between his hands.

"Not she, not that I ever saw," said John. "I was hurt some, but she danced between them musket-balls like a fairy. The last I saw of her, it was midmorning; she was all right in midmorning. Then Bradley, he got it in the leg, and I pulled him behind a wall… and then I reckon I swounded, Admiral sir. Next I knew, the fighting was over. I been searching for her ever since."

"So I am informed," said Morgan.

"Aye. Well," said John. He watched the dagger turning and turning in the lamplight. Morgan said nothing for a long moment, and then:

"You were Bradley's aide-de-camp, I believe?"

"Chief gunner and purser's mate, sir, and I carried the standard on the march," said John. "Me being taller than anybody."

"Why then, John James, you'll be a useful man to keep by me," said Morgan. "Captain Bradley being dead. For, look you, we're going up the river next, and I'll take care you're at my side by day and by night. We'll both keep our eyes open for the girl; and you'd best pray to Jesus we find her, and safe too."

"If we could but find her, sir, I'd forego my share of plunder," said John. "She weren't afraid of nothing, Admiral sir. I never seen a girl so brave."

Morgan turned away and reached for a sheaf of maps.

"In your opinion, now, John James," he said, in his sharp Welsh voice that made it o-pin-*yun*, "is the girl mad?"

John hesitated.

"No," he said at last. "Full of fancies, like a girl, and she hates Spain something powerful. But she's no Mad Maudlin, not she. You didn't see her fight."

Morgan eyed him strangely then. John almost thought he was going to smile, but he looked down instead and opened the sheaf.

"Send in Collier and Morris," he said. "And leave me now."

John saluted and left, brave as though his conscience was lily-white;

though he had to lean against the wall for a minute once he was outside, his knees were knocking so.

• • •

Morgan spent most of a week cleaning up Castle Chagres, until the bastion of San Lorenzo was as secure as before Bradley had taken it; more secure, for Morgan gave orders no thatch was to shade the ramparts, though the sentries' brains roast in the sun like chestnuts. The open ground before the ramparts, where so many had fallen, had become the cemetery, by reason of convenience. Bradley was laid to rest there, among a hundred brave fellows. Like John had done, Morgan walked among the last dead and looked each one in the face.

And he called the Reverend to him and thanked him personal for being the first to get to the bastion, and wrote him out a promissory note for fifty pieces of eight; the which Bob Plum and Dick Pettibone took charge of, lest the Reverend lose it in one of his transports of religious zeal.

Word had got out that the Admiral was looking for a girl who'd stowed away. One eager man came, hat in hand, to say as how he'd glimpsed a white figure paddling away upriver, when they'd gone to the boat landing to see what the Spanish had left behind. This eased John's heartache a little, and maybe Morgan's too.

Dick Pettibone, of all people, came weeping to confess something that had weighed on his mind: which was that he and the old woman, in one of her clearer moments, had fell to gossiping about how the girl must be taught once she was back in Jamaica. They'd spoken of corsets, and face powder, and deportment lessons, and table manners, and the frizzing and curling of hair, and how hard it was to teach a girl to walk in tight shoes with high heels. Dick thought the girl might have overheard and, being used to living wild, decided then and there to slip her cable.

Morgan sent Dick away without punishment, and bent his will to getting ready for the expedition.

THE RIVER

They left a garrison at Chagres Castle, under Captain Norman, and took the main force of fighting men up the Chagres. Morgan gave orders to travel light, on account of the boats and the river being something low that year, for want of much rain. No provender was brought along. They could forage as they went, Morgan said, at the villages and outposts along the river.

Twelve hundred men crowded into canoes, and rafts, and a few little river-craft the Spanish had left behind them.

• • •

For a while the tidal bore took them along the Chagres, flat and mud-colored under the glaring sun. It was pleasant to sit in the waist of the little cargo-boat and look out at the green jungle slipping by, and watch the curious birds and the little monkeys, bearded like old men, that watched them back in wonderment. John might have stretched out for a rest, if there'd been room; but he was crowded in with the Reverend on one side and Tom Blackstone on the other, and Morgan himself behind him by the tillerman.

As the sun rose higher, the force of the tide waned; now it wasn't so pleasant at all, with the sail hanging slack and the green caymans drifting past them, eyeing them contemptuous-like, as their way fell off. Morgan gave the order to set to the oars. John rose to strip off his waterproof jacket, and hit Jago in the eye with his elbow, at which Jacques had something to say. He didn't say much of it, though, before Morgan bid them be quiet, not loud but with such threat in his voice that they shut up one and all and bent to the oars.

An hour or more after noon John saw one bare trunk of a dead tree jutting up on the bank off to starboard, so scoured down by rain and wind it was silver-white, and having besides a funny sort of resemblance to something that doesn't bear mentioning in polite company. He nudged Blackstone and pointed, and there were some sniggers in the boat for a while, until it fell behind them. But a great while later there it was again, to larboard this time; and with a groan John realized that they'd just rowed a long weary way to navigate around a point of land they might have marched straight across in two minutes' time. The river snaked back and forth on itself like this the whole way.

Now and again one of the boats grounded, and all her crew had to clamber out amongst the mangrove roots and work her off, which was a muddy, nasty business, and many a man climbed back onto the thwarts and settled down, only to yell with horror as he spied a leech on his bare leg. They did no real harm; the *boucaniers* amongst them quite coolly took them off by holding the hot bowls of their pipes against the nasty things. John was grateful for his boots, all the same.

And now and again, and more and more as they went higher up the river, the way branched, with two or three or five riverlets flowing into it, and here were the deserted huts of Indians. John and his mates kept a sharp eye out, but no arrows came sailing out at them from anywhere. Men left off rowing and peered through the green shadows, scratching their heads.

Each time, though, Morgan conferred with the tillerman in a low voice and then directed them the way they must go on. He watched from the stern, his face somber, and John could tell he wasn't any too happy about the time this was taking.

By twilight, when the monkeys and the birds began to scream loud, they'd made no more than eighteen miles up the Chagres. Then around a bend, they came out suddenly on an open place and glimpsed roof-beams, and John nudged the Reverend.

"Best you start considering how sinful them Papists are, messmate," he said. "There's our dinner, but we'll have to fight for it."

"What is this place, Admiral?" Tom Blackstone inquired, looking back over his shoulder.

"De los Barcos," said Morgan, drawing his pistol. He was staring at the empty landing. John knew well enough that *barcos* meant boats, like as the place was a port; but there weren't any boats in sight but their own, and not a cry nor a rustle from the huts, but only a thin plume of smoke going up from a bed of gray ash where a fire had been. Even the birds and the monkeys had fallen silent.

"Two volunteers to go ashore," said Morgan, and Jago stood up brisk and jumped lightly to the bank, with Jacques scrambling after him. They walked in warily amongst the sheds and huts, but nothing attacked. Slipping into the trees they circled the place, before coming back and reporting all was deserted. Morgan gave the order to go ashore; a little late, for hungry men were already scrambling up the banks with cutlasses drawn, eager to kill something.

But, as it turned out, the Spanish hadn't left so much as a goat nor a chicken behind to be slaughtered. No maize, no manioc cakes, scarcely even a dry stick of firewood; poking around in the ashes of the open fire, John realized the villagers must have heaped everything they couldn't take away in the boats there and burned it. He noticed something more too; someone had been there since the fire had burned down, for here and there in the ashes were the tracks of small naked feet.

Morgan, following John's gaze, saw them too.

"Would you know the print of her foot?" he asked John, quietly. John swallowed hard and nodded.

"Well then, that's something," said Morgan, and laughed. He had a sick look in his eyes, as though it had just occurred to him (as indeed it had) that the Spanish might well have played this game at every village along the Chagres.

But he turned round and made a fine speech to the rest of his men, about what cowards the Spaniards were, to clear out so before an enemy, and how if they were like to be so bold at Panama herself, why, the privateers might just stroll in and help themselves to the riches there. If there was no food here, what then? He was no weakling, that a night of fasting would do him any harm, nor were they.

There was some grumbling, but most men didn't mind it too much, as it was such a relief to be ashore after being bent over an oar or a paddle all blessed day. So sentry-duty was assigned, and those not on watch at the boats pulled down some of the huts and built cheerful fires, around which they sprawled, lighting up their pipes.

Sleep came sweet and easy to most of them, even with the mosquitoes, but not to John. He lay awake a great while, looking up at the stars and wondering where the girl was, whether he had missed her by hours or days. He got up once and saw Morgan sitting awake in the lead boat, watching the fires ashore; he reckoned Morgan must be wondering the same thing.

· · ·

Whether or not he'd slept much himself, Morgan had them up early and back in the boats, rowing on. This day passed much as the first one had, except it was harder; for the river narrowed and grew shallower, and now and again they came to great snags of dead trees, that must be dredged and hacked and hauled to clear their way. The heat was fearful, except when cloudbursts drenched them; but they were cunning enough to catch the rainwater in every vessel they had, and eased their thirst at least.

The sun had sunk down low in the west when they spotted a great cross on a hillside, made of two logs stripped and carved; Morgan nodded and said, "This should be Cruz de Juan Gallego. Weapons at the ready, if you please."

But when they came up level with it, they saw no village; only a sort of landing and a couple of sheds, and two or three boats abandoned. John guessed that the cross marked only a place to disembark and portage, and talking with the men who'd been up the river before he learned that was so; also that the cross marked a grave.

They'd kept plenty of company with dead men, though, so nobody minded camping there for the night. Morgan did some close talking with the surviving guide who'd come with them from Old Providence, who told him the jungle opened out soon, easy for steady marching.

There were no attacks in the night, not even by the shade of Juan Gallego. Come morning, Morgan left a column of men to guard the boats and took the rest overland, to see whether they mightn't hack a path through the jungle. He kept John close by his side, and Jacques too. Jacques was the first to spot the cut and broken twigs that meant somebody had passed that way not long before; he pointed to them silently. Morgan looked, and said nothing. John thought he saw again the mark of a slender bare foot, tiptoe here and there as though the girl had been running.

A fairy-lass might slip through the trees easy, but an army of a thousand men is something else again. There were nasty things in the jungle too: spiders as big as kittens, scorpions, snakes, swarming ants whose bite was like the touch of a red-hot poker.

When they'd made not more than a mile or two in two hours, Morgan bid them turn back. The cargo-boats couldn't get any further up the river, but the canoes could just be floated; so upriver they went, paddle and dig, in shifts, and twice John fell into the muck and had to scramble back to his perch on the thwarts, with his knees sticking up about his ears, and was roundly cursed by his shipmates for being so big.

But by nightfall they had all made it as far as a place the guide called Cedro Bueno, where the jungle thinned out a bit. Here they camped, and here the mutterings of mutiny grew loud around the campfires; for in all that time they hadn't been able to eat a blessed thing but flower buds and snakes. John was sitting by Morgan when the party of men came to declare their grievances.

The leader was Hendrik Smeeks, because he'd been a barber-surgeon and had an education, and he spoke well. He had short words for Morgan, though: he said it was plain their designs were known to the Spanish, and that all that lay ahead was starvation and ambush, and they'd best turn back now and cut their losses.

Morgan heard him out, and then he began to talk. So artfully! Yes, he said, it would be a great thing if they were ambushed. The Spanish cowards surely had food with them, and horses. He could fancy a lovely bit of broiled horseflesh, sizzling from the fire, belike washed down with the curious dark wine of Peru, or maybe a maize-cake baked in the ashes. And what viands there'd be in Panama! Pickled fish, and sugared cates, beefsteaks, sherry sack such as the rich bishops and cardinals supped, white cheeses and oranges...

Tender and lewd as a procurer he spoke, and all men hearing him groaned with hunger, and felt the painful rumblings of their bellies. John's own mouth watered so he was near to drowning. Morgan said it was never his custom to be a tyrant; he preferred all parties in agreement whenever possible. So, he said, he'd put it to them: whether they would venture on to feasts and plunder, or slink back like starving curs. And if they were to go on, perhaps they'd agree to leave all but a few of the canoes and march overland, now that the way was open and plain?

Which last made excellent sense, to men sick of fighting through the river mud. So they shouted that they'd go on, and some abused Smeeks for a coward. But Morgan graciously bid them leave off, saying that Smeeks was surely as good as the next man. Smeeks stalked away from him scowling. He had his revenge in time, though it cost him dear.

• • •

The next day they set off, with the main body of the men marching and others following in canoes, very much easier now that the damn things weren't packed to the gunwales. A little after sunrise some of the *boucaniers* cried out that they'd spotted an Indian watching them from the woods, and took off in pursuit. They lost him, or there'd likely have been servings of long pork for breakfast, so sharp-set they were.

Around noon Bob Plum, marching near the front, shaded his hand with his eyes and stared hard into the distance.

"There's smoke up there," he said. Just as the words left his mouth, they heard a cry from the guide who had gone ahead in the lightest of the canoes: *Emboscada! Emboscada!*

"Take 'em!" said Morgan, and drawing his cutlass he led the charge, men following him like so many roaring lions. Oh, for grilled flesh, and maize-cakes, and wine! And now they could see the huts clear, and the smoke, and...

Nothing else.

The smoke hung low in the sunlight, putting a haze on things, but even so it was plain the place had been deserted. The Brethren milled around like ants, baffled and then angry. Morgan said something in Welsh, what, John didn't know, but it had a blistering kind of sound to it. He stalked over to the guide, who was just coming up to the bank in the canoe.

"What is this place?" he demanded.

"The outpost of Torna Caballos," said the guide. Blackstone, who'd been poking through some empty provision-bags, turned his head sharply.

Dick Pettibone found a crust of bread, just then, half-charred from being in the ashes, and straightaway another man made a grab for it. Dick backed away, clutching the crust; the other fellow made to open Dick's guts with his cutlass, and only the fact that Morgan drew his pistol and fired stopped him.

"Now by God, the next man to raise his hand will get a bullet between his eyes," said Morgan. "And I leave it to you all to imagine what kind of burial he shall have, look you. Go search the huts! See if any provision was left."

John saw that Blackstone had already slipped off to the huts, and he followed after.

"Wasn't this the place where you were bid to look for your lost prince? Torna Caballos?"

"The same," said Blackstone, throwing back the door of one shelter. Nothing but a dirt floor scattered with straw, and a few dirty hammocks hanging from the ceiling beam.

"Looks like you been done again, then," said John. Blackstone only gave him a disgusted sort of look and went outside to the next hut. From the shouts of disappointment echoing across the clearing, it was plain no food had been left anywhere.

At the fourth hut they tried, something was different; their boots thudded with a hollow noise as they stepped inside. John looked down and saw that the floor was made of wood.

"This must be the mayor's house, eh?" he said. Blackstone looked down absent-mindedly, then looked away; then looked back, with gimlet eyes.

"There's a cellar under this," he said, bouncing experimentally. Sure enough, there was a hollow sort of *boom* from under his feet. John took a straw and bent down, poking it between the planks. It vanished its whole length into the dark without touching anything. He reached for another straw, from the heap that had been placed conveniently on the floor, and Blackstone caught his arm. One scuff of his boot through the straw-heap laid bare the trap door underneath.

John drew his pistol. Blackstone drew his too. With his free hand he caught the ring and threw the door back, aiming down into the dark.

"Don't shoot!" cried someone from below.

John was so hungry, and so tantalized by the thought of hams or wine or whatever else might be hidden down there, that he jumped in straightaway. He landed fair on his feet and saw a fearful-looking Spaniard, and behind him a second figure sitting against the wall. So much he noticed before he saw the provision bags hanging from the ceiling, and as Blackstone descended the ladder John tore a bag down, and stuffed his mouth with dry bread and jerked meat.

The Spaniard had fallen to his knees in entreaty. As he saw John's boots he began to weep with relief.

"Thank God, you have come," he said. "I thought you were the pirates."

John grinned with his mouth full and was on point of telling the poor devil the truth of it, but Blackstone raised his hand.

"Where is His Highness?" he said.

The Spaniard got to his feet. Stepping to one side, he indicated the seated figure.

"Here, señor," he said.

Blackstone looked horrified, and John didn't much blame him. The man who sat there didn't fit John's idea of a prince. He was naked but for some raggedy breeches, without a hair anywhere on his body; not so much as an eyelash. His skin was white as salt and he had a swollen kind of look, like a drowned man. The blank moon-face was as placid as smooth water in a millpond.

Blackstone went down on one knee before him.

"Have I the honor of addressing His Royal Highness, Prince Maurice von Simmern?" he asked.

"He cannot answer you, I am afraid, señor," said the Spaniard.

Blackstone looked round, his eyes blazing. "What have you done to him?" he said.

The Spaniard gave a little cough. "*We* have done nothing, señor. His Highness' lamentable condition is entirely his own doing."

Blackstone got to his feet. "You had better explain."

John had begun to feel a little sick by this time, what with the food he'd gobbled down so fast and the queer way the cellar stank, so he didn't pay as much attention as he might have, but what the Spaniard explained was: that many years before the crew of a Spanish galleon weathered a fearful storm at sea, and put into an islet to repair their gear. There on the sand was a new-wrecked ship, the *Defiance*, and lashed to her mast was a man, still alive.

He was taken prisoner, along with a half-dead servant they found belowdecks, and shipped off for interrogation to Hispaniola. There, the viceroy learned that the prisoner was close kin to the English king in exile (as he was then). The Spanish hadn't loved Oliver Cromwell particularly, so the viceroy put the royal prisoner in rather better rooms than were usually given to English heretics, and then wrote to Spain to ask, what should he do next?

Unfortunately, the royal prisoner, instead of waiting and being ransomed like a sensible man, took it into his head to try to escape. That, at least, was what they learned afterward from the servant.

It seemed he had seen an English play wherein one *Juliet* avoided an enforced marriage by drinking off a potion that made her look dead. She was buried in the family crypt, and woke afterward, and all had been well but for her true love not being privy to her plan and killing himself before she woke.

Prince Maurice (for this was he) having no true love to worry him, resolved to escape in this manner: to appear to die, and then have his servant break into the crypt and set him free. He sent the man, who had leave to do his marketing and his laundry and such, into the nearest village to ask whether a potion mightn't be found to make a man appear to be dead.

There was a sort of herb doctor there and he had such a potion, all right, but it seemed the servant hadn't explained proper as to what it was needed for.

All went off as planned until the servant broke into the crypt to free the prince, when he was found to be alive, indeed, but in his present unfortunate state. They were recaptured by the viceroy's men, much to the viceroy's dismay. He had just got word back from Spain that Prince Maurice was to be set free and returned to the bosom of his loving family, in the hope that King Charles would remember this little favor if he was ever restored to his throne.

So he wrote again, explaining what had happened. It was a great embarrassment to the Spanish, who were always ready to abuse common Englishmen but felt that those of royal blood ought to be given certain considerations. They decided to keep the matter a secret; as far as the English knew, Prince Maurice was dead anyway. And, who knew? Perhaps the effects of the drug might wear off and the prince might one day be more presentable.

This proved not to be the case, however. The years went on, and Prince Maurice was moved from one prison to another on the Spanish Main, and now and again a rumor got out that he'd been seen somewhere. Then it became public knowledge that his brother, Prince Rupert, had offered a reward to know his fate.

Well, the Spanish weren't about to admit the truth, so the order went out that the matter was to be kept concealed. But then, some warden with a keen eye for the main chance saw a way he might turn a profit. He devised all the hugger-muggery with the boots, and wrote in secret to Prince Rupert's agents to see if they were in the market for one lost prince, somewhat the worse for wear.

"And it has been much more difficult than we expected, señor," said the Spaniard peevishly. "He is difficult to move about and to conceal, especially with those sons of whores the pirates making war on us, and then there has been the cost of his feeding. I hope you have brought the money, señor."

Blackstone turned and shot him dead where he stood.

"Neat," said John, in an admiring kind of way. "You get the prince and keep the money, eh?"

The sound of the shot brought men running to the hut, and in short order there were faces peering down through the trap. Prince Maurice just sat there; neither the shot nor the commotion that followed drew his notice.

• • •

It took rope and tackle to get the prince out of the cellar, but once he was set on his feet he'd walk, if prodded on the back, and stop if prodded on the front. The men crowded around him, curious, all save those who were busy in the cellar; and the less said about that the better.

"Aie! *Il est un zombi,*" said Jago, looking horrified. "They are the misfortune."

"What, you mean bad luck?" said John.

"We can scarcely have worse luck than he's had," said Blackstone. He saw Morgan approaching and went off to have a quiet word with him.

"Phew! He doesn't half stink," said one man, holding his nose.

"It is the smell of the living death," said Jago. "The Indians on Hispaniola, they teach the *médecins* among the poor people how to make this. It makes slaves of the dead."

"A dead man! Lord preserve us!" cried Bob Plum, backing up against the Reverend.

"This is sorcery," the Reverend said, with his hands beginning to shake.

"It's a big fat fellow who ain't been washed in a month, more than likely," said John. "And he ain't no dead man." He told them a little of the truth, and they were no less appalled.

"Prince Maurice!" cried Dick Pettibone. "Why, he was a lovely gentleman! Oh, to see him come to *this*!" He stepped close and shouted up at the prince. "Your Highness! Your Highness, do you apprehend me?"

The prince only stared. Whether there was some memory behind that egg-smooth countenance, of riding with his cavaliers at Lyme or piratical raids out of Kinsale, who can say? Morgan seemed to be wondering the same thing, as he approached and looked him up and down.

"Jesus," he said at last. "We'll fetch him along with us; but we are doing his brother no kindness, to bring him home so. Can he walk?"

John said he could, and pushed him a little; the prince started forward obediently, and likely would have kept going until he was in the river, had

John not run ahead and stopped him. Morgan shook his head.

"Jesus," he repeated. "Very well; form up! We march on."

• • •

The prince came with the Brethren, and only wanted for a bit of guiding now and then to keep him on the path. They camped that night at another abandoned village, where Morgan gave order that someone should wash the prince, as the smell was starting to offend even Brethren who'd gone a week without a bath or a change of clothes. Dick Pettibone volunteered, as did Bob Plum, once he'd been told that Maurice had been a good Protestant prince and none of your scurvy Papist gentry.

He proved a good beast of burden too. They found they could strap a pack to him and he'd bear it along without the least complaint. So they loaded him with powder and shot and he marched along of them. Blackstone started to object to this and then shrugged; for it really took more imagination than a man's generally given to see that fat, staring thing as a royal cousin.

That night they found another village, but lately deserted, and camped there. Next day they came to another, about noon, and here had great luck: for Jacques found a cache of foodstuffs, sacks of wheat and plantains, hidden in a little cave. Morgan had the whole mess cooked into a sort of porridge and served out equally to all parties, even those like Hendrik Smeeks, who had been seen picking his teeth as they left Torna Caballos. Dick Pettibone took it on himself to feed the prince with a spoon, like a baby, and the poor creature opened his mouth obediently and swallowed too, but gave no sign that he understood anything.

They marched on, more easily, for the country was more open and there were little deserted farmsteads now and again. One of these made a good campsite that evening, with plenty of dry firewood stored in an outbuilding. The Brethren sprawled at their ease around fires and there was plenty of big talk and praises for Morgan, now that they'd had a few scraps of luck; for everyone assumed the worst was behind them.

• • •

The first sign they were in the wrong on the point came when they'd been marching an hour or two next day. The land began to rise, and the going became harder. Around midday they came on another little farm and discovered the barn loaded with ears of dry maize. Most of the men wanted to stop right there and grind it into meal for cakes, and it was only by drawing his sword that Morgan kept them from doing so. He gave them hot words, and there were surly looks and mutters. The maize was portioned out equally to every man, and awkward it was to carry too. There were some who fell to chewing at it whiles on the march, and not a few rash fellows broke teeth doing that.

John was marching along beside the prince, who was moving a little slower as so many had sort of casually draped their bundles of maize over him on the march, when he heard the cry:

"Los indios! Emboscada!"

John drew his cutlass and ran forward, but it wasn't to be an engagement for blades; he caught a glimpse of lithe brown bodies retreating through the trees, and a man next to him dropped with an arrow in the eye, screaming no end. Still the Brethren raced on, shedding ears of maize as they came over the ground, and were only stopped by a bend in the river. Here they saw the last of a troop of about a hundred Indians scrambling ashore on the opposite bank.

John drew his pistol and fired. Some fellows even plunged into the river, assuming that since the Indians had crossed easy, it must be shallow here. But maybe the Indians had picked up the trick of walking on water; Morgan's men sank over their heads, and came up gasping and clawing at the mangrove roots.

The Indians jeered and shot at them from the other bank, calling names in Spanish. John bent to pull one fellow ashore, and just as he came level with John's face he gave a shivering cry and died, pierced through with an arrow. John dropped him and pulled back; as he did, he heard a shot ring out on the *other side* and saw an Indian drop where he stood, with the red blood starting down over his bare breast. Another shot rang out, another one fell, and the Indians took to their heels, vanishing through the woods.

And someone ran after them.

John gaped to see a pale figure darting off between the branches. He had only one clear sight of her, but it was certainly the girl, carrying a musket soldier-fashion as she ran. He stood, dumb, staring after her. When he turned away he saw Morgan staring too, as though doubting his senses, and knew he'd seen her as well.

"That was *her*," said John.

"She can shoot," said Morgan. And then he swore, not loud but a lot, some in Welsh.

• • •

That night the Brethren camped by the river. What weathercocks men are, John soon learned: for all the high spirits and bold talk of the day before were gone entirely, now that the enemy had drawn a little blood. Smeeks, who was getting to be a right sea-lawyer, sat muttering with his friends and casting black looks at Morgan.

Some said as how they'd best to turn back, now that the Indians had found them. If they didn't, the Indians would pick them off one by one. Other folk were plain hopeless and reckoned it was better to lie down and die right there, rather than fight their way back through the jungle.

Morgan must have heard it all, sitting upright by his fire. It was a strange thing, but John, looking across at him, felt pity for the man, alone there with his thoughts.

John began to talk loud about how the Indians attacking only meant that Panama was near to hand; that folk only fought when they had something to lose. He went on to take wagers as to whether they'd sight the church towers of Panama next day, or the day after, and whether it would be gold or silver or jewels they should lay their hands to first. He allowed as how it was a shame they'd lost a few men, but no one ever made buttered eggs without breaking the shells first.

Some men told him to go to hell, but some took heart and said he was right; weeping and wailing was bootless now, and they may as well laugh and hope for the best, by God.

And so they argued back and forth. And all the while the prince sat a little distance away on the bare earth, looking out of his empty eyes, like an image of Fortune's Wheel: *I was once among the great. Regard me now...*

• • •

Next morning they saw to their firearms before setting out, for it was plain there'd be fighting soon. Morgan had the canoes brought up to ferry the men across, and on they went, and not long after they saw a great pall of smoke hanging over the jungle ahead.

"What should this be?" Morgan muttered to himself. John clapped Bob Plum on the shoulder and said:

"Cooking fires! They're boiling up our dinner, messmates!"

Whereat the men all raised a great cheer and picked up the pace, jogging along with their muskets in their hands. They came to the palisade and stormed over it, whooping and firing, but no one fired back; and now they saw it was another deserted place, so recently left that the houses were still in flames, and abandoned cats and dogs ran here and there.

"Roof rabbits!" cried Jago, and raising his musket drew a bead on someone's Tibby and blew its brains out. Others fell to following his example, and presently there were little groups of men clustered here and there, cooking succulent bits of house pet over house coals. You'd have thought it was Christmas, they laughed and chattered so.

"Admiral sir!" Dick Pettibone came waddling up, sweating and panting. "Here's the king's stables, that aren't burned; and the lads have found, must be a dozen jars of wine of Peru."

"Oh Christ," said Morgan, not as though in thanks, and he strode over to the stables and John followed him close. There were the great clay jars lined up along the stable wall, with a bread-bag hanging in the rafters above them. Two fellows had already hauled out one jar and broached it, and as John watched they gulped down near a quart each of the dark, sticky stuff, scooping it up in their dirty hands. Morgan looked on them with despair in his eyes; for nothing breaks discipline on a march like strong drink, and here was enough to make his whole force stupid.

But Fortune did Morgan another good turn; for the two drinkers turned, first one and then the other, a queer shade of pea-green, and proceeded to puke their guts up. No surprise, guzzling down that much sweet wine on an empty belly. Morgan turned and shouted, "Treachery! It's poisoned, you stupid bastards!"

As the two groveled and moaned, and the others stood looking on in dismay, Morgan went to the other jars and smashed them, each one, with the hilt of his cutlass, and threw them over. There were some snarls, and one man ran forward to try to stop him. Morgan caught him by the front of his shirt and held him out at arm's length.

"You'd drink, would you? The whole town in flames about our ears, and the cattle driven away, and this one place left standing, with a drink for the thirsty privateers when they arrive? Fool! It's a snare!"

Such was the light in his eyes as he spoke, that the man stood down abashed, and so did all the rest who had come up to see; and by then the wine had all spilled out and soaked into the ground. So mutiny was avoided, and whether the wine had been really poisoned or whether no Spaniard had dared to set fire to royal property, who knows? It served

Morgan's turn. It taught John a lesson in quick thinking too.

• • •

Now, it happened that this was the place where the Chagres turned north, and Panama lay to the south; so being as it was all hard marching overland after this, and them having taken themselves possession of the palisadoed town, Morgan let them rest up here that day and through the night. Come morning they left the river.

John marched among his messmates in the advance party, peering up at the mountains that rose to either side. Their way lay through the bottom of a gorge that narrowed. Soon there was room for no more than four or five to march abreast. Ahead it narrowed still further, for they could see the mouth of an arch through which they must go single file, a tunnel cut out of the rock. Jacques muttered something uneasily.

"He says, this is where they will make their *embuscade*," said Jago. Jacques said more, very earnestly and in a tone of entreaty, to Jago. Jago laughed and said something back, seeming to make mock of whatever Jacques had asked him.

"Gentlemen! Say to one, say to all," said Blackstone. "Has he noticed something else about which we ought to hear?"

"No," said Jago. "Only, he is afraid for me. Wish me to walk a little under the cover of the trees."

Which some men sneered at, and made kissing noises; and so the sound was obscured when it came.

The clouds of locusts coming down on Egypt might have made such a noise, whirring and clattering. John never heard anything like it before or after. He looked up to see what it might be.

There must have been four thousand arrows dropping toward them out of the sky, coming nearly straight down, and no sign of the bowmen who'd loosed them. John never remembered afterward how he'd got under cover, but there he found himself amongst the trees, with other men crowded around him, shaking and swearing. Arrows were still falling, out on the trail, like so many jackstraws. There were four men lying dead that John could see and Bob Plum dragging himself toward the trees, with an arrow sticking up under his chin. Out in the middle of the road the prince marched on, unconcerned, though an arrow had hit him in the shoulder.

Dick Pettibone screamed, and he and the Reverend ran out to pull Bob to safety, heedless of the arrows still falling.

"Hold your positions!" shouted Morgan, for some men had begun to run back the way they'd come.

The Reverend was moaning and wringing his hands. Dick took hold of Bob's collar and hauled.

"Over there—" he said, panting. "We need privacy, Elias!"

"What are you playing at?" said John, for it was plain Bob oughtn't to be shifted much. "Get the bleeding arrow out first."

He drew his knife and sliced open the front of Bob's shirt. "No!" cried Dick, but too late; for John saw that Bob was already bandaged tight around the chest, and the arrow had stabbed down between this bandage and his skin, cutting only a shallow trench where it had passed.

"No, no, no—" said Bob, fending him off.

"Oh, don't be such a coward," said John.

You may think John a capital bull-calf, and you'd be right; for even now he only wondered, *When did Bob get wounded before?* And he cut the bandage to free the arrow, and the bandage fell away and there was the arrow lying between—

"Bob's a woman!" said John, astonished. He sat back on his heels, as Bob clutched the edges of her shirt and pulled them together.

"You have looked upon my wife," said the Reverend, and in a trice his big hands were about John's throat and his red eyes were peering down into John's own, and John felt his windpipe squeak shut before he could say anything in apology. Blackstone came running with cutlass drawn, and so did Jago and Jacques.

"Elias! Stop!" said Dick, and began to sing the song about the little white lamb. Bob, where she lay, chimed in feebly. The Reverend joined in at last, easing up his grip enough for John to pull free. He fell back, gulping for breath.

"Bloody hell," he said, rubbing his throat. Light was dawning at last. Looking at Dick, he said: "And—you're a woman too! Ain't you?"

"*Les femmes!*" said Jacques, horrified. Blackstone began to laugh.

Morgan himself came striding through the brush. "What is this? I'll have no damned fighting here!"

"Dick ain't a eunuch after all," said John.

"What?" said Morgan.

"We have two of the fair sex here, disguised," said Blackstone, smirking. Morgan looked at them, aghast; for of course now it seemed too obvious.

Dick folded his arms and glared at them all.

"You can't send us back now," she said. "Have we not been fit companions? Was not Mr. Hackbrace the first to the wall at Chagres Castle? We have fought bravely and well. Do we not deserve our shares?"

"We must apologize, ladies, for our dull senses," said Blackstone. "Else we'd have penetrated your disguises sooner."

"Spare us such feigned gallantries, sir," said Dick.

"You had better explain this," said Morgan to the Reverend, who was crouched beside Bob, vainly trying to tuck the cut bandage back into place. He merely raised a bewildered face. Dick said:

"We were attempting to repair our fortune, sir. We had lived humbly but honestly, until poor Elias yielded to the sin of Wrath and smote that man dead in Winksley, and we were obliged to flee England. We thought to make his temper, that had been the instrument of our undoing, also the means by which we gained a comfortable sufficiency. Yet Elias could not be trusted to go adventuring alone; only Clementine and I are able to soothe his rages.

"Wherefore, Admiral, we hit upon the stratagem of disguising ourselves and traveling as comrades. But for this sad mischance, none had ever been the wiser."

"Some at least ought to have guessed," said Morgan, giving John a look that made him squirm. He in his turn looked accusingly at Bob.

"So you're Clementine, then?"

"*Mrs.* Clementine Hackbrace," said she, pale but defiant.

"And I am Lady Phyllida de Bellehache," said she who had been Dick, and Blackstone left off leering for surprise.

"But—but you were a great society beauty!" he said. "I've heard of you! There was a scandal—"

Reverend Hackbrace was on his feet in an instant.

" 'Even a fool, when he holdeth his peace, is counted wise,' " he said in a warning tone, flexing his hands.

"Even so," said Lady Phyllida, putting her hand on her hip. "Time changes us all, does it not? And now, Admiral, you will comprehend our desire for blest privacy to tend to poor Clementine's hurts."

"That you may have," said Morgan. "But understand me, ladies: you would be soldiers, and now you must soldier on. I have no men to spare to convey you safe home."

"We ask none," said Lady Phyllida, with a toss of her head.

"Where's the prince?" said Blackstone, looking around suddenly. John pointed out through the brush, at the distant figure marching along and still drawing an occasional hail of arrows. Blackstone swore and charged after him.

Some Indians had broken cover to come and stare at the prince. One fell dead in his tracks with Blackstone's musket-ball between his eyes. The Brethren, seeing them, rallied and sent out a volley of shot, which killed two more; and though they retreated, Jago and several others rushed them, reloading on the run. Blackstone caught the prince and turned him round, and half-dragged him back to the cover on their side of the woods.

"Get 'em!" said John, drawing and running from cover; for just then a pitched battle seemed a more congenial place to be. He ran, and others ran with him, as Morgan yelled, "Take prisoners! Twenty pieces of eight for the first man to take a prisoner!"

Yet the prize went unclaimed. There was bloody battle in that pass before the tunnel, with nearly a score of Morgan's men killed or wounded, and more of the Indians slain, since all they had to fight with close to were spears. They broke and ran at last, swift as deer through the tunnel, and by the time enough of the Brethren came pouring after them they were beyond range.

• • •

Strangely enough, the mood in camp that night was more cheerful than otherwise. This though it poured rain half the night, and with no shelter but a few shepherds' huts. Maybe it was the fact that battle had finally been joined, which likely meant that Panama was near; maybe it was the news that two ladies had been discovered within the party. Morgan had a field shelter rigged with branches, and set John to guard it, along with the Reverend, and there Mrs. Hackbrace and Lady Phyllida sat and conversed pleasantly. Mrs. Hackbrace, once her wounds were tended at last, was found to be not much hurt.

Notwithstanding what he'd said, Morgan was minded to send them back down to Chagres Castle in a canoe, with Jago and Jacques, who could be trusted not to commit outrages on their persons. But in the end he relented. For one thing, the ladies had held their own so far, and nobody else could sing the Reverend out of his rages. For another, they had been the only ones willing to see to the washing of the prince, and he soiled himself pretty regularly.

So when the army moved on next morning, Lady Phyllida and Mrs. Hackbrace marched with them.

· · ·

John marched by Morgan. The land was all cleared now, the road wide; there were the prints of booted feet that had gone before, so they knew it was not just Indians now but the Spanish too, who retreated from them. Morgan watched the forest with a scowl, and let it be known again that he'd pay for a prisoner to question. The *boucaniers* slipped ahead and ferreted through the brush, but the Indians were too swift and silent, the Spaniards too long gone.

And then, as they struggled up the switchback road that scaled a green mountain, there was a shout from ahead. Jago came sprinting back, glad-faced, waving; Morgan broke into a run, and John ran beside him, and the whole army mustered its strength and sprinted, until at last they broke like a wave over the mountaintop—

And there was the sea.

Men sighed, and not a few dropped to their knees. John stared at the placid blue expanse, where a ship and half a dozen boats were gliding. That was the first time in his life he beheld the great South Sea. A salt wind came out of it, rolling up the face of the mountain toward them, and blew their hair back out of their faces. Morgan's cloak rustled with the breeze, and all their banners snapped.

"We've done it!" said Morgan, turning to them all. How his eyes burned! "Here we stand, my boys, in despite of hunger and thirst and all that they dared to send against us. And we're the first. Not Drake nor Hawkins nor Baskerville ever got so far. That great ocean there is henceforth *ours*."

Well, that got the Brethren cheering, and John with the rest; though it did seem to him that if boats were putting out from Panama, they might well be carrying the city's wealth on them, to get it out of danger. He dropped his gaze from the sweet line of horizon to where the mountain-side fell away below them into hills and broad meadows. He saw a white flash among the green. He peered harder, and saw the little figure running, holding her musket well away from her body.

"Sir!" He caught Morgan's arm, and pointed. Morgan turned swiftly and saw her.

"By God, she's beaten us," he said under his breath. "There's a girl for you, eh? Let God preserve us both, I'll no nurses for her, nor corset-stays and tight shoes. She shall ride horses if she choose, and shoot, and climb trees. Who'd lock up a brave heart?"

THE CITY

The Brethren came down the mountain in good order, at least until they found a meadow where cows and horses grazed together. Then no starving man could think of anything but butchery, and Morgan let them do as they liked. The *boucaniers* among them dropped the animals with a few neat shots, and waded in with cutlasses drawn. Others scrambled for firewood. In short order they were stuffing themselves with grilled beef, and roasted horsemeat and asses' flesh too, and nothing in the world had ever tasted so good to John. Morgan himself laid hold of a great gobbet of meat and wolfed it down nearly raw.

The Reverend cut three or four steaks and carried them back on a plantain leaf to Lady Phyllida and Mrs. Hackbrace, who fell to in a most unladylike way, tearing at the meat with their bare hands.

Blackstone, something loath, sliced up a sirloin into little gobbets and fed them on knife-tip to the prince. John came to watch; for there was a sort of grim fascination in seeing the royal jaws champ, mindless as a millstone grinding, and not seeming to mind what he ate nor his arrow-wounds nor the flies that buzzed about him.

"What'll you do with him, do you reckon?" said John.

"There's a question to revolve in one's mind, by God," said Blackstone. "I can't think His Royal Highness will be greeted with glad cries of welcome from his brother, can you? Not in his present condition."

"Perhaps he could be made to look a little better," said John. "We could get him a wig, eh?"

"We might dress him up," agreed Blackstone. "Christ knows there's many a courtier with no more sensibility; no, nor so well-mannered. This poor block will never be prating about his dogs, or his horses, or his debts, and so might pass for a wise man. Even so… it's a dangerous thing to trust to

217

the gratitude of princes."

"You'd know, I reckon," said John. "Ain't there a little matter of four thousand pounds you was supposed to pay in ransom? Or did you lose it gambling?"

"Not I," said Blackstone, and for a moment looked as though he were going to draw on John. "Bastard. No, that's safe in sealed bags, and you needn't inquire where. But you do have a point, sir."

He fed the prince another scrap of meat. "Yes, Your Highness, we shall have to fetch you home after all. You're a right royal embarrassment; but your family's known worse, I think."

• • •

In grease, blood and great contentment the Brethren marched on, bearing with them whole legs and sides of beef. Morgan, with John, looked keenly to see the girl, but it seemed she kept ahead out of sight.

So did the Spaniards, though Morgan sent out an advance party of fifty men to seek out prisoners. Some of these encountered mounted men, who shouted insults but did not stay to give satisfaction; no, they spurred away as though they fled the Devil himself. Which indeed some of them may have thought was the case. If they'd caught a glimpse of Morgan marching along, with his black beard glistening with horse's blood and the light of happy Hell in his eyes, they surely mistook him for Old Nick.

By the time the sun was beginning to dip low in the west, Morgan had still not laid hands on a living soul; and then the towers of Panama were sighted, with one tall cathedral-tower above the rest. The Brethren cheered and danced, and lifted Morgan on their shoulders as though he had already waded with them into the counting-houses of Panama, spurning heaps of doubloons as he came.

Standing above them so, Morgan took a sight through his spyglass, and lowered it with a sober face; but then he grinned down at them all.

"Well, my lads, there is an army camped not three miles off. It may be they are those same fearful fellows who have run ahead of us this whole way. You mark me! By cockcrow we'll see they've run again, and left their empty tents fluttering, eh?

"Let's rest here, my lads, and eat good beef, and build great fires to warm ourselves. Blood and gold come morning!"

They cheered him like madmen, did the Brethren, though John had his own thoughts: that it mightn't be so wise to make holiday with the

Spaniards sitting within easy march. And so he followed uneasily as Morgan walked through the camp they made, from bonfire to bonfire where men sat roasting meat. Some took out the campaign trumpets and drums, and made brave music, singing loud. Some men danced, giddy as though their bellies were full of good rum. John looked out into the dark as it fell, expecting every moment to see Spanish horsemen riding forth on them.

"Jesus bless us, boy, anyone would think you were at a funeral," said Morgan. "Afraid, are you?"

"I am, Admiral sir," said John.

"Why then, you have excellent good sense," said Morgan, clapping him on the shoulder. "And, look you: that army over yonder has good sense too. Sober little clerks defending their investments, see, and officers who like to serve their time behind a desk, and patient blacks and Indians who'd rather serve the devil they know than be so imprudent as to rise against him. They are watching and listening, make no mistake.

"And what do you suppose they're seeing? Filthy beasts, in their hundreds, dancing around great fires. What do you suppose they're hearing? Howls of laughter and song. These are no soldiers; they're madmen. They want gold, and for the love of it they followed me up that stinking river. They want it, and tomorrow they'll follow me to get it, over the bodies of the slain. Musket-balls won't stop them. Toledo steel won't stop them. Would *you* stand in their way?"

"I reckon I wouldn't, sir," said John.

"I dare say that army won't, either. Not after a few hours' sober reflection," said Morgan. He grinned. The firelight gleamed on his eyes, and his teeth.

There was a clatter of hooves, and a trumpet-call, clear and long and loud, from out in the dark; but the voice that followed was shaking badly.

"Dogs! English Dogs! We will meet you!"

And the Brethren catcalled back, and fired into the night, and danced obscenely by the fires; sure invitation, John would have thought, for Spanish snipers, but none fired upon them. Instead, the sound of hoofbeats retreated away into the dark, and not long afterward came the thunder of cannon from the city walls. The which was so stupid (the enemy being so far out of range) that the privateers were cheered even more.

Near to where John stood with Morgan, three or four men got up a morris-dance, and sang:

> *What happened to the Spaniard*
> *Who made so great a boast, oh?*
> *They shall eat the feathered goose*
> *But we shall eat the roast, oh!*

That was the only time a shadow fell across Morgan's face. He looked out on the prancing demons he'd charmed so far through desolation, and said:

"God send she has the sense to keep well clear of these."

"She's done it so far, sir," said John. Morgan looked at him thoughtfully.

"I may get my death tomorrow," he said.

"Never say it, sir! You got the Devil's own luck," said John.

"Oh, yes, no question of that; but luck plays a man false, now and again. I think *your* luck will hold, John James. These poor sots and cutthroats will rush into the cannon's mouth heedless, but you will think twice about wasting your life. Should I fall, find my girl. Take her away with you, to Jamaica or even to England, and treat her well."

"Sir, I swear it!" said John. "But I ain't got your luck, all the same."

Morgan sighed.

"Then I will give you half my luck," he said, and reaching out with the heel of his hand struck John between the eyes, a sharp blow that made him see stars. "There. Do you feel fortunate now?"

"I think so, sir," said John, blinking and wanting to laugh, except it hurt.

"Christ Jesus, what I wouldn't give for a glass of rum," said Morgan, looking out at the fires.

• • •

John made himself a sort of tent that night, draping his coat over a green bush and stretching out underneath. He lay there a while, thinking on the morrow. He remembered that there'd been an alehouse in London called the Green Bush, and he thought how funny it was that here he lay now, in a green bush, only he wished it was the other one.

Whereupon he heard his mother's voice in his ear again, pleading-like, telling him how he might open a nice little tavern of his own someday. It was a fine living, for a sober man; why, he could set up at a crossroads, with a painted sign to hang out front, and a clean little brew-house out back, and three snug rooms upstairs with clean linen, so as to attract gentle guests. He would wash the windows often, so as to let in a lot of light, which would shine on the copper pans… and in his own chamber there'd be a grand big bed, just the place for a neat, little wife… a sea-coal fire all cheery in the grate…

But the sea-coal sent up green flames, and the hanging sign was a hanging man. John heard Morgan's voice then, smoothly arguing down his mother.

A tavern at a crossroads! Aye, and there he'd dream of jungles, and battles, and blood and gold. The gentle guests would shout for him, and order him to take away the chamber-pots and make the beds. His hand would grope for a cutlass to change their tune, but he'd not find one, never again. Gray England would send her winters over him, not the stink and glare and salt sea-haze of Port Royal. And every seventh day, he'd sit in a pew and drone hymns, and mutter *Amen*, like to die of boredom. What kind of life was that, demanded Morgan.

Well, but there'd be the neat, little wife. She'd be a pink-faced country girl, pious, in yards of white cambric to be groped through before he could get proper hold of her a'nights, and that only when there wasn't babies coming, which there would be most of the time… lying mouth to mouth with her he'd be dreaming all the while anyway of a girl with flaming eyes, slender and terrible, white as mist, with long, wet hair and the smell of the sea on her…

She began to do things, lying on him, and he was panicked lest his mother see or, worse yet, Morgan, but he couldn't stop the girl. He didn't want to stop her.

John woke, gasping, to find that she had her white arms around his neck and was smiling down at him, not an inch away from his face in the darkness. They wrestled close, for five or six minutes, and it was like going to Heaven.

When John could draw breath to speak at last, all he could tell her was how he loved her. She stroked back his hair from his face, still smiling.

"And I love thee," she said. "You're my own man, John. I will be your right bride all the days and nights of your life, and never leave you. Wherever you may sail, I'll be at your side. Let the world quake for fear of us!"

John said something half-witted back in reply, about all the things he'd do for her, like pile the riches of the world at her feet. Then, enough of his conscience woke for him to croak something about how Morgan was worried for her, and only wanted what was best for her.

"Oh, he'd keep me close," said the girl, laughing. "I know him. But there's none like Morgan for burning, and plundering, and living free; and am I not his daughter? I must be free too, John."

Now this news terrified John, as he recollected all that had happened and all Morgan had said, and finally understood the truth. He felt a dull ox not to have guessed it before now; but he loved her all the more, and told her so.

Three times more before the night was out, they struggled together again, in bliss and joy. John drifted off at last, asleep in her arms, so happy. He dreamed of a fair ship, sweet-steering and swift, laden to the decks with loot.

But when he started awake, in an hour when the stars had dropped far down into the west, the girl had slipped away from him once more.

• • •

Morning came chill and pale, with cocks crowing indeed. The Brethren woke beside the ashes of their fires, under a pall of blowing smoke, and formed up, and marched off to do battle. Before they had gone two miles, they saw it was even as Morgan had told them: the Spanish forces had fled in the night, leaving their empty tents and gear. There was only a fat, old man riding sadly away, with his priests running after him. It was the viceroy himself, deserted, riding back to pray for his city.

And the Brethren looked at Morgan with wide eyes, remembering that he had prophesied it would happen so, and some among them crossed themselves. John didn't, but he reached up and touched the place Morgan had struck him, and smiled sheepishly to think of the luck he'd have from now on.

He looked about him for the girl as he marched, bearing Morgan's standard; but if she followed the army, she was keeping herself well hid. That pleased him. Safer, he thought, for her to stay unseen, and shoot from afar off. Jacques was already in tears, his little, red eyes like rubies, because Jago was in the vanguard with him, and it was no use to march in front and try to shield him with his body. Jago towered over him by a head.

Forward they went, through the bright day, under a clear, hot sun, and clearer and sharper grew the towers of Panama. By noon they could make out the defending army, drawn up under the walls, on a wide open plain.

Now, John marched with Morgan's troops, that formed the right wing of the main body of men; that was about three hundred, with three hundred more on the left wing under Captain Collier, or Colonel Collier as he was now, because Morgan had assigned ranks so all would be done army-fashion.

Three hundred more were in the vanguard, the *boucanier* sharpshooters mostly. The rest followed in the rearguard. Blackstone was in Morgan's column, by John; it had been agreed to keep the prince to the rear of the column, with the ladies. The Reverend needed no goading now, not since the cathedral tower had come into plain view. He was marching along with his eyes fixed on it, muttering to himself about catamites, and the sale of indulgences, and graven images. Every so often he shook as though he had the palsy, and flecks of foam began to appear at the corner of his mouth.

Pretty soon the guns on the walls started up again, *thud-thud-thud,* and men remembered the bombardment of the night before, and a few laughed for scorn. That fell off as they came within range at last, and the first balls went shrieking through the air and ploughed up earth and bushes to one side and the other. The vanguard kept their heads up now, as they marched, watching for the shots coming in.

Now the Spanish troops could be seen clearly. John glanced over at Morgan and saw him pulling on his beard as he studied the field; for the Spanish outnumbered them, being maybe fifteen hundred men to their thousand-odd, and there was beside a great herd of lowing cattle being kept in place by Indians with goads. The Spanish right flank was drawn up behind a little hill, with a ravine before them. The wind was out of the west, and blowing the cannon-smoke across the Spanish lines.

Morgan called a halt to the march, and sent for Collier, who presently came sidling through the ranks.

"Now, Ned, what say you?" Morgan jerked his thumb at the enemy positions. Collier looked pale, but he grinned.

"They have the sun in their eyes," he said hopefully.

"And smoke too," said Morgan. "Still…"

"What do you reckon they've kept all those cows for?"

"Why, to fright us with," said Morgan, and now he grinned too, and raised his voice. "Bless my heart, lads, what sport is here! They'll drive their beefsteaks at us, to make us run away!"

Which brought a roar of laughter from the Brethren, and heartened them no end, to think anyone could be so stupid as to attack starving men with meat on the hoof. Someone started up the old song again, *They shall eat the feathered goose, but we shall eat the roast, oh!* Morgan turned back to Collier and pointed at the little hill.

"Look you, how safe their right flank sits back there. I am thinking, though, that they will have the Devil's own time getting reinforcements to the center, going down into that ravine and up out of it again. It would be easy to turn their flank, see, if we could gain that hill."

"By God," said Collier, in admiration.

"Do you think you might take your lads up it, Ned?"

"None readier!"

"And so we shall have the advantage," said Morgan, with a kind of a purr in his voice.

Collier hurried back, and when Morgan gave the order to advance again, the left flank went wheeling away to storm the hill.

A squadron of Spanish cavalry galloped forward now to attack the vanguard. Glinting eyes, beating hooves, manes flying and the men bending low above, grinning to charge on so many poor bastards without pikes to fend them off. Morgan craned his head to see what the commander of the vanguard would do, and nodded when he saw him forming the French sharpshooters up into a square, where they dropped each to one knee and raised muskets, and blew the slow-matches bright, waiting for the range—

And Morgan glanced over at the left wing, that was storming the hill now, and John followed his gaze—

And they both, in the same moment, saw the girl running with Collier's wing.

Morgan turned to John, staring, but said nothing. John couldn't have heard him if he had, with the roar of the battle commencing. John blurted something—he never afterward remembered what—and thrust Morgan's standard into someone else's hands, and took off through the lines after the girl.

He'd never run so in all his life, dodging and ducking through charging men, for the attack had begun in earnest. The Reverend went howling past him, clawing slower men out of the way to get at the enemy. But John ran after the force that was surging up the hill now, unstoppable as a wave, and up he went too and he could see the girl again, and the noise of the charge shook the ground under his boots.

He came up alongside—oh, who wouldn't have noticed she was a woman now, with her shirt torn open and her white breasts bared, and her hair streaming out? *But hadn't she cut her hair?...* Yet the men around them never seemed to see, they were so fixed on taking the hill.

A kind of growl seemed to rise out of the earth, as they gained the top, and it mixed with the volley of shots below, for only now had the cavalry charge reached the vanguard. John heard the screams of men and horses caught by musket-fire. He reached out his hand to the girl. She turned her face to him, and there were no eyes in her face but only flames.

She lifted her arms and jumped, or seemed to, for up she rose before him like a kite, and her spread arms and wild hair flowed out like wings or a cloak.

Up she went like the smoke of a fire, and seemed to cover half the sky. Her face was Death itself, and in her left hand she bore a flaming brand, and her right bore blue steel with lightnings playing about the blade. She laughed fit to crack the sky open.

Out she flew as Collier's men fired down on the Spanish right flank, slaughtering them like they were chickens in a pen. But she soared on to the walls of Panama itself, and it seemed to John the cathedral tower trembled, and where she came fire sprang up and climbed like roses.

John fell to his knees there on the hill, clutching his heart. When he lifted his eyes again there was no sign of her, but only clouds of smoke shot through with curious colors, writhing and descending on the city.

He turned and looked down on the plain, that was now a flailing slaughterhouse of cattle and horses and men. There was Morgan's standard, and there hard by stood Morgan himself, staring up at John.

He had seen her too. John knew it by the look on his face.

• • •

The Spaniards fled, or died. Morgan led his forces on, pursuing close, into the very streets of Panama, but it was already in flames. The people of the city ran to and fro, confusedly, and some tried to put out the fires. Some few attempted to stand against the Brethren that came racing across the little bridge, and so into the city, but in the end most fled.

John crawled down from the hill, weak and sick as though he'd had a fever, and staggered after the army. Looking up, he could just see the backs of Lady Phyllida and Mrs. Hackbrace, scrambling over the dead as they followed the privateers in. They had left the prince far behind. He walked on in his slow way, deaf to the moans of the wounded and dying on both sides.

Someone was screaming to John's left; he turned and saw Jago on his knees, holding Jacques close and rocking to and fro with him. Jacques' red eyes were still open, and staring. He'd been cut in the sinews of his neck, likely some cavalryman's blade going straight down to the heart.

Jago was crying so, John didn't know what to say to him. He only stood and stared, and wondered at the things that make a man leave Paradise once he's found it.

. . .

John walked on. He caught up with the prince, who'd have marched straight into the sea if John hadn't caught him by the arm.

"This way, Your Royal Highness," he said, giving him a shove toward the main road. They trudged along, side by side, toward the city. Flames swept up from most of it now, smelling sweet as incense, for its houses had been made of cedarwood; or maybe that was the churches burning. Women were screaming. There were desperate shouts in English, orders to leave the wine and put the fires out, as Morgan's officers tried to restore order; but the Brethren were ignoring them, laughing, doing just as they liked.

Blackstone was on the bridge, crawling along on hands and knees. He'd had one foot blown off, by a cannonball seemingly. He'd tied it off himself, but it was still bleeding.

"Good day to you, sir," he said, as John drew abreast of him. "And to you, Your Highness. I fear we'll be late to the ball."

John swore. He tore the shirt from a dead man that lay a little distance off, and wadded it on the stump where Blackstone's foot had been. Then he was flummoxed, for he couldn't think how to hold the wadding on.

"You oaf," said Blackstone, laughing. "Isn't it obvious? Steal another man's boot."

So John helped himself to the dead man's left boot as well, and when Blackstone's stump was crammed down in it the bandage stayed in place well enough. John hauled Blackstone up with his arm around John's shoulders, and they hobbled on.

"You know, there's six hundred pieces of eight for you if you lose your leg," said John, with his voice sounding small and funny in his ears. "The articles says so."

"I don't recall whether there was payment for losing one's foot, how-ever," said Blackstone. "And, you know, that's just the sort of thing clerks stick at."

"I reckon so," said John.

"Do you know Watkin's inn, hard by St. Paul's?"

"What, in London?"

"No, you fool, the one in Port Royal."

"Oh! The Bluebell. No, I never been in there."

"Well, I'll thank you to take the prince there, if you get out of this alive and I perish. Ask for Mistress Clarissa Waverly. She'll pay you for your trouble," said Blackstone. "Tell her I died singing."

"Are you likely to do that?"

"It would make a grand gesture, don't you think?" said Blackstone.

• • •

Panama burned to the ground. The Reverend, having left a trail of dis-membered enemies in his wake, personally set fire to the cathedral, with its great square tower. One time it had been the tallest building in the New World; and for all the Reverend's pains, it was still standing after the flames had hollowed it out, though its bells had dropped all the way down the shaft and lay in a molten mass on the stones below. He raved and tried to tear down what was left with his bare hands. His wife and cousin had to get through seven verses of the hymn about the little white lamb before he could be dragged away weeping.

Morgan was by no means pleased with this, for any gold altar plate or cloth-of-gold vestments that might have been left behind were now so many molten lumps and ash. But the Reverend had been the first man into the city, and fought bravely, so he was put down for another fifty pieces of eight, when all the plunder should be counted up.

• • •

What with the fires, and the looting, and the fighting that was still going on here and there as some of the townfolk tried to defend themselves, it was hours before Morgan could restore any order; and that only because half the Brethren were too stupefied with wine to cause any more trouble. It was nightfall before John could see Blackstone and the prince squared away, in the hospital that had been left standing. It was another hour before he could persuade himself to walk to Morgan's headquarters, set up in a plundered convent.

Morgan was in there with his officers, around a table with a map of the city spread out upon it. They were talking over whether it was worth it to blow up any more buildings, or whether the fires were likely to burn themselves out now; and if so, how to organize parties in the morning, to begin searching the wells and gardens, or any other places treasure might have been hidden.

John limped in and sat quiet in a corner, as they went over business. They concluded with talk about who should interrogate the prisoners, and whether any of the Inquisition's gear had survived the fires, as it should be handy in questioning. Collier agreed to go find that out; whereat they all saluted Morgan, and left him.

Morgan, rolling up the map, looked over at John. John stood and made to say something smart. He choked up instead.

Morgan just went to a cabinet, and got out three bottles of wine. He set them on the table and opened them, one after another.

"Come, boy, and drink for me," he said. "I don't believe I could get drunk tonight if I emptied every bottle in this Goddamned city. How do you like my luck, eh?"

John swabbed his face with his sleeve, and said he was sorry. He drank most of a bottle, and only then had the courage to say:

"What *was* she?"

"A ghost," said Morgan. "Blood-drinking Revenge, having put on a pleasing shape to accomplish her ends. A man's sin, come to smile in his face and call him Father. Christ, boy, how should I know?"

EPILOGUE

They were twenty days in that place before leaving.

Blackstone's leg mortified, and had to be cut away joint by joint. Each time John stood by him and reminded him how he'd surely get his six hundred pieces of eight now, no clerk in the world could quibble over it; but Blackstone died in the end, so it came to nothing after all. Though he did manage to gasp out a few verses of "The World Turn'd Upside Down" before he went, and so had his grand gesture.

A day or so later, it fell out that some witty fellows decided to crown the prince as ruler of Panama. They made him a crown of twisted vines, with spikes of burnt wood sticking up from it, and an empty sack for a cape, and gave him a cup full of ashes to hold; and they set him on the back of an ass, and led him about carousing, until they all fell down dead drunk.

John was away, running an errand for Morgan. By the time he returned and heard what they'd done, the prince was nowhere to be found. John cursed them, and ran here and there asking who'd seen the prince. At last an Indian prisoner said as how he'd sighted him, still mounted on the ass' back, riding away on the long road out of the city. A party sent out on horseback failed to find him.

For all John was ever able to learn, the prince is riding still.

• • •

The Spaniards, having had plenty of warning that Morgan was coming, and being reasoning men, had emptied what treasure was in the storehouses and sent it away in ships before the Brethren ever got there, as John had feared. So every last ditch and outhouse and cesspool was raked through, and some jewels and candlesticks were found, as well as slaves and prisoners to be ransomed. When it was all packed up on mules and brought back to Chagres, though, when it was counted out and reckoned up according to the number of survivors, it was found that each man's share amounted to no more than two hundred pieces of eight.

There was some debate whether Lady Phyllida and Mrs. Hackbrace were owed shares, being women. There was no question Mrs. Hackbrace had slain a score of men taking the bastion at San Lorenzo, however, and Lady Phyllida, while not so quick on the kill, had made herself useful in other ways, so in the end the ladies were paid fairly.

Then Hendrik Smeeks started up mutinous talk again, the sense of which was, that Morgan had taken the lion's share of the plunder for himself. So Morgan had every last coin portioned out publicly, and then had each man searched to be sure he kept nothing back. He let himself be searched too, before them all.

Having settled that, the company was disbanded. All parties took ship at Chagres Castle, and sailed home. Some went to Port Royal, and the French among them went to Tortuga; others sailed south, to try to better their luck with piracy.

Morgan got home in the *Mayflower*. Five hundred of the English Brethren came with him, spending their money so free it was soon gone.

Then Fortune's Wheel began to turn in earnest, for word came that England had signed to the Treaty of Madrid. A new governor was sent out to Jamaica to arrest Modyford, and Morgan in his turn was arrested and shipped off to London.

But Morgan's luck stood by him again. Let the Spanish ambassador rave away how he might, Harry Morgan was cheered wherever he went in London. Folk called him Drake come again. The canny king listened, and in the end sent Morgan back with a knighthood and the lieutenant-governorship of Jamaica to boot.

And yet...

Hendrik Smeeks, home in the Low Country, declared himself a reformed man. He took pen in hand to write a book purporting to tell the true history of the privateers (whom he was careful to call *pirates*). He made the Spaniards the heroes, brave and dutiful to a man, and slandered Morgan no end, beginning by saying he had been brought out to the West Indies as a bond-slave. He went on to invent all manner of abominations committed by Morgan. However, it was that claim of his having been a slave that provoked the lieutenant-governor's wrath. He sued Smeeks' publisher, and won damages, and forced a retraction.

And yet...

That was the end of Morgan's adventuring on the Spanish Main. He never sailed forth with his captains anymore, but stayed home and drank rum punch, playing at politics in Port Royal. The Brethren of the Coast never went out in such numbers again, and when they did sail, it was as outright pirates. A man might have his fill of blood and gold, fire and glory, but when he looked at himself in the shaving-glass of a morning he saw a thief and a murderer, and no hero.

For most of them, it didn't matter much.

Prince Rupert never found his lost brother, though there were rumors Prince Maurice was still being seen in unlikely places for years afterward. Rupert continued to advertise for news of him, as he advertised for his lost dogs. Some of the dogs, at least, found their way home again.

John made his way in time to the Bluebell, where he asked whether there was a Mistress Clarissa Waverly there. After some wait he was shown up to see a fine lady, and told her a tale. She might have wept, and he might have comforted her. She might have dried her tears and considered his youth, and his size, and his willingness to be of use. And there may have been certain talk of four thousand pounds in gold, in sealed bags; and there might not have been.

Whatever other adventures John had, he did become a bricklayer for a while, and laid many a herringbone floor in old Port Royal. But his mother never spoke in his ear again. Now it was Morgan's voice he heard there, in warning or counsel; the more so after Morgan died, long years later.

But one night the girl came to John in his sleep, bidding him follow her. He woke, and thirsted for rum, and ached for the smell of smoke and the sight of gold glinting, of white sails filling with a fair wind. He wondered whether he might find her again, a slender wraith wandering some lonely beach.

He ran to Lynch's wharf and signed on with the captain of a rakish craft, who asked him few questions and answered none. They sailed by night; come morning the colors were run up, a black ensign bearing a skull and crossed bones.